SPIN THE BOTTLE

CAMPUS GAMES BOOK #2

STEPHANIE ALVES

Copyeditor: Amanda Oraha
Cover designer: Stephanie Alves

ISBN: 978-1-917180-07-8

This book contains detailed sexual content, graphic
language and some other heavy topics.
You can see the full list of content warnings on my website
here: stephaniealvesauthor.com

Happy Reading!

Also by Stephanie Alves

Standalone

Love Me or Hate Me

Campus Games Series

Never Have I Ever (Book #1)
Spin The Bottle (Book #2)
Would You Rather (Book #3)
Truth Or Dare (Book #4)
The Final Game (Book #4.5)

This is for all my big girls who think they don't deserve love.
Yes, we fucking do.

Playlist

SPIN THE BOTTLE - Stephanie Alves

GORGEOUS - Taylor Swift ♥

DISTRACTION - Kehlani ♥

BUTTONS - The Pussycat Dolls ♥

BETTER - Khalid ♥

NASTY - Ariana Grande ♥

JUST FRIENDS - Why Don't We ♥

NO STRONGS ATTACHED - B Monae ♥

COME THRU - Summer Walker ft Usher ♥

HONESTY - Pink Sweat$ ♥

BOYFRIEND - Ariana Grande ft Social House ♥

GOODNIGHT N GO - Ariana Grande ♥

JUST MY TYPE - The Vamps ♥

BIRTHDAY SEX - Jeremih ♥

CLOSE - Nick Jonas ft Tove Lo ♥

TOUCH IT - Ariana Grande ♥

GET YOU - Daniel Caesar ft Kali Uchis ♥

SWAP IT OUT - Justin Bieber ♥

1

The game begins

Leila

As much as I love a man on his knees, this isn't exactly what I had in mind.

His grunts make me wince when I notice the green liquid dripping off his jacket. My hand flies to my mouth, my eyes widening when I see the aftermath of my bad decision from last night.

"I'm so sorry." I crouch down, extending a hand to the man on the ground, cursing at me, the world, and smoothies.

He shakes my hand off, glowering at me. "Just drop it," he says, shaking off the spilled drink from his t-shirt. "I'll get up on my own." He lifts off the ground, staring down at this drenched t-shirt.

"I really am sorry." I attempt to smooth over this situation, but the way he scowls at me lets me know nothing I do can rectify this, especially when he curses at me before walking off.

"What just happened?" I hear Rosie's voice coming from my phone, clutched in my hand beside me.

I lift it to my ear and exhale, letting my eyes close. "I'm a disaster this morning."

"Fill me in," she says. "I heard a bunch of grunts and cursing."

The spilled drink on the ground brings a sigh out of me as I head towards the classroom. "I wasn't looking where I was going, is what happened." I let out a breath. "Bumped into some guy; he fell over; I died of embarrassment. The end." I let out a sigh. "That's the last time I hook up at a party." She snorts on the other end, which makes my lips twitch. "Fine, it's the last time I leave so late," I amend.

"Who did you leave with?"

I chew on my bottom lip. "Some jock."

"Nice name," she muses. "Has a ring to it."

I let out a laugh. If only I had snuck out a little earlier, I wouldn't be in this mess. "I can't believe I forgot to turn my alarm on." I walk a little faster, pulling my phone away from my ear to check the time. "Now I'm late, and I lost my green smoothie."

"You still went to get a smoothie when you're late?"

"I need all the energy I can get if I'm going to be bored to death for an hour."

She laughs. "So dramatic. Is it really that bad?"

"Extremely," I sigh. "Remind me again why I haven't dropped out?"

"Your mom would kill you?" she offers.

Right. Well, it's not like my mom doesn't have another daughter she prefers, anyway. "And I care because?"

"Because even if you try to not let it affect you, you know you care about what she thinks."

Well, damn. She's right again. "Are you sure you want to go down the designer route?" I joke. "You'd be a good therapist." My shoulders drop when I see the door to my impending boredom.

"Of course I would, but then who would dress you?"

I snicker, reaching for the door handle. "I've got to go; I'm about to go in."

"Have fun."

Not likely.

The line goes dead, and I pocket my phone. My breath shortens before I take the plunge and pull the door open, heading inside. The room quiets when over 50 heads turn to look at me. This, right here, makes me want to die.

Their eyes on me feel like a huge spotlight of judgment. You would think with my line of work, I'd be used to the attention, but I'm not.

My confidence slips a little, the roaring in my stomach an indication of the anxiety brewing inside of me.

"Leila. I see you don't value my time," Professor Wilson says, making the spotlight on me even brighter.

I swallow, blink, and slip my mask back on, squaring my shoulders and give him a smile. "Sorry, sir. Won't happen again."

"Doubt that," a low voice says to my right. My eyes drop, seeing Jordan Wright sitting at the table closest to the door. He doesn't look my way, though. He never does.

The one and only person I can stand in this class, Mia—who happens to be sitting near him—shoots me a smile and calls me over. I take a seat next to her, placing my bag on the floor.

"Where were you?" she whispers, nudging me on the shoulder when the professor turns back around.

"Forgot to set my alarm," I offer with a shrug.

With a smile on her lips, she shakes her head, probably knowing there's more to the story. She'd be right.

"Having a great product isn't always the end result," Professor Wilson drones on, making my eyes glaze over. "Marketing is the main focal point of any business. You could

3

have the best product in the world, but no one would know if you didn't market it."

Yeah, I've heard it all before. It would be easier to figure out what exactly I preferred over business, but therein lies the problem. I don't know what I want. I've always admired my dad running a business. It seemed so cool when I was younger, but then my mom got me into modeling, and that became my life.

She stopped pushing me into modeling once I had gone through puberty and gained a lot of extra pounds that made me inadequate for the modeling she wanted. Modeling was fun and I loved dressing up and posing for the camera; so I didn't give up. I found a plus-size modeling agency and haven't looked back since.

But by then, my mom had already made up that I wouldn't go anywhere if I didn't lose weight, so she pushed a college degree on me. I didn't mind it, I could do both, but the problem was, I didn't know what I wanted to do once I got here, so I settled on something I already had knowledge of. Business. Too bad it's a bore.

"The papers on the end of the table have the assignment on them," Professor Wilson says. Mia reaches for the papers on her end, handing one to me and Jordan. She hands one to the guy sitting next to her, Toby... something. She tucks her straight hair behind her ear, smiling at him when she hands him the assignment. Hm, little Mia has a crush.

"New boyfriend?" I tease, dropping my voice so only she hears.

She glances up at me. "It's nothing."

I shrug. "I could smell the sexual tension from here."

4

She shushes me, a small laugh escaping her while she stuffs the assignment in her bag.

When the door opens, everyone's head turns to the noise.

Aiden Pierce.

Redfield's basketball captain.

I grew up watching basketball. Every Sunday, when my dad was home, we'd sit on the couch and watch the game while he snuck me some alfajores from his food truck. My mom would have slapped me on the back of my head if she caught me eating them.

And when I came here, the tradition still stood. Even though I couldn't be with my dad on Sundays, I would still attend every basketball game I could, which means I've watched Aiden play. A lot.

And as much as I don't like admitting it, he's good, like really fucking good. It could be an advantage because the guy is as tall as hell, but it's not; he has skill. I can appreciate that.

But what I'm not a fan of? How everyone treats him like he's a God around here. Girls fall at his feet, fanning themselves whenever he's near, and he eats it up; of course he does. A guy like that can get any girl he wants with a snap of his finger.

"Aiden," Professor Wilson sighs. "Class started thirty minutes ago."

"Sorry, sir," he says with a shrug. "I had early practice this morning. It ran over."

Professor Wilson sighs again and turns back around.

Add that to the list of things I'm not particularly fond of.

He gets special treatment.

"We've already assigned assignments," Professor Wilson says. "Grab one from the table closest to you."

Which would make it mine.

Oh joy.

Aiden sits beside Jordan, grabbing the piece of paper Mia hands over to him. He winks at her and stuffs it in his bag.

"We didn't have practice this morning," Jordan whispers, which makes my ears tip up.

Aiden grins. "He doesn't know that."

A liar too. How the list keeps expanding. A scoff escapes me before I can stop it, which makes both Jordan and Aiden turn to face me. My skin burns under the examination of his blue eyes burning into mine. It's not fair. He can't be tall, talented, and attractive. Pick one.

His eyebrows lift when he sees me.

Seeing as our best friends are dating, you'd expect us to have met before, but that hasn't happened yet.

The corner of his lips tips up in a smirk, which makes my eyes drift to them. Good lips too. Asshole. "Leila Pérez."

My name on his lips has my head spinning. I lift an eyebrow at him. "Do I know you?"

He laughs, fixing the hat on his head. "You're Rosie's friend, right?"

"Yeah."

He smiles, leaning forward on the table. "She's told me about you," he offers.

I nod. "Unfortunately, I can't say the same."

He laughs, which makes me glance at him. "What's with the hostility? Did I do something?"

I blink. "I'm sorry. Did you want me to get on my knees and bow for you?"

His tongue darts out to trace his bottom lip, and he lets out a low laugh. "Well..."

6

I roll my eyes. "Forget it."

"The assignment is due in two weeks," Professor Wilson says. "I expect you all to put in the work. Class dismissed."

Thank God. I pick up my bag, stuff the paper inside, and push the door open. I reach for my phone to meet up with Rosie, but a familiar, annoying voice stops me.

"You've been avoiding me."

I lift my head, seeing my roommate from hell standing in front of me, her arms crossed as she looks at me.

The lack of my smoothie is really taking its toll on me. I don't have the energy to deal with this today. "I've been busy."

"Your plants are all dead," she states, making my heart break a little. "You haven't been over all week, and they're not mine to take care of. Where the hell have you been sleeping?"

"With friends."

Her face contorts, judgment and disgust painted all over it. "Sleeping around for a bed? Really?"

I would have thought I'd be used to the judgment from her already when she has said so many more degrading things before, but the shock is still there. "I don't have time for this." I try to push past her, but she stops me.

"If you're not coming back, I need your room."

"For what?"

She shrugs. "For my stuff. It's hard living from one dresser."

I restrain the urge to roll my eyes. "Oh, the travesty."

"And your clothes take up *so* much space," she emphasizes, making me want to punch her. Just a little. Fine, a lot. "Can you do it?"

"Do what?" I don't even know what she's talking about; I just want to get rid of her.

7

"Move out."

Move out? Lord knows I want to, but I pay for that room. Granted, I barely use it anymore, but I can't crash at Gabi and Madi's forever. "And where am I going to go, Tiffany?"

She shrugs. "With those friends of yours. Or you could ask for a transfer."

"Trust me. I've tried." No one wants to switch, and there are no available rooms left, which means either I move out or I'm stuck with her.

"I don't care what you do; just do it. Honestly, the quicker, the better."

Like that's an option. "I've got to go." I push past her and pull up my phone, texting the girls. Guess I need to find a new place to stay.

2

I know your secret

Aiden

There's nothing I miss about Texas. It's always way too hot, too many bugs, and, oh yeah, my family lives there.

For eighteen years, I've wanted to escape that hellhole, and now that I have, nothing in my body misses home. I hated it there.

But here? I'm a completely different person. I'm someone. Even though I know who I really am, these people don't. The girls looking at me right now? All they see are my good looks and skills on the court. They don't see beyond the image I've tried so hard to keep. I fucking love it.

I lift my chin at the group of girls walking past me, the redhead in the mix keeping her eyes on me until she leaves the room.

Jordan nudges me on the arm, bringing my attention back to the assignment in my hands. "Can you talk to Grayson about it?" he asks.

"He doesn't do that anymore," I tell him, stuffing the paper in my pocket.

He stops in his tracks. "You've got to be kidding me."

I shrug, opening the door. "It's business class. It's not hard." Grayson's side hustle of doing assignments for people stopped months ago. Even though I've never used his services, many of my teammates have, and now that he's not doing that anymore, they have to actually work for their grades.

He laughs. "For you. I don't have time for this shit. I have practice all week."

"Coach still busting your balls?" I ask him, knowing damn well he is. Jordan's good, but he can get distracted. Can't fault Coach for wanting him to be more prepared.

"You have it easy." His eyes narrow, and he lets out a laugh. "He treats you with kid gloves."

"That's not true." His eyebrows lift, and I shrug. "Don't be jealous just because I'm the best player on the team," I joke, pushing through the doors to the courtyard.

He scoffs. "Best player, my ass."

I let out a laugh. I might be teasing him, but I work hard for that spot. Being captain isn't a joke to me or a pastime. Basketball is my number one priority. My only priority. So even though he might not agree, I will get there. I will be the best on the team, and I will get drafted. It has to happen; otherwise, I have nothing.

He lifts his chin. "You want to come over and play some games?"

"You sure you want to get another beating?"

He laughs. "Fuck you. You got lucky."

"Right." I let out a breath, shaking my head. "Can't. I have work tonight."

He laughs, like working is a joke to him, and it might as well be. "Dude, come on. You can get out of it."

"I can't."

His eyebrows lift, humor coating his expression. "Are you broke or something?"

My stomach cramps when I let out an uncomfortable laugh.

He claps a hand on my shoulder. "See you at practice." He heads away to the frat house where he lives, where I tried to apply freshman year and got turned down, or I quit. The logistics are still blurry. That whole night is blurry; all I remember is chants and alcohol and a line of coke in front of me with my name on it, watching as the other pledges snorted the line, huge grins on their faces.

But I'd seen what it could do to someone once the high wore off and once they became addicted to it, hooked on it, dependent on it.

By the time I've reached my place, I've re-lived that whole night in my head. I blow out a breath, shaking the image from my head when I hear my name. I blink, seeing Grayson getting off the back of his motorcycle, a bouquet of flowers in his hands; no doubt for Rosie. That girl gets more flowers than the dead, I swear.

"What's up?"

"You blanked out for a sec," he says, his eyebrows bunched, looking at me with worry.

I run a hand down my face. "It's all good," I tell him, or maybe I tell myself. I don't know.

"You working tonight?"

I nod. "I have class in like an hour, and then I head straight there."

He nods. "You want me to pick you up later?"

"Nah." I shrug. "I'll walk."

"You sure?"

I roll my eyes. "Yes, Jesus, go see your girlfriend. She's probably waiting naked in bed for you," I joke.

He doesn't think it's funny, though. He narrows his eyes at me. "Don't think about Rosie naked, asshole."

11

I snort. "Too late." I'm fucking with him. Rosalie is pretty, and my best friend definitely agrees, seeing as he's deeply in love with her, but she does nothing for me. She's way too tiny and way too good. I like a girl who can keep me on my toes, someone who will play with me, who'll make it worth my time. Too bad I haven't found her yet.

I let out a laugh when he flips me off, walking inside the house. I follow him in, heading to the kitchen to grab a glass of water and down it.

My phone buzzes, making my head twist to where the screen lights up on the counter. I set the glass behind me and grab it, opening up the text.

Unknown:

I know your secret

What the fuck? My eyebrows bunch up, my eyes burning a hole into the screen. I head towards the door, push it open and look around at… nothing. No one's there.

I look down at the phone in my hand, my eyes scanning the words, reading them over and over in my head.

There's only one secret I can think of.

Aiden:

Who is this?

In less than thirty seconds, I get another text, but there's no name, no words, just a picture.

My throat burns at the picture in front of me.
How the fuck did they get this?

Aiden:

What do you want?

3

Ex - roommates

Leila

Fridays are good for one thing.

Well, two. But the first is definitely my girls. I barely see them during the week, between classes and meetings with my agent, it doesn't leave much room for anything except a bath and heading into bed early.

The second thing?

Well…

Gabi flops onto the bed, pressing her hands under her chin, her blue eyes shining up at me. "Wanna go to a party?"

That's the second thing.

I've never been one to turn down a party, contrary to Madeline, who drops her head back and groans.

"When?" I ask, trying not to laugh at Madi shooting me a glare.

"Tomorrow. Grayson's house."

Madi shakes her head. "I need to study."

Gabriella turns her body, facing Madi, who's sitting on Rosie's pink couch. "You've been studying all week," she says. "It's a Saturday. Loosen up, woman."

She narrows her eyes at Gabi. "I have an assignment."

Gabi kicks her feet over the edge, sitting on the edge of the bed. I glance over at Rosie, who's smiling already. We all know how this is going to end. Gabi begs, Madi gives in, Gabi wins.

"It's one night," Gabi says to her friend. "I promise we'll leave early."

Madeline laughs. "We both know that's bullshit. If you stay late, I'll have to as well." Madi and Gabi moved into an off-campus apartment for their sophomore year. And knowing Gabi, she'll either make a huge noise and wake Madeline up anyway, or end up passed out at the party.

"I promise this time," Gabi says with determination. "We'll leave at two."

"Twelve." Madi rebuts.

"One?" Gabi compromises. Madi stares at her, mulling it over until Gabi groans. "C'mon."

"Fine," Madi says with an eye roll, giving in just like we all knew she would. We can't say no to Gabi; she's our weakness.

"Fuck yes." Gabi turns her head. "Who else is in?" She eyes Rosie.

"The party is at Grayson's house," she says with a shrug. "So, I'm already going to be there."

"Are you sure you can spend one night without your boyfriend?" Gabi teases her.

"She's in love," Madi replies. "Leave her alone, you bully."

"Hey." Gabi's head snaps to Madi. "That's how I show my love."

"I know I haven't been around as much," Rosie replies. "I'm sorry about that. It's just…" She smiles, lifting a shoulder apologetically. "I spent so long seeing people in love and wanting that for myself, and now that I have Grayson, I never want to leave him."

I smile at my best friend. I know exactly what she means, wanting to be around that person all the time. I thought I was in love once, gave so much of myself to that person, just for it to end up being a lie.

Gabi eyes me warily, probably knowing what I'm thinking about. "You're in, right?" she asks. "You're coming?"

"Of course." I shoot her a smile, trying to forget all about what went down in high school. "I'm there."

She grins. "I knew I liked you."

"Speaking of…" My eyes search for Gabi and Madi's, both of them looking my way. "Can I stay over again?"

"Of course," Madi says. "You're a better roommate than this one, anyway." She gestures with her head to Gabi.

"Take that back." Gabi narrows her eyes at Madeline, who's smirking. She shakes her head, laughing at Gabi's expression.

"Actually," Rosie says. "I've been meaning to talk to you about that."

"About what?"

"Well, I know you can't change roommates, but would you like to move in here?"

I blink. Move in here? "You're serious?" She nods, a smile tugging at her lips. Shit. That would be amazing, but… "Where would you go?"

She shrugs, tucking her blonde hair behind her ear. "I was thinking of moving in with Grayson."

My eyes widen. "Really?"

"Whipped," Gabi sings.

She shakes her head, a smile on her lips. "Yeah," she says. "I practically sleep there all the time anyway, and he's asked me once or twice."

My eyes widen. "And you said yes?"

"Not yet. But if you want this place, then it's yours."

I smile at my best friend since high school. "I would love to, but I don't think I can afford this place." I *know* I can't afford it. This apartment is 1000 square feet of wealth. The couch Madi is sitting on probably costs more than everything I own. There's no way I could ever pay for this place.

Rosie shrugs. "My mother pays for it," she says. "She'll never know."

I eye the girls, and their expressions say everything. *Do it*, they scream with their eyes. I glance at my best friend once more, mulling it over, knowing everything in me wants to say hell yes. "You're sure?"

She nods. "I'm very sure. It's a win-win, Leila, just say yes."

I blow out a heavy breath, unable to contain the grin on my face. "I don't have to put up with Tiffany anymore?"

"Thank fuck," Gabi mutters. "She was a disaster. I knew it from the moment I saw her."

"You can't judge someone by how they look," Madi says. "She could have been a really nice girl."

Gabi shrugs. "But she wasn't," she says. "She said the only reason I was bi was because I'm a whore." Damn. I didn't know that. "She looks evil and is evil."

Tiffany was one of the worst people I've ever had the displeasure of being around. She was judgmental and had no regard for my personal space. And now, hearing that she offended my friend? I owe Rosie big time for finally being done with her.

"And you didn't slap her?" Madi asks, her brows lifting.

Gabriella flicks her brown hair behind her shoulders, letting out a sigh. "It's not worth it. People are just going to say what they want no matter what I do." She glances at Rosie, a smile on her lips. "You're moving in with Grayson."

We all note how Gabi seems to want to change the subject, so Rosie smiles, a blush peeking on her pale skin. "Yeah," she breathes out. "I am."

I nudge her. "How do you feel about that?"

She blows out a breath, a huge grin on her face. "Good," she says. "I can't wait."

Her phone rings beside her, and by the smile on her face, I can already guess who it is.

"Is that lover boy?" Gabi asks.

Rosie lifts her eyes, a laugh escaping her. "Don't call him that," she says, scrunching her nose. "But yes." She drops her eyes again, texting away. "Do you guys want to come over later?" Rosie says, lifting her head to look at us.

"To Grayson's?" Madi asks.

She nods. "We can watch a movie or something, to celebrate."

"Well, since someone's dragging me to a party tomorrow, I only have today to study," Madi says apologetically. "I won't make it. I'm sorry."

"That's okay," Rosie says, eyeing Gabi. "What about you?"

She shakes her head. "Dance practice," she says.

Rosie frowns, looking at me.

A laugh escapes me. "Sure, I'll be there. I just have to get my stuff from my dorm before I do."

Gabi lets out a snort. "Good luck dealing with her."

I don't need luck. I need resilience.

4

New roommates

Aiden

"Fuck, you're so beautiful."

I stop in my tracks, the bucket of popcorn almost spilling. There's some seriously heavy breathing going on in there, and honestly, I don't know what to do.

I mean, I don't really want to go in there and walk in on… whatever the hell they're doing, but I also want to fuck with them.

"Aiden's here," Rosie gasps. I shake my head, stifling a laugh.

"He's in the bathroom," I hear Grayson reply. "I just want to kiss you. It feels like I haven't seen you in so long."

Thank God. They're just kissing. I push open the living room doors and hear shuffling, watching as Rosie almost jumps out of her skin when she hears the door open.

I settle myself in between them, placing the popcorn on the glass table in front of us and place my arms around each of their shoulders. I let out a sigh. "What we doing, roomies?" I say to both my roommates because it turns out Rosie is moving in with us.

Grayson throws my arm away from him, getting up from the couch. I'm unable to stop laughing when he scowls at me. "You couldn't have given us ten more minutes?" he asks, throwing a throw pillow at me.

A snort escapes me as I catch the pillow. "Please. We both know it would have taken more than ten minutes."

He shakes his head and laughs, sitting on the other side and pulling Rosie to his side. Those two have been glued to each other's side since they got together. I've got to say, I like seeing Grayson happy. Dude didn't even think he was capable of love a few months ago, and now look at him; he looks like a lovesick puppy.

"What are we watching?" I ask, grabbing a handful of popcorn from the bucket.

Rosie smiles at me. "A walk to remember."

Grayson snickers. "You staying for the movie?" he asks me.

I shrug. "Finished my workout, got nothing to do."

He shakes his head. "Good luck, bro," he says, humor coating his tone.

"For what?"

"It's a chick flick about a girl who's dying."

"Fuck."

"Yeah."

"They're going to cry."

He laughs. "As I said. Good luck."

I came from a family of brothers. Two older brothers who definitely didn't watch rom-coms. I have no idea how to deal with crying girls. I pick up another handful of popcorn and stuff it in my mouth when the door rings. Grayson glances at me, and I take that as my cue.

I head towards the door, reach for the door handle and pull it open. My eyebrows lift when I see the same girl from class last week. Her eyes round at the sight of me, and I don't know what that means exactly. I smile at her, waiting for her to smile back, but she doesn't. She narrows her eyes at me a little. Huh. Not the reaction I'm used to.

"Leila." I note the way her eyes widen at the sound of her name coming from my mouth. "You stalking me?" I joke.

She lets out a breath. "Rosie invited me over."

I find it funny how this girl seems unaffected by me. It's strange. I like it. I lick my bottom lip to hide the grin I'm sporting. She acts like she doesn't know who I am, but I know better. I know it's bullshit. Everyone around here knows who I am.

Not only that, but I've got something on this girl. Rosie has let slip many times how obsessed with basketball Leila is. How she comes to all of my games, she never misses one, apparently.

She blinks, propping a hand on her hip. "Are you going to let me in or just stand guard at the door?"

A smile spreads across my face, turning into a laugh. "Are you that eager to come inside?" I tease her, loving how her warm complexion brightens, red coating her cheeks, even if her eyes burn with anger. It's still cute as shit.

"If this is some little game you play, I'm not interested."

Damn. She seems pissed. "Well, shit." I fix my hat nervously. "This isn't the exact reaction I'm used to."

She shrugs. "Just not a fan of yours," she says.

"Really?" A smirk paints my lips. "According to your friend, you come to all of my games."

She closes her eyes, cursing under her breath. When she opens her eyes again, the regained fire is back in her eyes. "Don't get an ego boost," she says. "I don't come for you."

I laugh, letting out a low whistle. "Consider my ego boosted." I shoot her a wink. "The more you talk, the more I can see how obsessed you are with me."

There's no reason I should let this one girl's opinion of me affect me. So, she doesn't like me; big fucking deal. A lot of people don't like me. It shouldn't hurt. It doesn't.

She scoffs. It's the closest I'm getting to a laugh from her. "I just happen to like basketball; it has nothing to do with you."

I hum, crossing my arms. At least she likes basketball. My kind of girl. "That's too bad." I smirk, continuing to tease her. "I'd love to look up at the bleachers, seeing you in a cute little outfit and some pom-poms, screaming my name."

I see her cheeks flush and I resist the urge to laugh. She already doesn't like me. I shouldn't be giving her more incentive. She blinks, squaring her shoulders. "That will never happen."

I shrug, but before I can say anything else, Rosie appears at my side. "Oh hey," she says. "You came."

I tut. "And here I thought you were here for me," I joke, placing a hand on my chest, feigning hurt.

"What are you guys doing?" Rosie asks.

I turn my head to look down at her. She's so tiny, it hurts my neck. "Having the time of my life talking to your friend here." I smile down at her, but she doesn't look convinced, turning to Leila for confirmation.

"He's killing my will to live," she says dryly.

The more she talks, the more I want to rally with her. I want to get to know her. I don't know why she doesn't seem to like me, don't really care. Something about her intrigues me.

Rosie laughs, steps back inside the house and to the living room. I step inside, holding out my hand, allowing Leila to enter. She walks past me, her body brushing against mine as she walks in front of me. My lips twitch when she looks behind her shoulders, narrowing her eyes when I trail behind her.

"Did you get your stuff?" Rosie asks once they're in the living room.

"Yes," Leila says, sitting beside Rosie, fanning her long brown hair behind her back. "She wasn't lying. My plants were all dead."

"How long did you leave them?" Rosie asks her.

She shrugs. "A week?" Her face crinkles up with a wince. "I just couldn't handle her anymore."

"Bad roommate?" I ask, dropping down on the couch beside Grayson.

She eyes me warily for a second. "Yeah," she says. "The worst."

"Damn. That sucks." I note how she spoke to me without a remark. Yet. "Is that why you're celebrating?"

She smirks, the side of her lips lifting. That's still a smile, right? That counts. "We're celebrating because you've got a new roommate."

I can't help but grin. "Would that be you?"

She rolls her eyes. "I mean Rosalie."

"Right," I murmur. "And where will that leave you?"

"Far away from you," she replies.

Grayson eyes me, noticing the way she's ribbing me. "Have you two met before?"

"We're in the same class." I shrug. "I'm sure we'll get acquainted soon."

Her eyebrows lift. "Not if I have anything to do with it. You probably won't show up anyway."

I go still. "What does that mean?"

23

She sits upright, tilting her body forward to face me. "How you blatantly use your reputation as an excuse to slack off."

"Slack off?" I repeat. "I work hard."

"I'm sure," she says with an eye roll. "So you didn't lie about having practice that morning?" Her head tilts, thinking she's got me.

I didn't have practice. I worked late the night before, slept through my alarm. Can't tell her that, though.

Grayson brings his knuckles to his mouth, hiding his laughter. I'm sure he's loving this, seeing a girl who can't stand me.

When I don't answer, she shakes her head. "Who knows? Maybe you won't even have to work." She waves a hand to Grayson. "You'll probably get him to do it for you."

"Nah," Grayson replies. "I don't do that anymore."

"About that." I extend my legs, crossing them on the table. "Jordan has been hounding me to get you to do it. Why don't you?"

He shrugs. "I don't have a reason to anymore. I needed the money; I wanted to leave. I don't want that anymore." He looks to the side, down at Rosie, who's looking up at him like he hung the moon. "I finally have a reason to stick around. Don't want to do anything to risk it."

A snicker leaves my lips. "That's cute as shit. But unhelpful."

"He's just going to have to do it himself," Leila says. "As will you."

I tip my body forward, glancing at her. "Wanna be study partners?"

The craziest thing happens. She laughs. Like an actual laugh. Sure, she's laughing at the idea of working with me, but

24

fuck, it's a pretty sight. Might be the only time I get her to laugh around me, so I eat it up, watching how the corner of her eyes wrinkle, and her pink lips tip up in a cute smile. She's pretty, that's for damn sure. "I work alone."

I tut. "Not very social of you."

"I have no problem being social," she replies. "Just with dealing with arrogant assholes."

I rub my chest. "Ouch." I let out a laugh, knowing how wrong she is. At least I have her fooled, right?

"Oh, please." She rolls her eyes. "We both know nothing I say is going to hurt you. You don't care what I think."

"I don't?"

She shrugs. "Would you care if I said last week's game was way out of character from you?"

Fuck. My smile is completely wiped away. My teammates, Coach, and now her? I have never lost before. Not once. And the one time I do, it's completely obvious. Whoever texted me telling me to throw the game must have gotten what they wanted because they haven't texted back.

I avoid looking at this girl who seems to enjoy laying it on me and shrug. "So you really do watch my games," I tease her. Can't really disagree with her. It *was* out of character.

I hear a sigh from her that makes my eyes flash to hers. "Cocky as usual. Even when I'm criticizing you, you seem to hear a compliment."

I can't help but grin when I glance at her. "You seem to enjoy it, who am I to stop you?"

I don't even notice that there's no one between us when I shift closer to her. Her eyes widen, looking around the room for her best friend, who just left with my best friend. She groans, tipping her head back. "They just left to hook up, didn't they?"

My shoulder lifts. "Seems like it."

"Great." A soft sigh escapes her lips.

I lean forward, grabbing another handful of popcorn. "Well, I'm not letting these go to waste," I say before stuffing them in my mouth. I try to keep my eyes on the tv, scrolling through the movie categories, but the way Leila is looking at me, tracking my every movement, is distracting me. I turn to face her, making her eyes snap to mine.

They're green. Never noticed that before, but my god, they're so green. Like freshly cut limes and just as bittersweet, so big and round, with long lashes framing them. She blinks, snapping me out of checking her out, and I hold out the bucket to her, shaking it. "You want some?"

She shakes her head, pulling out her phone and scrolling through it.

"Calling for reinforcements?"

She glances at me. "Seeing as my best friend is off celebrating with her boyfriend, I guess there's no reason for me to stick around."

"You don't need to leave," I tell her. I kind of like having her around. "We can watch a movie," I suggest.

She blows out a breath, moving to the edge of the couch. "I should go," she says instead, which blows. She holds up her phone. "Madi texted, and she wants to go shopping for the party tomorrow."

She's lying. I know damn well she didn't get a text, and that Madeline is currently studying, according to Rosie, which means she's lying to me. The girl doesn't even know me, but if she really doesn't want to be around me, who am I to stop her? I nod, leaning back on the couch. "So, I'll see you tomorrow then?"

"Shit." She exhales, squeezing her eyes shut. "I forgot the party was here."

I let out a laugh, seeing her fists bunch up beside her. I'm not really one for parties, especially when everyone's mood is down from last week's loss, but seeing as I'm captain and I have to keep up morale, it's kind of my obligation. But knowing she's going to be there tomorrow? This is going to be fun.

"Sure is. So why don't you answer that fake text and go shopping?" Her eyes widen when the words come out of my mouth, making the green of her eyes that much more prominent. I smirk at her reaction. "Buy something pretty for me, baby."

Those bright green eyes narrow, scowling at me, and she picks up her bag, throwing it over her shoulder. I keep my eyes on her until she's out of the room and I hear the door close.

I run a hand down my face, laughing to myself. Who the hell is this girl? And why do I want to get to know her?

5

Spin the bottle

Leila

"One more," Gabriella says, holding out her red cup.

"Nope." Madi grabs her cup and places it on the table behind her. "You promised we'd leave at one."

"One thirty?" Gabi asks, blinking up at her.

Madi glares, shaking her head. "One."

"Fine," Gabi concedes.

My eyes look around the dark tiles of the kitchen, now littered with drinks and snacks. Grayson is going to have fun cleaning this place up tomorrow, considering how big this damn house is.

"Is Rosie here?" I look around the party, trying to spot her face in the crowd.

Madi hums. "I saw her with Grayson like ten minutes ago." She laughs. "Those two were two minutes away from public indecency."

"Is it considered public indecency if it's inside your house?"

"It is if there's an audience."

"No," Gabi replies. "That's just a good time." She grins, wrapping her arm around mine.

Madi groans. "You're drunk? Already?"

Gabi waves her off, attempting to stand up straight, leaning all of her weight onto me. I snicker, glancing at Madi. "No,"

Gabi says. "I'm fine, look." She tries to take a step forward and almost trips us both over. I grab onto her, keeping her steady. "Okay," she breathes out. "Maybe."

"That's a yes," Madi says with a sigh.

"And you're too sober." Gabi grabs her cup, holding it out to Madi. "You want a drink?"

Madi smiles. It's hard not to. Gabi is the kind of girl who can make you laugh even when you don't feel like it. "I can't," Madi tells her. "I'm driving tonight." I admire Madi. Never stepping out of line, always in control. It's got to be exhausting, though.

"C'mon," Gabi urges. "We can walk home instead."

Madi snorts out a laugh, shaking her head. "You can barely stand."

Gabi waves her off, grabbing my drink from my hand and downing it before I can stop her. Jesus. "Okay," I tell her. "You're cut off."

She eyes me, her eyes dipping down to my outfit. "You look hot in green."

I breathe out a laugh. "Thanks."

"You know what would be fun?" she asks, sighing dramatically.

"Sleep?" I offer.

"No," Gabi says with a headshake. "A hot tub."

I scrunch my brows at her. "A hot tub?"

She nods. "Do you want to go swimming?" she asks, grinning at me.

Not particularly, no. But I'd rather not kill all of her dreams. I sit her down on the nearest chair, avoiding the mass amount of people walking past us. "Sure," I tell her. "But there's no hot tub."

"Yes, there is," she says. "Travis and I took a dip a few weeks ago last time we were here."

I look up at Madi, seeing her eyes widen. "They have a hot tub?" she mouths at me.

I shrug. "I have no idea. Don't ask me."

Our heads turn when chants come from the other room.

"What's going on?" Madi asks.

A girl turns to face her, sipping her drink. "They're playing Spin the Bottle."

"Damn, we should go," Gabi suggests.

"Who's playing Spin the Bottle?" A dumb-ass frat guy asks, throwing his arm around Madi. He licks his lips, looking down at her. "I wouldn't mind kissing you," he says, blowing Madi a kiss.

She slaps his hand away, taking a step away from him. "No one is playing."

"We're not?" Gabi asks, frowning at me.

Brad grins at Gabi. "I'll play with you if you want."

What a sap. I roll my eyes. "Get out of here, Brad."

He laughs at me, running a hand through his styled brown hair. "Don't come running back to me when you want to get some." He winks my way and finally walks away. Not without causing damage, though, because now the secret's out.

My lips thin, feeling their eyes fall on me. I can already feel it. The questions, the judging, the disgust.

"You slept with him?" Madi asks.

I blow out a breath, closing my eyes. "It was dumb, I know."

"He's an asshole," Madi replies.

I nod. "I'm well aware."

"He made fun of you," Gabi says, her mouth turned in a frown.

30

That one's like a punch to my stomach. "Yep. Know that too. Thanks for bringing it up."

Call it a lapse in judgment, if you will. It was dumb; I know that. I regret it every day. But that's what happens, isn't it? Guys like Brad call you names to your face and beg to sleep with you in private.

I love the girls, I really do. But none of them know what it's like being a bigger girl. I don't have the same experiences they do, and that includes putting up with comments about the way I look and completely ignoring how they made me feel when they come back around and flirt with me.

I don't want to get into it with them. I know it should probably be one of the worst mistakes of my life, but ultimately, he was half decent, and it made me feel good about myself, even if it was just for a brief moment.

"Come on," I urge Gabi to stand, wrapping my arm around hers to keep her steady on her feet.

"So, we're playing?" she asks, grinning at me like an idiot.

I laugh. "Yeah, sure, why not?"

We make our way over to the living room. Madi follows us behind, walking over to where all the noise is. A crowd surrounds the circle of people on the ground, two of them meeting in the middle for a kiss.

I spot Grayson sitting on the couch with Rosie propped on his lap. I snicker, making my way over to them. "Having fun?"

He sighs. "We were already here when they came in."

Rosie turns to face me. "Grayson doesn't want to play."

"Hell no," he says, clutching onto Rosie. "I don't want to kiss anyone but you."

"You wanna join?" I ask Rosie, wanting to see what Grayson will do.

She eyes him for a second, mischief sparkles in her eyes, no doubt wanting the same reaction I do.

He narrows his eyes at her. "Don't even think about it, angel."

"But I've never played Spin the Bottle before," she replies, her lips painted with a smirk.

Grayson leans in, planting a soft kiss on her lips. "I know you're just fucking with me," he says. "But I still don't like it." She smiles up at him, his eyes on her, completely consumed by each other. "We'll play together sometime," he tells her.

Gabi plops herself on the ground, joining the group. She turns to face me, and I roll my eyes, giving in and joining her. I sit on the ground with her and a bunch of people I don't want to kiss.

My head lifts when the door opens again, spotting the one person I was hoping I wouldn't run into tonight.

Aiden Pierce steps into the room, looking around the group.

"Oh shit," his teammate, Ethan, says, looking around the room. "What's going on in here?" Where Aiden goes, everyone follows, which means not only his teammates but a bunch of other people have joined in.

"You want to join?" one girl asks, smiling up at Carter, another one of Aiden's teammates. He smiles at her, shaking his head.

Aiden makes eye contact with me, his eyes widening when he sees me. "Leila." His deep, gruff voice makes me shiver when I see everyone's eyes on me. "You came."

I decide to play coy, blinking up at him. "And you are?"

There's a low howl coming from his teammates, the girls in the room shooting me daggers with their eyes. Not Aiden, though; he laughs, a smile spreading across his face.

I watch as Jordan nudges Aiden, eyeing me carefully. "What's her deal?"

I scoff, Aiden's eyes still on me. His tongue traces his full bottom lip, wetting it, and he shrugs. "Leila here is my biggest fan. Isn't that right?"

Gabi laughs beside me, and I glare at her. "What?" she asks innocently. "It's funny." Traitor.

My head snaps when I see Aiden sitting on the ground, everyone making room for him. "Are you playing?" he asks.

"Not if you are."

"Oh, c'mon." He stretches out, his dark brown hair hidden behind that baseball cap he always wears. "Don't chicken out."

I open my mouth to reply, but his phone buzzes in his pocket. I watch as he pulls it out and scans the screen, his jaw clenching when he reads whatever is on that phone. His eyes blaze, looking around the room.

I raise my eyebrows. "You look pretty scared to me. Are you sure you want to do this?"

He tucks his phone back in his pocket, his lips twitching a little, but just as quickly, his face drops, and I watch as he swallows, making his Adam's apple bob with the movement. "You want to play?" he asks, his eyes darkening. "We'll play."

His hand reaches out in front of him, those long fingers grabbing the neck of the bottle. I glance up at him, seeing him staring back at me, smiling slightly, before the bottle spins on the ground between us.

"You're watching that bottle pretty damn close," Aiden says, his voice making me glance up at him. "Any particular reason?"

I swallow, looking into his eyes as he grins. Yes, there's a reason. I hate to admit this, but something about him makes me nervous. And the thought of what might happen scares me. Will it land on someone else? Or will it... I gulp.

Please don't land on me.

Please don't land on me.

Please don't—

"Look at that." I watch Aiden's head drop to the ground, looking at the bottle that is—

Fuck.

The neck of the bottle lands at my feet, pointing directly at me. I glance up at him, his blue eyes shining with humor.

"What are the chances?" Aiden asks, a husky laugh coming from him.

"Stop being cocky," Grayson tells him.

"It's my nature," Aiden replies, looking up at his best friend. His eyes land on mine, tilting his head. "Are you up for it?"

"On second thought, this game is stupid." I let out a breath, turning to face Gabi. "Do you want to take my place?" She smiles knowingly but shakes her head.

"No way," Aiden interrupts. "You are not backing out now. Are you really that scared of me?"

"I'm not scared," I tell him, leaning forward. "I'm just not interested." I'm such a liar. The idea of kissing him has my blood pumping, but I can't let him know that.

He shakes his head. "I find that hard to believe."

I scoff. "That's just because you're conceited."

He tuts, leaning in closer. "Not conceited, baby. Just confident."

"If she won't kiss you, I will." A girl beside him says, glaring at me. I look to Aiden, raising my brow, seeing if he'll take the bait, but he doesn't even look at her.

He tilts his head, looking amused. "It's just a kiss," he says with that husky voice of his. "I promise it won't get you pregnant." He smirks. "I know I'm good, but—"

"Seriously?" I laugh. "You really can't accept that I just don't like you?"

"And you can't finish the game and kiss me?" Those words on his lips have my breath hitching in my throat. I can tell he notices because his smile widens, eyes dipping down to my mouth. Is this really happening?

"Just kiss him," Madi says, making me rip my eyes from Aiden and to her. Her long legs are crossed as she shrugs, her plump red lips lifting in a smirk. "He'll never shut up if you don't."

"Listen to your friend," Aiden coaxes. My head snaps to the man in front of me. Did he get closer? "She knows what she's talking about."

I narrow my eyes at him. "Do you even remember my name?"

He licks his bottom lip once again, making my eyes drift down to them. "Of course I do, Leila," he emphasizes, making me look at his eyes instead of his lips. "Did you just want to hear me say it?" he teases. "You can hear me say it all you want. Just kiss me first."

I want to scorn him for being such an arrogant piece of work. I want to say it will never happen. I want to say something, but instead, I lean in.

Dios. I'm going to regret this.

6

Make a move

Aiden

I really wish I could say I feel guilty about kissing Leila. My stomach should be churning, riddled with guilt. I should pull away and tell her I can't do this. It should feel wrong, bad. But the last thing I feel is guilt.

It's hard to feel bad when her pink, plump lips meet mine in a soft kiss. The way she allows my mouth to move over hers, so in sync, letting our lips get tangled as she returns the kiss. Holy fuck. I bite back a moan when her tongue swipes over my lip, sliding in my mouth.

My hands press deeper into the floor, leaning into her, tempted to pull her flush to me. I want to feel the way her breath gets caught in her lungs; I want to slip my hands into her hair and feel her body close to mine. I want to slide my tongue inside her mouth and taste her. I want to deepen this kiss, but before I can do any of that, I feel her pull away from me.

"Wha—"

I open my eyes, suddenly reminded of the circle of people surrounding us that just watched that kiss. I was so lost in the moment I completely forgot we had an audience.

My fingers reach up, grazing against my lips, still feeling her on them, still tasting her. Shit. That was a good kiss.

"Well." Grayson clears his throat. "That was something."

"I've had better," Leila replies, her eyes on the ground.

I've had better?

I let out a bitter laugh, running my tongue over my bottom lip. "That's bullshit."

Her head snaps up, red coating her face. There's no way she didn't like it. I know she felt as affected as I did by that kiss.

She shrugs. "You're a bad kisser, Aiden. Hate to break it to you."

Whispers fill the room as I process what she's telling me. "I'm a bad kisser?" I ask her in disbelief. "Never had any complaints before."

She rolls her eyes at me. Fuck, why do I find that so sexy? "That's because they just wanted to hook up with the captain of the basketball team. A bunch of yes men telling you what you want to hear. I'm not one of them."

Yeah, I can see that.

This is going to be so much harder than I thought.

She turns her head to face her friend. "You owe me," she says, her friend snickering when Leila stands. "I need a drink." She doesn't even acknowledge me when she walks out of the room.

My mind is spinning. Who sent me that text? What do they want from me? I look around the room, but no one is looking at me, too invested in the game still going on. Fuck this. I lift myself off the ground, stepping closer to the door.

"You okay, man?" Jordan asks, landing a hand on my shoulder.

I nod. "Yeah, I'm good. Just thirsty." I push the door open, leaving the crowded room and heading to the kitchen.

"Pierce." A guy I've never seen before claps my shoulder. "Tough luck, man," he says

"Uh, yeah, thanks." My face falls at his disappointment. One game. I lose one game and everything changes.

I squeeze past the people dancing in the kitchen, trying to find a flash of green. That tight green corset top she's wearing has engrained itself in my mind. But I don't see it anywhere. I don't see her long brown hair flowing behind her back; I don't see those black denim jeans clung to every dip and curve in her body. I don't fucking see her.

Where did she go? Did she leave?

"Hey." I feel a soft hand run down my arm and turn my head. A blonde girl I'm pretty sure was in Jordan's bed last week, shoots me a smile. "Aiden, right? I'm Valerie. I'm in the Kappa Gamma house on Greek row," she says like that's any sort of relevance to me. Her hand leaves my arm and pulls out a piece of paper from her jean pocket, holding it out to me. "You should call me sometime."

I take the piece of paper from her, scanning it when she leaves my side. My eyebrows lift at what she wrote beside her phone number. 34D. No name, just her bra size. I shake my head, crumple it up and stuff it in my jeans.

My head lifts, trying to see where the hell Leila went. She's not down here. Is she upstairs? I grip the railing, climbing up the stairs until I see a flash of green against a wall. Can't see much of her, though; another guy's body is in the way.

I cross my arms, leaning against the wall while listening to her laugh. It's not the laugh I've heard before, though; it's strained and tense, almost uncomfortable.

"You know I can make it worth your time." My eyebrows lift, wondering what Leila will say. Does she like this guy?

"The first time was more than enough." So she's slept with mystery dude before. Interesting. "Just let it go." Her hand presses against his chest, pushing him back.

"C'mon," he growls, stepping closer to her. "It was good, right?"

"You know," I start, approaching them. The guy turns his head around, eyes widening when he sees me there. "When a girl pushes you off her, it usually means she isn't interested."

"Oh shit, Pierce," the guy says, letting out a strained laugh. "Tough game last week, huh?"

My brows furrow. "What were you two talking about?"

He laughs. "Crazy thing. I forgot where your bathroom was. I was just asking this girl here." What a load of bullshit.

I hear Leila scoff and look up to see her roll her eyes at him. I don't bother acknowledging him when I take a step closer to her, noting how she swallows when I get close to her.

I cock my head. "You okay?" I ask her.

"She's fine. I really was just lost."

"There's a bathroom downstairs," I cut him off. "Go."

I don't even bother turning around to check; the way her shoulders sag in relief tells me he's long gone.

"What was that about?"

Her eyes meet mine in defiance. "He wanted to know where the bathroom was."

I find it amusing how she's relentless in going against everything I say. "Please," I scoff. "We both know that was bullshit."

"You really think you can do whatever you want, don't you?" she asks me, her eyes burning with that fire I'm used to seeing from her. "You just tell people to leave and expect them to listen."

39

I shrug, leaning into her. "It worked, didn't it?"

She nods. "You're right," she says before shaking her head. "But it won't work with me. I don't see what the appeal is. You're all the same."

"And who do you want me to be?" She doesn't answer, though. Her head turns to the side, away from me. I trace her face with my eyes and see she's biting down on her bottom lip. "Why did you leave?"

She looks back at me, her throat bobbing as she swallows. Her mouth parts as a shaky breath escapes her, which makes my eyes dip down to her lips again, and she instinctively licks them. "Are you thinking about that kiss?" I ask her.

"You mean how bad it was?" she retorts. "Yeah, can't forget it."

I laugh; it's impossible not to. "Cut the shit. The way you slipped your tongue in my mouth says the opposite."

Her face heats as the words slip out of my mouth. She clamps her mouth shut, knowing I'm right. She liked it. She fucking liked the kiss we shared.

I wonder if it had gone on for longer if she would have grabbed my face, moaned into my mouth, sucked on my bottom lip. Fuck, I'm getting off track.

"Can I get your number?" I ask.

Her face contorts with laughter. "Why would I do that?"

I reach up, brushing a strand of hair behind her ear. "So I can see you again."

She shakes her head, looking down at the ground between us. "Sorry, I'm not interested." She's such a liar, can't even look me in the face when she says that. The way she kissed me tells me she's very much interested.

I take a step back from her. "You know, this playing hard-to-get thing you've got going on isn't cute anymore."

She looks up, narrowing her eyes at me as she crosses her arms, making her cleavage pop up through that bright green corset top clinging to her body. God. "Then stop playing," she replies.

I lift an eyebrow. "So you admit it, you are playing with me."

She sighs, turning her head to the side. "I didn't say that."

"So you'll give me your number?"

Her head turns back to me, brows furrowed once again. "I didn't say that either."

"Alright," I relent, laughing. "Then what are you saying?"

Her eyes lift. "I'm saying if you really want something, then maybe you have to chase it a bit." She drops her arms and pushes past me, and I let her. Watching as she walks away from me, I press my fist to my mouth to stifle my laugh.

She wants my attention?

She's fucking got it.

7

I'm not a patient man

Aiden

I've always liked sweating.

Working my body to the max, exerting all of my energy into something, anything. It always helped clear my mind and made me focus on that one and only thing I was doing, nothing else.

I guess it's why basketball came naturally to me when I was young. I had nothing else that was worth my time except a ball and a hoop. I remember seeing the kids from my school playing, watching their games, thinking I could do that. I could be out there playing with them and win.

But I had never been part of a team before; the closest I got was a guy who had been watching me play at the park and asked if he could play against me. I wiped him clean off the floor, scoring every time. It was easy. As natural as breathing.

It was the one thing I had to look forward to. Through all the hits and punches and dirty looks, there was one thing I liked. I was good at it, and I worked hard to get where I am. Basketball is my future. It's the only thing I have going, and I won't mess it up, no matter what I have to do.

The ball pressed up against my chest flies into the air, and Jordan catches it instantly.

"Good pass, Pierce," Coach shouts. Jordan dribbles the ball, attempting to score, and I jump, attempting to block, but then I feel the ball hit my fingertips before it goes in.

"Fuck."

Jordan laughs. "Bad luck, Cap."

My brows lift. "Try again." I throw the ball back to him, but the whistle blows before he shoots again.

"That was good, boys," Coach says, bringing out the ball rack. "Get in the showers."

I pick up the ball closest to me, watching the guys head past into the locker rooms.

"Pierce." My head snaps up. "A word." Coach Thompson looks down at his notepad.

I place the ball on the ball rack, heading towards him. "Yes, Coach?"

"Last week," he starts, my heart accelerating. "What happened, son?"

I don't answer. I can't. I don't have the words. When he lifts his head, the disappointment is there, and it crushes me. "I don't know what happened or if it was just a fluke," he says. "But you were off your game." He shakes his head. "That was an easy block; you should have been able to knock it out of the air."

I know. My head shakes, not knowing what to say. The night before, I couldn't sleep, knowing I had to throw the game. I could have blocked that ball in my sleep, but I couldn't. I had to make sure my future was solid, even if it meant losing a few games. "It won't happen again." But as I'm saying the words, I'm not sure they're true.

He nods. "The team is counting on you, Pierce."

"Yes, Coach."

He places the notepad under his arm, patting me on my arm. "Now go. Get in the showers."

I blow out a breath, running to the locker room. My future is on the line. Everything I have worked for is at risk of being taken away from me if I don't do what they want.

"Look who it is," Ethan announces when I walk in. "He let you off again, huh?" He doesn't let me reply, letting out a scoff instead. "Figures. Let me guess, you sucked him off good?" His brows raise. "Tickle his balls, did you?" He emulates by wiggling his fingers.

A towel whips him in the head. "Shut the fuck up, Ethan," Carter Ruthers, one of the best players I've played with, says. "Show some fucking respect."

It shouldn't bother me that Ethan Campbell hasn't respected me ever since I became captain, but it does. The way he treats me brings me back to high school when the coach suggested I try out. It was useless; no matter how good I played, no one wanted me on their team, but Coach did. He saw something in me that was worth it and let me join the team. I owe everything to Coach Thomson.

I'm here now. I'm here, and I'm ready to do whatever it takes so that I never have to question what hunger is like again. So if I have to deal with Ethan's snarky comments every now and then, so fucking be it. The rest of the team respects me, Coach respects me; that's all I need.

Ethan's jaw clenches, and he spins, cursing when he heads into the showers.

Carter walks over to me, shaking his head. "He's just being an asshole today," he says, sitting down on the bench, running a towel over his wet hair. "Coach busted him for coming in drunk again."

44

I scoff, ripping my jersey over my head, I jam it into the locker. "That has nothing to do with me."

"Maybe not," Jordan says, closing his locker. "But he's pissed you get off scot-free every time."

I pull my t-shirt back on, tugging it down over my torso. "I'm sick of taking the hit for other people's actions." I slam my locker a little harder than needed, grabbing my cap and placing it on my head. "If he has a problem with Coach, then he needs to take it up with him."

My phone rings in my hand, the screen flashing with the last person I want to speak to. "Fuck, I've got to go." I grab my gym bag, fling it over my shoulder, and head outside, letting out a curse before I answer, bringing my phone to my ear.

"I don't have it all yet," I tell him, knowing the reason he's calling.

"That's bullshit," he spits out. "I know you're lying."

I squeeze my eyes shut. "Brandon, I don't have it. I have a shift tomorrow. I can send it over once I get paid."

A few seconds tick by, silence filling my ear, and then, "You know mom is sick, right?" My jaw tightens. He always does this, brings up Mom, knowing I can't say no when it comes to her. "She's barely getting out of bed, definitely not going to work. How do you expect us to eat?"

Why does it have to be on me? Why is it always on me? "You could get a job," I grit out.

A scoff on the other end hits my ear. "And leave Mom alone? Jerry is trailing around again. I can't do that."

My heart pounds when I hear that asshole's name. "How?" I ask my brother, a nauseating pit forming in my stomach at the sound of his name. "I thought you and Cameron handled him?" He hasn't been around in so long; why now?

45

"We did," he says. "But things got complicated."

God fucking damn it. "What happened?"

"Nothing that concerns you, little bro." His laughter makes my stomach churn. "Just do your job and get us our money before Mom dies."

"She's not sick, Brandon, don't feed me that shit." I stop speaking when I hear some of the guys leaving the gym, their voices getting closer until I hear their footsteps trail off as they walk away. "She's high," I tell him when I'm sure no one's around. "She's killing herself, and you're helping her."

"I don't know why you care so much." He sniffs. "You're the one that left." His demeanor changes, his voice growing bitter and heavy. "You left us in this hole, and because of you, Mom is sick. She doesn't fucking care about you anymore, Aiden. You're dead to her. You left." I hear his voice change into something so familiar it hits me in the gut. "The least you can do is get us our fucking money."

I sigh, rubbing a hand down my sweaty face. "You're high." Of course he is. Why am I surprised? So much for the money I sent for his rehab.

Another dark chuckle on the other end. "Just get us our money." He hangs up, and I pull back, staring at the screen.

"Fuck." The bastard knew what he was doing bringing up Mom. He knows I have a soft spot for her, even if she's practically disowned me for leaving. I needed out. I needed a life, and that was no life worth living.

The screen flashes with another text, and I open it.

Unknown:

> Have you got it yet?

I bite down, grinding my teeth to a pulp. I should have done it already. I need to get it over with. Just give them whatever they want and be done with whoever this is.

Aiden:

> Working on it.

It takes a second for whoever is on the other end to read it and start typing. I squeeze my fists, anticipating their response.

Unknown:

> I'm not a patient man.

It's a guy. At least I know that.

I pull up the text thread with Carol, my manager, and shoot her a text.

Aiden:

> Do you have any more shifts?

She replies within a minute.

Carol:

> You're already working
> five days a week.

Aiden:

> I'll take whatever you have.

I watch the three little dots dance on the screen, my fingers gripping my phone. "C'mon," I mumble to my phone screen. "Just give me something."

Carol:

> I have Saturday available.

"Carol, you're one hell of a woman." I grin, tapping away on the screen.

Aiden:

> I'll take it.

8

I don't give up

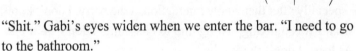

Leila

"Shit." Gabi's eyes widen when we enter the bar. "I need to go to the bathroom."

"Are you serious?"

"I'm sorry?" Her face contorts.

I roll my eyes. "How many times do I have to tell you to pee before we leave? I swear, it's like you're my kid." I sigh, pressing my fingers to my forehead.

She snickers. "Can I call you Mommy?" I let out a laugh, giving her a push. She presses her lips together, trying to stop laughing. "I'll be quick. Just order me something." She waves a hand. "Whatever will get me drunker." She starts to walk into the bathroom but then spins. "Actually, just order me a Cosmo. I need to stay up late tonight."

"Hot date?" I tease.

She smiles, then shakes her head. "Nah." Her hip nudges the door open, and she walks in. I pat my jean pocket, making sure the money is still there. I turn, heading to the bar when I see—

"You've got to be kidding me."

Aiden's head lifts, one hand clutching a glass, the other around the beer tap. He grins when he sees me, then props the drink in front of a customer. He places his hands on the counter. "How I love to be the reason for your disappointment," he says, his smirk letting me know he finds my attitude towards him amusing. "Are you stalking me again, Leila?"

I cross my arms, leaning my hip against the edge of the bar. "More like trying to forget you."

He hums, leaning forward on the counter. "Hard to forget, am I?"

I'm not even going to dignify him with an answer. I bite my bottom lip, knowing he's right. The guy is hard to forget, especially after that whole interaction at the party. I don't know what I was thinking, daring him to chase me. I don't want that. At least, I don't think I do.

I blow out a breath. I don't know what I want when it comes to Aiden. And therein lies the problem. "So you're a bartender?" I ask him, sitting on the stool, visibly wincing. Fuck I hate barstools. They are not big girl friendly. They painfully dig into my thighs, not to mention my ass barely fits on the seat.

"You okay there?" he asks.

I peer up at him. "Peachy."

He smiles, his tongue tracing his bottom lip. *Don't look at his lips.* He moves over to the glasses, grabbing a tall one. "Beer, right?" he asks.

I furrow my brows. "Yeah. How did you know?"

"Lucky guess." He fills the glass, staring down at the amber liquid filling it.

"You're full of surprises."

He lifts his head, eyeing me for a second before his head drops back to the task at hand, a laugh escaping him. A breathy, low laugh that has my stomach spinning. With a shake of his head, he says, "I've got to say, even though you seem to despise me for some reason," he glances up at me, "I always seem to have a good time whenever you're near."

A full glass of beer gets placed in front of me. "You're a masochist, huh?" I ask, taking a sip. "You like when people torture you?"

He laughs. "If torture is anything like you, then hell yes."

A bubble of laughter escapes me, and I press my hand to my mouth, swallowing down the liquid. "Does that actually work?"

"What?" he asks.

I gesture to the—if I'm being honest—drop-dead gorgeous face of his. "The whole blue-eyed, cool guy flirting thing you do."

He seems to mull it over, tilting his head. "I would say all the time. But lately, I've struck out."

I eye him wondering if he's talking about me. Hoping he's talking about me. It's a good feeling saying no to someone like Aiden Pierce. Someone that can have anyone, that everyone wants. "It won't work on me." Although as I say the words, I'm not entirely sure it's true.

He shrugs, the big muscles on his shoulders lifting. "I wouldn't be so sure about that."

I take another sip, the burn of the alcohol hitting my throat. "Have you forgotten I don't like you?"

He shakes his head, a grin on his lips. "That's not an issue."

My brows furrow. "Why not?"

He licks his lips, his eyes dropping to my lips. "Because I find it hot as fuck every time you roll those pretty green eyes at me." My throat clamps up as I stare at up at him. "Plus, your supposed dislike isn't even valid. You don't even know me."

I place the beer on the counter, glancing up at him. "I know enough," I say with a shrug.

51

"What exactly do you know?"

I tilt my head. "We'd be here all night."

"Humor me."

Alright then. I clasp my hands together in front of me, noting how he leans in a little when I do. "You're a classic playboy. You have the whole school in the palm of your hand, every girl in your bed, and the hot athlete thing clearly works for you. Not to mention you use your talent to get away with anything and everything. And even though you seem charming with that smile and those eyes, you don't fool me."

His lips curve into a grin. "I've got to be honest. All I heard was that you think I'm hot, talented, and charming."

I roll my eyes. "Of course you would."

He laughs, filling up another glass. "And you think by that little statement you have me all figured out?"

I give him a shrug. "As much as I need to."

He shakes his head. "You want to bet how long it will take before you give in?" he asks.

My eyes narrow. "Don't act like you're in control. We both know this little game is all on me."

"And we both know you want me just as bad." His tongue darts out to lick his lips. "You're just kidding yourself when you tell me the opposite."

My throat bobs with the harsh swallow, and I grab my drink to give myself something to do to avoid his lingering eyes, the smile on his lips, and the way he's absolutely right.

He sets the glass on the counter and eyes me carefully, his lips curved in a smirk. "I really want to ask for your number even though you'll probably turn me down again."

I scoff. "I'm not giving you my number."

Aiden's eyes narrow a little, his eyes darkening as he pulls closer, leaning forward until there's a measly few inches between us. "Here's one thing you don't know about me, Leila," he says. "I don't give up. Ever." I swallow hard, watching how he follows the movements of my throat before his eyes meet mine again. So blue.

I want to breathe, I do, but… it's currently stuck in my throat. "There's also something else," he says, his eyes dropping to the curve of my lips that are now parted and so dry. I lick them instinctively.

"Yeah?" It comes out raspy, thick with the tension between us. I clear my throat.

He smirks, pulling back completely until I can inhale a much-needed breath. "I never lose," he says.

That snaps me out of whatever the hell just happened and I clear my throat once more. "I guess you're going to have to get used to losing," I tell him. "Because you will this time."

He tuts. "I'm not so sure about that. You seem to be under the pretense that I'm trying to prove something here, that because you said no, it makes me want you more." That is exactly what I'm thinking. "But that's not it at all," he says. "You fucking intrigue me." His eyes dip to my lips again. "And I really want to kiss you again. All I need is your number and I'll make it happen."

His words blur my vision, making me lose focus. This isn't who I am. I don't get nervous or tongue-tied and I definitely don't let the guy control the situation. I square my shoulders, playing along, and lean in, my eyes focused on his lips. A grin undeniably appears on my lips when I hear his breath hitch, his lips parted slightly.

53

I take my time to look up at him, staring into his eyes. *Focus.* "And what will you give me in return?" I ask him, my hand dancing on the counter, getting closer to his shirt.

He lets out a heavy breath. "Whatever you want."

My fingers get closer to the fabric of his white t-shirt, itching to grab it in my fist. "Anything?" I ask him, my fingers slightly grazing the fabric.

Another shaky breath. "Everything."

I hum, looking up into his eyes. I know how much guys love looking down at girls, it makes them feel powerful, like they're in control, but not this time. "That's too bad," I mutter. I pull back completely, dropping the act. "I don't want anything from you."

He lets out an exhale, turning into a laugh. "The way you were undressing me with your eyes says the opposite," he says.

I let out a scoff. "You're delusional."

He opens his mouth but before he can speak a girl slides in beside me. "Aiden," she purrs, her voice so sweet, just as sweet as she looks. Slim figure, tiny and drop-dead gorgeous, just like the girls I've seen Aiden with.

I'm not stupid. I am so far out of his usual type, which makes me wonder why he's pushing this so hard. Memories of my ex come flooding back, making me bite my bottom lip.

"I didn't get a chance to talk to you at the party last week," she says, pouting. My eyebrows rise, glancing at Aiden. I can't lie, I'm very interested in what he'll say, how he'll react. I keep my mouth shut, sipping on my drink, waiting it out.

He smiles at her… of course he does. Aiden is just a golden ball of sunshine and smiles that people eat up like sunlight. "I'm sorry," he says. "I didn't get your name."

A snicker comes out of me, and I end up drinking at the same time and cough uncontrollably. The girl and Aiden both look at me. I hold up my hand, attempting to stop dying over here. "I'm fine."

Aiden presses his lips together, failing to attempt to hide his laughter.

The blonde shakes her head, turning back to face Aiden. "My name's Alicia, we met at Carter's twenty-first, remember?"

He squints and then nods. "Yeah, of course." I press my lips together. Liar. "Alicia, right. I'm a little busy right now. Can I get you anything to drink?"

She shakes her head. "I ordered like twenty minutes ago. From you."

"Right," Aiden says, rubbing the back of his neck. "I'm sorry, busy night."

"Oh," she says, deflating a little. "That's ok."

He smiles at her again. "It was nice to meet you."

She gives him a grin, leaning forward so her cleavage spills out. My eyes widen. Damn. The girl has an impressive rack. I glance at Aiden for a second. I've got to give it to him, he doesn't even glance down.

"Hey, man," Andre, his teammate, slides up to the bar, tapping on the counter. "Scotch. Neat."

"Sorry, I have drinks to pour." Aiden gives her one of his signature smiles and moves behind the bar, grabbing a glass and filling it with the dark auburn liquid, sliding it over to his friend. By the time Aiden turns around, she's gone.

"Thanks, man," Andre says, taking the drink from him and sliding a ten across the bar before he leaves.

"You alright there?" Aiden's voice makes my eyes lift, meeting his. "Didn't think beer would be a choking hazard."

I roll my eyes, a laugh bubbling out of me. It must be the alcohol. "I'm good." I take another sip. "You seem to have options." I eye him, seeing if he'll catch on.

He smiles, nodding. "I have many." Well shit. At least he knows it. "Too bad the one girl I seem to want is hellbent on denying there's any attraction between us."

I don't know what to say. What can I say? I could try to lie, tease him about it, but at this point, we both know I'm lying.

"Shit. Gabi's Cosmo."

He smiles, heading back to grab a glass and starts making the drink. I lift myself off the stool, grabbing my glass and let out a breath, picking a twenty from my jean pocket and sliding it in front of me.

He pushes it back. "It's on me," he says, placing the red drink in front of me.

My eyebrows lift. "In exchange for my number, right?"

"Damn." He drops his head, a chuckle escaping him. "Why didn't I think of that?"

"Because you're not a complete asshole?" I offer with a tilt of my head.

He grins, rubbing his thumb across his bottom lip. "Glad to see you're coming around."

"Eh." I shrug. "You're not all bad." I spin on my heels, heading to the table where Gabriella is sitting at, eating pretzels. Her eyes widen when she sees me approaching, and she reaches for the glass. "Finally," she says. "That took forever."

"Sorry. Long line." She accepts the drink from me, her eyes closing when she takes a sip.

I take a seat beside her, placing my beer on the table. I presumptuously look over my shoulder and see Aiden looking at me. He flashes me a grin, and I roll my eyes, turning back around.

"Damn," Gabi says. "I could kiss whoever made this." She takes another sip.

Yeah, me too.

9

Swallow my pride

Aiden

"You hesitated." My head turns to the paused screen, pointing at it.

Ethan narrows his eyes at me. "Only for a second. I caught it, didn't I?"

I nod, not giving him the satisfaction of telling him he's right. He caught it, but that could have been luck. Next time he might not be so lucky. "That one second could have cost us." I point at the screen where a player from the other team is surrounding him. "They were ready to attack, and Jordan was open."

His brows lift. "So much talk from someone who lost two weeks ago."

My jaw hardens, not liking how he's undermining me in front of my team. "Just get your head in the game."

He snorts. "Okay, Troy Bolton."

The guys chuckle along with him. Fuck, I'm losing them. I know Ethan wants this position. He's older than me, has been on this team longer than me, but ultimately Coach picked me. Freshman year, I was handed the captain position with the responsibility of bringing this team to a win. Some of the older guys weren't too keen on having to listen to orders from a freshman, but they fell in line. Ethan, however, hasn't.

"This isn't a joke," I grit out, hearing their laughter come to a halt. I don't want them to hate me. I know what it's like being on a team when everyone looks at you like you're trash, like you don't belong there. You start to believe it more and more, and I won't ever go back there.

I don't want to be an asshole captain, but I also need them to respect me, to listen to me. "That almost cost us a win."

"Relax, Cap," Jordan says, making my head snap to his. "It was one game. We were up against Crestview." He lets out a laugh. "It wasn't like they had it."

"Do I need to remind you we won by five points? Five. It could have easily been them. Don't get too comfortable." I watch as Jordan settles into the couch. My shoulders slump, looking at the rest of my team. "Do you all feel like this?" I ask them. "Do you not care if we lose?"

"Of course not," Carter replies. "We want to win, Pierce. You know we do."

"Then listen up." I turn off the tv, turning to face them. I was given captain for a reason. I take this shit seriously, and I will do whatever it takes for my team to win. It's on me, the championship, the playoffs. It's all on me.

"I'm your captain," I tell them, pointing at my chest. "It's on me to get you that win, to make sure you've all got your head straight. This is what's going to get us there. But I'm not the only one on the team. You all need to pull your weight." I raise my eyebrows. "You got that?"

"Yes, Captain."

"Good." I nod, waving my hand. "You can leave."

I watch as they leave, murmurs going off as they exit the living room. I sit back down, tuning into last week's gameplay. We won. That's all that matters. But we almost lost. Almost is

59

too close. After what happened at the last game, I can't let the team down again. I pause the screen where I'm about to shoot, my feet are too far apart. I need to reel it in.

I take my stance, pause again. Shit, that was too low, I need to aim higher. I click again, unpausing the screen, watching as I sink the ball into the net. It went in, the winning shot. I blow out a breath watching as we celebrate on the court.

I tune into the rest of the team coming onto the court, celebrating around me. My eyes narrow, watching their faces. Could it be one of them? Could this be about revenge?

I take my cap off, running a hand over my hair. I have no idea what they want from me. I groan into my hands. I don't know how I'm going to get what I need. It seems impossible at this point.

The door opens, and I lift my head to see Grayson walk through the door. I let out a breath as he walks in. "Have they left?" I ask.

He shakes his head, scoffing. "Hell no, they're raiding the fridge." He takes a seat beside me.

"Great." I barely have enough to buy groceries as it is.

"It's on me, don't worry. I'll replace everything they ate."

I'm already shaking my head as the words leave him. "Hell no, you barely eat here, Grayson. It's on me."

He lets out a scoff, nudging me on the arm. "You know that's not true; when you cook, you make extra for me, don't try to act like you're the only one using that damn kitchen."

I snort. "Yeah, I use that kitchen to cook. You, on the other hand…" I shake my head. "The kitchen? Really? Your bedroom is right upstairs," I point out.

He laughs, sinking back into the couch. "You heard that, huh?"

My brows lift. "This house is big, but the walls are thin. My room is above the kitchen. Please remember that now that Rosie's moved in."

"Yeah," he says, sitting up. "About that. I know I should have run it by you first." He glances at me. "But it won't be that much different, right? I mean, she practically stays here all the time."

I turn to my best friend. "You don't need to run it by me, Grayson. It's your house."

"And yours," he adds.

"Right." I roll my eyes. Grayson wants me to believe this house is as much mine as it is his, but we both know it's not. He's the one with the rich parents to put him up in this big ass place. If it wasn't for him, I'd either be slashing all my earnings for a dorm or giving up my morals for a place at the frat.

He saved me from making the biggest mistake of my life. One I never thought would cross my mind. If it wasn't for him... fuck, I'm so grateful for this bastard next to me. He doesn't know how much.

I nudge him with my shoulder. "So, Rosie's moving in." I flash him a grin. "You ready for that?"

He blows out a breath, a smile forming on his face as he nods. "I never thought I'd have a girlfriend," he says, shaking his head. "I never thought I'd want to spend so much time with one person." His face hardens. "I just don't want to mess it up. I can't lose her."

There's no way to stop the smile that forms on my face. "You really love her."

The frown disappears as he lets out a laugh. "Yeah," he says. "I really do."

61

"That's great, man," I say. "You know, for someone who didn't believe in love, you are a sappy shit."

He snorts. "Fuck you." He shakes his head. "What about you?"

My brows knit together. "What about me?"

He shrugs. "Haven't seen any girls around lately. You seeing someone?" he asks me.

I shake my head. "I don't have time for that." For a while, actually. I think he's been so caught up in Rosalie that he hasn't noticed I haven't had a girl around in a long ass time. Basketball is what I need to focus on. It's the only thing that matters. The rest is a waste of my time. And I need to make sure it stays that way.

I swallow my fucking pride and turn to my best friend. "Do you have Leila's number?"

His eyes narrow at me as he furrows his brows. "What are you doing?"

"What do you mean?"

He shakes his head, still scowling. "You know what I mean, Aiden. What the fuck are you doing?"

"What?" I say, giving him a shrug. "I can't ask for a girl's number now?"

He blows out a breath. "After you just said you're not interested?"

"I didn't say I wasn't interested. I said I didn't have time."

"So you're interested in Leila?" he asks me straight up.

"Maybe."

"Aiden," he warns, shaking his head. "I repeat, what are you doing? Don't play with her, man."

"Who said I was playing with her?" I don't like how he assumes the worst of me. I would never play with a girl's emotions. What's the harm in asking for a phone number?

"She's my girlfriend's best friend. You hurt her, Rosie gets hurt. Which means I'm going to have to take sides," he shakes his head. "I love you, bro, you know that. But I love her more."

I grin. "You love me?" I let out a laugh. "Thanks, but you're not exactly my type."

He laughs. "You need your ass kicked."

Like he could kick my ass. "Sure," I scoff. "So, do you have it or not?"

His eyes hood before he sighs and shakes his head. "Even if I wanted to give it to you, I don't. I kind of stole her number from Rosie's phone once and Leila made me delete it."

Fuck.

"Can't you just get it again?"

"Hell no," he says. "I'm not doing that shit again. Leila's super private about who she gives her number to. Something I didn't know before. Trust me, I'm not making the same mistake again."

I pick up my cap and put it back on my head. If I can't get it from him, I have to find another way.

"Fine," I say, standing up from the couch. "I'll get it myself."

I start to walk to the door, but Grayson's voice stops me. "I can't tell you what to do, but don't do something that you know will hurt her, Aiden."

10

Never going to happen

Aiden

A fucking water leak.

With a game next week, I need to be on top of my schedule, and things like this derail my plan. Training at another gym is not what I need right now. I push the door open and head inside. I scan the area, feeling my spine tighten with the list of things that throw me off balance.

The place is crowded, with only a few machines available, and none of the ones I need. Coach told us to use the football gym if necessary, but after the last encounter I had with Ben Reed, that was a no.

The guy can't help himself from making crude comments about women, goading and instigating until someone snaps. If Grayson hadn't pulled me off him last year, I could have lost my scholarship, I could have lost everything I have worked so hard for in the matter of a few seconds. And I can't let that happen.

So, I suck it up, pull out my headphones and turn on my music, walking over to one of the only machines available. The treadmill. Fuck, I hate running, but I need to keep my body in shape somehow. This will have to do.

My head snaps up when I feel eyes on me. I slowly turn, making eye contact with the girls walking by. They smile at me and turn, whispering to each other.

I let my eyes fall to the screen in front of me, trying not to get distracted. I loved the attention when I first got here. I came from nothing, an absolute nobody, but then everything changed. Suddenly I was wanted and attractive, and girls wanted to sleep with me.

It was a surprise, but I went with it, had a girl in my bed every night and a new one knocking on the door by morning. It was everything freshman me could have wanted, but it got old, and ultimately, basketball has to come first. It's what I'm working towards; it's what's going to make sure I never end up like my brothers or my mom back home. It's my freedom.

I pick up speed, my legs extending the entire length of the treadmill as I start to jog. I keep my eyes on the screen, watching the speed increase, feeling the burn in my legs.

I lift my head and keep my eyes locked forward, trying to forget about everything but the burn. My eyes look up, catching the poster of the team, with my face front and center. The captain. The one that's supposed to lead the team to victory. The one living a lie. I shake all thoughts out of my head. That's not fucking helping.

My eyes drop as I try to focus on something else. Anything. They drop and land on the person in front of me, watching as she climbs the stair master. The long, brown ponytail flicking behind her shoulder with every step she takes.

I narrow my eyes. Is that…?

My eyes widen as realization kicks in.

What are the chances?

I can't help but let my eyes drift to the pronounced curve of her ass in those gym leggings as she climbs the stairs, causing a grin to form on my face.

Her head stays high, her hands on her hips as she steps on the machine. I don't even know what speed I'm on or how long I've been on here.

But by the time she steps off the machine, my legs feel like jello. My hands hold on to the railing as I watch her lean down, grabbing a towel to wipe away the sweat on her face.

It doesn't take long for her to find me, her eyes meeting mine. She stares, blinking a few times, making sure she's seeing right. I let out a laugh. "Hi," I mouth at her, flashing a smile.

She shakes her head, not taking her eyes off me. I pick up speed, full-on running as she checks me out. Her eyes roll as she bends down, giving me a shot of her round ass as she picks up her gym bag and leaves, heading towards the weights.

Damn, I guess it's time to lift.

I turn off the machine, coming to a stop before I jump off, walking over towards where she's holding a weight bar on her shoulders, dropping into a squat.

Holy— I turn my head and find the bench press empty. Perfect. I lie down on the seat, shuffling back. My hands grip the bar, and I lift the weight, dropping it down to my chest. A grunt leaves me as I lift it back up and repeat.

I don't get past three reps when a shadow casts across my face making me look up, seeing no other than—

"Leila," I flash her a grin, setting the bar on the rack. She's upside down and angry, but somehow, she still looks hot.

"Are you following me?" she asks.

I sit up, grab my water bottle off the floor, and take a gulp. I tilt my head as I look back at her, resisting the urge to laugh when I see the scowl painted on her face, her hands propped up on her hips. "Just purely coincidental," I tell her.

"A coincidence?" she repeats.

I shrug, my eyes trailing down the sliver of tanned skin below her black sports bra. "Water leak. My gym closed down. Had no other option."

I lie back down on the bench, gripping the handle. My eyes look up, seeing her still standing above me. "Besides, I don't get a view like this in my gym," I tease her.

Her hand presses against the handle, not allowing me to pick up the weights. I grunt, smiling at her. "Are you going to spot me, baby?"

Her green eyes narrow at me. "Don't call me that."

"What do you want me to call you?" She rolls her eyes, letting out a frustrated groan and walks away. Where the hell did she go? I drop my hands from the bar, attempting to sit up, but before I can, a hard press of her hand against my chest pushes me back down. I look up, seeing her standing above me, legs on either side of me. Holy fuck.

"Why don't I believe you?" she asks, practically straddling me.

I try to lift myself up, but she presses me back down. I grunt, feeling her heat over her leggings. Jesus. I let out a laugh, my hands drifting up to her hips. "Careful, Leila." Her eyes widen when I grip her hips. "You're playing a dangerous game." One I'd love to play, but the way she stands and steps back tells me she didn't think before she straddled me on a gym bench.

I finally sit up and look up at her. The blush on her cheeks makes my chest pound. I would bet it has nothing to do with her workout and everything to do with me. "That was quite a show," I tell her, standing up from the bench. "We could do it again if you give me your number," I suggest, lifting my brows.

She assesses me for a second, shaking her head. "Why are you pushing this so hard?"

My brows furrow. "What?"

"At first, I thought it was a pride thing. I said no, so it made you want me, but now I don't know."

A pride thing? "C'mon, Leila. Don't act coy. I know you want me too."

She looks up, pulling her bottom lip between her teeth. I note how she hasn't denied it, but then her eyes narrow. "And what's in it for you?"

I shrug. "The pleasure of your company."

She lets out a scoff. "You never quit, do you?"

"I told you," I say, stepping closer to her. "I don't give up. And I don't lose."

She tilts her head. "And if I say no?"

My hands itch to touch her face, but I keep them by my side, stuffing them in my pockets. "You won't. You want this as much as I do."

Her eyes keep my hold for what seems like eternity, until she finally sighs and steps back, reaching into her bag. Holy shit. She holds out her hand and glances at me. "Phone," she orders.

I pull my phone out of my pocket, grinning when I hand it over to her. "As you wish."

She lets out a scoff, the corner of her lips turning up into a smile and starts typing away on my phone. A few seconds later, she hands it back to me, and a laugh escapes me when I see what she saved her number as.

"'Never going to happen'?" I ask, reading out her contact name.

She nods, giving me a smirk.

I shake my head, taking a step close to her, towering over her and tut. "Hate to break it to you," I whisper. "But it just did."

I pull back, admiring how her breath accelerates and her face flushes. She picks up her bag and heads into the lockers. "Don't make me regret it," she says without turning around.

I drop my eyes to my phone, staring at the screen with her number. I grip my phone in my hand, looking up to see she's gone. "You will," I mutter to myself.

11
Find me

Leila

"God, I needed this." I drop down on the couch beside Madi.

"That bad?" Gabriella asks.

I shrug. I love modeling, but coming back after is always great. Hanging with my girls, getting shit-faced at some random party, nothing beats it. "It was fun," I tell them. "But those girls can be draining."

"Aw," Gabi coos, blowing me a kiss. "You missed me."

I can't help but laugh. "Desperately."

Madi nudges me on the arm, her brown eyes shining with a mischievous glimmer. "Don't feed into her ego," she says. "Her head is already too big."

A scoff comes from Gabi who's downing her beer. "You wish you could be me."

"I really don't."

"Here," Gabi cracks open a can of beer, handing it over to me. "It's the least I can do since you were so miserable without me." I take the can from her, taking a sip. The cold liquid drips into my throat, the burn on my throat almost instant. "Better?" she asks.

I nod, taking another sip. "I'll get there." I look around the room at the couples cuddled together on the couch, the girls dancing to the music. "Rosie didn't come out again, huh?"

"Nope," Gabi says. "She's an old lady now."

"I know she has Grayson now, but I just miss her," I admit with a shrug. "She hasn't been coming out with us as much."

"She's in love," Madi replies. "You can't fault her for that."

I hum, shaking my head. "Of course not. Just because my love life went to shit, doesn't mean she shouldn't be happy."

"Don't even mention him," Gabi says, narrowing her eyes at me. "He doesn't count."

I let out a laugh, taking another sip of the beer. "He does, unfortunately."

"Nope. I'm not letting you get sad," Gabi says, shaking her head. "No more talking about shitty ex-boyfriends. Come on." She stands up from the couch, holding out her hand for me to take it.

"Where the hell are you taking me now? I'm not playing any more drinking games with you," I warn her, lifting my brow.

She smirks. "Why? You seemed to have fun last time."

I glance at Madi who's got an equally cocky smirk on her face. "I think I need new friends," I mutter, downing the rest of my beer.

"Oh, come on," Madi says, crossing her legs when she turns to face me. "You're acting like it was so awful." She rolls her eyes. "You know damn well you enjoyed that."

I shrug, looking down at the empty beer can. "I have no idea what you're talking about."

Gabi's laughter makes my eyes snap to her. "Please," she says, sitting back down. "You were like half a beer and thirty seconds away from stripping him right there in front of everyone."

"That's an exaggeration." I roll my eyes.

"Was he good?" she asks, lifting her brows.

71

I bite my lip. Okay, I might have fibbed a little at the party. He wasn't bad, not even close. But it threw me all the way off, I didn't want to be the kind of girl who melted in the sheer presence of Aiden, but then his lips landed on mine and… it was better than I expected, to say the least. "He was decent," I murmur.

Gabi hums. "That means he was *very* good." Her eyes shine with intrigue, and I can't help the flutter in my stomach at the thought that Gabi might actually be interested in him. I mean, who isn't? My eyebrows lift in shock before I can stop it, and by her reaction, I'm guessing she notices. "Relax," she says, her lips twitching with amusement. "I'm not interested in him. He's all yours."

I feign indifference, lifting my shoulder. "I don't care. I'm here to drink, not focus on some guy I barely know."

Especially because, after everything, he didn't call. Over a week has gone by and… nothing. I really expected him to. He was so persistent, so demanding. I hate to admit how much I liked it. How much I liked having someone work a little to get me, instead of me having to do all the work.

I let out a sigh. "I'm going to the bathroom," I tell them, standing from the couch.

"Want us to go with you?" Gabi asks.

I shake my head. "I'm good."

"If you need us, call," Madi shouts back as I head through the crowd, trying to find a bathroom that doesn't have a long line.

I find an empty bathroom and shut the door, letting out a breath when I stare at myself in the mirror. I've been here countless times before.

I turn my hips, admiring my black dress hugging my figure in the mirror. I have nice hips, full and curvy. I run my hands over my body. "I love my body," I recite to my reflection. "I love my curves. Every dip, every roll, every stretch mark."

One day, I'll believe it. I hope.

I love my friends, love them dearly, but they don't see that when guys approach us, they don't approach us, they approach *them*. I get a weak smile, a pity drink, and maybe a couple of words from the guy who was stuck with me.

They don't see that when guys talk to them, they get asked out on dates, I get asked back to their rooms for a one-night stand.

I hated being the approachable one, the non-desirable one, so I flipped the switch. I flirted with guys, I approached them, I made the first move, and it worked. I was always in control and I didn't have hopeless, unrealistic expectations.

Until Aiden.

He came in and everything changed. He pursued me, he asked me out, he goaded me into kissing him. It was new, interesting, fun. But now, he got what he wanted. He won the game, and I made it easy for him.

I fix my hair, glancing at myself one last time before walking out the door. I barely take two steps before being hit with a hard chest of muscles. "Shit, I'm sorry." I look up and blink.

His hands grip my arm, keeping me in place. "Falling for me already," Aiden teases, smirking down at me.

I look up at him, my neck straining when I do. I'd never admit this to anyone, but I love how tall he is. I'm used to being the tallest person in the room, it's nice having him tower over me. "What are you doing here?" I ask him, taking a step back.

He takes a step back too, leaning on the wall opposite me. "Same reason as you," he says, crossing his arms. "I'm here to have fun."

I let out a scoff. "My fun stopped the minute you showed up." Alright fine, I'm a little bitter that he didn't call. I don't even know why. I'm not sure I would have answered either way.

Aiden laughs. "So stubborn. Is that why you gave me your number?" he asks, making me freeze. "Because I'm not fun?"

I tilt my head. "I don't know," I say with a shrug. "Is that why you didn't call?" His smile drops, and his face blanches. "Because I'm *so* fun?"

He frowns a little, a line forming between his brows. "Leila—"

"Just forget it. I don't care. Lose my number and forget about me." I step forward, ready to leave this hallway and him behind when his hand captures mine, spinning me around so my back hits the wall.

"I can't do that, Leila," Aiden whispers.

My brain is foggy with the scent surrounding me. A mixture of clean soap and a deeper, woody scent blurring my senses and making me aware of his body heat encompassing me.

"I can't forget about you." His deep voice rumbles through me, making my skin break out with goosebumps. I try to take a breath, but my heart's beating so fast. I feel his breath on my skin and my eyes close of their own accord, a whimper escaping my lips.

Fuck. My eyes snap open, looking up at his bright blue eyes, where he's standing above me, crowding me. His hand reaches up, rubbing the dark brown strands of my hair between his fingers.

74

I gulp, watching him entranced with my hair; he brushes it back behind my ear and leans in. "I wish I could forget about you. Fuck, I wish I could just let you go, but I can't do that anymore."

"I'm sure you'll find a way," I manage to say.

He chuckles, his eyes dropping to my lips. "God," he rasps. "What are you doing to me?"

"Nothing," I reply, forcing my throat to move. "I don't even like you."

He laughs. "Such a liar." His tongue dips out. Licking his bottom lip, making my eyes drop to his lips. Oh, he is good.

"You say you don't like me, that you don't want me, tell me something," he says. I take that as my opportunity to breathe. "If I put my hand up this dress, what would I find Leila?" His tone is so casual, so simple. "How wet would you be?"

Jesus. He's not even touching me and I'm weak. I don't give him the satisfaction though, I stare at him with indifference, squeezing my legs together, trying to ease the ache as I blow out a breath. "Bone dry."

Another dark chuckle from him that does nothing to stop the lust brewing. "It's so hot when you put me in my place," he says, smirking down at me. "But I'd love to see you smile at me like you do with your friends." His thumb ghosts my lips, barely grazing them. "Just once."

Holy shit, this man is good. Too good. I shake my head, regaining some control, and force my limbs to move, bringing my hands to his chest, my fingers itching to touch him. The material of his t-shirt a thin barrier between all those hard muscles of his. I lean up into him. "What do you have in mind to make me smile?" I ask him.

He grins, no doubt loving this reaction from me. "I want to kiss you again."

I almost bunch his t-shirt between my fingers and pull him into me, but I drop my hands instead and sigh. "Pass."

His brows bunch up. "What are you doing?" he asks. "I know you feel this. You wouldn't still be here if you didn't." He leans down until his blue eyes burn into mine. "If you want me to chase you, just say the word."

He's got me there. I want this. Him. I want one night with Aiden. I want to know if the rumors I've heard about him in bed are true, I want to be the girl in his bed, even if it's just for one night. Doesn't mean I'll make it easy for him.

I lick my lips. "I'll tell you what." His brows lift, intrigue painting his expression. "You can kiss me," I lean up into him, wrapping my arms around his neck, loving how his breathing accelerates and his hands drop to my waist. I reach up until my lips graze his ear and whisper, "If you find me."

I drop my arms and head out of the hallway before he can say anything else. I race through the crowd, heading up the stairs, glancing behind me but I don't see Aiden anywhere. I keep going. If he wants to chase me, then let him chase me.

I look around for an empty bedroom, but the last one I can find is off-limits when a couple walks inside. The bedroom door closes, leaving me out in this empty hallway alone. I bite my lip, wondering where Aiden is. Do I even want him to find me?

Yes.

I might tease and joke around with him, but we both know the attraction is there. I want to kiss him again. I want to feel his lips on mine and pull him into me, hearing every moan and gasp that comes from him. I want to know what one night with him will be like.

I push open the bathroom door, ready to go inside when I feel a hand wrap around my wrist. I don't even have to look. I know it's him.

"Looks like I found you," he whispers, his breath hitting my skin, so close I can almost feel what his lips would be like if he pressed them into the sensitive skin of my neck. He turns me around, a cocky grin on his face. "Do I get my reward now?"

Yes. Fuck yes. Just kiss me. I lick my lips. "That was the deal."

He smiles, but it drops just as quick when he shakes his head. "I'm not going to kiss you," he says, making my face drop. "I want to taste your lips again so badly," he grits out, running a hand down his face. "But I can't in good conscience kiss you, Leila."

"Why?" I ask before I can stop myself.

He smirks. "Because, gorgeous," he says, making my chest pound. "Consent is important to me. I love teasing you, but I'm not going to kiss you unless you tell me you want it." If he's trying to make me less attracted to him, it's having the opposite effect. "I don't want to push you into anything you don't want to do," he says with a shrug. "And if you say you don't like me, then I can't kiss you."

I want it. I want it so bad. I feel the heat and the tension between us, and I just want to rip it apart. I want his lips on mine, his tongue in my mouth, and for him to take me to bed tonight.

I watch as he smirks at me, his eyes dropping as he checks me out. "You look so fucking beautiful."

I don't know what to say. I'm stuck in this hallway, watching as he turns around and gets ready to walk away from me.

"Aiden." He turns back around, his eyebrows lifting, wondering what I'm going to say. But I don't know either. What do I say? What do I want?

I take two steps forward until I'm right there in front of him, but I say nothing. I stare up at him, wanting him to just read my mind and know how much I want this. Kiss me. Kiss me, Aiden.

"Yes, Leila?" he asks, the edge of his lips curving in a smirk. "Is there anything you want?"

I roll my eyes. "Oh, for fuck's sake." I grip the back of his neck and bring him down, crushing my lips to his.

This, I'm good at.

The talking, not so much, but this? This I can do.

I lift onto my tiptoes, brushing my lips with his, feeling his tongue prod the entrance of my lips. I open up for him, welcoming him, wanting him, and he enters.

His tongue swipes over mine, our mouths working together as the kiss gets hotter and deeper. My teeth graze his bottom lip, sucking on it as I pull away and bring my tongue back into his mouth. A groan builds in his throat, but I swallow it down before it can escape. He's consuming me, in this moment all I can feel is him, all I can taste is him, all I can think of is Aiden.

"God, Leila," he rasps between kisses and pushes us so I'm pinned against the wall once again. His hand grips my face as he deepens the kiss, making love to my mouth. Fuck. The way his tongue sucks on mine makes my knees wobble and my clit ache, so badly. I involuntarily grind up, making contact with the bulge poking through his jeans.

He pulls back for a second, his dark, lustful eyes burning a hole into mine. His eyes widen as if he doesn't believe I just did that, but I'm not backing down. I started this, and I'm going to finish it. I'm going to end up in Aiden's bed tonight.

He dives back in, crushing his mouth back down to mine. His kiss is better than actual fucking. I could do this all night. But I need more.

My hands play with the hem of his t-shirt, letting my fingers span the hot, hard flesh of his stomach. His abs ripple beneath my fingertips. God, he feels so good.

His big hands leave my face, making their way down to my waist. I don't even care to think of what he's feeling or if his hands are touching the rolls in my back. I don't care. He grips my waist with a fervor I can feel in my core every time he touches me.

His lips leave mine, trailing down my jaw and neck. His tongue plays with the skin, licking and sucking, the feeling making me lose control in my legs.

"Aiden," I whisper, needing him to do something. Anything.

He moans against my skin. "My name sounds so good coming from your lips," he grunts, thrusting a little, making our crotches align. My head lulls back, consumed with the small pleasure the friction provides.

"I need more," I gasp when his fingers brush against the hard nipples poking through the thin material of the dress.

He gives me one quick kiss. "You want me to fuck you?" he smiles against my lips. "I'm so close to lifting that dress and feeling how wet you really are for me," he says, going in for another kiss before he licks my bottom lip.

79

I don't answer him, I just bump my hips up, grazing his hard dick once again. "I'd prefer a bed," I breathe out.

"Fuck," he whispers. "Come back to my place?" he asks.

I nod. I'm not completely moved into Rosie's place yet. "What about Grayson and Rosie?" I ask him, letting out a moan when he pushes his erection against me. "I don't want anyone to know."

His tongue traces my ear, biting it. "Then we'll have to be quiet."

I'm used to that. Being quiet, keeping it a secret. It's nothing new to me. "Fine. Just go before I really do fuck you in this hallway." I push him away, fixing my hair and dress.

He chuckles, fixing his cap and adjusting his jeans. My tongue darts out to lick my lips as I look at his crotch. "Don't worry," he says. "I'm not finished with you yet."

12

Ask nicely

Aiden

This wasn't the plan. This wasn't supposed to happen. I should be racked with guilt, but the prospect of feeling her lips again, tasting her, having her, makes me forget about everything but the girl in front of me.

My eyes drop to the curve of her ass, jiggling in that tight dress of hers with every step she takes. God, she felt so good underneath my fingers, all soft and pliant. Not the usual stubborn, cold girl she normally is around me.

I felt her move against me, enjoy me, take pleasure from my body. And now I want more. I want to rip off that dress of hers and trace her body with my tongue, feeling every dip and curve. I want to hear that breathy moan again. I want to know if she's a screamer, or if she moans quietly.

I grab her hand when I see Grayson's house and don't bother letting her go. I'm not letting go of her anytime soon.

"What are you doing?" she chastises, whisper-yelling at me, looking around to see if anyone is noticing, but she has nothing to worry about. There isn't a soul around here.

I open the door and pull her inside, and I'm back on her as soon as her back hits the door, bringing my lips to hers. Fuck, she tastes so good. Like sugar, pure fucking sugar. She's so sweet when she's not telling me to fuck off.

STEPHANIE ALVES

"Admit it," I nip at her bottom lip. "You like me."

Her eyes shine with defiance. "I don't."

I lift an eyebrow, smirking down at her. "But you want me."

Her tongue traces her bottom lip, her eyes drifting to my own. "Maybe."

I grin, and pull her into me until she moans when she feels every hard inch pressed against her. "Definitely."

Her chest rises, her heavy breathing the only sound ingrained in my mind. I want to hear more from her. My hand lifts her dress, grabbing her full ass in my hands, and I knead the skin, pushing her into me. My hard dick scrapes against her soft body, eliciting a groan from me.

"Are you planning to fuck me, or just tease?" she asks breathlessly.

My laugh ripples through her skin, hidden in her neck. "Are you really that impatient?" I kiss her again, unable to keep my hands off her. "Or are you just desperate for me?"

Her eyes hood when she licks her lips, shaking her head a little. Her eyes drop and before I can see what she's looking at, her hand covers my dick over my jeans, grasping it in her fist. Oh shit. "I'm desperate for this," she says, bringing those soft, juicy lips to my neck, working her tongue over the skin.

"Fuck." I let out a harsh breath. "I can't wait to be inside you," I admit as she licks and sucks on the sensitive flesh of my neck.

Her lips meet mine in a hot kiss, her tongue lashing against mine as our lower bodies grind together. She runs her tongue over my lip before pulling back, looking up at me through her lashes. "Then take me upstairs," she whispers.

I grab her hand, loving the feel of her hand in mine and pull her up the stairs, careful not to make any noise.

When I reach my bedroom, I pull off my shirt as soon as the door closes, desperate to feel her. I want her body pressed against mine, feeling her soft skin against mine.

I can barely think as she devours me with her eyes. Those green eyes trace my body like I'm a painting. The way she looks at me has me wanting to do a hundred pushups a day just to keep her looking at me like that.

"You don't have any tattoos," she points out, her eyes scanning my chest.

Can't afford them. "Disappointed?" I ask her, anticipating her response. She shakes her head instead, bringing a snicker out of me. "Speechless already?" I joke. "I haven't even started."

Her tongue traces her bottom lip, licking it before she pulls it in between her teeth, cocking her head and running her eyes down my body. My cock twitches.

"I put on a show for you," I start. "Now it's your turn." I take a step closer. "I want to see you."

Her eyes hood a little, shaking her head. "Not yet," she says, pulling on the end of her dress, making the material even tighter against her body. Her soft stomach prods the material, making me wonder what it would feel like under my fingers, under my tongue. I want to kiss every inch of her. Jesus.

She takes a step closer, my dick twitching in my pants with each step. When she's right in front of me, her head tilts up, those piercing eyes tantalizing me. I don't even feel her hands at first, completely entrapped in her gaze, but as soon as she starts running her hands all over my chest, exploring me with her fingers, my dick wakes up.

It's impossible to restrain the sound that comes out of me when her tongue meets my chest. Her soft lips press against my skin, pressing kisses all over my pecs. "Oh fuck." There's nothing but her lips and tongue on my skin, and I'm dangerously close to blowing my load. I flex my abs for her, wanting her tongue on every part of me, and when she makes her way down, running her tongue over the ridges of my torso, my head lulls back. Fuck, why does that feel so good?

The soft moan that escapes her lips brings out a rough breath from me. "If you lick my abs like that, I can't imagine what your mouth will feel like on my dick."

She pulls back, practically on her knees, looking up at me, so submissive, so innocently, those big, round eyes peering up at me. "Want to find out?"

Hell. Fucking. Yes.

She rips off my belt, unbuckling me until I kick off my jeans. My eyes roll back at the feel of her hands rubbing my junk through my boxers. A second later, she pulls them off, and I throw my head back, eyes closed, anticipating the feel of her mouth on me.

"You've got to be kidding me."

I instantly open my eyes, looking down at her, watching her look at my hard dick with furrowed brows. "What?" I ask her. "What's wrong?"

She looks up at me, eyes narrowed. She looks pissed. "You're hot, talented, tall as shit, and have a big dick?" She exhales, looking away from me and my huge dick, apparently.

A laugh bubbles out of me. "You're scared of my dick?" I tease.

She rolls those pretty eyes of hers. "I'm not scared of it," she says, crossing her arms, taking a sneaky glance at my dick that's still very much hard and right in front of her face. "It's just unfair to everyone else. You can't have it all."

I cock my head, laughing at her expression. "You've never seen a dick as big as mine, huh?"

She gives me a sideways glance. "What makes you think that?"

My eyebrows raise. "The way you're terrified of it," I say, grabbing it in my hand and give it a stroke. Her eyes widen, staring right at it, and she licks her lips. I don't even know if she realizes she's doing it. She watches as I lazily stroke my cock, and I let out a grunt when I see her lick her lips once more. "You don't have to do anything if it's intimidating for you. I could just make you come."

"You'd do that?" she asks, glancing up at me with uncertainty.

I squint at her. "You mean eat your pussy until you come all over my tongue? Fuck yes."

"No," she says, shaking her head. "I want to…" She doesn't finish her sentence, just stares at my dick again.

"Leila," I sigh. "I'm serious, you don't have to—"

Oh. Fuck.

Her soft hand wraps around my shaft, shuffling closer to me and bringing her tongue to lap at the tip. "Shit," I moan, feeling her wet, hot mouth wrap around me. Her tongue strokes the length of my cock before fitting it between those pretty lips of hers.

"Fuck," she grunts with her mouth full of me. "I can't take you all the way," she says, slobbery as shit when she pulls her mouth off me. It's easily the hottest sight I've ever seen.

My knees buckle. I don't know if I'm going to be able to stay upright. My head is already shaking as she keeps stroking me. "You don't have to."

85

But she doesn't listen, instead she tongues the tip again. "I want to try," she says making my eyes roll to the back of my head. "Just don't push my head down."

"I won't." She gives me no time to prepare. She stuffs me as far down her throat as she can, making me grunt at the feel of her hot wet mouth around my cock. Fuck, this is heaven. This right here.

When I die, I want this.

"Oh, fuck. Leila."

She gags a little and pulls me out of her mouth, spit drooling down her chin. She takes a breath and looks up at me. "Don't say my name," she grunts, squeezing my dick. "The walls are thin, remember?"

Shit. Grayson and Rosie are in the next room over. I press my lips together when she takes me in her mouth again, twirling her tongue around the tip. Shit, I'm way too close.

I grab her hand and pull her off the floor. I'm naked in front of her, and she's still wearing all her clothes. Too many clothes. I grip the hem of her dress, wanting to pull it off her body, wanting to see her, but she stops me.

"There's no need for that," she says.

I frown, my body feeling like a furnace. "I want to taste you."

She smiles, patting my chest. "That's nice." Nice? "But I can assure you I'm good to go. Just fuck me," she says, bringing her lips to mine in a hot kiss. My god, her lips feel so good against mine, soft and tender, her teeth grazing my bottom lip every once in a while.

"If only I knew this is what would get you to be nice to me," I murmur, pulling back. "I would have done it sooner."

She pushes me away, a slight smile on her face as she rolls her eyes. "God, you're so full of yourself."

I grip her waist, pulling her flush to me. "You could be full of me too." Her breathing stops, catching in her throat as she licks her lips. "Get on my bed."

She falls onto my mattress, lifting her dress to her hips, the black lace underwear on her smooth, tanned body making my mouth water. God damn. I want to taste her so bad.

I approach her, pull the underwear down her legs, throw it to the floor, and stare at the bare skin between her legs. Her pussy glistens with the evidence of her arousal. "Hmm." I grip her thighs with my hands. "You little liar." I want to lick her so bad. "You're dripping, Leila." She whimpers, making my dick twitch. "Not bone dry at all."

She twists under me until her sweet ass is in my face, her knees bent as she lies on her stomach. "I want you from behind," she tells me.

She's trying to kill me. Seriously, someone check on my poor dick, it's so painfully hard. I reach over to grab a condom from my dresser, roll it on and give it a slow stroke before bringing it to her entrance. She stills, sucking in a breath when she feels me. "Are you okay?" I ask her, rubbing her back with my hand, wishing it was her soft skin instead of the dress under my hands.

"I don't need a pep talk," she says, bumping her hips up and grazing my dick. I grunt, gripping her hips to keep her steady. "I need you to fuck me."

I start to push in, slowly. Fuck, she's so tight. Her head drops to the mattress, as she breathes out a moan. I keep pushing into her an inch at a time until she whimpers. "Is it in?"

she asks, lifting her head, attempting to look behind her shoulder.

I knead my hand over her hips, staring at where I'm disappearing inside of her, the sight making me lightheaded. "Not all the way," I tell her.

"God," she cries, dropping her head again. "Go deeper."

"Leila."

"Deeper," she tells me again.

I push in another inch and when she moans again, low, agonized. I stop. "I don't want to hurt you."

"You won't."

I love watching her stretch around me, but the way she tightens around me when I feed her another inch and sucks in a harsh breath, stops me from giving her more.

Her head lifts, looking at me behind her shoulder, her eyes hardening. "Either fuck me," she says. "Or I'll go back to the party and find someone else who will."

I thrust the last couple of inches inside of her and a strangled cry escapes her as she drops her head, my dick all the way in now. "Holy fuck," she says breathlessly.

Holy fuck indeed. I let out a breath, my cock strangled inside her. "Are you ok?" I ask her.

"Yes," she moans. "Oh my god. Start moving."

I pull out halfway and thrust back in, her hot pussy gripping me when I do. "God damn," I breathe, watching her body move with mine as I thrust against her. My condom-covered dick slick with her juices. "Fuck," I grunt. "You're stretching so well for me, gorgeous."

She moans again, meeting my thrusts, her ass jiggling with every slap of my skin against hers. I lean forward, gripping her throat and twist her neck to bring her mouth to mine. I need to kiss her, to see her. As much as I love this position, I want to look at her when she comes.

Fuck, I bet she's so pretty when she comes.

"God, you feel so good," I grunt, looking down at where I'm pushing inside of her. "So tight." I squeeze my eyes closed, the feel of her too much to bear. "I'm struggling to hold on."

"Are you going to be a two-pump chump?"

Her little remark makes me laugh when I lean over her, nipping at her ear, loving how she moans when I thrust deep inside of her. "I knew you'd be like this," I admit. "Stubborn and bossy in bed."

My hands grab onto her ass, clutching the soft skin rippling with each thrust. "You needed someone like me, didn't you?" She moans again, burying her head into the mattress. "Someone that will fuck you into submission until that attitude of yours is nothing but a jumble of words begging me to let you come."

"No," she says in a breathy voice that turns me the fuck on.

"No?" I repeat. "Do you want me to stop then?"

The groan she lets out makes me chuckle, and when she looks behind her shoulders, her eyes are narrowed. "Are you saying you can't do the job?"

She's such a little tease. "Of course I can, gorgeous." I run my hands over her plump, round ass. "If you beg."

"You've got to be kidding me." Her eyes narrow even more.

I tut, pulling out of her halfway. "I don't kid." When I thrust back in, she lets out an urgent cry that makes her squeeze around me. "You want to come? Ask nicely."

She shakes her head, whining into the bed. So stubborn. "I am not *begging* you."

"Don't act like your pussy doesn't drip when I tell you what to do." When she shakes her head, I let out a laugh, withdraw a

89

few inches and push back into her, loving how she tightens around me, crying out into the pillow. "Come on," I coax her. "I chased you, told you how much I wanted you." I pull out all the way and tap my cock against her dripping wet pussy. "Now it's your turn." When I slide in again, it feels like heaven. I want to drag this out, I want to know she wants me as much as I've been craving her, but as soon as I'm deep inside her, I don't give a fuck if she begs anymore. Hell, I'm close to begging her myself.

She shakes her head again but when I withdraw again, she caves, letting out another moan. "Fuck. Please," she cries. "Please." The plea from her lips sounds like a melody, my cock twitching inside of her. "Please make me come."

If only she could see the smile on my face. "That wasn't hard, was it?" She gasps when I give her another inch, whining for more. "I knew you could be good for me," I murmur into her ear, my teeth grazing against her jaw.

When I grab onto her hips and shove my dick all the way inside of her, she throws her head back, meeting every thrust. "I'm so close," she whimpers, dropping her head once again. "Don't you dare stop."

Shit, so am I.

I bunch her dress up around her midsection, wanting to watch me pound into her, her low breathy moans bringing me closer. The pleasure racking throughout my body, tingling in my balls the louder she gets.

My hand reaches out, covering her mouth. "Shhh," I whisper in her ear. "We don't want our best friends to know how nice you are when your pussy is filled with my cock, do we?"

She moans again, the sound muffled with my hand. "Yeah, you're so nice to me now, Leila. Taking me so fucking well." I grunt, thrusting in all the way, wanting deeper inside of her.

A soft bite hits my palm as she cries out, bumping her hips back. Her body melts into me as she comes, her pussy tightening around me when she does.

"Fuck," I grunt, speeding up my thrusts until I spill myself into the condom inside of her. I keep thrusting, squeezing every drop of cum out of me, my breathless moans filling her ear.

She softens beneath me when she comes down from the high, and I lift myself off her, pulling out of her warmth, instantly wishing we could do it again.

I watch as she turns around, adjusting her dress to cover her, staring up at me with a hazy look in her eyes. Her breath comes out harsh and heavy as she calms down from the orgasm.

I pull the condom off my spent dick, tying it up and disposing of it. When I turn back around, Leila is off the bed, pulling her underwear back on and putting her shoes back on.

My brows furrow. "Where are you going?"

"I'm leaving," she says, not looking back at me as she adjusts her hair in my mirror. "See you around." She pulls the strap of her bag over her shoulder, trying to push past me.

"You're not going anywhere."

"Aiden," she sighs, her eyes dropping to my dick that's already hardening. Can't blame me, just look at her. "I'm not really in the mood for another round."

"No. That's not what I meant. It's past two in the morning, Leila. You're not walking back home. Stay here tonight." I grab my boxers, pulling them on.

"You mean," she says her eyes narrowing at me, "with you? As in sleep in your bed?"

91

My lips twitch. "Yes?" Is that such a hard concept for her to grasp?

"No." She's already shaking her head. "No, that's not a good idea. I'll be fine. I'll just get an Uber." She tries pushing past me again, but I stand in front of her.

"Seriously, Leila. I won't be able to sleep knowing you walked out of here alone in the middle of the night. Stay."

Her eyes look past me to the bed that's still made, the cover all rumpled. "Aiden," she starts.

"Stay. Just for tonight."

Her eyes narrow a little, brows knitted as she considers me, looking from me to the bed until she lets out a little sigh, taking off her bag. I shouldn't be smiling, I know that, but it doesn't stop me from doing just that when I watch her reach down to remove her shoes. I beat her to it, dropping down on one knee and wrap my hand around her ankle.

"I'm not five," she tells me. "I can take off my own shoes."

I snicker, running my hand up her long, smooth, tanned legs. Such a stubborn woman. Even after we just gave each other mind-blowing orgasms, she goes right back to defying me. "I know you can. Doesn't mean I don't want to." These legs. I want them wrapped around my head next time.

I remove her shoes, setting them down beside the bed. "You want a t-shirt to sleep in?" I ask her. The image of her lying next to me in one of my t-shirts has me wishing she says yes.

"No," she says instead. "I'll be fine in this."

I'm not going to push her. Not when I've already got her to sleep here. With me. In my bed.

I lift off my knee, towering over her and dip down to press a quick kiss against her lips. Her eyes widen when she realizes

92

what I did, but before she can say anything, I take hold of her hand and pull her with me. "Let's go to bed."

13

No repeats

Aiden

The ringing of my phone jolts me awake, my eyes blinking, adjusting to the dark surroundings.

What time is it?

I grunt, wiping a hand down my face. The ringing permeates my ears, sounding louder and louder the longer I take to pick up. I roll over to the side, eyes barely open, still foggy and answer the phone, bringing it to my ear.

"Yes?" I grunt.

"Are you trying to piss me off?" my brother says on the other end. "Where is our money?"

God damn it. My eyes snap open, my whole body going stiff at his voice. The cold tone enough to make me uneasy. I pull back, looking at the time on my phone, grunting when I see it's still early as fuck. "It's four in the morning, asshole. You're high already?"

He sniffs. "Shut the fuck up," he grits out. "Where is our money?"

My eyes narrow even though he can't see me. It's way too early for a migraine. "You mean my money?"

His laugh makes my whole body shiver. I'm twenty years old, for fuck's sake. I shouldn't be scared of my own brother, especially since he's miles away, but I can't forget what it was like growing up with him, with all of them.

The dark, snarky laugh echoes through the phone. I can almost picture the grin he has on his face. It's the same grin he used to have right before I got a beating. "You don't make shit. You owe us. College or not, you've got to pay your dues, little bro."

"I told you," I sneer. "I haven't gotten paid yet."

"I'm getting very impatient waiting around for you."

I shake my head, knowing he's not going to let this go anytime soon. "How's Mom?"

"What's it to you?"

A sharp exhale escapes me, running my hand down my face. "I care about her."

"Yeah, seemed like it when she begged you not to leave and you did anyway."

Fucking— "Can you just put Mom on the phone? Is she awake yet? Where are you?" It's just over three am back home. What is he doing calling me at this time?

"It doesn't concern you. All you have to do is get us our money before I come and get it from you."

My body freezes at the thought of seeing any of them again. "You can't even drive, asshole."

"How hard could it be?" He lets out a scoff. A cocky prick too.

"How are you going to afford a car?"

He sniffs again, I can almost picture the way he cracks his neck when he gets nervous. "I'll figure it out."

My eyes glaze over. "You mean steal."

"I said I'll figure it out," he grits out. "You don't need to worry about anything but getting us our fucking money."

The line hangs up a second later.

"Fuck," I yell, scrubbing my face in my hands. "Fucking asshole. Shit."

I place my phone back on the nightstand and fall onto the bed, pulling the pillow over my head. When am I ever going to be rid of them? Redfield was supposed to be my ticket to freedom, but I'm still under their control, under their grasp. I twist over, burying my head into the pillow, my hand grazing against something, and I turn my head, spotting a hair clip lying on the pillow beside mine.

My eyes squint as I grasp it in my hands, bringing it in front of my face. I run my hands over the white clip.

Leila.

She left.

She left after I told her not to go.

Did she regret what we did last night? Does she hate me again? God, it was so good having her underneath me, moaning and breathing and kissing me. And now she's gone.

I hate the thought of her leaving in the middle of the night. Alone. Did she even sleep or just wait for me to pass out before she dipped?

I close my eyes, picturing her in my head, tucked in that tight, black dress of hers, hair spread all over my pillow as she tried her hardest not to look at me.

I didn't look away. Couldn't. The whole time I spent tracing her features in the dark, the way her lips parted when she let out a breath, the way she tucked her hands underneath her head when she was pretending to sleep.

I really thought she'd spend the night with me, and we'd wake up together in the morning. I'd make her breakfast, talk about last night, about how much I want to do it again.

But none of that can happen because she left.

I sit up, grab my phone from my nightstand, and find her name.

Aiden:

You left?

I don't even know if she's awake right now. Don't even know if she got home safe, if she's ok.

Last night was...

I can't get it out of my mind.

Aiden:

Text me if you're alive.

I press send, and let out a sigh, pulling the covers over me and let sleep take over.

By the time I manage to get myself out of bed, it's way past breakfast. I pull the covers back, needing some water, some fresh air... something.

I trail down the stairs, heading to the kitchen, when I hear Grayson's voice echo through this big ass house his parents bought for him.

I barely make it two steps into the kitchen when I see Grayson and Rosalie acting all cute and shit as he hugs her from behind, Rosie squealing when he buries his head in her neck. I cross my arms, just watching them for a second, and then clear my throat.

His head snaps up, and Rosie gasps as she turns around. A laugh escapes me watching her try to hide her flushed cheeks from me.

Grayson, as usual, scowls at me. "We weren't even doing anything," he grits out.

"PDA gives me hives," I joke, grabbing a glass from the cabinet.

He snorts out a laugh. "I thought the same before I met her," he says, glancing over at Rosie. A shy smile grows on her face and she leans in to give him a kiss, wrapping her arms around his neck.

I groan. "Come on." As much as I love those two, some things need to be kept private.

They break apart and Rosie offers me a smile. "You wouldn't be like this if you found yourself a girlfriend," she says, lifting her brows.

I laugh. "Got it." That's not going to happen anytime soon. Girlfriends are distractions, another thing to take my time away from what really matters. Basketball.

She shrugs before dumping a bag of popcorn—plus candy—into a bowl. "I'll be with the girls," she says to her boyfriend, before giving him a quick kiss and heading out of the kitchen.

My ears perk up. The girls?

Grayson grabs a beer from the fridge, cracking it open, the sound making me flinch.

It never goes away. The noises my brain reprogrammed to mean a beating was coming, the sound of their footsteps when they were having a bad day. The way a can of beer was opened right before you got bruised ribs. It plays in my mind, every time I hear it, like a horror movie I can't turn off.

"You good?" Grayson asks making me snap out of the memories.

I shake my head, try to regain a little control. "Yeah," I breathe out.

His eyebrows knot together as he takes a sip of the beer. "You look weird."

"What do you mean?"

His hand gestures to my head. "Your... hair. It's weird."

I laugh, running a hand through it. "I need a haircut."

He nods. "You do." He brings the can to his lips again, licking them when he takes a sip.

"So Rosie invited her friends over?" I ask.

"Yeah," he says, nodding. "She said we're spending too much time together, and she needs some girl time." He rolls his eyes.

"She's right. You two have been glued to each other's side."

"I get it," he says, running a hand through his long, dark hair. "I do. It's just... When I'm not with her, I miss her."

"She's in the other room, bro." When he glares at me, I let out a laugh. "So is that why you're in here? You've been kicked out of your own living room?" I ask him, filling up the glass with water.

He shrugs, taking another sip of his beer. "It's her house too now." He says, a smile sprouting on his face. "I like having her here. So if she needs to spend time with her friends without me there, then so be it."

I nod, only one thought running through my mind. "And all of her friends are here?" I ask him, taking a sip of my water.

His face drops. "Aiden," he sighs. "Are you kidding me?"

"What?"

He sets the can on the counter behind him, crossing his arms as he narrows his eyes at me. "This is about Leila, isn't it?"

I take another sip, my throat all of a sudden feeling dry as hell. I lift my shoulder in a shrug. "I was just wondering if she was here."

He laughs, shaking his head at me. "That's not all, is it?" he asks, raising an eyebrow. No, but I don't let him know. Leila was so demanding on this being just between us, I wouldn't want to give her any more ammunition. I sip my water instead. He knows, though. He nods a few times and grins at me. "So, everything I told you last time went in one ear and out the other?"

I scoff. "The day I listen to you will be a cold day in hell," I joke. "I didn't get involved in your relationship with Rosie, don't get involved in mine."

He presses his lips together, trying not to laugh. "From what I can tell, she can't stand you."

"Yet." I grin.

He shakes his head, laughing. "And that's bullshit," he says. "You told me to stay away from Rosie, that she couldn't handle what we were doing, and I should cut it off with her." His eyes narrow. "Remember?"

I shrug, rubbing the back of my neck. "I didn't know the girl," I sigh. "And I sure as hell didn't know you'd turn into a sappy shit."

"Fuck you." He laughs. "If I listened to you, I wouldn't have her."

I nod. "And you didn't listen to me," I tell him. "So why should I listen to you?"

He shrugs. "Fair enough." He reaches behind him, grabbing his beer.

"So, is she here?"

He sighs, wipes a hand down his face mumbling under his breath. "Yes," he exhales. "She's in there." He points at the living room door, taking a swig of beer before he starts walking out of the kitchen, turns back and glares at me. "Just make sure you know what you're doing."

"I do," I tell him.

His eyes narrow for a second, assessing me before he sighs and walks away.

I down the rest of the water, heading towards the living room. The sound of laughter hits me before I've even opened the door. It makes me wonder what Leila sounds like when she laughs, when she really opens up and lets herself be happy.

My knuckles hit the wood before I push the door open, peeking inside. The noises stop as they look back at me. I offer them a grin. "Hey."

"Did Grayson send you to spy on us?" Rosie asks.

I hold up my hands, shaking my head. "I came by my own accord. I swear."

"Well since you're here," Rosie's friend Gabriella says, picking up a can of beer and throwing it at me. "Here."

I catch it with ease and look down at it. My jaw clenches at the feel of it in my hand. "I'm good," I say, putting it down on the table. "Training." It's easy to blame it on training instead of having to go into a whole spiel about why I don't drink.

STEPHANIE ALVES

"Ugh," Gabi groans. "Athletes and their rigorous diets." She shakes her head. "I couldn't do it. I love chicken nuggets too much."

I let out a laugh. I like that girl. She's funny. Too bad the only girl I came in here to see is avoiding me like the plague. She's sat on the edge of the couch, sipping on her beer without a care in the world, like we didn't hook up last night and she left in the middle of the night.

I watch as she glances at me for a second, meets my eyes and snaps her head back into position. "Is this a slumber party?" I ask them.

"We're watching a rom-com," Rosie says. "We never got to celebrate me moving in."

A groan leaves me before I can stop it. "Yeah, on second thought, I have a lot to do. See you, ladies." I close the living room door behind me and head upstairs, getting into the shower.

Our whole house back home could fit into my room here. One single small as fuck toilet and a shower that I barely fit into. And now, here I am in a big ass stand-in shower with huge glass panels. It blows my mind how just a few years ago, I was living so differently.

I turn off the water and climb out of the shower, wrapping a towel around my waist.

"I was beginning to think we had scared you off." I blink, seeing Leila in my room, on my bed. She's sat on the edge, staring up at me. I don't miss the way her eyes widen, dropping to my body, water still dripping on my skin.

"I'm not easily scared off," I tell her, drying my hair with one towel, while holding onto the other. I watch her eyes dip to the deep-set v cut of my abs, my dick merely a few inches

102

below it. Her throat bobs as she gulps and then she looks back up at me. "Didn't think you wanted to see me again." *After you ran off.*

"I don't."

"Then what are you doing here?"

She frowns, biting the inside of her cheek. "I don't know."

She's trying so hard. So fucking hard to act like she doesn't want me, like she didn't enjoy last night, and she wouldn't want to do it all over again. I know that's a lie. I shake my head, trying not to laugh at how much she's fighting with herself over this. "What would your friends think if they found you in here?" I ask her, raising my brow.

She shrugs. "I told them I was using the bathroom."

"There's a bathroom downstairs." She looks away from me, staring down at the ground. It's weird, seeing her act shy and speechless around me. I don't like it. "What are you doing here, Leila?" She glances up at me, her lips parted like she wants to say something, but nothing comes out. She presses her lips together and looks away again. I approach her on the bed, her breath hitching when I rub my thumb over her chin, lifting it so she can look at me. "I want to see you again."

"You're seeing me right now."

I smirk, letting my knuckles graze the soft skin of her cheek. "Not in the way I want to see you."

She shakes her head and stands up from the bed, putting distance between us and clears her throat. "That's not going to happen."

"Why not?" I ask, taking a step closer to her.

"Because," she says, stepping back, "I don't do repeats."

I stop in my tracks, my brows furrowing as I look at her, trying to make sense of what she just said. "You don't do repeats?"

"Yes." She crosses her arms. "We had a good night, but that's enough for me."

Enough for her? I haven't been able to stop thinking of every detail of last night. Her soft body, her hands all over my skin, and she's telling me one night was enough for her?

"That's not going to work for me," I tell her shaking my head. "I want to see you again, Leila."

She laughs, the sound hitting me in the chest. "Why? We both got what we wanted last night. Now we can go our separate ways."

I take a step, crowding her. I hear her sharp intake of her breath and it fills me with memories of last night. Every glorious sound she made. "If you think I got what I wanted, you're dead wrong."

Her throat moves as she gulps, looking up at me. She licks her lips quickly, dropping her head. "We were both drunk, Aiden. It was just a hook-up."

"I wasn't."

"What?" she asks, lifting her head.

"I wasn't drunk," I clarify.

She laughs, pressing her hand against my chest. I feel her fingerprints for only a second before she removes them again, replacing the warmth of her touch with the coldness of her words. "Right," she says not believing me.

"I didn't have a lick of alcohol, Leila."

She shakes her head. "You don't need to lie to me, Aiden."

"I don't drink." Her eyes narrow as she looks for any disbelief in my expression. She doesn't find it though because I'm not lying.

"But… you work in a bar."

My shoulders lift. "It pays well." And it was the only job willing to accept me. "And you weren't drunk either. You had one beer."

"How did you—?" she asks, shaking her head. "How did you know that?"

My lips twitch. "Because I was looking at you all night," I admit. "Couldn't take my eyes off you."

She gulps again, her eyes softening before she sets them back in place, giving me a look of indifference. "That doesn't change anything," she says. "I'm still not going to sleep with you again."

I look down at her, wondering if it was all one-sided. Did she really not feel anything? "That's it?" I ask her. "This is enough for you? One night and nothing more?"

She's lying. She's lying before she even speaks. But I see the resigned decision settle in her features, and she outright lies to me when she says, "Yes."

"Well damn." I take a step back from her, very aware of how little clothing I have on. "Then I guess you got what you wanted." I hold the door open for her, watching as she turns back one last time before leaving my room. I push the door closed and blow out a breath.

This was good. This was a good thing. A smart decision. I can't let myself get sidetracked by anything else. I got what I needed. She got what she wanted. And now we're done with each other.

As it should be.

105

14

Bar fights and catcalls

Aiden

The bar is packed.

My teammates are surrounded by drinks and girls—while I wish I was home. I need to be out here with them, celebrating, making sure the team is strong because, if not, then none of them will respect me.

"Want one?" I turn my head to Jordan, holding out his empty beer glass. "Lacy here was just about to order another round."

I swallow, staring at the drink in front of me. "I'm good."

"You never drink, Cap," he says, the girl on his lap snickering into his neck. "What's up with that?"

My shoulders lift in a shrug, avoiding his eyes and the girl laughing along. "We have a game next week."

Ethan scoffs, and I twist my head towards him. "Such a pussy," he murmurs. "You need to loosen up."

My jaw clenches when the rest of the team quietens, all looking back at me. I knew I shouldn't have come here. Today is my day off. The one day I don't have to work at The Barrel Room and they drag me to another bar instead. Most of Redfield usually hang out at Murphy's which is closer to campus and packed with athletes every night.

Seeing as I had to work pretty much every night, they started to get suspicious about my whereabouts, wondering why I would never go out with them, so here I am, hanging out in a bar with drunk girls and horny guys and I fucking hate it.

I grab my glass of Coke and lift it to my mouth. "I'm captain. I need to keep a clear head."

Carter nudges me on the arm. "You good?" he asks.

"Fine." My hands clutch the glass, taking another sip. "Just tired."

"Tonight's your day off, right?" I nod, dropping the glass to the table. "And you're spending it in another bar?" he jokes.

I chuckle, rubbing my jaw. When I lift my head, my laugh settles, watching the one girl that seems to pique my interest. Her friends walk in behind her. Rosie's decked out in a short pink dress, reminding me of the first time she ever showed up at the house.

Her friend Gabi taps on the bar, getting the attention of the bartender by taking off her jacket, leaving her in a crop top and some jeans.

And Madeline looks as elegant as she always does, wearing a long white dress complimenting the tone of her dark skin, her brown hair flowing down her back.

But the one girl that has my undivided attention, the one girl that I can't seem to stop looking at is, Leila. Her ass is so prominent in the tight jeans she's wearing, almost looking like they're painted on, and the black, low-cut top does nothing to hide her full figure, her tits the center of attention.

Fuck, she's gorgeous.

"Hey." My eyes snap away from Leila to the girl standing in front of me, short brown hair above her shoulders, wearing a

107

skimpy outfit that my teammates are drooling over. "Aiden Pierce, right?"

I press my lips together, giving her a smile. "Yeah, that's right."

She nods, giving me a smile of her own. "My friend was wondering if you would give her your number."

My brows raise. "Who's your friend?"

She turns, pointing at a girl sat at the bar, sipping on a cocktail. She tucks her blonde hair behind her ears, her face tinting with pink when my eyes meet hers. She's pretty, but she's not who I can't stop thinking about.

It would be so easy. I wouldn't even have to give her my number, I'd just nod, and she'd be in my bed by tonight. Don't want that though. I want one person who's hellbent on keeping me at a distance. "I'm sorry," I tell the girl. "I'm not dating right now."

She laughs. "She doesn't want a date."

Of course, she doesn't. I don't think I've ever met a girl who was interested in me beyond just sleeping with me or bragging to their friends. "I'm not doing that either." Her face falls and I'm quick to add, "You're both beautiful, but I'm focusing on basketball right now." *Or trying to.* I don't want them to think there's something wrong with them, there's not, I'm just not interested.

"Your loss." She turns around and heads towards her friend.

"What's wrong with you?" Ethan asks, raising his eyebrows. "She was hot. They were both hot."

"Then you can have them."

He scoffs, lifting off the chair and downing the rest of his beer before heading towards the two girls.

I can't help myself, my head turns to where Leila was standing before, but this time she's not alone. Some guy is standing with her, talking and laughing with her. I see him take a sip, his eyes dipping down her body, checking her out.

I'd be pissed if she wasn't constantly looking at me. When my eyes meet hers for the umpteenth time, she twists her head away from me, nodding along to whatever the guy is saying. She doesn't want me, my ass. She can't keep her eyes off me, just like I can't.

That night replays itself in my mind frequently. More than I'd like it to. I can't stop thinking about her, about the noises she made and how she keeps me on my toes. I've never met someone like her, don't think I ever will.

"That's my girl, jackass." A loud crash rips my gaze from her to the two guys rolling around on the floor. I lift off my seat, my eyes widening when I spot Ethan straddling the guy, swinging his fist, punching the guy.

"Campbell!" I shout through the noise, pushing everyone aside until I get to them. "What the fuck are you doing?"

My arms reach for him, attempting to rip him off the guy, but when he turns and sees me, the anger is directed at me, nudging me off him. "Fuck off," he says, lifting off the guy and pushing at my chest.

"What are you doing?" I repeat, narrowing my eyes at him. "What the fuck happened?"

He shakes his head, pushing at my chest again. "I don't listen to you. You're not my captain." With that, he turns and walks out of the bar, murmurs spreading across the room.

I wipe a hand down my face, turning to Carter. "What the hell just happened?"

109

He gestures with his chin to the short-haired girl who approached me, who's now clutching at the bloody guy on the floor, calling him 'babe.' "I guess Ethan flirted with the wrong girl."

"Everybody out!" The bartender shouts, escorting everyone out of the bar.

I blow out a breath, and when Jordan and Andre come out, looking at the smashed glass and blood on the floor, they turn to me. "What just happened?"

Once again. This is all on me. I'm team captain. I should have a hold on my team, and instead, I let everyone down. I shake my head. "I messed up."

15

So much fun

Aiden

I feel a nudge on my shoulder, and Grayson nods towards the tv. "Go that way," he tells me.

I press the controller, moving to the left, squatting down until I can get a clear target. "There's no space."

"Right there," he tells me, gesturing to the guy coming around the corner. "Shoot."

I shake my head, moving more to the right. "You're blocking me."

In the next breath, Grayson's character gets shot, giving my location away. We both die, and Grayson curses, letting the controller fall to the side. "You had a clear shot."

"You're kidding, right? You were covering him."

He shakes his head, running a hand through his hair, and Rosie walks in, glancing at the tv. "Hey, what are you guys doing?"

"He's ruining my street cred," I tell her, laughing when Grayson flips me off. "My stats are going to suck."

"We were playing a game, angel," he tells her. "Want to join?"

She shakes her head. "I don't think I'd be very good."

"Easy fix," I tell her, shuffling so she can sit next to her boyfriend. "Sit."

She sits between us, and Grayson passes the controller to her, she stares at the buttons, clicking away, and I laugh. "See. You're already better than your boyfriend."

"Cocky son of a bitch." Grayson lets out a laugh, teaching Rosie the controls and starts a new game. Poor girl dies instantly, moving around in a circle. I press my fist to my mouth, stifling any laughter when Grayson scowls at me.

"I suck," she says.

"You don't," I tell her, starting up a new game. "That was pretty good for the first time."

"You did well, Rosie," Grayson tells her, smiling at her. "You're always so good at everything you do. Such a quick learner."

She blushes and his cocky grin makes me blink. "Are you guys dirty talking right in front of me?"

Grayson glances up at me but doesn't reply. He doesn't have to, by the way Rosie giggles, shuffling closer to him makes me think that whatever just happened was some sort of weird dirty-talking foreplay. I groan, standing up from the couch. "That's my cue. I'm out of here."

"Finally," Grayson breathes out, grabbing Rosie and bringing their mouths together.

I shake my head, leaving them alone to do whatever it is they're about to do and head upstairs.

I strip off my t-shirt as soon as I get inside, turning on the shower and letting the hot water drip down my body, engulfing me. It's so good. I don't think I'll ever get used to hot water whenever I want. When I first got here, I must have raised the water bill by a fuck ton because I couldn't stop taking showers.

I had never felt so... clean. We barely had hot water growing up, and when we did, the water was cut off for lack of paying the bills. I would sneak into school earlier than everyone else and take a shower at the gym, but then some guys from the team caught me, and I wasn't allowed to shower there anymore. It sucked having to be the school's reject, having to put up with the shit-talking and people thinking I was gum on the bottom of their shoe.

Which is why I will always be grateful to Grayson for taking the heat off of me freshman year. I don't know how they found out, or who it was but rumor was one of the freshmen lived in a trailer park and had a junkie mom. I was terrified that people would find out it was me, that the few weeks I had in college being treated like an actual human being was all going to come to an end, but then Grayson stepped in and let everyone think it was him.

I love that motherfucker. I owe him so much but as much as I try to pay my way, give some money towards rent or some bills, he won't accept it. He knows the shit I have to deal with back home and doesn't let me spend a penny. So the least I can do is buy groceries and cook us a decent meal that doesn't come in a box.

I turn off the shower after what feels like an hour and pick up the towel, running it over my hair. Fuck, I need a haircut. I hate the long strands. Hate feeling it under my fingertips.

I throw the towel onto the bed when I notice something on my nightstand that I'm not quite sure why it's still there.

Leila's hair clip she left here the night we... the night she dismissed so easily.

I pick it up and turning it over in my hands, wanting to know what she's doing right now. I've barely seen her. I kept my word, she wants to be done with me, to act like that night never happened then so be it.

113

Too bad I can't do the same. I can't act like it never happened. The times I see her in class, I can't take my eyes off her. She always sits next to this girl she seems to be friends with. I watch as she talks to her, laughs with her, smiles at her. She has such a pretty smile. If only it was directed at me.

She needs this back, right? I clutch the clip in my hands, picturing what her hair looked like that night, pinned back with this butterfly clip, the rest flowing behind her back, those rich, chocolate strands of hair that were so soft between my fingertips. I want to run my hands through it, to clutch the strands and pull her into me until those pink, plump lips part and let me inside, tasting how sweet she is when no one else is around. So sweet.

I pick up my phone from the nightstand, scrolling through until I find her name, letting out a breathy laugh when I see the name still set as what she changed it to.

Never going to happen.

That's too bad, Leila, it already did, and like the gluttonous asshole that I am, I want it to happen again.

I pull on my sweats and throw on a clean shirt, stuff my phone in my pocket and head downstairs, not even daring to go near the living room. I send Grayson a text, smiling when I see his reply and I open the front door and head outside.

I've never been here before, but I know I have the right place when I see the big ass spiral doors at the front. Grayson came here all the time when he was seeing Rosie. Difference is, Rosie wanted to see him too. Leila doesn't want anything to do with me.

This might be a mistake, but I knock on the right number before I can talk myself out of it. I can hear shuffling on the other side and then the most gorgeous pair of eyes stare back at me when she opens the door and blinks, twice, three times.

"Aiden?"

"Hey."

She blinks again, making me grin a little. "What are you doing here?" she asks.

I grasp the small butterfly-shaped clip in my pocket and pull it out, holding it out to her. "You left this at my place the other night." She glances down at my hand, grabbing it. "Thought I would bring it back." It's such a shit excuse, but it's the only thing I could think of.

"I didn't even know this was missing," she says, glancing down at the clip and then back at me.

Right. Of course she wouldn't. "Well, I thought you might need it." I rub the back of my neck. Fuck, this is not going how I wanted it to.

She squints. "That's the only reason you're here?"

No. "Yep," I say instead, stuffing my hands in my pockets. "I just wanted you to have that back," I gesture to the clip clutched in her hands. "And now you do. So…" Well, this was a fucking dumb idea. I turn around, heading out of here before I embarrass myself further.

"Wait."

I look behind my shoulder at her, clutching the clip in her hands, fiddling with it. "You want to come in?" she asks.

I blink, my eyes widening a little. "Yeah. Sure." She steps inside, holding the door open for me and I enter, looking around the place. Damn, there's a lot of windows. This place screams rich trust fund kid. "Wow, this place is nice." Understatement. It's so white and clean, glass vases everywhere, covered in green. Plants are spread all over the place, on the counters, tables, by the windows.

"Yeah," she says a low chuckle coming from her. It makes me twist around to see her. Did she just… laugh? "Well, I have Rosie to thank for this. If not, I'd be living with my roommate."

"She sounds awful," I say, remembering how she wasn't her biggest fan.

"She was the worst." She rolls her eyes which makes me smile. I really like when she does that, I don't even know why.

"What did she do?" I ask her, leaning against the wall. "She steal your soap?" I tease, grinning at her.

She shakes her head, dropping the clip on the table near the door. "More like set fire to my dorm and roll around with her boyfriend in my bed."

My brows lift. "Damn. I'm sorry, that does sound bad."

"Yeah." She scoffs, crossing her arms. "That's why I'm thankful for this place." She turns around and grabs a glass, looking behind her shoulder at me. "You want something to drink?" she scrunches her nose. "Fair warning, I only have water and orange juice."

I laugh, liking this side of her. "I'm good."

She nods, fills up her glass with water and takes a sip before she turns around and leans against the sink. I watch as her eyes drop, giving me a once-over. Very obviously checking me out. Oh, Leila, you are not as done with me as you think. "So, what are you really doing here?" she asks.

"I came to bring your hair thingy."

She rolls her eyes, setting the glass on the counter. "We both know you didn't come all the way here to give me my stuff. Why did you even keep it?"

I shrug, deciding to be honest with her. "I wanted to see you again."

My eyes trace the movement of her throat when she gulps, licking her lips. "I told you I don't do repeats."

Trust me, I can't stop thinking about it. "I know."

"I said I couldn't do this again, Aiden."

There's no way I can stop the smirk that's currently on my lips. "Couldn't, huh? Not didn't want to."

"Aiden."

"I've been racking my brain over what happened between us the other night, and I know you liked it. I know you wanted me."

"Of course I did," she admits. "For a night."

"So this is your thing?" I ask her straight up. "You sleep with guys and then leave. Never see them again?"

Her brows raise, a frown painted on her lips. "Don't you do the same?" Well shit. "I don't see why you'd have a problem with that."

"I didn't think I would, but when it comes to me? Fuck yes, I have a problem with it."

She sighs. "I don't get why you're so hung up on this."

I take a step forward, watching as she stills. "I can't stop thinking about you."

She presses her lips together, almost stopping herself from speaking. She shakes her head and lets out a breath. "That will pass."

"I doubt it."

"You just need to get laid," she tells me which makes my pulse skyrocket.

"Can't do that."

"Why not?" she teases, smirking. "Lost your mojo?"

I almost laugh, loving when she teases me, but I shake my head instead. "I can't stand the thought of sleeping with some other girl when I'd just be comparing her to you." I watch as her lips part and her breathing gets faster. "I'd picture your breathy moans under me, the way those big, round, green eyes have lived in my mind for weeks, there's no way I could think of anyone else when all I see is your flushed cheeks and the way you moaned my name."

"You don't think that," she forces out after a few seconds of silence ticking between us.

A breathy laugh escapes me when I step even closer to her. "I do." My eyes drift down to where she's gripping the edge of the sink behind her, almost having to hold on. She's so damn pretty, dressed in an oversized white shirt and some little shorts underneath.

"I don't do relationships," she spits out, all breathless.

"Neither do I," I tell her, looking down at those sour green eyes. "Basketball takes up all of my time," I admit. "I'm not talking about a relationship, Leila. I don't even know what one would look like."

"Then what?" Her tongue pokes out, running over her bottom lip. I'm dying to taste her lips again.

I cup her face, loving how she melts into my touch, and looks up at me. "We had fun, right?" Those beautiful eyes stare back at me for a second before she nods, licking her lips again. I do something a little risky and graze my fingers along the material of her shirt, unbuttoning the first button. The little gasp

I elicit from her making me lose focus. "We had so much fucking fun." I unbutton the second button, the edge of a lace bra peeking through.

"What do you say we make this a regular thing?" I ask her, unbuttoning another button.

She stills, sucking in a breath when she places her hand on top of mine, stopping me. I think I've gone too far, scared her off when she says, "Like friends with benefits?"

I shrug. "Something like that."

"I've never done that before," she admits, her honeyed breathy voice making my dick hard.

"First time for everything."

"We're barely even friends," she teases, bringing out a soft chuckle out of me. Fuck, I really have missed having her around.

"We can be whatever you want to be. What do you say?"

I can see the wheels spinning around in that pretty head of hers. "We need to establish some boundaries," she says, pressing a hand against my chest, playing with the material of my t-shirt. "Rules."

"Rules?"

She nods, glancing up at me. "For example, rule number one. No one finds out about this."

"Why? Are you embarrassed to be seen with me?" I lift my brow.

She rolls her eyes. Fuck, that makes me want to kiss her so bad. Knowing she's willing to get rid of her 'no repeats' rule makes me ecstatic, if I have to put up with some other ridiculous rules then so fucking be it, as long as I get to kiss her again. "So cocky."

I tut, letting my hands drift to her hips, her full body filling my palms. Missed this. "Not cocky, baby. Confident."

"Don't call me baby," she chastises, narrowing her eyes at me. "No nicknames."

"None at all?"

She seems to mull it over, shrugging. "As long as they don't gross me out."

"I'm sure I'll come up with something." I give her a grin. She shakes her head but I can see the small smile on her lips. "We keep it a secret and no nicknames. Got it. Anything else?" I just want to kiss her. I want to pull her into me and brush my lips against hers, taste that pure fucking sugar I can still taste on my lips.

"No sleeping over," she says, making my stomach drop a little. I'm not the biggest fan of that rule.

"You're joking."

She shakes her head. "It's too intimate. We need to make sure we keep this casual."

"Fine," I concede. "Anything else?"

She lifts her arms, wrapping them around my neck. Fuck, just kiss me already. "We don't get jealous, and we don't put pressure on this," she says. "When one of us is free, we fuck."

I scoff, drifting my hands to her ass. "Don't flatter me with such romance."

"You don't want romance," she says, leaning up into me. "You want quick, easy, dirty sex in the dark, and I'm willing to make that work."

"You're serious?" I ask her, wanting to rip every shred of clothing from her. "You want to do this?"

She shrugs. "You weren't completely horrible last time."

I laugh, leaning down until my lips barely brush against hers. "I'm going to remind you how good I made you feel, gorgeous."

I smash my lips against hers, loving how she groans and pulls me into her. She wants closer. More. And I'm willing to give her whatever she wants.

16

Can I slap her?

Leila

My dad would smack me on the back of my head for saying this, but my god, I do not miss New York.

My dad moved here when he was twenty and fell in love with the city. Although I wish I was like him in every way, I do not feel the same way. New York was my home growing up, but I'm so glad to be done with it.

But being back here is rewarding in a way. It's always great seeing my favorite front desk lady who grins as soon as she sees me approaching. "Leila!" Her eyebrows shoot up at the sight of me. "I'm so happy to see you."

"Lilly!" I mock, approaching her desk. "I know," I sigh. "I miss you."

She smiles, looking down at her computer. "Max is still setting things up. I'm sure he'll love to see you."

Max is one of the best photographers I've worked with. Kind too, which is hard to find in this line of work.

I pull out a little Sephora bag and prop it on her desk. Her eyes drop to the bag, then back at me. My shoulders lift in a shrug. "I had extras," I lie. "I need someone to get it off my hands." I push the bag towards her, noting how her eyes track the movement. "Do you want it?"

Her eyes hood, trying hard to keep her bright pink lips pursed, but she ultimately fails, a smile growing on her face. "Leila," she scolds. "We both know you did not have extras." Her head dips to look inside the bag and her eyes widen. "Oh my. Is that the new lipstick I've been seeing everywhere?" Her hand dips inside, picking up the small tube. "Maybe I can take it off your hands," she says, lifting her eyes to look at me before she admires the rest of the products.

I laugh. "You're welcome," I say. "Do you know if any of the other girls are here yet?"

She rolls her eyes. "You know they like to be fashionably late," she tells me, opening one of the perfume boxes. "They'll probably all come together giggling in about thirty minutes." She sprays the mini bottle, taking a whiff. Her eyes roll back as she inhales. "Seriously, Leila. You're the best."

"I had extras, that's all." I shrug.

"Right." She scoffs.

I laugh. "You deserve it." I shoot her a smile, admiring how she goes crazy for all the crap these companies give me.

She clutches the perfume bottle to her chest, smiles at me and shakes her head in disbelief. "You're a Godsend. Honestly."

I wave my hand. "Stop. You're going to make my ego even bigger," I joke.

She laughs, setting the bag underneath her desk. "Have fun," she says.

"I'll try." I smile before heading into the elevator. My agent has been begging me to book this gig, I didn't have many other choices, so I said yes. So far, it's been fun, but knowing that soon I'm going to have to stand in little to nothing in front of the camera makes my heart race.

The elevator doors open with a ding and I blow out a breath, painting a smile on my face. I take less than two steps when a tap on my shoulder has me turning around. My smile instantly grows when I see who it is.

"Leila," Lucas says, smiling at me. "God, where have you been?" His arms open, pulling me in for a hug. This guy has been a solid in my life for so long, one of the best people I have met.

I shrug, letting out a laugh. "Not all of us are famous models like you, I've been in college."

It's hard balancing college and modeling, especially when my agency is in New York. Being able to take time away and catch a flight is nearly impossible. It's helped that I haven't had many jobs lined up. Either a blessing or a curse, depending on how you want to look at it.

He pulls back, rolls his eyes. "I'm not famous."

I let out a scoff. "Sure."

He laughs, shaking his head. "Listen, I haven't really had a chance to talk to you with all the… press," he starts, avoiding my eyes.

"You mean the scandals," I joke.

He shakes his head, letting out a laugh. "You know how they can be."

"Ruthless," I finish for him. Some of the headlines about him don't really paint the best picture, but come on, with that perfectly styled hair of his, and those big brown eyes, what else would you expect?

We've been friends for the longest time. We were signed to the same modeling agency, and he was the one and only friend I had when we would do shoots, but Lucas outgrew our agency and now is a very well-known model.

He's very attractive, and the fact that he's Brazilian makes it the cherry on top. The frown on his face makes me wonder if he's really that upset about the headlines, but it isn't a big deal. It's impossible to go anywhere without girls swooning the moment he enters the building, it's expected that he reciprocates.

"Anyway," Lucas says with a shake of his head. "I've been meaning to ask you something. I know you're a private person, and I respect that, but Adriana won't stop hounding me for your number. I told her I didn't have it, but she insists that I'm lying. Too smart for her own good."

My heart warms at the mention of my favorite little girl. She's the kindest, sweetest soul I've ever met.

"She's uh…" he mutters, rubbing the back of his neck. "She's been having some problems with kids at school and I thought," he shrugs, "I thought you could help her. Maybe give her some advice or…" He shakes his head, blowing out a breath. "I don't know what to do," he admits.

I feel my heart break for that little girl. I know exactly what she's going through, having to put up with comments about her body and having kids laugh in her face. Kids are assholes. The pain wracking through my body must be written all over my face because he's quick to add, "She'll be fine, Leila. She's strong, but I don't have any experience with this kind of stuff, and I remember how you handled it, and I thought you would be a good choice."

How I handled it.

He means how I handled the fact that I was bullied on set by the other models. He means when they removed the food from the table so I wouldn't eat because 'I had already eaten enough

125

to last me a lifetime.' He means when they would make pig noises whenever I walked by.

Only he doesn't know that I didn't handle it well. At all.

To him, maybe it didn't seem that way since I kept to myself, ignored them and tried to not let it affect me, but when the shoot was over, I shut myself in my room with a whole box of Oreos and binged while I cried. The whole night.

Nobody knows that I'm weak though. They don't know that I don't have control over my emotions, even though it seems like the complete opposite.

And the fact that Adriana is getting bullied breaks my heart for her, for me, for every little chubby girl who had to grow up and hate her body.

I can't even count how many times I grabbed a pair of scissors and wished I could cut my body, mar myself to fit in, to look good. To love myself.

I blow out a breath, feeling my heart race and the tears threaten to spill over. "Yeah," I say, giving him a smile. "I can do that." I reach into my bag and pull out my phone.

His eyes widen. "Seriously?" he asks, pulling out his phone. "I know it's a lot to ask, Leila."

"It's okay," I say shaking my head. "This trumps any dumb reasoning I may have."

"It's not dumb. You have a right to want to keep your life private."

I scoff. "Kind of impossible to do when I'm a model." A plus-size model, I want to add. The distinction is very important. People think that because my career is in the public eye, they have a right to judge me, to comment on my body, my face, my hair, whatever the hell they decide that week.

I take his phone from him, inputting Adriana's number in my phone, jolting when I hear the elevator ding behind me and the room fills with laughter and murmurs.

"Your best friends are here," Lucas whispers, grinning like an idiot.

I narrow my eyes at him. "Funny," I deadpan.

He snickers, grabbing his phone back. "Thank you, Leila. Seriously."

"No problem." I give him a smile. He pulls me in for a hug, and I wrap my arms around him, squeezing him.

"Oh my god, is that Lucas Silva?" I hear whispers behind me.

I pull back and smirk at Lucas, knowing he heard that too. "Don't start," he scolds.

I hold my hands up. "I wasn't going to say anything." I definitely was.

"Right," he says with an eye roll. "I should probably get going before I'm raided by fangirls."

He presses his lips to my cheek and turns around, walking into the elevator. As soon as the door closes, the questions come in.

"Was that Lucas Silva?" Jennifer asks me. Her blue eyes trailing down my body as she assesses me.

I nod, giving her a tight-lipped smile.

"How do you know him?" she asks.

I shrug. "We're friends."

Her brows knit, her face scrunching as she looks up at me. "Really?"

"Yes," I say, with a straight face. I walk away, heading into the studio where Max is crouched down, setting up the studio.

"You know," I hear behind me. "I've heard stories about Lucas." I turn my head, raising my eyebrows at the blonde who just doesn't want to leave me alone today.

"His usual girls aren't really, you know…" Her eyes scan my body once more. Did she not get a good enough look last time? "You're not his usual type."

Can I slap her?

I force a smile on my face, hoping it somehow kills her instead. "Like I said, we're just friends." I turn my head back around before she can say anything else, and I hear heels tap on the floor in the opposite direction.

"You were right." I shoot Max a smile when I approach him. "That was the best wine I have ever had."

He laughs, clutching a hand to his chest. "I told you. Did you share it with your friends at least?" he asks, lifting himself off the floor.

My lips twitch. The bottle of wine he gave me last time we worked together was gone in a day. Rosie twisted her nose at it, Madi had two glasses, and Gabi and I devoured the rest. "Barely."

He nods, lips twitching. "Marcel was adamant France had the best wine, but as soon as he tasted real Italian wine, that shut him right up."

"How is Marcel?"

He groans, waving a hand. "Good. Busy with Macy." My eyes soften at the mention of Max's adorable baby. God, just looking at her makes my ovaries cry. "I see the look on your face," he says pointing a finger at me. "Don't get any ideas. Changing diapers is not fun."

A laugh bubbles out of me. "Got it." I take a step back onto the backdrop. "Where do you want me?" I ask.

He shuffles his hand, directing me to the left and then calls in the other girls. They all line up, adjusting themselves where Max tells them to go.

I feel a nudge to my elbow. "Is it true?" Amina asks, her dark brown eyes widening as she looks up at me. "You're dating Lucas Silva?"

Good god. "Who told you that?"

She gestures with her head to Jennifer who's standing front and center. "You've got to be kidding me," I mutter to myself.

"So, is it true?" Amina asks again once the flash has gone off. "It's not like you to keep this from me."

I sigh, taking a minute to adjust to the next pose. "No," I mutter, trying not to move my head. "She saw us hugging and apparently ran with it."

Amina laughs. "That girl is dripping in jealousy."

"Beautiful," Max shouts at us, the flash going off once again.

"He's a close friend," I tell her. "Nothing more."

She scoffs. "That man is so fine. Can't really judge her for being jealous."

"That's a wrap."

I exhale all the air in my body, smiling at Amina when the shoot is over. "You ready?" she asks. "Next shoot is the big one."

I swallow down the urge to puke, forcing a smile. "Of course."

Her eyes hood. "You don't have to lie to me," she says. "We're the only big girls here." A laugh escapes me at how bluntly she puts it. "I know how you're feeling but you can't let it stop you."

I sigh. "I don't know how I feel about it all."

129

She nods. "I get it, I mean when I told my boyfriend, he was worried about what people would say but do you know what I told him?"

"What?"

"I said why do I have to feel anxious about showing my body when they do it every day?" She waves a hand. "So they're skinny." She shrugs. "We're hotter."

I give her a push, a laugh bubbling out of me. "You're not nervous at all?" I ask her, admiring how at ease she is with all of this. People expect me to be confident every single day of the week and act like all the negativity doesn't affect me, but it's not that easy.

I have spent the better part of my life hating my body and spending every birthday wish on being skinny. It's hard to just let it go overnight, it takes time.

Sometimes I wonder if I'm ever going to get there. If one day I'm going to wake up and be completely in love with myself, if every time I look in the mirror, I don't scan for imperfections and things I wish I could change. I hope so.

She grabs a handful of chips, dropping one by one in her mouth. My stomach cries at me. Shit, when was the last time I ate? I make myself look away from the food and focus on Amina.

"Why should I be? People are going to talk shit whether I'm fully clothed or half-naked regardless." Damn. When she puts it like that. "You want some?" she asks. My instinct takes over, my head shaking before I can even decide if I wanted some or not. She eyes me carefully but shrugs it off, dropping the rest of the chips in her mouth.

"So how's college going?" she asks, sitting down on the couch.

I drop onto the seat beside her, rolling my eyes. "I don't know how I put up with it every day."

She laughs. "Best thing I did was drop out. No responsibility and no headaches."

I bite my lip. I don't know if I could do that. I love going to classes, having something to do.

"But I do miss the parties," she says.

"Yeah." I let out a laugh. "They're not so bad."

17

Hands behind your back

Aiden

"Ruthers! Keep up the pressure on defense." Carter turns his head at Coach's directions and blocks a pass. He grabs the ball, looking around and I turn, trying to get the ball, but I'm being blocked. Ethan crowds me, blocking Carter from throwing me the ball. Carter passes it to Jordan, and in less than a second, he has the ball in his hands, spinning around, trying to find someone who's open.

"C'mon," Coach shouts. "Move that ball with purpose."

I manage to find myself open, calling out his name for him to pass the ball. Jordan glances at me but he shakes his head, looking around. What the hell?

"Jordan. I'm open, man." He doesn't even turn around, dribbling the ball away from me.

"Pierce is wide open," Coach tells him. "Don't wait to make a pass."

He looks back, throwing the ball to Andre who doesn't catch it in time. Ethan snatches the ball, spins on his heels and shoots. We all stare at the basket as the ball sinks, scoring for the opposite team. Fuck.

The whistle blows and the opposition celebrates, patting each other on the back.

"Wright. What the hell happened?" Coach asks Jordan. I blow out a breath, wiping the sweat from my forehead. I don't know what happened, but I was wide open and he made a bad call. "Don't wait around next time," Coach tells him. "You have to keep up the intensity. You can't let the opposite team get comfortable."

"Yes, Coach." Jordan replies, glancing at me.

"Practice is over," Coach says. "Get out of here."

"Unlucky, Cap." Ethan Campbell grins, running back to the lockers.

When I push through the doors to the locker room, Ethan walks out of the showers, towel wrapped around his waist and stops in place when he sees me. "You're losing your touch, Cap." He shakes his head. "Are you sure you're up for the job?"

My jaw clenches when all of my teammate's eyes are on me. "It was one mistake," I grit out. "I get I made a bad move when I lost the game, but it's been over a month."

He scowls at me, opening his locker and pulling his clothes on.

"It's just weird, that's all," Carter says.

I furrow my brows at him. "What is?"

"That you haven't made any more mistakes like that one," he says with a shrug.

Yeah, I got that. Such a silly mistake that cost us the win. I don't lose. Ever. That one game has doubted their trust in me. It's fucking working. Whatever the blackmailer wants, it's working.

I turn, ripping off my shirt and stuff it in my locker. "It slipped."

He's silent for a while before he turns to face me. "You coming to hang out with us at Murphy's tonight?" Carter asks, throwing on a t-shirt.

I place my cap on my head, shutting my locker. "Not tonight. I'm gonna head home."

He nods when I walk out, slinging my gym bag over my shoulder. My phone buzzes in my pocket and I pull it out, grinning when I see the name on the screen.

Leila:

You free?

Aiden:

For you? Always.

I smile when I press send, watching those three little dots dance on the screen for what seems like forever.

Leila:

My place.

She doesn't have to tell me twice. Leila and I have been secretly hooking up for weeks now. Whenever one of us has the chance, we're jumping each other's bones. It's amazing. Never having to worry about what I'm going to say to the girl once we're done, or if she's just going to want free tickets, or ask me to set her up with my teammates, which most of them do.

Leila is not that kind of girl. She's looking for the exact same thing I am and that's what makes this situation work so well. Which is why I head home as fast as I can, taking a quick shower before I'm knocking on her door.

She opens it, and her hand wraps around my arm and pulls me inside. "Did anyone see you?" she asks, closing the door behind me.

"No." She's on me in an instant, grabbing the back of my neck and pulling me down to kiss her. "Umffff." I groan into her mouth. Holy fuck. I'm never going to get used to how she kisses. It's fucking erotic, sucking, biting, and licking my lips like I'm a feast she wants to devour. My hands grab her full ass, pushing her into me. A low, throaty groan rumbles in the back of her throat. "Fuck." I knead her into me. "You're so needy today."

She moans again when I kiss her neck. My dick hardens in my pants instantly. I want her so bad. She wraps her arms around me, her mouth back on mine as she moves backwards, stumbling onto the couch.

"Bed," I mumble into her mouth.

She shakes her head. "There's no time."

I laugh into her skin, groaning when she lifts her hips, grazing against my hard dick. "It's right there."

She shakes her head again. "I've been thinking of this for days." Holy shit. My dick just got harder if that's even possible. We haven't been able to see each other in a couple of days. She's been gone for a photoshoot, and I've either been working late or have practice, and I need her as bad as she needs me. But

135

that being said, she's tall, I'm tall, a couch isn't going to be the best bet.

"And I can do so much more for you in a bed." I punctuate my sentence by pressing myself against her, loving how she drops her head back, her eyes rolling to the back of her head when I do.

"Fuck," she moans, pressing her hands against my chest.

I pull myself off her, grab her hand and push us through the door. She untangles herself from me, falls onto the bed and shuffles back.

"So pretty, laying there for me," I murmur, looking down at the beautiful woman spread out on the bed in front of me. "Will you be soaked when I pull your panties off?"

She shakes her head, her tongue drifting out to lick her lips. Her hands pull at the hem of her pants, pulling them off slowly, so fucking slowly until they hang halfway down her hips. "I'm not wearing any," she says.

My cock twitches in my pants. "Show me," I tell her, desperate to see her. "Take off your clothes and spread those pretty legs for me."

Her brows lift. "How about you just fuck me instead?"

I tut, shaking my head as I lean closer to her until I'm towering over her, placing my hands on either side of her hips on the bed. "You do as I say or you don't get off. What's it going to be? Do you want to talk back to me again or be a good girl and follow my instructions?"

She lets out a shaky exhale and then her hands drift lower, the material of her pants falling down until her tanned skin is on display, completely bare to me. "That's it," I coax her. "Take it all off."

I help her out, pulling on the leg off her pants until they're on the ground and she's laying underneath me naked and so ready. I can smell her arousal, dying to taste her. I flick her top. "This too."

Her nostrils flare. "Aiden."

My frown is instant. This isn't the first or the second time she hasn't wanted to take her top off. I don't push her on it, not wanting to ruin the mood. I lean down instead and bury my lips in her neck. "Do you know how bad I want you?" I ask her, my fingers spanning the width of her thigh, her skin so soft underneath my hands.

I drag my fingers through her slick folds, a soft groan coming deep from my throat when I feel how bad she wants me too. I press my thumb against her hard, swollen clit and her hips jump off the bed instantly. Her lips part and a sexy little moan comes from them, making me lose focus for a second.

"I can't decide if I want to fuck you fast until you're shaking or so slow you cry out for more." I brush my lips against hers, my finger pressed against her wet pussy, the sounds in this room so filthy.

She breathes hard. "Fast," she says, shaking her head. "I want to come so bad."

"Don't worry that pretty little head of yours," I tell her, keeping my thumb on her clit and bring my middle finger to her sopping wet entrance, pushing inside of her in one quick thrust. Her hands grab onto my arms, gasping when I fuck her with my finger. "I'm going to make you feel so good, no matter what I do."

I push another finger into her, stretching her out, getting her ready to take all of me, and in a matter of minutes, she's shaking, clamping her legs closed around my hand. She drops her head back, moaning, a gush of wet heat coating my fingers as she comes so beautifully. Flushed cheeks, lips parted as she screams out in ecstasy, her eyes squeezed shut.

When she comes down from the high, I grip her waist and flip her over without any warning, placing a pillow under her hips. "Don't move," I tell her, running my hands over her full ass.

I get off the bed, looking at her sweet ass in the air for me and strip off my pants and boxers in one go, throwing them onto the floor.

"Condom," she reminds me, looking at me from behind her shoulder. "In my nightstand."

I let out a dark chuckle. "You know damn well those won't fit me." She rolls her eyes and turns back around, knowing the condoms she has are way too small. I grab the condom I brought and rip the packet, rolling it on my length, giving it a few strokes before I'm standing at the foot of the bed.

I grip her waist, pulling her until she's less than an inch away from me. She gasps when she feels me there.

"Spread yourself open for me," I tell her, running my cock over her wet cunt, letting it get drenched in her juices.

"You're not the boss of me," she mutters, looking at me from behind her shoulder.

I break out into a smirk, pressing into her. "Do you not want me to fuck you?" She rolls her eyes in pleasure when I run my cock through her folds, and when I retreat, she grabs her ass cheeks and spreads them until I can see her pretty, pink pussy dripping and ready for me.

My brows lift, a cocky grin on my face when I start to push into her. In a matter of seconds, her head drops to the bed, groaning when I fill her up. "Not got much to say now, do you?" I continue to push deeper into her, my eyes rolling to the back of my head when I feel how tight she is around me. "You've got an attitude until you're stuffed with my cock." I push a few inches deeper until she moans, dropping her hands.

"Did I tell you to move?" I ask her, squeezing her ass, watching as she swallows me inside of her. "Hands behind your back."

She groans and I think she's going to defy me again but she places her hands behind her back, crossing her wrists. I keep one hand holding onto her hip and grab both of her wrists with the other, thrusting all the way in. She lets out a desperate moan when I'm deep inside of her.

Holy fuck. The feeling when I first push all the way in is the best, feeling her contract around me, stretching to accommodate for my size, it's fucking perfection. I wait until she's adjusted to me before I pull back a few inches and thrust back in, the skin of my thighs slapping against her ass. The sound is music to my ears.

I watch, entranced at where we're connected, watching her stretch to take me, bumping her hips back to fuck me. Her hands are still on the small of her back, pinned there by my hands.

"Oh fuck. I'm going to come."

"God yes," I breathe out, letting go of her hands. I press into the bed, thrusting inside of her, feeling her squeeze every inch of me. It's so good. So damn good. "I love hearing you come." I exhale, pressing my lips to her shoulder, giving her another deep thrust until she's moaning so loud. Best part of her having her own place is she can be as loud as she wants. I love every noise that comes from her. It drives me insane.

"I'm so close, please, Aiden."

139

My dick twitches inside of her. "Oh fuck. Say my name again."

She drops her head. "Faster. Aiden, please."

I lift onto my knees, holding onto her hips as I thrust faster and harder, feeling my balls tighten. In a matter of minutes, she's there, crashing onto the bed and burying her screams into the mattress, and I'm right behind her, my thrusts getting sloppy, faster, harder, mindlessly fucking her until I groan, spilling into the condom inside of her.

I wait until we're both breathing evenly again, but I don't pull out of her just yet. I can't. I just keep thrusting slowly inside her, unable to stop the pleasure from coursing through my body.

"Fuck, you feel so good," I tell her, groaning as I push inside of her, and out, and in again. "I just came and I could go again."

She rolls underneath me, causing my dick to slip out of her until she turns and faces me, giving me a smile while she licks her lips. So damn pretty.

I fall onto the bed beside her and blow out a breath. Holy shit. I knew we had insane sexual attraction between us, but every time we fuck, I'm astounded at how good it is.

I've never really been into cuddling and Leila seems to be on board when she sits up, shuffling to the edge of the bed, looking at me behind her shoulder. "Are you free on Friday?" she asks.

Disappointment builds in my chest when I shake my head, my eyes dipping down to her plump ass before she pulls her pants up. "I have a game."

She picks up my jeans, frowning when something falls out of the pocket. I watch as she opens up a piece of paper, her eyes widening as she reads it. "34D?" she asks, raising her brows.

"Sounds impressive," she quips, pressing her lips into a flat line. "Did you call her?"

I scratch the back of my neck, noting how she seems off. We haven't really talked about what we're doing here. Are we seeing other people... are we not? "That's been there since my party." I completely forgot about it, and even now I couldn't pick the girl out of a line-up.

She nods, throwing my jeans onto the bed. "Get rid of the condom before it spills," she says.

"Or you could just lick it off me." Her chest rises, her lips parting a little. I'd love to see that. Her on her knees taking all of me inside her pretty pink lips. When her cheeks flush and she turns around, I can't help but grin, resting my hands behind my head and stretching my legs out. "Jeez," I groan when my feet hang off the edge. "Your bed is tiny."

She looks at me behind her shoulder. "Good thing you're not staying."

I let out a laugh, running my hand over my face. "Jesus. Give a guy a minute to breathe before you kick him out."

"Noted," she says. "I'll keep that in mind when the next guy shows up." She smirks at me, but I don't like the words coming out of her mouth, joke or not. I glare at her, and she presses her lips together, trying to hide the huge grin on her face. "Kidding."

She throws my t-shirt onto the bed, and I take the hint, getting up and throw out the condom. I grab my pants from the bed and pull them back on. I want to let it go, but my mind won't let me, so I just come out and say it. "Are you?"

She turns around, brows furrowed. "Am I what?"

"Kidding," I explain. "About another guy showing up."

She lets out an exhale. "Yes."

141

"How about tomorrow? Or the day after that, or any other day?" I ask her, throwing my t-shirt on. "Are you seeing anyone else?"

"What are you asking me, Aiden?"

She knows exactly what I'm asking her, but I play coy. "I was just wondering."

Her brows raise. "I didn't say anything about your big-breasted friend earlier."

The way she puts it has me pressing my lips together in amusement. "That's different. I don't even know her name."

"I'm sure that hasn't stopped you before," she retorts with a roll of her eyes.

"Did you?" I ask her, anticipating her response. "Want to say anything about my *big-breasted friend*, as you so eloquently put it?"

Her brows raise. "We said we would put no pressure on this."

"There isn't."

"We said this wasn't a relationship."

"It's not." I shrug. "Doesn't mean I like the idea of another guy's hands on you." Frankly, it makes me feel angry as hell, even though I know I don't have any right. We have nothing but a strictly physical relationship; it's what I signed up for.

"You're acting possessive," she says, pulling her long hair into a bun. "This isn't what fuck buddies do."

My nose scrunches, disgust on my face. "I don't like that term."

"Then what would you prefer?" she asks, planting her hands on her hips. "Friends with benefits?" My eyes darken as I look down at her. I shouldn't hate those words. That's what we are, technically, but I don't want to just be another friend to her. The idea is laughable really.

I approach her, grabbing a handful of her ass and pull her into me, letting her feel the effect she has on my body, how much I want her. "Do your friends know what you sound like when you come?"

She swallows, her lips parting slightly and then shakes her head.

"Then I think we've established where we stand."

Those pretty green eyes roll and she lets out a sigh. "We haven't established anything other than the fact that you're stubborn."

I laugh. "When it comes to you?" I say, leaning down until I brush my lips against hers. "Always."

She pushes me back on a hum. "You seriously need to go. The girls are coming over soon."

I smooth my hands down her arms, kissing her cheek, and then her other cheek, trailing closer and closer to her mouth. Her breathing picks up, the slight rise and fall of her chest bringing a low chuckle out of me. I look into her eyes when I lean in, mere inches from her lips, but before she can lean in and kiss me, I pull back, admiring how flustered she is. "See you later," I whisper, "friend."

18

Eat you alive

Leila

The FaceTime call comes just as I'm settling in to watch a movie, needing a break from studying. I pick up the call, smiling when I see him grin. "Hey." Lucas smiles, holding the phone up to his face. "How are you?"

"I'm good," I tell him. "Just studying." I give him an eye roll which he snickers at.

"Can't be that bad."

I shrug. "It's alright. Just boring as hell."

"Really?" he asks. "Damn, aren't you glad I called then?"

I laugh. "So glad. Have you heard from James yet?"

His face drops a little and I instantly want to retract my question. "Yeah, he's good I think." I watch as he rubs a hand down his face. "Just waiting for the results now."

"I'm so sorry," I tell him. "James is such a good guy. I hate that he's going through all this again."

"Yeah." He lets out a breath. "I thought he was doing better." He shrugs.

"And Adriana?" I ask him, knowing the topic of his friend is hard. "How is she doing?"

His face lights up, a smile painted on his lips. "She's so much better," he says. "She won't stop talking my ear off about you. Honestly, Leila, I can't thank you enough."

"It was nothing. I love that girl."

"And she is so completely in love with you. I swear she sees you as some sort of celebrity. She tells me all the time how she wishes you were her sister instead of me." He lets out a laugh. "I try not to take it personally but…"

"She loves you," I'm quick to say. "She wouldn't confide in you if she didn't. You're a good big brother, Lucas."

He smiles. "I try. I just don't have much experience in these kinds of things. And speaking of," he says, grinning at me. "I heard about the photo shoot. I'm so proud of you, Leila."

I roll my eyes, feeling the blood rush to my cheeks. "It's nothing."

He lifts his brows. "It's everything. Are you kidding me? Sixteen-year-old Leila wouldn't be caught dead doing a swimwear shoot. You're going to be an inspiration to girls like Adriana everywhere."

Those words lift a huge weight off my shoulders. That's all I've ever wanted, isn't it? I wanted what I never had when I was younger. I wanted to see girls in the magazines and think, 'that's what I look like.' And now I get to be that to someone.

"Thank you." I close my eyes, tipping my head back. "It's a little nerve-wracking."

He shakes his head. "You'll be great. I know it."

My head snaps to the side when I see Madi enter my apartment, waving the key in the air. I gave each of the girls a key to my place mostly for safety purposes but also because… I love their company.

"Hey," I smile at her.

"You have someone over?" Lucas asks.

"It's just my friend," I tell him.

He hums. "Is she hot?"

I snicker, watching as Madi's eyebrows raise as she takes off her shoes, leaving them by the door. "Very. She'd eat you alive though," I tell him. Madi smiles beside me.

"I doubt that," Lucas says.

I narrow my eyes at him. "You don't need help getting women."

A heavy sigh escapes him. "You believe everything, huh? You're like my mom when she reads something she saw on the internet."

I lift my brow at him. "I've seen it," I remind him.

"Of course," he says, rolling his eyes. "How can I forget? The media are always right."

"I still love you." I blow him a kiss, watching as he scowls at me. "Even if you have playboy tendencies." Madi in the corner of the room catches my eye, and I quickly turn to Lucas. "I've got to go. Talk to you soon."

"Tchau."

"Who was that?" Madi asks, sitting beside me on the couch when I hang up. "Aiden?"

I freeze, glancing at her. "Why would it be Aiden?"

She shrugs, smirking. "After that kiss…"

I shake my head. "That was ages ago. Nothing happened." Fine, I'm lying, but this thing with Aiden is too confusing to even make sense of myself, never mind telling my nosey friends. "And nothing is ever going to happen, not with someone like him."

"You've slept with athletes before." She tucks her feet under her legs. "What makes him so different?"

I blink at her. "The fact that he's way out of my league?"

She scoffs. "That's an excuse if I've ever heard one. There's no league, Leila. There is attraction, and that boy wanted to ravish you at that party, no doubt about it."

"That's not true." But as I'm saying the words, I think back to the other night, every gasp and moan and groan and his hands. His huge hands all over my body, feeling, squeezing.

"And last week? Where did you go? You told us you were going to the bathroom and then next thing we know, we get a text saying 'had to go, don't wait for me'?"

I shrug. "I had a test I had to study for."

She presses her lips together. "We just finished midterms. Try again."

"I…I…" Think of something. Anything.

"I?"

I blow out a breath. "Damn, woman, get off my case."

She laughs, shaking her head. "I rest my case."

"You'd be a damn good lawyer, almost crapped my pants."

She sighs. "Don't start. I already have my parents on my case."

I hold my hands up. "No pressure from me. So what are you doing here?"

She flashes a stack of papers in my face. "I need to rehearse. I have an audition next week and I can't concentrate. Gabi is playing video games with some guy, and if I didn't love her so much I would have told her to shush, but… she seemed so happy."

"When is Gabi ever not happy?"

Madi shakes her head. "This was different. She was blushing, Leila. It was weird. I didn't have the heart to stop her."

Gabi blushing? That's new. "I'm intrigued."

147

"Me too." She holds up the papers again, giving me a sweet smile. "Will you help me?"

"I'm not an actress."

"You don't need to be," she says. "You're just a stand-in."

"My dream job," I muse.

"Please?"

I smirk at her. "Flutter your eyelashes at me again and I might reconsider." She scowls instead, eliciting a laugh from me. "Fine. Get up."

She hands me my piece of paper and tells me what to read. Madi really goes all out, putting all her energy into reading the lines.

"Again," she says when she's done. This time she does it differently, a more emotional take on it. She has me staring at her in disbelief. My best friend is so talented.

She blinks once she's done. "Which do you prefer?" she asks.

"The second."

"Really?" She glances at me, eyes widening.

"Why are you so worked up over this?" I ask her. "You're an amazing actress. It will happen, you don't need to stress so much."

"I love you for saying that." She looks up at me. "But it's not that simple. The more time I don't land a gig, the more my parents hassle me about it. I just want to shut them up, you know? Show them that I'm serious about this and it isn't just a hobby."

"I get that. But just because it hasn't happened yet, doesn't mean it won't."

She looks down at the piece of paper she's holding and shakes her head. "From the top." I let out a sigh and her eyes soften. "We'll get ice cream later," she says. "My treat."

My nose scrunches. "Can't."

"Why not?"

"I have a photo shoot soon."

Her face drops. "Leila, It's just some ice cream. It won't kill you. We're getting ice cream and that's it," she says. "I won't hear a no for an answer.

I want to say no, but my stomach rumbles at the mere thought of having an ice cream. I sigh, giving in and say, "Deal."

She smiles, clearing her throat. "From the top."

19

Beer and jealousy

Leila

When Gabi invited me to go to a bar with her, I didn't expect to see all the basketball team here, and oh look, most of the football team is here too.

"Oh shit, it's packed today," Gabi says when she pulls me to an empty booth near the back.

I turn my head, raising my brows at her. "You didn't think of that before dragging me here?"

She shrugs. "I wanted to celebrate. It's a big deal."

I narrow my eyes at her. "Since when do you care about basketball?"

She shrugs, grinning. "Free drinks," she explains. "Scoot over. My legs are killing me." She exhales when she sits, stretching out her legs under the table.

"Rough day?"

"Dancing," she says, glancing over at me. "My dance teacher told me I need to be more bendy," she says with a nose scrunch. "Honestly, the splits can kiss my ass."

"Damn." My eyes widen. "You can do the splits?"

She shakes her head. "Not yet, but give me like two months and a whole tub of Advil and I'll get there."

I chuckle, watching her devour the pretzels on the table in front of us. My eyes drift to the guy standing in front of us, looking down at her with a grin on his face. "Hey," he says, flashing her a smile. "Can I buy you a drink?" He runs his hand through his hair, messing it up.

Her eyes widen, and she smiles at him. "Sure." She glances at me, and I bite my lip, shaking my head. Guess her plan worked. Gabi nibbles on her pretzels, smiling when the guy comes back, holding the drink of her choice, a Cosmo, dropping it in front of her and sitting on the other side of the booth.

As much as being a third wheel to my friend and a flirty guy sounds *so* fun, I decide to get out of there and give her some privacy.

I tap Gabi on her arm, leaning in to whisper. "I need to get out."

Her frown is instant. "Are you okay?" she asks.

I nod, reassuring her. "Just going to get a drink."

She lifts herself off the seat, grabbing her purse. "Want me to come with you?" she asks without looking back at the guy.

I smile at her, shaking my head. "No. Stay; I'll be right back."

She gives me a pointed look. "If you need me…" *Call me.* She doesn't finish the rest but I know. I give her a reassuring nod and head to the bar, letting out a breath when I know Aiden is probably working tonight. I don't even know if that's a good thing or a bad thing. His comment about me seeing other guys has been running all over my mind every time I see him.

He hasn't asked me again, and I haven't brought it up, but it's still there, every time he comes over, every time I see him around campus. I'm still not quite sure why I didn't tell him the truth. There are no other guys, I'm not even thinking of other guys. And that's the problem. This was supposed to be a fun, casual, no strings arrangement, but the more time I spend with Aiden, the more I miss when he has to leave right after.

We made the rules clear, well, I did, but they still stand, and they're there for a reason. I don't want to lose control or let myself repeat my past mistakes. It won't ever happen again. But I can't lie, the thought of Aiden with another girl makes my stomach feel all weird and jumpy. It's not jealousy though. It can't be.

I wave down the bartender who smiles at me when she approaches me. "What can I get you?"

"A beer please."

"You got it." She turns around, grabbing a glass and fills it up.

"Full house today." I don't really come to this bar, knowing this is where all the athletes hang out, but when Gabi showed up at my apartment, all dressed up and made up, I couldn't say no.

"They're celebrating," she says. "They just won a game."

"By 58 points," the guy beside me says, drinking his beer. "You saw the game?" he asks me.

I nod, giving him a smile. "They were amazing today."

He shakes his head. "Pierce is a fucking legend."

Yeah, he is. He played so well today. I was on the edge of my seat almost the whole game, fighting the urge to shout his name.

"Here you go," the bartender says, glancing up at me. "Word of advice, they're giving out free drinks like candy."

I laugh, grabbing my glass when she places it in front of me. "Yeah, I know." *Not to girls like me, though.* I pull out my wallet but she holds up her hand.

"They've bought so many drinks tonight," she tells me. "This one's on the house."

"Really?"

She nods, shooting me a smile. "Definitely," she says. "Now get going. You're way too hot to be sitting here talking to me."

I shake my head, let out a laugh, and sip on my beer. She gets called over for another drink, and I turn, looking around the packed bar.

It doesn't take me long to find him. He's right in the middle, surrounded by his team. Oh, and girls. Of course. I take another sip watching as he laughs, rubbing his jaw that feels stubbly when he kisses me whenever he forgets to shave. His body is sprawled out, legs wide open as he munches on the pretzels in front of him.

My eyes drift to the pair of long legs next to him. I don't even know those girls. I don't think I've seen them around the school before, but they seem to know him. The way one of the girls, with long, blonde hair, rubs his arm, smiling and giggling at him makes me realize who Aiden Pierce really is.

He's a big deal. Not just at Redfield but everywhere. The guy can play basketball as well as some of the pros, and I have no doubt in my mind that he's going to be famous one day. And girls like that are going to be all over him all the time.

He turns his head, his eyes landing on mine. I don't look away; I just take another sip, craving the burn of the alcohol. His eyes stay pinned on mine, and he licks his lips, letting his gaze fall to the length of my body, plainly checking me out. I feel drunk under his ogling, my breath hitching when I watch his eyes meet mine again, a cocky smirk on his lips. I love his eyes on me, love how he's looking at me like he can't wait until we're alone.

But then I see the girl rub his arm again, watching how her boobs strain the top she's wearing, exposing her tiny waist, and I shake the thought away, turning back around and finishing off my beer in one. *He'll probably hook up with her tonight*, my brain tells me, making me mad for even thinking it. So what? It's what we both agreed on, right?

I leave my empty glass on the counter and push my way to the bathroom, holding the door open when a girl exits, leaving the place empty. I turn on the faucet, washing my hands, my eyes drifting up until I hold my own gaze in the mirror. My eyes are cute; I have plump lips and an impressive rack. I know I'm pretty, but I'd be dumb if I thought I could compete with those girls out there.

My head snaps to the left when the bathroom door opens and my eyes widen when I see who it is.

"This is the ladies' room."

He smirks, looking around the empty bathroom. "Hello," Aiden calls out. "Any girls in here?" His brows lift, tilting his head, a smile on his face when he doesn't hear anyone. "No? Good. Just the girl I wanted to see."

My heart starts to jump when he approaches me. "Someone could come in here."

He turns, locking the door. "This okay?" he asks when he turns back around.

I shake my head, trying to make sense of what's happening. "What are you doing in here?"

He takes a step closer to me. "You were avoiding me."

I scoff, crossing my arms. "It looked like you had your hands full."

He lets out a laugh, tilting his head. "You're jealous," he states, making me blink.

154

"I am not jealous." My eyes involuntarily roll when I drop my arms, pushing at his chest.

"No?" he asks.

"No," I confirm. "I was just wondering."

"About?" he asks, taking a step closer to me.

"What you said last week."

He rubs his jaw. "I've said so many things," he says. "You'll have to remind me."

I lift my brows. "You asked me if I was seeing anyone else," I remind him.

He drops his hand, his brows furrowing. "Yes?"

"Are you?" I ask before I can stop myself.

The line between his brows deepens when he takes a step closer to me. "You're jealous," he says again. "Tell me why."

I sigh. "I'm not jealous."

"Tell me—"

"Because she had her hands all over you," I blurt out, instantly regretting the words that came out of my mouth.

His eyes widen, and I groan when I see the smile slowly appear on his face. "You're jealous," he says again.

I glare at him. "Can you stop being cocky about this? Fine, you're right. I hated seeing her grabby hands all over you, rubbing up on you and laughing like you're the funniest guy ever when I know you're not that damn funny. I hated how my stomach cramped every time you looked at her or smiled at her or laughed with her, okay?" I throw my hands up. "Is that what you wanted to hear?"

He grins. "I'm pretty funny," he retorts.

I scoff. "Funny looking."

"That's not true." He laughs again. "And you're jealous."

I sigh loudly, burying my head in my hands and letting out a groan. Why did I open my big mouth? "Leila," Aiden says. I shake my head, groaning into my hands. I've already died of embarrassment and admitted that I'm jealous. I don't want to look at him, I can't.

I feel his hands on mine, slowly peeling my hands away from my face until I look up at him, he's got a sympathetic smile on his face, and when I look up into his bright blue eyes, I swear my stomach does a little flip. I don't like that, at all.

"Leila," he starts, still holding onto my hands. "I wanted to break that guy's face for talking to you."

My brows furrow as I look up at him. Guy? What guy? I shake my head, remembering the guy from the bar. "That was nothing," I tell him. "He was talking about the game. Said you were a legend."

His brows raise. "He did?" He smiles when I nod. "And what about you?" he asks. "Did you see the game?"

I nod. "Of course, I did," I tell him. "You were great."

"Thanks, gorgeous." He's still holding onto my hands when he dips his head. "It doesn't change things though," he says. "Whether he was talking about me or not. I wanted to kill him for talking to you. You smiled at him. You never smile at me."

I frown. "I do."

He raises his brow. "Hardly," he says. "It fucking killed me watching you smile at some stranger." His hold tightens on my hands before he drops them and his hands find a home at my waist. "You're not the only one who got jealous tonight."

I don't know why I like the idea of Aiden being jealous of another guy, even if it is just the guy from the bar who was drooling over Aiden. It feels good knowing I'm not alone in this. "What does this mean?" I ask him. "We had rules."

He shrugs, his hands running down my waist. "It doesn't matter what we said. Your feelings can change at any time."

"No." I shake my head, hating those words and how my heart thumps when he says them. "No, they can't."

"Why are you against relationships?" he asks me, holding his hands up when he sees my eyes widen at his question. "I'm not putting pressure on you. That's not what's happening. I just wanted to know why you're so against them."

"That's not important." I close my eyes, trying to erase the image of my ex-boyfriend from my mind. "This isn't a relationship."

"Right," he says, his hands drifting down to my lower back. "Just fucking, right?"

I wrap my arms around his neck, loving how his eyes fall to my lips, licking his own. "Just fucking."

He squeezes my hips, pulling back. "And you're asking me to be exclusive?" he asks. "Because I don't have a problem with that, Leila."

I blink. "You don't?"

He shakes his head. "I haven't been with anyone else since that spin the bottle game."

I breathe out a laugh, knowing that's complete bullshit. "You don't need to lie to me."

He pulls back, frowning. "I'm not lying," he says. "The only lips I've tasted since are yours."

I shake my head, unable to believe what he's telling me. "How is that even possible? You get so much attention every day. Did you even see the group of girls around you out there?" I ask, gesturing towards the door.

"I saw them," he says with a lift of his shoulder. "But it was you I couldn't keep my eyes off of. I don't want anyone's attention but yours."

My heart stops. It skips a beat at his words. I don't want to get attached. I promised myself I wouldn't let it happen again, that I wouldn't be hurt again. But it's so hard to forget every reason when he's in front of me telling me these things.

"Leila," he says, leaning into me. "We're fucking exclusive. No doubt about it." He sighs. "The thought of another guy's hands on you makes me want to rip out their throats. I need to know I'm the only one touching you, kissing you." His hand reaches up and grabs my face, smoothing his thumb over my cheek. "Fucking you," he whispers, dipping his head, flattening his tongue against my neck. "I licked you," he says. "You're mine."

Those words make me shiver, staring up at him. "I'm not yours."

His brows raise, an amused smirk on his lips. "Don't even try it, gorgeous. We both know you're mine." His hands run down my body, flattening his palms against the curve of my ass. "Say it," he tells me. "Tell me no one else touches you."

I gulp, his touch making me weak. My brain wants to rebuff, to tell him he has no hold on me, but when those eyes look down at me, I know he's right. "No one else touches me," I tell him. "Only you." I lick my lips, my brain screaming at me not to say what I'm about to say. But it's already too late. "I only want your hands on me."

He wastes no time, leaning down and bringing his lips to mine in a desperate kiss. His lips brush against mine, moaning into my mouth when his tongue wraps around mine. This kiss is fast and punishing. It's so good. It's always so good.

158

"You taste like beer," he mumbles against my lips.

"Fuck. I'm sorry." I pull back, remembering how he told me he doesn't drink. But he keeps his hold on me, shaking his head.

"I don't care," he says, leaning into me. "Don't stop kissing me."

His hands drift down to cup my ass, pushing me against him until I gasp into his mouth when I feel every hard inch of him pressed against me. "You can still feel me inside of you, can't you?" he murmurs against my skin.

God yes. He's so long and thick, I still feel him days after we sleep together. I bump my hips up, grazing against the thick bulge in his pants. He groans, pulling back and dropping his forehead on mine. "Leila," he whispers. "I don't think I can wait until tonight."

I laugh, taking a breath and pat him on his chest. "Not going to happen tonight, buddy." I don't miss the way he narrows his eyes at the term. "I have to get back to Gabi. She's probably already wasted by now."

He tips his head back, sighing when I untangle myself from him, turning around and fixing my hair in the mirror. "And I don't have a condom."

He exhales, wiping a hand down his face. "Me neither."

"Tomorrow?" I ask him, looking behind my shoulder.

He smiles, wrapping his hands around my waist from behind. "Whenever you want," he whispers, pulling my hair to the side and pressing his lips to my neck.

We both jump at the knocking on the door and I turn to look at him, our eyes wide as we untangle ourselves and fix our clothes.

I quickly unlock the door and open it without thinking, seeing Gabi on the other side. Her shoulders drop, a relieved sigh coming from her. "There you are. I've been looking for you. Why the hell was this locked?" And at the same time, the giant behind me approaches the door making Gabi's eyes drift up. Her brows lift. "Oh."

Shit. Another rule broken.

Gabi smiles, glances at me. "You ready to go or do you want to hang here?" Her eyes dip back to Aiden who still hasn't said anything and is still right behind me.

"I'm ready to go," I tell her. I head out of the bathroom and wrap my arm around hers. "What happened with that guy?" I ask her.

She shrugs. "I got the drinks," she says. "But the guy was boring."

I look behind my shoulder, spotting Aiden still in the same spot, his hands tucked in his jean pocket. He grins and mouths 'tomorrow.' I roll my eyes and turn my head back around, pulling my bottom lip between my teeth to try to stop the smile from blooming, but it's too late. I'm already grinning like an idiot.

"Don't worry," Gabi whispers, nudging me. "I'll keep your secret."

20

Focus

Leila

I hear his grunts before I see him. The sound of the ball hitting the floor echoes throughout the court.

I shut the door behind me as quietly as I can. I've seen Aiden play before, I hardly miss a game, and when I go, I can't keep my eyes off him. He's so quick and clever out there. His maneuvers one of the best I have seen.

His sneakers squeak against the floor as he runs towards the net, bouncing the ball before he shoots, landing a three-pointer.

He's so good. I decide to tease him though, waiting until I'm close to shout, "You can do better than that." I stand near the seats, watching how he turns his head, brows furrowed as he tries to look for me.

His face lights up when he spots me, squinting at me. "Leila?" he says, a grin on his face. "What are you doing here?"

I shrug, not wanting to tell him I missed him. I've hardly seen him this past week, but telling him I miss him would only put pressure and expectations on this, and I like how it is between us. It's easy, fun. "I wanted to see you play," I say instead. "And by the looks of it, you've got more practice to do."

He laughs, taking a step closer to me. "Are you criticizing my basketball skills?" he asks, lifting his brows.

I smile at him, his eyes widening when I do. "You know I used to watch basketball all the time with my dad, don't you?"

"Yeah," he says, raking a hand through his hair. "But watching and playing are very different." He runs his hands over my waist. "I bet you couldn't even score one basket."

My brows lift. "You're serious?"

He nods, grinning. "You're a short little thing, not even half my height. No way you could sink a ball."

I push at his chest. "I'm the tallest of my friends. You're just huge."

He lets out a laugh, running his hands over my waist. "Tell me how huge I am again," he murmurs, leaning down to brush his lips against mine. "Fuck. I've missed you." He has? Before I can say anything, he plants another kiss on my lips.

I hum, pulling back. "You need to practice."

He shakes his head, nuzzling his lips against my neck. "I need to kiss you." His lips trail to my jaw, leaving soft kisses before making his way up until he's back on my mouth. God, this man can kiss. Just the brush of our tongues together makes me weak, lightheaded. He does things to me I don't even know how to explain. It's like I'm alive with him, like every one of my bones vibrate whenever he's around.

"No," I say, attempting to catch my breath. "I'm not letting you waste time with me."

"Worth it," he mumbles, kissing me again. "You're the best kind of distraction."

I let out a laugh, pushing him back again. "I'm serious," I say, giving him a smirk. "From what I saw, you need all the practice you can get."

He laughs again, tightening his hold on me. "You bust my balls more than Coach. Come on then, baller," he says, grabbing the ball from the ground and holds it up against his chest. "Let's see what you got."

Okay, I might have underestimated how easy it is because when Aiden throws the ball to me, I flinch, watching as it rolls outside the court.

"What the hell was that?" he asks in a fit of laughter, curling up.

"You're trying to kill me," I wheeze. "That came at me way too fast."

"What happened to 'you could do better?'" he asks, still laughing. "Not as easy as it looks, is it?"

I shake my head, determined to prove him wrong. "Let me try again."

He shakes his head, grabbing another ball. "Come here."

"Throw it to me. I can do it."

"Leila, gorgeous, I say this in the most respectful way possible, but you can't catch a ball to save your life. Come here before you hurt yourself. I'll teach you."

I raise my brows. "You'll teach me?"

He nods, pulling on my arm until I'm standing in front of him, circling me with his arms as he holds the basketball in front of me. "Hold the ball." I do as he says, grabbing the ball and hold it out in front of me, and he covers my hands with his. "Good," he says, his breath hitting my neck and my body very aware of how his groin presses against my ass. He lets out a shaky breath. "Focus," he says.

"I can't." It's hard to concentrate or do literally anything else when he's so close to me, whispering in my ear, his deep, gravelly voice making me feel a little dizzy. Fuck, is it hot in here?

"Look at the basket," he whispers. I turn my head, focusing on the basket in front of me. "Now bring the ball closer to your chest, like this," he positions our hands so the ball is pressed against my beating heart. "Now shoot."

He drops his hands and I throw the ball, watching as it hits the backboard and falls to the ground, not going inside. I turn my head, frowning at him. "Okay, fine," I concede. "Maybe it's a little harder than I anticipated."

He laughs, twisting me around and bringing his hands back to my waist. "You did good. For a beginner."

I wrap my arms around his neck, his blue eyes pinned on me, making me feel dazed, feeling unsteady on my feet. "You're so talented." I let out a sigh.

His brows furrow. "That's the first compliment I've ever heard from you. Are you okay?"

I nod, looking up at his beautiful face. God, why is he so beautiful? A strand of his brown hair falls onto his face, little beads of sweat coating his pale skin. "And you're so pretty."

He lets out a scoff, rubbing his thumb over my cheek. I love when he does that. "You're the pretty one."

I shake my head, wincing when I feel the room spinning when I move my head. I blow out a breath when I open my eyes and look up at him again. He's so handsome, and so nice. Why did Aiden have to be so nice? Why couldn't he have been a hot asshole? It would have made this so much easier.

My knees buckle and I stumble against him, Aiden's hand gripping my waist. Why do I feel so dizzy? When I look up at him, he's frowning. Why is he frowning? I want him to smile. I love when he smiles at me.

"Leila," I hear him say. I can't see his face properly, though. He's all blurry, fuzzy. Are those stars? "Leila. What's wr—"

My eyes flutter open when I start to regain consciousness, a foggy haze coating my blurry vision as I try to move. A heavy grogginess weighs me down and I struggle to shake it off, my head throbbing painfully when I do.

I blink slowly, trying to make sense of blurry surroundings, my vision gradually starting to clear, a dull ache pulsing through my skull when I attempt to sit up, realizing I'm in some sort of clinic.

"Careful," I hear a female voice somewhere around me. I feel a hand holding me upright, helping me to sit up. "You need to take it easy."

Her concerned face looks down at me. I hear another voice, a distant buzz in my ears. I open my mouth to speak, but my throat feels dry and scratchy. The woman turns around, holding a plastic cup with water in front of me. "Here," she says, "This might help."

I grab the plastic cup, gulping the water down, trying to piece together what happened. I don't remember anything except going to the basketball court and seeing—

I see Aiden standing above me, leaning over to cup my face in his hands. "Fuck, Leila." His voice is thick and full of emotion.

I blink up at him, adjusting to the light coming through the giant windows. "What happened?" I ask him.

He rubs his thumbs over my cheeks, his brows drawn together, like he can't bear to let go. "You don't remember?" he asks.

"No?" I look back at the woman, watching as she takes off her blue gloves and gives me a sympathetic smile.

"You passed out," Aiden says, making me look back at him. "You were stumbling over, talking absolute crap and then you fell in my arms."

I gulp, clenching my fists together. "For how long?"

He shakes his head, blowing out a breath and shrugs. "I don't know, like ten minutes? I brought you here as fast as I could." He scans my face, running his hands all over me. "Are you ok?"

"It can happen," the nurse says, both our heads turning to look at her. "If you haven't eaten in a while, your blood sugar can drop." She picks up a flashlight in her hands. "Just let me check your reflexes. Look directly in front," she says, flashing the light in my eye. She moves the flashlight around, assessing me. "Good," she says, turning the light off. "You're going to be fine." She smiles at me.

"So, she'll be okay?" Aiden asks.

The nurse nods. "Her body just felt weak, that's all," she tells him, turning to face me. "Just make sure you don't wait too long before eating. Your boyfriend was very worried about you."

"Oh, we're not—"

"Thank you," he says to her instead. "Can we just have a moment?"

"Sure," she says. "You're all set. When you're ready, you can leave." She closes the door when she exits, leaving just the two of us in the room.

Aiden takes a step back, blowing out a harsh breath. "Are you feeling better?" he asks me.

I nod. "I'm fine. I'm sorry."

His shoulders drop. "Don't apologize for passing out, gorgeous." I grab the plastic cup and sip some more water, watching how Aiden rubs his jaw, glancing at me. "What did she mean before?" he asks.

My head lifts. "About what?"

"About you not eating."

My face drops, my blood cooling as he stares at me. "Aiden—"

"Have you been starving yourself?" he asks.

"Aiden, no."

"I swear to god, Leila. If you've been malnourishing your body because you want to lose weight, I'm going to fucking lose it."

"I didn't—"

"Why would you do that?" he asks, throwing his arms up. "You need to eat. You need food," he says, taking a step closer to me. "You're hurting yourself by doing that."

"I haven't been starving myself."

He stops, staring at me. "You haven't?"

"No," I say on a sigh.

He visibly relaxes, his shoulders dropping as he blows out a breath. "Then what did she mean when she said you weren't eating?"

I shrug. "I forget sometimes."

He narrows his eyes at me. "You forget sometimes," he repeats. "How the fuck does that happen, Leila?" he asks, running a hand through his hair. "How do you just forget to eat?"

167

I close my eyes, pressing my fingers to my forehead. "Stop," I whisper. "Please don't be mad at me. I just... I feel so lightheaded."

"Fuck, Leila." He drops to his knees in front of me, grabbing my face in his hands. "I'm not mad at you. I just got so scared. Don't do that again." His voice breaks. "You passed out. That's some serious shit."

"It's not that serious. It's happened before," I say trying to appease him.

His hands freeze on my face. "You're saying you've forgotten to eat before?"

"Sometimes." What I don't tell him, what I *won't* tell him is that a small part of me feels proud when I forget to eat. My stomach cramps at the admission. I don't think I even realized it, but I feel like I've succeeded when I forget to feed myself.

"That's not going to happen ever again," he tells me, lifting himself off the floor and grabs onto my hand, pulling me off the exam table.

"Where are we going?"

He stops and turns back to look at me, his jaw clenching. "We're going to get you a massive fucking plate of food and I don't want to hear a single word about it. Got it?"

My eyes widen at his authoritative tone. It's kind of hot. My lips twitch when I nod and say, "Yes, sir."

A light smirk appears on his face when he looks down at me and he blows out a breath, pulling me into him and wrapping his arms around me. "Remind me when you're feeling better and we'll circle back to that sir comment."

"I'm feeling better right now," I say, looking up at him.

He smirks, shakes his head and leans down, pressing his lips to my forehead. "Come on, let's get you some food."

21

Face masks and polaroids

Aiden

My neck hurts. It's so tense I honestly think I'm going to pop a vein.

Stuffing my empty wallet back into my pocket, I blow out a breath when I grab the piece of paper that lets me know all the money, I worked so hard for, is gone. I leave the bank, pulling out my phone from my pocket and type out a quick text.

Aiden:

It's sent. Try to make it work until next month.

I exhale when I press send, knowing they'll probably blow the money I sent on more poison for their bodies and then demand more.

I don't know how much more of this I can take. I barely have any left over from working at the bar and I don't have time for a second job, practice takes up so much of my time as it is.

I might have gotten rid of one evil in my life for now, but my brothers and my mom are a whole other story. As much as I resent them for beating the crap out of me when we grew up, it doesn't stop me from wanting to help them out any way I can.

We didn't even have food growing up, if the money I make can get them a loaf of bread that isn't expired, I'll do it. I'll keep sending them money if they need it.

I spot an older lady carrying a cart full of plants, my shoulders drop, my face breaking into a smile at the sight, reminding me of Leila. Her apartment is filled with plants, big ass ones, small ones. I can't lie, it's so fucking cute watching her water them and talk to them as if they're her babies. She glares at me whenever I catch her do it, but I can't help it. It's adorable.

It's a sign from the universe, right? I tell myself exactly that when I push the button on the elevator, taking me to her apartment. I knock on her door, waiting for her to answer.

"Who is it?" she says from the other side.

I smile at her sultry voice, a melody to my ears. She could yell at me and I'd still follow her like a puppy. That girl has me wrapped around her little finger and she doesn't even know it.

"Aiden," I reply to the wooden door. A smirk tugs at my lips when I hear her mumble a curse, but when she doesn't open the door, my eyes narrow. "This would be where you open the door."

I hear a sigh and then the door opens and a green face pops through the door. I press my lips together to stop my laugh, but I fail, shaking my head. "I'm sorry, I thought this was Leila's place. I guess not."

"Ha." She narrows her eyes at me. "Very funny."

"What the hell is on your face?" I ask her, unable to stop laughing.

Her eyebrows raise. "You've never heard of a face mask?"

I shake my head. "What the fuck is that?"

"Men," she sighs. "I don't have time for this. You could have texted."

My eyebrow lifts. "And you would have answered?"

She contemplates it for a second, shakes her head. "We don't have any plans."

"I wanted to see you," I offer with a shrug. "Can I not come and see you?" Another sigh leaves her mouth as she closes her eyes. How does this girl look so fucking good even with her face painted green?

"I'm sorry, now is not a good time."

"What do you mean?"

"You can't come in," she says.

"Why not?" She looks to the side, avoiding me. My heart starts to race, my palms getting sweaty. "Leila, if you have some guy in there—"

"What?" she interrupts, looking at me. "No. I don't. Why would you think that?"

I shrug. "You're being weird about letting me in."

"Aiden," she sighs. "I'm on my period. There, are you happy? You can't come in because we can't fuck."

My eyebrows raise at the bite in her tone. "That doesn't matter."

Her eyes narrow. "Did you not hear me?" she asks. "I said we can't fuck."

"And I said that doesn't matter. I wanted to see you. Doesn't matter what we do, I just want to be with you."

"You wanted to see me?"

"Yes."

"With clothes on?"

"Yes," I exasperate, throwing my hands up. "Is that so hard to believe?" She stares at me, lips parted as she looks at me with disbelief. "Are you going to let me in or not?"

She steps back, opening the door wider so I can come into her apartment and close the door behind us. When I face her, my hands itch, very unaware of what I can do in this situation. "Do you need ice cream or something?" I ask her. "A foot rub maybe?"

She tilts her head at me. "Do you have any sisters?"

"Two brothers," I tell her. "Don't know shit about what's going on with your body," I admit. "But I'll do whatever you need to make it better."

Her lips press together, trying to hide her smile and then she shakes her head. "I'm good. I'm on my last day." When I nod, she squints at me. "You really want to be here?"

I laugh, closing the space between us. "I *need* to be here right now. There's nowhere else I want to be." I lean down to kiss her, the cold green goo on her face landing on mine. I pull back, wiping it.

I must be fucking dreaming because I hear the most beautiful sound I've ever heard. My eyes widen when I look back at her and she's laughing. She's laughing. With me. Holy shit. My heart is about to leave my chest. This beautiful woman is laughing, and she scrunches her nose when she does. God, she's adorable. I'd never tell her that because she'd probably cut my balls off, but she's so fucking adorable I want to kiss her. So. Fucking. Bad.

I lean down, brushing our lips together. She hums in my mouth, pushing me away. "Your face is covered in it," she says in a fit of laughter. The corner of her eyes wrinkling with joy. God, I've never been so happy before.

"I don't care," I mumble before I lean down and kiss her again.

"Aiden," she says, pulling away again. "I have to clean you up."

"Do whatever you want to me," I mumble, lost in her scent, in her lips. She smells like fresh peaches; it's intoxicating. I kiss her again. "I don't care. Kill me. Skin me alive. Just let me kiss you some more."

She yelps when she feels my lips back on hers but I don't give her any time to think, I wrap my arms around her waist, feeling her soft body under my fingertips. Her lips feel like velvet, her tongue brushing against mine.

Kissing Leila feels like the world around me has stopped. All the noise and pressure ceases to exist when her lips are on mine. I'm breathless when I pull back and when I look down at her, those pretty pink lips of hers are tipped up in a smirk. "What?" I ask. "Why are you smiling?"

"Your face is green," she says, chuckling as she looks at me.

"Oh." I laugh, wiping some of the stuff off my face. "Right." I look at my fingers, inspecting it. "What's this for, anyway?"

"I have a photo shoot tomorrow," she tells me. "I'm doing some prepping, getting my skin to look good."

I want to tell her she always looks good, but her words run through my mind. "Tomorrow?" I ask her, wondering when I get to see her again.

She nods, sitting on the couch, tucking her leg under. "I'm a little nervous," she says, glancing up at me.

"Why?" I sit beside her.

She lets out a breath. "It's a swimwear shoot." I don't miss how she pulls her bottom lip between her teeth. A nervous Leila

173

isn't something I'm used to seeing. She's always so strong, so confident, a bossy little shit putting me in my place.

But the thought of her being on a magazine in a swimsuit for guys to gawk at her makes my jaw—hell, my whole body—tighten. This is not good for the tension in my neck.

"Why are you nervous?" I ask her. "You're going to look hot." I can already picture it. Her soft, lush, tan body in some little skimpy bikini. God, if only she knew the dirty thoughts running through my head right now.

She rolls her eyes and turns her body to face me. "I've already agreed to fuck you, Aiden. You don't have to keep complimenting me."

I furrow my brows. I don't like how she makes it seem like a chore for me. It's the easiest thing in the world, telling her how gorgeous she is. "I like complimenting you," I tell her. "I want you to know you're beautiful."

"I know that." She glances at me from the side, pulling her bottom lip between her teeth.

I laugh. "Do you? Because you seem to hate when I say anything nice."

She shakes her head, smirking. "That's not true. I'm a praise whore."

I wrap my arms around her shoulder, pulling her into me, her head resting on my chest. *Fuck, stay there forever. Please.* "Oh, I know, gorgeous," I whisper in her ear. "You love when I tell you how much I love watching you swallow my cock in your tight pussy," I murmur, my breath hitting her jaw. "You love when I tell you how good you feel." She shivers against me. "You love when I worship every inch of you."

"This isn't fair," she whispers, breathing hard. "I can't do anything about this." She whimpers frustrated.

I laugh, pulling back. "Fine, I'll stop." She takes a deep breath, turning her head and smiling when she sees my face again, which probably still has that green goo. "Put some on me," I tell her, patting her cheek.

"You want a face mask?"

"Hell yeah." I grin. "You can't be the only one that looks good in this relationship." Her face drops and I curse inwardly at myself. Why did I just use that word? I clear my throat. "You know what I mean."

"Yeah," she says, her eyes dipping a little. She pulls away from me, getting up from the couch. "Be right back with your face mask, sir." She winks.

I adjust myself on the couch. "I like the idea of you calling me sir," I say, raising an eyebrow.

She narrows her eyes. "Don't get used to it." She turns around, heading out of the living room, my eyes tracking her movements.

Those hips, that ass. God. The tight, black leggings she has on make my dick twitch. I look down at my pants and let out a sigh. "Not gonna happen," I mumble to my dick, tipping my head back and closing my eyes. How did I get here? From one silly game to sitting here craving her company.

The couch dips, my eyes fly open and I see her sitting next to me, holding up a long tube. "You good?"

I nod, smiling at her. She's so pretty. I don't ever want to close my eyes if it means I could look at her forever. "All better now." She chuckles, opening the tube and pours out the green mixture onto her fingertips. Her fingers swipe across my face, wiping the stuff all over. "Fuck," I curse. "It's cold."

She laughs, shaking her head. "Such a baby. Be still."

175

"I can think of something that would make me behave," I tell her, grinning.

"And what's that?

"If you sat on my lap," I say, smiling as I rake an arm around her waist, pulling her up.

"Aiden, no." She gasps, pushing my arm away. "I can't sit on your lap."

"Why not?" I ask her.

She rolls her eyes. "Just sit still, idiot."

I raise my brows at her, wincing when I feel that cold liquid on my face again. "You're not getting a tip if you keep talking to me like that."

She laughs and lifts an eyebrow. "And what tip would that be?"

I laugh, my heart jumping in my chest. My girl knew exactly what kind of dirty joke I was about to make. I stare at her in awe as she wipes that green shit on my face. It's cold and itchy, but I wouldn't want to be anywhere else.

"There," she says when she's done. "You're gorgeous, darling." She says in the worst southern accent I've heard.

"So are you."

She wipes her hands on a rag, and I just stare, admiring her beautiful face, her eyes a close match to the green painted on her skin, except for the golden specks in them.

She turns, grabbing a small camera from her table, facing it towards me.

My eyebrows raise. "Are you taking a picture of me?"

She looks at me from behind the camera. "Stay still."

I let out a laugh, giving her a smile until the shutter goes off. "I didn't know you took pictures."

She shrugs, pulls out the Polaroid, and gives it a shake. "I prefer being in front of a camera rather than behind it, but yeah." She glances at me. "My parents had stacks and stacks of photo albums and I always loved going through them. So I decided to take more pictures." She tucks her leg underneath her. "Most of them are of my plants."

The mention of her childhood brings an odd feeling to my stomach, wondering what it would be like if I had a different family, a different life. "Let me see," I say, gesturing to the Polaroid in her hands.

She holds it out, grinning when we both look at my green face covering the picture. "I look as bad as you do," I tease, nudging her.

She shakes her head, scrunching her nose. "You look worse."

I grab the camera from her hands, turning it over until it's facing us, and wrap my arm around Leila. I pull her into me and bring our lips together. The shutter goes off, and when I pull out the picture, I can't stop staring at it. She's so beautiful, even with her face painted green. "This one's mine," I tell her, pocketing the picture.

"Why do you get to keep it?"

The smile on my lips belongs to this girl and this girl only. "I want to look at it every day," I admit.

When she looks at me, her lips twitch in a smile, and she lets out a sigh. "You're going to make some girl so happy one day."

A weird feeling settles in my stomach at her words. "What about you?" I ask her, my brows dipping. "Don't I make you happy?"

She parts her lips, both of us staring back at each other, but before she can say something, her stomach rumbles, and she freezes, and her eyes widen when she looks up at me. "You heard that, huh?"

I nod. "You hungry?"

She shrugs. "I'm fine."

I glare at her. "When was the last time you ate?" I ask her, anticipating her response. After what happened in that doctor's office, I'm not letting her 'forget' ever again. She shrugs, which makes me mad because I hate that she's not taking care of herself. I sigh, get up from the couch, and head to her kitchen.

"What are you doing?" she asks, peering at me from the couch.

"Making you food. What do you have?" I ask, opening her fridge. Nothing. That's what. Besides some fruit, eggs, some veg, cheese, and two bottles of beer, the fridge is empty.

I close the fridge, turning back around to face her. "Woman, do you not eat? Where is your food?"

She shrugs, wiping off the mask on her face with the rag. "Wasn't exactly expecting company," she says.

"And what were you going to eat?"

"I would have figured it out," she says, cleaning the rest of the mask off.

"Come on."

She glances up at me. "For what?"

"You obviously don't know how to cook," I say. "I'm going to teach you."

22

Cooking is dangerous

Leila

"I know how to cook."

He turns his head back, lifting his brows. "Really?"

"Yes." I roll my eyes. "I'm Colombian, cooking is like a rite of passage in my family. Not to mention my dad owns a food truck. He taught me how to cook when I was ten."

"He did?" he asks, and I don't miss how his face drops a little.

"Yeah." I approach him. "He's a great cook. Too bad he hates making vegetarian stuff." It took watching him behead a chicken to change my mind about eating meat. I laugh, remembering how he looked at me as if I was crazy when I announced I was going to be a vegetarian. It didn't stop him, though. He learned new recipes, new ways of making food without meat.

Aiden grabs the eggs from the fridge, along with the cheese and mushrooms, and places everything on the counter. I watch as he rolls his sleeves up, washes his hands, and grabs a chopping board that's definitely not mine. I guess Rosie left it here.

"You're really going to cook for me?" I ask him, admiring how he dominates the kitchen. My god, this man is so hot.

He laughs, grabbing a bowl from my cabinet. "You make it seem like I'm doing something extravagant. I'm just cooking you food."

"Why?"

He turns his head, lifts his brows at me, his face covered in a green face mask. "Because, gorgeous," he says, stepping closer to me. I can't even start to explain what he does to me every time he uses that nickname. "I want to take care of you. I want to make you happy other than just giving you orgasms."

Big, red alarms flash in my mind, reminding me I'm *only* supposed to want the orgasms. A laugh bubbles out of me. "I do love the orgasms, though," I sigh.

He narrows his eyes, taking a step closer. "Just orgasms in general or the ones I give you?"

I slide my hands up his chest, feeling every hard ridge of his body. I lift onto my tiptoes, reaching his ear. "Just orgasms in general."

He laughs, brushes his lips against my jaw. "Too bad I can't prove you wrong. But I will. I'll make you see that no one can make you feel like I do." His lips graze mine and I close my eyes but before I can deepen the kiss, he pulls back with a satisfied smile. His thumb wipes the mask that transferred to my face. "This shit really gets everywhere, huh?"

I laugh while grabbing a rag to wipe his face clean staring into his bright blue eyes as I do. "There," I say when his face is mask free. "All done."

He smirks. "How do I look?"

There's not a word in the English language for how handsome this man is. I can't let him know that, though, so I lift my shoulder, shrugging. "Meh."

He laughs. "Meh?"

I love how he knows I'm teasing him. It could be because he's cocky, or he just knows that he's one of the most beautiful men I have ever seen. "I've seen better."

He chuckles, shaking his head and pulls me into him. "You always know how to flatter me," he says, rubbing his thumb over my cheek, staring into my eyes. I don't know how long we stay there, just looking at each other. "C'mon," he says. "I need to get food in you."

I nod again, unable to say anything, watching him walk past me into the kitchen, washing his hands before he holds the mushrooms up. "Do you want to help me?" he asks, placing them on a cutting board. I nod and he slides it over to me. "Cut them up into chunks," he tells me.

"What exactly are we making?"

"Well, seeing as you barely had anything," he says, glancing over at me with a pointed look. "The best I could come up with was an omelet," he offers with a shrug.

I glance at him, unable to stop the smile that sprouts on my face when I watch him crack an egg into a bowl. How is it a few months ago I was so annoyed with this guy, under the impression that he was just a huge playboy and now he's standing in my apartment, cooking me food? I was so wrong about him. "How did you learn how to cook?" I ask him, running the mushrooms under water.

When I turn to face him, his jaw is clenched, the muscles so tight. I frown. "I'm sorry, did I say something wro—"

"It wasn't something I wanted to do," he says, staring down at the bowl in front of him. "It was something I had to do."

"What do you mean?"

He squeezes his eyes shut, opening them up a few seconds later. "My family are drug addicts, Leila." His head turns to

181

look at me, the dread in his face so apparent. "I come from a dirty, small trailer in Texas, smaller than your bedroom. I didn't come from a family like yours with a dad to teach me how to cook. My dad fucked off before I was even born." He turns back away from me, looking down at the bowl. "My mom is an addict, and my brothers are following mother dearest's footsteps."

He drops the bowl and turns his whole body to look at me, crossing his arms before he blows out a breath. "I've never touched drugs," he explains. "I saw what it was doing to my family. Didn't want any part of it. That's why I don't drink either."

I want to say something, anything, but I just stare at him as his jaw clenches and he looks to the side. "But I got into their stash when I was young." My hands squeeze the board, my other gripping the knife. I can't take my eyes off him. I can't look away from the pain in his eyes, the way his throat bobs as he gulps. I can feel the words burning his throat before he even says them.

"I was passed out for a good hour before any of them found me." I want to throw my arms around him, to take all the pain away but I stay rooted in place as he keeps looking at me, staring so intensely. "I was admitted to the hospital. I woke up delirious, attached to all these machines. I was a kid," he says, squeezing his eyes shut. "I didn't know what was happening or what I did."

He shakes his head. "And when I got home," he says, looking to the side again, his fists ball up beside him. "When I got home, my mom beat the shit out of me for costing her medical bills."

His eyes open, glancing at me. "I had to learn how to cook because if I hadn't, I would've died." This is the longest I haven't spoken. I can't say anything though. He doesn't need me to say anything. He needs me to listen. "I burnt my hand right here," he lifts his hand to my face, pointing at the scar on his palm, "making toast when I was nine."

I look back into his eyes when he drops his hand. "I found the bread in a dumpster behind a store. It was past the expiration date, but unopened and still looked fine." He shrugs. "I hadn't eaten in days and we had no food at home, so I took it and attempted to make myself some toast on the stove, because we didn't even have a toaster. My mother was passed out on the couch, high out of her mind and didn't even notice. Eventually I got better. I learnt a lot in home EC and made it work."

He glances at me, but I don't say anything. He lets out a sigh, turning back and cracking another egg. "I'm sorry for spilling all of that on you. I haven't told anyone that before."

I turn back, too, grabbing a mushroom and cutting it into chunks. "Did you want to tell me?" It's the first words I've spoken since he's told me. I still don't know what to say. He's a completely different person than I originally thought. I thought he was privileged, and that he was given everything he ever wanted. That's the furthest thing from the truth.

The knife scrapes the board, filling up the silence in the room. "I wouldn't have told you otherwise," he says after a few minutes.

"I'm sorry," I mumble.

"For what, gorgeous?"

The nickname makes my stomach flutter, but I shake it away when I turn my head to look up at him. "For thinking you were an asshole."

183

He lets out a low chuckle, shaking his head like the moments before never even happened. "That's just your lack of judgment. My shitty upbringing has nothing to do with it."

I smile at him, watching him whisk the eggs. "Where are your brothers now?"

He lets out a breath, eyeing me. "Cameron is in jail," he tells me. "For robbing a quick-mart. And Brandon and Mom…" he trails off with a shrug. "They're back home, spending the money I send them on drugs."

My eyebrows lift. "You send them money?"

His jaw clenches as he looks down at the bowl. "We didn't have anything growing up," he says. "As soon as I came here and got a job, I thought I'd help them, thinking it would go towards food or bills, but it didn't. And now they just want more and more."

"What happens if you stop?" I ask him.

He shakes his head. "I can't."

"Why not?" Aiden works hard for his money, the thought of him having to give it away makes me so sad for him.

He blows out a breath. "It wasn't just my mom who liked to lift her hand at me. My brothers beat the shit out of me growing up, for anything and everything. Sometimes it was because they were high, other times, because it was fun for them, I guess," he admits. "I know I shouldn't be scared of them, but I still am."

My hands shake, thinking of the little boy who had to go through that, who just wanted to eat. Who had to learn how to cook, burns and all, to make sure he survived. I gulp, and at the same time, a blinding pain hits.

"Ow," I shout, dropping the knife and stepping back from the counter. "Shit." I grab my finger, pressing down on the blood drizzling out of the slash.

184

Aiden drops everything, grabbing my hand in his as he inspects the damage. "I thought you knew how to cook," he says as I curse in pain.

"I thought I did too." I groan, feeling the throbbing in my finger increase. "Cooking is dangerous."

He laughs. "You're dangerous." He grabs my finger and brings it to his mouth, sucking on it.

"Did you just—" My eyes widen.

He chuckles, pulling my finger out of his mouth. "It stops the bleeding." He pulls me, sitting me down on a chair. "Here," he says. "Where do you keep your bandages?"

"I don't have any. Check the bathroom, maybe Rosie had some." He nods, heading out of the room. I stare at my bleeding finger, watching as the blood drops out.

"Give me," Aiden says, walking out of the bathroom with a bandage. I hold out my finger to him. He crouches, wrapping the bandage around my finger. "There," he says, pressing a kiss against the wrapped finger and smiling at me. "All good."

I can't help the grin on my face when he looks up at me. Who the hell is Aiden Pierce? And why do I want to get to know him when we're not naked? This was not supposed to happen. Lines are blurring, things are getting too complicated. And I don't want to stop it anymore.

23

Family visits

Leila

Being back home is so bittersweet. I miss my dad, I miss the weekends we used to spend together, I miss watching him at work in the food truck on my way back from school. But I also hate that this is the one place that always brings back bad memories.

This house was where I binged for the first time, hating my body every time I looked in the mirror, devouring an entire box of cookies just to starve myself the very next day. This house is where my mom looked me straight in the eyes and asked me what she did to deserve a daughter who didn't look like her or my sister.

This house is where I learned that my body was not accepted, that my value as a human, as a woman was diminished because of my size, because of the way I look.

But one look at my dad when I open the door has every bad memory floating away. I miss him so much. His grin warms my heart when he pulls me in for a hug. "Leila, it's so good to see you."

"Me too." I pull back. "I miss you, Papi."

He gives me a smile. "I wish you'd stay until your birthday next week."

He always made a big deal out of birthdays, inviting all the neighbors and the family over for a huge feast. It's honestly so disheartening that I won't be able to spend my birthday with them this year.

"I'd love to, you know I would. But I have class."

"Hmm. ¿Y como van?" *And how is it going?* he asks, making me wince.

"Good."

He gives me a pointed look. "No mientas." *Don't lie.*

I let out a laugh. "Boring. But it will be fine."

He nods. "I know you picked business because of me, but you don't need to do everything I do, Leila." He shakes his head, closing the door behind me. "You are not me; you're your own person."

"I know that," I glance at him. "I wanted to make you proud." I've always admired him, starting his own business, and even though it's not my dream, I was always interested in how it worked.

"You do. Estoy muy orgulloso de ti. Mi Tigresa." *I am very proud of you. My Tiger.* "And this photoshoot, huh?" He laughs. "I know how difficult that must have been and I am so proud of you for following your dreams," he says, wrapping his arm around my shoulder. "Even though I wish you would do it with your clothes on."

I laugh. "Thanks, Papi."

"Did it go well?" he asks.

I nod. "Yeah it was fun." It always is. Every time I stand behind a camera, it gives me a rush just like the very first time. It went great, apart from the other girls making little comments here and there about their bodies. The way they looked in the mirror and tore their perfect, thin bodies apart right in front of me, Amina, and some other bigger girls was such a slap in the face.

"And how are you feeling about it?" he asks.

I shrug. "Good," I admit. "I know I would have loved to see someone that looked like me in those magazines, and now I can be that for someone."

He nods. "Tan orgulloso," he repeats. "Viene. Your mom has been up early making arepas."

My eyes widen, my stomach rumbling at the thought of having home-cooked food. "She has?" I ask skeptically, knowing my mother wouldn't want me to eat those, even though they're my favorite.

He glances at me, pushing open the door to the backyard where my family is. "I helped." Which means he cooked them, and Mom was not happy about it. Dad has always tried to keep the peace between Mom and I, and failed—miserably.

My sister turns around at the sound of the door opening and her eyes widen. "You're here."

I nod, giving her a smile. "I'm here." We were inseparable growing up, but when we grew up, she had different interests, and we drifted apart. "Hey, Daniel," I glance up at Laura's boyfriend, whom she's been glued to since high school. They met, fell in love, lived happily ever after. Even though she's my younger sister by two years, her love life is better than mine ever was.

"Hey, Leila," he greets, leaning down to kiss my cheeks. "Haven't seen you around lately."

"Well, some of us go to college," I offer with a smile. Laura and Daniel decided college wasn't for them. My mom was not happy, and neither was my dad, but being my mom's favorite child, she won her over when she told her she'd decided to follow her dreams and be a hairdresser. Daniel got a job at the dealership his uncle works at straight out of high school, and together they make a perfect couple.

He laughs, his brown eyes a perfect match to the hair on his head. "I heard about the photo shoot," he says, flashing me a wink. "Congrats."

I press my lips together, giving him a smile. "Thanks."

My head turns, seeing my mom, who looks as beautiful as ever. Long, brown hair that my sister and I both inherited; Laura cut hers short, just above her shoulders. The dress my mom is wearing falls just above her knees, wrapping around her slim waist that she wishes I had too. I give her a smile, still finding myself missing her even though she makes me feel so bad about myself. "Hey, Mama."

Her smile doesn't quite reach her eyes when she pulls me in for a hug, kissing my cheeks. "Mija. So nice to see you. Te ves muy feliz." *You look very happy.*

"I am," I tell her, hoping she doesn't go into a rampage about my body. "I'm happy."

Her brows raise. "¿Novio?" *boyfriend?* My stomach drops.

I shake my head, inhaling before I sigh. "No, Ma, no boyfriend."

She shakes her head. "If only you would just—"

"Ven comer." *Come eat.* My dad interrupts whatever my mom is about to say, calling us over to the folding table he set up in the middle of our backyard, decked with arepas and filling, a big salad bowl on the side and some plantains and fries.

As soon as we sit, my sister tells me all about her trip to Europe she took with Daniel, how they saw the Eiffel Tower and tried snails and I listen to it with a smile, all while my mother glances at me with a clear effect of telling me that this could be me. That the life my sister is living could be mine.

I leave my half-eaten arepa on the plate, noticing how my mom's eyes widen with every bite I take. My stomach cramps, but I don't even have an appetite anymore. I got so used to Aiden making me eat and acting like there was nothing wrong with eating that I forgot. I forgot that my fatness offends my mother, makes her hate me, makes me worthless.

I've tried so hard to fight for myself. I look in the mirror every day, grab my rolls, and whisper words of love. I've been trying to love myself, love my body, embrace it for what it is, that I forgot what it was like.

The feeling of disgust of being in my own body. Feeling like I occupy the room with my loud voice and my big body. Feeling like I'm unworthy of love.

It's all coming back to me, and that happy feeling I had before, it's long gone. In less than twenty minutes, my mom managed to destroy my self-confidence once more.

I try to smile when my dad puts some of his fries on my plate when my mom turns around. But I don't eat them. I leave the fries to harden and get cold on the side of my plate.

"When does the magazine come out?" It takes me a while to realize my sister is talking to me and I blink, trying to shake all the negative thoughts out of my mind.

"Next month."

"Are you going to be on the cover?" Daniel asks.

"No. It's a feature piece."

My mom shakes her head, digging into her salad. "I don't know how you're not embarrassed."

"About what?"

She looks up, rolls her eyes. "Leila, por favor. No seas tola." *Don't be dumb.* "Everyone is going to see your *body*," she says, that last word covered in disgust. She drops her fork, pressing two fingers to her forehead. "If you would just…" she shakes her head, not bothering to finish her sentence, but I know. Eat healthier, work out more, whatever stupid thing she sends me that she saw on the internet. She looks at me. "You could be so pretty."

I've been heartbroken before. What my ex-boyfriend, Jake, did took a toll on me. I really thought I loved him and that he was genuine, and then when I found out it was all a lie, my heart shattered into little pieces.

But this right here? What my mom just said to me? It hurts a million times worse. What's left over of my heart sinks to the bottom of my stomach as everyone at the table stops eating, stops talking, and stares at me.

You could be so pretty.

"Mama," my sister says, grabbing her attention.

"¿Qué?"

"We're celebrating her birthday, lay off."

My mom scoffs. "Her birthday isn't for another twelve days."

"Camila," my dad says. "That's our daughter. How can you tell her she's not beautiful?"

My mom holds her finger up. "Yo no dije eso." *I didn't say that.* "I was just telling her she could be so much prettier if she lost weight."

"Camila!"

"This is your fault," she says to my dad. "You think I don't know the secret snacks you give her when you think I'm not looking?" She glances at me. "How can you blame me for that?"

She lets out a heavy breath, gesturing to Laura. "Look at your sister, Leila. She has a boyfriend, a good job. That could be you."

"I can still have that."

She scoffs again. "The one boyfriend you had thought you were a joke. Despierta mija. You will never have that if you don't make a change."

I can't sit here and listen to my mom berate me and tear apart the tiny little piece of confidence I've tried so hard to build up the past year I spent away from home. I stand up, the chair scraping against the ground as I do. "I need to go to the bathroom." I head inside, closing the door just in time to hear my parents arguing.

I take the stairs, finding the old bathroom and lock the door, sitting on the edge of the bathtub. The tears fall freely as my brain replays every bad word I've heard about my body.

So much potential wasted.

If only she wasn't big.

Do you really think I would ever want you? It was a joke.

You could be so pretty.

A knock at the door makes my head snap up, staring at the wooden door in front of me. "Leila?" my sister asks. "Can I come in?"

I shake my head, wiping my tears with the back of my hand. "What do you want?" The bite in my tone is obvious.

She opens the door and peeks in. "I'm not here to make it worse," she says, shutting the door behind her. "I promise."

I sniff, wiping the wetness from my face. "I'm sorry." My shoulders drop, feeling the tears brew up again. "I just…"

"I know."

"How can she say that?" I ask my sister, a tear rolling down my cheek. "How can she sit there and talk about me like that?"

"I'm sorry," my sister says, frowning. "None of us believe that, Leila."

I laugh, tears streaming freely down my face. "Please. I know what everyone thinks when they look at me."

"That you're stunning? Yes, that's what they think."

"Laura." I glare at my sister, knowing she's trying to make me feel better but also knowing that it's all a bunch of lies.

"Leila," she mimics. "I know you're not a nun at college."

I shrug. "So? Doesn't change anything."

"It means guys want you."

"For sex," I explain to my sister. "You will never understand, Laura. You'll never know what it's like being kept in secret all the time and then being looked at with disgust the next day, avoiding you at all costs, afraid that anyone finds out they like fat girls." I shake my head, letting out a breath. "I wish I was you."

She's quiet for a moment before she sighs. "No, you don't."

I laugh bitterly. "I can't begin to count how many times I have wished to be you."

"Daniel's cheating on me."

I lift my head, the silence between us deafening. "What?"

She sighs, closing her eyes and tipping her head back on the door. "I don't mean to avert from your problems, but hearing you speak about being kept in secret and wishing you were me... I just had to tell someone."

"Really?" I ask her.

She shrugs, frowning. "I think so. He's been coming home late, always having a different excuse." She drops her head. "I don't know what to do."

"I'm so sorry."

She lifts her head, wiping the tear that's falling down her cheek. "I didn't tell you that because I need you to feel sorry for me. I wanted you to know that Mom is wrong. Life can be shitty no matter what you look like."

My shoulders drop. I miss my sister. Growing up, I diverted more to my dad, having more common interests with him, and my sister grew closer to my mom. "Thank you." I glance up at her. "Why didn't you tell me?"

She shrugs, picking at her nails. "I didn't want to bother you."

"You're my sister," I tell her, standing up from the bathtub. "You can never bother me."

She smiles, giving me a laugh. "You're going to regret that," she says. "I'm going to be calling you every week now."

"Please do. I've missed you."

She smiles, pulling me in for a hug. "I've missed you too." She pulls back and fixes her short hair in the mirror, wiping her face and making it look like she hasn't been crying.

My phone buzzes in my hands and I look down, the name on the screen making my heart pound. It's only been a few days since we last saw each other and I'm already anticipating seeing him again.

Aiden:

I know this is breaking the rules.

My heart beats as the three dots jump on the screen, my hands clutching the phone tighter.

Aiden:

But I really fucking miss you, Leila.

"So, no boyfriend," Laura says, making my eyes snap to her. She grins, glancing at me in the mirror. "But there is someone. I can see it in your eyes."

She turns around and I sigh, my eyes dropping back to the text that is undeniably making my insides flutter. "There may be someone."

She grins. "I knew it. Tell me everything."

I shrug, turning off my phone. "There's nothing to say. We're just sleeping together."

She shakes her head. "That never works. Do you have feelings for him?"

I try not to think too much about it. I didn't want to get attached to Aiden, but I think it's too late. Just being in New York for a couple of days without seeing him is making me desperate to go back home until I can see him, kiss him. "We'll see." It's the first time I've ever admitted it and the confession makes my heart beat even faster. I do have feelings for Aiden. Undeniable, strong feelings that I can't push away anymore.

My sister laughs. "Keep me updated."

A grin sprouts on my face. "Will do."

195

"Come on," she says, opening the door. "If Mom says anything, I'll distract her."

I scoff. "We're going to need a tornado to distract her."

24

I'm in control

Leila

Redfield has become my home away from home.

Even though I miss my dad and home-cooked meals, this group of people has become my second little family. I wouldn't trade them for anything in the world. And now that Rosie is dating and has moved in with Grayson, I guess he's now part of our little posse.

Gabi, however, doesn't really seem to appreciate that little fact, given how she's glaring at him. "You've been hogging her."

"I haven't hogged her," Grayson replies.

Gabi raises her eyebrows. "I know you're like in love, and I'm happy for you, but do you really need to be here?"

"In my house?"

"Yes."

Grayson laughs and holds his hands up. "I thought we were cool. I gave you candy."

"It ended," she says with a shrug. It's entertaining as shit watching Gabi mess with Grayson.

He snorts. "I'll get you some more."

"You've been blackmailing him?" Madi asks her.

Gabriella rolls her eyes. "He had to earn my approval somehow."

"How about because I love your best friend?" Grayson offers.

Rosie turns her head, smiling at him, and Gabi's eyes soften, as we all do when we look at them. They're so pure, so in love, it's adorable. "Fine," Gabi says with a sigh. "You're off the hook."

Rosie snickers. "As much as I love watching you threaten my boyfriend, we all know you're a big softie."

"Boyfriend," Grayson repeats, looking all lovesick when he looks at her. I swear he has hearts in his eyes. "Love that word."

I don't even know why I do it, but instinctively, I glance at Aiden who's sitting on the end of the couch, to find him already looking at me. The word boyfriend rings through my mind when those blue eyes twinkle; he smirks when I hold eye contact.

He stands up and my eyes follow his movements, watching as he lifts himself off the couch and announces, "I'm going to get some snacks."

"Do you have any gummy worms?" Gabi asks, raising her eyebrows at him.

He shrugs. "We might do."

Gabi grins. "I want them."

He laughs. "I'll see what I can do."

"They're gross," Madi replies. "How can you like them?"

"At least they're not those disgusting vegan candies Leila likes."

"Hey," Rosie says. "I like those too."

Aiden glances at me before he heads out of the living room. I blow out a breath when he leaves. Whenever he's in a room with me, my eyes follow him, looking for him everywhere. There's so much tension whenever we're in the same room

198

together and knowing that we're not alone, that we're hanging out… together… with other people, it's scary.

Gabi grabs a can of beer off the table, cracks it open, and takes a sip. I lick my lips, wanting one, but I also want to kiss Aiden later, and I can't do that if I taste of beer. I haven't stopped thinking of what he told me about his family.

I would have never guessed Aiden came from nothing, that he had nothing. He always seemed so sure of himself, so confident. He dominates every room he's in, guys and girls following him wherever he goes.

A part of me feels like it's a good thing that he told me, that he trusted me with that part of him, but another part feels like it's a waste of time because, eventually, it will be for nothing. Aiden will move on, with someone else, and I'll be stuck harboring all of these little facts about him, knowing more about him than I do about anyone else.

When he comes back into the room, I glance up, watching how he throws a pack of sour gummies to Gabi.

"Fuck yes," she says, catching them. She grabs a can of beer and holds it up. "You want one?" she asks him.

His smile drops, his hand nervously rubbing the back of his neck. "I'm good."

"C'mon," Gabi says. "I have to say thank you somehow. One beer won't derail your training."

I don't know what comes over me, some kind of protective urge to get him out of this situation but I blurt out, "He doesn't drink."

All eyes turn to me, Gabi's lips turned in a smirk. Since she's in on my little secret, she knows how I know that about him, but the rest of the group doesn't, which is why they're all

199

looking at me with confusion. Aiden's smiling though, a hint of a smile on those beautiful lips of his as he looks at me.

"You don't?" Madi asks him.

He shakes his head. "No."

"Why not?"

He shrugs, clearly not knowing what to say, so my big mouth interrupts again and says, "It's not a big deal. I'm laying off the beer too."

Now, Gabi's eyebrows raise. "You? Not drinking?"

"Yeah, why not?" I might enjoy a beer here and there, but if it means they'll lay off Aiden, then I guess I'm quitting drinking.

She smirks, shaking her head. "It's interesting, that's all."

Aiden drops onto the couch beside me and my eyes widen as I look at him, glancing around to see if anyone notices, but they don't, wrapped up in their conversations. "You're not drinking, huh?" he asks.

I shrug. "It's not a big deal."

He laughs, running a hand over his mouth. "You know I don't expect you to do that for me, right? I'll still kiss you if you drink."

I glare at him, hating how he's caught on to my reasoning for laying off the alcohol, but when he scoots closer to me, I see him holding a pack of the vegan candies me and Rosie love. He rips it open and holds it out to me. My eyes widen at him. "What are you doing?" I whisper.

His eyebrows raise. "Eating?" He shakes the package at me again, and I shove it away. "C'mon," he says. "Gabi said they're your favorite."

"She's exaggerating."

His smile drops, and I can see the worry kicking in, wondering if what the nurse said was true after all and he pushes the package closer to me. "Take one, Leila."

"Aiden."

He shocks me by saying, "Defy me and see what happens."

My eyes snap to his, feeling the burn from his gaze, and I lick my lips. "What are you going to do?"

He smirks, lifting his brows. "Do you want to find out?"

Yes. I love how he throws me around in the bedroom, taking control and making me think of nothing but pleasure whenever we're together. But when I hear Gabi laughing, my panic kicks in, and I put some distance between us. "You can't do anything. We're in public," I whisper.

His smirk widens. "We're in my house, Leila."

I roll my eyes. "You know what I mean."

"Then eat." He shakes the package in front of me again. I glance back at him, but the way he looks at me makes me sigh, grab a few out of the package and drop them into my mouth.

They're so good. I can't remember the last time I had them, or any candy, for that matter. Every word my mother spoke to me this past weekend erases from my mind when Aiden smiles when I grab a couple more. He follows suit, grabbing a handful from the package and munching away. For like two seconds before his face contorts, and he stops chewing. "What the fuck is this?" he asks, his mouth full of the sour candy.

"You don't like them?"

He grabs a napkin, spitting into it. "This is the worst thing I've ever put in my mouth." He cringes, shaking his head and spitting out the remainder of the candy.

"You're so dramatic, they're not that bad."

"Holy shit," Aiden wheezes, unscrewing a water bottle and downing it. "Are you trying to kill me?"

I laugh while his face turns red, glaring at me. "You'll be fine."

He shakes his head. "If I don't make it to practice tomorrow, it's your fault."

"You ready for the game next week?" Grayson asks him.

He nods. "Of course," he glances at me, "If Leila doesn't kill me first. We'll get that win."

"You're up against UCLA," I point out. "They're good."

"They are?" Rosie asks, not knowing anything about basketball. I always tried to drag her with me to the games in high school, but the girl was never interested.

"Yeah," Aiden replies. "But I'm not worried."

I scoff. "Cocky as always."

I steal a furtive glance at him, his gaze meeting mine, and he smirks, his tongue glides over his lips as he stares down at me. I have to remind myself I'm in a room full of people—my friends—before I do something stupid like kiss him. But... I really want to kiss him.

"They have a great defense," he replies, with a suggestive smirk when his eyes drop to my lips. "But they can't shoot for shit." His eyes fall on mine once again and he smiles. "I've got it handled."

"You can take them," Grayson tells him, his voice cracking through me and Aiden like an ice bucket drenching us. "You're one of the best players I have seen."

Yeah, he is, and Aiden knows it too, which is why I say, "Don't feed his ego."

I can feel Aiden's eyes on me from my side and Grayson laughs, shaking his head. "Too late for that."

My head snaps to the man sitting beside me, watching as he grabs the package of the 'toxic waste' as he puts it, and shakes it in front of me. I shake my head and he narrows his eyes. If he thinks he can tell me what to do, then I can play with him too.

I grab one of the candies from the bag, open my mouth, and place it on my tongue. His eyes widen as he watches me wrap my lips around the blue candy, sucking half of it into my mouth. I know I've affected him when I hear a breathy rasp come from his lips, which spurs me on, looking up into his eyes when I pull it out of my mouth, only to swirl my tongue around it.

"Oh fuck," he whispers, the bag dropping onto his lap, his chest rising the harder he breathes. I grin around the candy, knowing I have him right where I want him.

"Leila."

I pull the candy out of my mouth, my eyes widening as my head snaps to my right where Gabi's calling my name. "Hmm?"

I hear the giant beside me snicker, running a hand down his face to cover his laugh, and I try not to look back at him. "How was the photo shoot?" Gabi asks.

"It went well," I tell her.

She gives me a smile. She knows how nervous I was before leaving for New York, but once I got there and was surrounded by supportive people, it went better than I imagined. Now the hard part is going to be when it releases. I'm trying not to think of it too much, but it's hard when it runs through my mind constantly. "I'm going to buy a hundred copies," Gabi tells me.

"That's a bit excessive," I say, laughing. "I'm sure one will do."

She shakes her head. "It's called supporting your friends." I love her, I really do. God, how was I so lucky to find three of the best friends I could ever have?

"When does it come out?" Madi asks.

"In two weeks." The anticipation is killing me. I don't know how I'll feel once it's out there and people see me with less clothing than anyone ever has, even Aiden.

"That's so exciting," Rosie replies, grinning at me. "I can't wait."

"Me neither," Aiden whispers beside me, making my eyes dart briefly in his direction to find him grinning. "It's all I can think about."

This man. I squeeze my legs together, wanting to ease the pressure of having to sit beside him and not being able to do anything about it. His eyes glance at my legs pressed together and his knowing laugh makes me lift off the couch, his eyes darting towards me. "I need to use the bathroom," I announce.

"You can use the upstairs one," Rosie replies. "I just bought some lavender soap."

I nod, stealing a quick peek at Aiden hoping he gets the message and head upstairs, shutting the bathroom door behind me. I leave it unlocked, staring at the white wooden door, hoping Aiden understood what I was telling him.

I haven't seen him since before I left for New York, and being in the same room as a bunch of people who don't know that we're sleeping together is hard to do when all I want is to pull him into me and kiss him.

When the door opens and he walks in, I blow out a breath, my shoulders dropping. "Took you long enough," I manage to murmur before I wrap my arms around his neck and lift onto my tiptoes, bringing his mouth to mine.

I've tried to deny my feelings for him, but I can't any longer. I've missed him. So. Fucking. Much. I miss how he kisses, how he moans into my mouth whenever I wrap my tongue around his, or when I graze my teeth against his bottom lip before slightly sucking it, or when I wrap my fingers in his hair, moving his head to where I want him.

The noises he makes drive me crazy, making my body desperate for him in a way I've never been desperate for anyone before.

"God," he groans, burying his lips into my neck, leaving soft, open-mouthed kisses all over my skin. "You've been dying for me, haven't you, baby?"

I don't even correct him on the nickname, I just whimper instead, wanting, needing his lips back on mine. "This is your fault. You've been shooting me bedroom eyes."

He chuckles, pulling back. "You were sucking on that candy like it was my dick; let's not tell lies." I don't care. I don't care who teased who. I just want him. So bad.

I suck in a breath when he squeezes my ass cheeks. "Shit, I'm so sore."

"Fuck, I'm sorry," he mumbles into my neck. "I'll be gentle next time."

My hands push at his chest, rolling my eyes. "From the gym," I correct him.

He chuckles, but a low groan comes out of him when I grind myself against him, his hard dick pressing against every soft part of me. "We don't have much time," he tells me. "I told them I was going to get a drink."

"You had water right in front of you."

"Exactly."

"Fuck." I groan, tipping my head back and Aiden uses that to his advantage, kissing my skin until I feel dizzy all over. "Do you have a condom?"

"In my room?"

"Shit."

He laughs, his hands drifting until he cups my ass. "I can still make you come without fucking you." Next thing I know, he presses me against the sink and dips to his knees right in front of me.

My heart hammers in my chest, and before he can go any further, I shake my head, pulling him up until he's upright. "Let me."

"Leila—"

I don't let him finish, I sink to my knees instead, grabbing his dick from the outside of his sweats. That shuts him up, and lets out a groan when I tug his sweats down, then his boxers.

I watch in delight as his cock springs free, already dripping at the tip. I never thought dicks could look good until I saw his, but my god, one look at it and my mouth waters.

Another harsh exhale comes from him as he tips his head back. Shit, his dick is so huge. I think that every time I see it. Every time he strokes it before putting a condom on, I gulp in anticipation. I know how good it feels, how full it makes me, and I can't wait to stuff him down my throat.

He grabs his dick in his hand, giving it a slow stroke as he looks down at me. "You did so well with that candy," he says, grinning as I open my mouth for him. He places the tip of his dick on my soft tongue. "Let's see how well you suck my cock."

I wrap my lips around the tip, giving it a tentative suck, mentally preparing myself. I've never really had a gag reflex, but his dick makes it impossible not to gag when I try to fit him all the way. He's too big for that; it doesn't work. But I can still make him feel good, even if I can't deepthroat him.

I spit in my hand and grip my fist around his cock, seeing his stomach twitching when I do. My tongue swirls around the head of his cock, my fist stroking him simultaneously. He whimpers, thrusting his dick an inch deeper into my mouth, making me gag. I grip his cock in my fist tighter, making him groan, and he opens his eyes, looking down at me. "Don't do that," I warn him. "You might like telling me what to do, but I'm in control here."

He nods, licking his lips as he brushes the hair out of my face. "I can't fucking help it," he says. "You look so good with my dick in your mouth." The praise makes me shiver, and I wrap my mouth around him, slowly sucking the head, and his eyes close once more. "Oh shit," he moans. "That's so good, Leila."

My name in his mouth makes me throb, wishing I had more time with him than these quick little secret hookups. The moans leaving his lips every time I slide my tongue up his shaft increases my pleasure.

I moan around his dick as I bob my head on him. A hand wraps in my hair, and I look up at him. He lets out a moan, a sound so sexy I swear I had a mini orgasm. "Don't look at me like that. Fuck. It's too.... Ugh." Every sound from his lips encouraging me to keep going, suck him deeper, work my tongue over him faster.

I tongue the slit, dragging my tongue to the underside of his cock. His butt clenches, his dick getting impossibly harder in my mouth. "Fuck, Leila. You're so good at that," he moans.

"Where the hell did you learn that?" Another grunt. "Wait, no, don't tell me. I don't wanna know."

I look back up, seeing his eyes squeezed shut in pleasure as he keeps his restraint, careful not to thrust in my mouth. I work him deeper inside, sliding my hot, wet tongue over him as I stroke the base, and in seconds, he loses that gained control. He bucks his hips slightly, and I feel the hot spurts of his cum hit the back of my throat. He grunts, mumbling my name as he comes in my mouth. I swallow every drop, pull him out, and lick the liquid dripping from his dick, cleaning him up.

He pulls me up from the floor, wiping my lips with his thumb. His eyes roll to the back of his head when I wrap my lips around it, cleaning it off. "Holy shit," he leans in and whispers in my ear. "Next time, it's my turn to taste you."

I turn the faucet on, place my hair to one side, and swish water around my mouth, then spit it back out into the sink. Aiden's arms wrap around my waist, and he buries his lips into my exposed neck. "So beautiful," he murmurs. "Missed you."

I let my eyes to close as I feel his hands on me. He places a kiss on my neck and another and another. I melt into him, my hair draped over my shoulder as he kisses my neck. "What's this?" he asks.

"Huh?" I say deliriously.

"You have a tattoo?" His fingers run over the ink on my neck. "I haven't seen this before."

I let out a laugh. "Well, it's not like you're looking at my neck when you fuck me."

He turns me around, frowning down at me. "Not for lack of trying," he says. "I want to look at every single inch of you, Leila." The meaning of his words brings a soft flutter to my stomach as his hands run up my arms, cupping my face.

My throat bobs, staring up at him. I pull back, turning around and washing my hands with the lavender soap, needing something—anything—to do that will get me out of this conversation.

"It looks good on you." I feel his hands pull my hair to the side, his fingers tracing the tattoo. "A tiger paw?" he asks me.

I look up, meeting his eyes in the mirror. "It's for my dad. *Eres una Tigresa*. He's always said that to me," I tell him, smiling when I think of my dad. "It means tiger in English." I let out a laugh. "I always wanted a cat," I tell him. "But my sister's allergic and we could never have one." I turn around, looking up at him. "And around the same time, I learned tigers were just big cats, so one year, for Halloween, I dressed up as a tiger and the name stuck."

He smiles at my reflection. "Tiger, huh? I can see that. Strong, confident… Vicious, scary," he jokes.

My head shakes when the smile on my lips gets too big to hide. What are we even doing anymore? So many rules have been broken, and the longer I spend with him, the less I can remember what I'm fighting so hard against.

His words from earlier pop up into my head, making my smile slip and my hands grip the sink behind me. "You said something just now, and I was wondering…" His brows pull together and I look down at the ground. "Does it bother you?" I ask. "How many guys I've been with?"

His hands are on me instantly, lifting my chin until I'm looking into his hypnotizing eyes. "No," he says with a frown. "I don't need names or a number, Leila. Hell, I don't even need to know if they were good or not." Not. Definitely not as good as him. "I'd be a hypocrite if I cared about that," he says. "You

209

had a history before you met me. We've both been with other people, we can't change that."

His thumb strokes my cheek. "I've been with just as many girls if not more." He pulls me closer to him, his hand finding a home at my waist. "But that's irrelevant now. All I think of is you." He smiles at me. "I'm not worried about any other guys either." With a smirk, he leans down and whispers, "We both know they were just practice until you met me."

I laugh, shaking my head. "You're so cocky." He grins, leaning down until our lips are an inch away. "Come on," I tell him, opening the bathroom door and stepping out. "They'll start to get suspicious."

"They'll get suspicious if we walk in together too," he says, kissing my neck. "Just a little longer." My eyes drift closed at the feel of his lips against me. Am I ever going to get sick of him?

"Aiden," I moan when he kisses down my neck.

"Yes, gorgeous?" he murmurs between kisses.

God, that nickname. "We need to go," I plead, my voice unrecognizable, strained and thick with pleasure.

He pulls back, sighing. "You go first," he tells me, wiping a hand down his face. "I need to cool down again." My eyes drop to the tent he's pitching in his jeans, making my lips curve up. He laughs when he sees my reaction. "You like driving me crazy, huh?"

I nod. "Just like you do to me."

A guttural groan comes from him when he takes a step away from me. "Go, before I change my mind and lock us in my room forever."

I twist on my heels, peeking behind my shoulder when I reach the staircase. Being locked in his room for the night doesn't scare me anymore. What does scare me is how much I want it.

25

Love's awakening

Aiden

The week before a game, I go into training mode. No parties, no fast food, no distractions. Just the gym, work, basketball, and going through game videos. It's always been that way, until last night.

It was late, I had just finished training, and instead of going home and getting an early night, I went to Leila's.

Nothing could have kept me away from her, not the voice in my head telling me I needed to focus on the game. Not the routine I had since freshman year to ensure I maintained my winning streak, and that I played the best I could. Absolutely nothing could have stopped me from wanting her, craving her. And as soon as she opened the door and pressed her lips against mine, nothing else mattered.

Rules. They're meant to be broken, right? At least that's what I told Leila when we woke up in bed together this morning, her lush thigh wrapped around my waist, her head pressed against my chest. It was one of the best mornings I've ever had.

It wasn't long until I was buried inside her, hearing her sweet, hushed moans as we had slow, hot morning sex. As I said... best morning ever. After it was over though, she got all defensive and panicked, pushing me into the shower, telling me last night shouldn't have happened.

I know I told her I didn't want a relationship, and I didn't, hadn't even thought of it until she brought up the topic. But now that we've spent so much time together, I can't bear the thought of ending it with her and watching her move on with someone else. It physically pains me to think of some other guy's lips on her, of his hands on her.

I might have agreed to a casual, no strings attached arrangement before, but that's not what I want anymore. Not even close to it.

I hear Leila's voice coming from the kitchen. My brows furrow as I push open her bedroom door only to see her sitting at the kitchen table talking to someone on her laptop. In Spanish.

I lean against the door frame, arms crossed, and listen to her speak. I can't make out what she's saying, but my god, it sounds sexy as hell. I've never heard her speak her mother tongue before, only some words here and there, mostly curse words, but hearing her speak this beautiful language, with who I assume are her family, has me grinning as I listen to her.

Spanish was my worst subject in school, resulting in not being able to understand a word of what's coming out of her mouth, until I hear one word that sticks in my brain.

Cumpleaños.

Birthday?

She chuckles at the screen. "Gracias, Papi." Okay, well I understood that. It's Leila's birthday? There's no way. She would have told me, right?

I hear her blow her family kisses and then close the laptop, dropping her head onto the counter. I approach her, leaning down to kiss her jaw. Her head snaps up, letting out a sigh when she sees me. "I thought you were still in the shower."

"It's your birthday?"

Her brows furrow. "How—" She rolls her eyes. "You were eavesdropping?"

"I didn't mean to," I tell her. "I love listening to you speak Spanish."

She smiles, lifting off the chair and wrapping her arms around my neck. I love how touchy she's become. How things have changed since we first started sleeping together. "Yeah?" she asks, looking up at me with those green eyes. "I could teach you some words."

"Like what?"

She hums, whispering against my lips. "Bésame."

So hot. "What does that mean?"

"Kiss me," she explains.

Gladly. I press my lips to hers, kissing her, getting lost in her sweet taste and scent. It surrounds me. "What else?" I ask her, wanting to hear her speak some more.

"Fóllame."

She shivers against me when I wrap my arms around her waist. "And what does that mean?" I whisper against her lips.

She licks her plump lips, staring up at me. "Fuck me." She wastes no time, grabbing the back of my neck and bringing our mouths together, making me forget what I was going to say. She always manages to make my mind hazy, unable to think of anything but her.

Her frown when I pull back amuses me. "Not so fast," I say, smoothing my hands over her bare hips, feeling her soft skin under my fingertips. "You weren't going to tell me it was your birthday?"

She lets out a sigh, unwrapping her arms from around me. "Didn't think it was necessary."

My brows furrow. "You didn't think I needed to know that today was your birthday?"

"No."

Ouch. My stomach drops, feeling the pain from her words. It's clear that she's not where I am at all. How am I supposed to tell her I want more when she clearly just wants sex from me? "Why not?"

She sighs, taking a step away from me. My hands twitch, wanting her back. "Because I don't really care for it."

"Why?" I ask her, crossing my arms.

Her shoulders lift in a non-committal shrug, playing with the hem of her pajama top. "It was different when I was growing up. My dad would go all out, you know? Plan a huge surprise when I woke up, balloons, a cake, the whole joint. But now... it just seems useless."

Hearing about her birthday celebrations when she was a kid makes me happy that she had that, that she had love and fun in her life. It might make me a dick but it makes me a little jealous and sad for younger me. Growing up, I didn't even know when it was my birthday because no one cared. "It's not useless. It's the day you were born. Is that why you're upset?" I ask her, watching her pull her bottom lip between her teeth. "Because you won't be able to spend your birthday with your family?"

Her nose scrunches. "A little," she admits. "But I also feel like it's a huge relief I'm not home for my birthday."

"Why?"

She sighs, closing her eyes. "Because my mom hates me."

I shake my head. Who the hell could hate her? "I'm sure that's not true."

She glances at me, dropping her eyes to the ground a second later. "It is. She hates my body. Hates that I don't look like her or my sister," she says, her voice breaking my goddamn heart. She sounds so small, so sad. Fuck, I just want to hold her and tell her that her mother doesn't deserve to look at her if she can't see how beautiful she is. Drop dead fucking gorgeous.

"You're not serious." The thought of someone as close to Leila as her mother telling her something like that shatters me. I see how self-conscious she is whenever we sleep together, I can sense how she gets stuck in her head sometimes, how she pulls on her top whenever it lifts, or how she prefers the dark. "Is that why you don't take your top off?" Her eyes widen when the question comes out of my mouth. "Because of your mother's comments?"

She shakes her head, her throat bobbing when she swallows. "That's different. It's got nothing to do with her."

"Then why?" I ask her, approaching where she's standing. "Do you not trust me?" I've told this girl more than I've ever told anyone, including Grayson. Does it hurt that she doesn't feel comfortable to return the favor? Yeah, it hurts like a bitch.

"It's complicated," she says.

"Then uncomplicate it for me." She shakes her head which makes me a little annoyed. "I just want to know you, Leila. I've told you all about my family, I have nothing to hide from you. I just want you to let me in."

She drops onto the chair with a sigh, burying her head in her hands. "I had a boyfriend in high school." I hate him already. "His name was Jake. He was a football player, and just like every other girl, I was interested in him. He was a quarterback, popular, hot as hell."

I scoff. "Not as hot as me." She glares at me, or she tries to, her lips giving her away with the small smirk on them. "Continue," I tell her, leaning against the couch.

"Obviously every girl was into him, and then one day, out of nowhere, he noticed me. He talked to me, flirted with me, and then asked for my number." I can't help but think it sounds familiar to how we started. I hate that. I hate the thought of her associating me with him, with whatever he did to make her hide a part of herself.

"He asked me out but told me it had to be in secret because the other guys would give him shit for dating someone that looked like me." My fists curl up by my sides, wanting to find this asshole and punch him. "I was fine with it. I knew I didn't look like the other girls. And then we started dating," she continues, glancing up at me. "He was my first," she explains. I can see the pain on her face and I'm not sure if I even want to listen to the rest of it. It's hurting me just knowing she was hurt.

"He told me to keep my top on because it wasn't necessary to see any of that," she says, using air quotes. I want to kill him. "I felt horrible, but I agreed. I didn't like that part of myself… I still don't." she mumbles that last part so quietly I almost didn't hear it. "And then once he finished, he left, saying he had practice."

"Please tell me that's it," I plead her. "Please tell me he didn't do anything else."

She turns away from me, dropping her eyes to her lap. "When I went back to school, he had exposed all of our messages," she tells me. "It turns out he didn't like me like I had thought, it was a bet between his friends." She laughs, bitterly. I watch as a tear falls onto her lap and she wipes it away quickly, shaking her head. "He said to me 'I can't believe you thought I actually liked you.' He slept with me as a joke."

"You're fucking with me." My blood pressure rises with every word that comes out of her mouth. "Tell me you're joking."

She shakes her head, shattering my heart into pieces. "*I* was the joke. They were betting on who can get the fat girl to think they like her." The look on her face kills me. "I lost all of my friends. No one wanted to be around me, except for Rosie. I was so embarrassed." She looks up at me with glassy eyes, brimming with tears. "So, when I got to college, I decided to flip the switch," she tells me. "I knew I wasn't the relationship girl. I knew guys wouldn't want to be with me." She wipes her face, squaring her shoulders. "So, *I* approached guys. *I* made the first move, and I kept the rules the same. Only one-night stands, always from behind so I wouldn't look at them, in private and I'd never see them again."

Yeah, I remember her no repeat rule very clearly. "I got what I wanted, and I didn't get attached," she says with a sigh. "It was working until…"

"Until me," I finish for her.

"Yeah," she offers with a small smile.

"Do you regret it?" My heart beats with anticipation. "Do you regret us?"

She shakes her head, her smile slipping. "No."

I lift off the couch, crouching down to where she's sat and grasp her face in my hands, wiping away the tears with my thumb. "I don't want you to hide yourself from me," I tell her, my heart bursting at the seams when she smiles at me. It's my favorite sight in the world. "You are the most beautiful girl I have ever had the privilege of being with, Leila. There is nothing about you that I don't like." She drops her head, but I lift her chin, wanting those green eyes on me. "You hear me? Nothing." She nods and I lean in, pressing my lips to hers for a quick kiss. "I wish you could see yourself how I see you," I tell her, staring into her eyes. "You're so beautiful, sexy as hell," I punctuate my sentence with a kiss. "And you've quickly become my favorite person to be around."

Her eyes widen and I can tell she's a little scared by my statement. Maybe I'm moving too fast. Fuck. I clear my throat. "We need to celebrate."

"What?" she asks, when I pull back, her brows knitted together.

"Your birthday," I clarify. "You can't be with your family today, but let me do something for you."

She shakes her head. "You don't need to do that. The girls and I already planned a movie night."

There's no way I'm going to let her do nothing on her birthday. "You do that every weekend. Let me take you out."

I can see the panic starting to kick in. "Aiden."

"Please." I grab onto her hand, pressing my lips against her knuckles. "Just let me do this for you, Leila." She frowns, looking down at me. "I never had a birthday," I tell her. "Never had a cake, no balloons, no presents." Her shoulders slump, her lips pursed together. "I grew up knowing no one cared about me and that no one even bothered to make that day special. But I'm not going to let that happen to you." I lift her off the chair, wrapping my arms around her waist. "Let me do this for you."

Her lips part but instead of saying yes, she sighs. "I don't think that's a good idea."

"Why not?"

She untangles herself from me and breaks my heart by saying, "Because it sounds too much like a date."

Well, if I wanted to know her feelings on the matter, I do now. I scratch my jaw, staring at this beautiful girl in front of me who acts like going on a date with me would be the end of the world. "Would that be so bad?"

"We have rules," is the response she gives me.

"No, you have rules." I take a step closer to her. "I just went along with them."

Her throat bobs. "You said you didn't want a relationship."

"I didn't," I tell her with a lift of my shoulder.

"And now you do?"

I exhale, harshly. I just want... her. "I don't know," I tell her honestly. "All I know is I want more than this, Leila." Her chest rises and falls rapidly as she struggles to catch her breath, processing what I've just told her. I reach for her hand, interlocking it with mine. She's so soft against me. "I want to hold your hand in public," I tell her, lifting her chin with my thumb. "I want to kiss you whenever I feel like it instead of having to sneak around and wait until it's dark to have you." Her tongue darts out to lick her lips. "I want to sleep over and wake up with you. I want more."

I wait for what seems like forever, time ticking before she pulls away and turns around completely. "I don't know."

I sigh, rubbing the back of my neck. I pushed her too hard. "You don't need to make any rash decisions right now, Leila. I don't want to ruin your birthday." She turns back around, her arms dropping to her sides. "Just let me take you out. Just tonight." I watch as her shoulders slump but before she can tell me no, I whisper, "Please." I'm not above begging. I'll crawl on the ground and beg for that girl if that's what it takes.

"Okay."

My heart stops. "Really?"

She nods, biting on her bottom lip. "Just for tonight." It's a start.

I erase the distance between us and brush her hair from her face, kissing her cheek. "Get ready," I whisper. "I'll pick you up at seven."

"Where are you taking me?"

I have no clue, all I know is that she deserves everything. "It's a surprise," I tell her instead. "Let me plan everything. All you have to worry about is looking pretty for me."

A low laugh rumbles out of her and without even thinking I pull her into me, getting lost in her lips, my hands running down her body, pulling at her waist until she moans into my mouth, which wakes my dick up. "Fuck. I should go before I take you back to bed." And I still need to figure out what I'm going to do for her birthday.

"And I have to get pretty," she says, grinning at me.

I shake my head, my eyes dropping the length of her body, lingering on every single inch of her. "Job done." She's so much more than pretty. She's gorgeous, beautiful, smart, funny, sexy as hell and can make my day with just a roll of those lime green eyes.

I pick up my hat, place it on my head, and lean in for just one more kiss. Reluctantly, I pull away from her, heading towards the door. I turn back one last time and my chest hurts at the sight of her.

Fuck.

She's perfect.

"I…" My lips press together to stop other words from escaping. "I'll see you tonight," I tell her before walking out of her apartment, the door closing behind me.

I blow out a much-needed breath, running a hand down my face at the words repeating themselves over and over in my head.

I never thought I'd be in love. I'm not a cynic like Grayson once was, I know it exists for some people, but I just never thought I'd ever experience it. Growing up I didn't know what love looked like, I'd never seen it. Not from my mom or my brothers, it just didn't exist in my family. I honestly never thought I would tolerate, let alone like someone so much to the point where I'm desperately in love with them.

But the proof is right there, inside apartment 305 that holds a million and one plants all over the place, that holds the woman I love.

Just my luck I fall for someone who doesn't want a relationship.

26

Close call

Leila

The text comes just in time.

After I've finished showering and shaving every inch of my skin—sweating in the process—I read Aiden's text which makes me shake with anticipation.

Aiden:

> I'm almost there.

Leila:

> How do I know what to wear if you won't tell me where we're going?

The three little dots dance on the screen until his text comes in, making me smile.

Aiden:

> I can promise you; you'll look beautiful in anything you wear.

My head shakes, pressing my lips together as I type back.

Leila:

That's sweet. But so unhelpful.

Aiden:

Wear something fancy.

And with easy access.

I snicker, shaking my head. Ok, I can do that. I drop my phone on the bed and open my closet, looking around for a dress for tonight. My eye catches on the short black long-sleeve dress with a heart neckline Rosie designed for me a few months ago, and I pull it out, holding it to my body.

I rip my towel off, standing in front of my mirror in only my underwear. The lacy black underwear accentuates my tan skin, fitting perfectly on my curves. I can't wait for Aiden to see it tonight.

I slip the dress on, adjusting it so it sits right and pull out the rollers until my hair falls over my shoulders in curls, framing my face. I've never been on a date, and the thought of going on a date with none other than Aiden Pierce makes my insides churn.

I barely have time to put on my heels when I hear a knock at my door. I glance at my reflection once more, fixing my hair before I head out and open the door.

I almost swallow my tongue at the sight of Aiden standing at my door, dressed in a white shirt that clings to his muscles and black pants that have my mouth watering when I look up at him.

"Fuck," he whispers under his breath.

I snicker. "Took the words right out of my mouth."

"You look…." He grips my waist, and pulls me into him, bringing his mouth to mine, moaning into my mouth. "I don't think I'm going to make it through dinner." A groan rumbles from him. "I'm struggling right now."

"I've never seen you dressed like this," I tell him, entranced by how good that shirt looks on him. "And you cut your hair." I run my hands over the shorter strands.

"Do you like it?" he asks.

I never thought I'd see Aiden Pierce wanting my approval on… anything, least of all, how he looks for our date tonight. Is this really happening? I nod. "You look so good."

He smiles, shaking his head, dropping his eyes to my body. "You're so beautiful," he murmurs. "How did I get so lucky?"

My smile drops at the reminder of everything he said this morning, of everything he wants, and everything I'm still reluctant to give him.

"Not tonight," he's quick to say. "We can talk about it another day. Let's go."

"Aiden, you've got to be kidding me," I say when we step out of the Uber. "This is too much."

225

He shakes his head. "It's not nearly enough. Come on." He holds out his hand in front of me and without even thinking, I freeze up, staring down at his open hand. I've been keeping up my guard for so long that the possibility of it being torn down makes my heart race. "No one knows us here," he says, and when I look up at him, his forehead is wrinkled, frowning at me.

Our fingers intertwine together, and he gives me a little squeeze before he pushes open the door, walking us in. Shit, this place is huge, and fancy as hell.

"Reservation for Pierce," Aiden says when we approach the host. He looks down the list, scanning for Aiden's name.

"Right this way, sir," he says, leading us to a table at the back, beside one of the huge windows overlooking the city. He hands us the menu when we're seated and tells us a server will come and take our orders soon.

When he leaves, I glare at Aiden. "I can't believe you did all of this." I shake my head. "I would have been fine with a pizza and a movie."

Aiden smiles at me, grabbing my hand on the table. He's sitting so far away, it's going to be agonizing spending the rest of the night unable to touch him, kiss him. "You deserve so much more than just fine, Leila." Those intoxicating blue eyes bring me a kind of peace whenever he looks at me. "You deserve everything."

My poor heart can't handle it; it's racing, almost beating right out of my chest.

He shakes his head, pulling away from me. "No, this isn't going to work."

My brows knit together. "What do you mean?"

He sighs. "I'm not going to be able to sit across from you all night without kissing you." He stands up, grabbing his chair. "I need closer," he says, moving his chair beside me. When he sits back down, he blows a breath and grins. "So much better."

I don't even have a chance to say anything before a server appears at our table, flashing us a smile. "Good evening," she says, holding a notepad in her hands. "What would you like to order?"

I open the menu, scanning through it quickly since I spent the entire time ogling Aiden. "Are there any vegetarian dishes here?" I ask her, trying to find something that sounds good.

"All of it is vegetarian."

I lift my head. "Excuse me?"

She smiles. "This is a vegetarian restaurant."

I glance at Aiden who shrugs, glancing at me. "Didn't want you to have limited options," he replies making my heart beat even faster.

It pains me that we're not alone right now. I scan the menu again, picking one that sounds the best. "I'll have the tomato pasta, please." I hand the server the menu, and she looks at Aiden.

"The risotto sounds good. Thank you," he tells her, handing the menu to her.

"Great choices," she says. "I'll be back with your food."

I can't think when he looks at me, but I manage to shake my head when I look around the place. "This place is too expensive, Aiden."

The frown on his face has my stomach in knots. He grabs my hand, looking at me and says, "I don't want you to think I can't take care of you, Leila. I will do anything it takes to make

227

you happy. I don't want you pitying me or thinking of me any differently because of my family."

"I don't pity you," I tell him. "I just don't want you to spend all your money on me. I don't need fancy dinners or extravagant dates." My throat constricts with the words that threaten to climb up and I blow out a breath. Just for tonight, right? We can pretend just for tonight. "I only want you."

His eyes widen. "You mean that?"

There isn't a hint of hesitation when I say, "All I want is you."

His smile is one of the first things I noticed about Aiden. It was one of the things that annoyed me about him when we first met. He seemed to get anything he wanted by flashing a smile and it aggravated me, how everyone seemed to melt at the sight of it. But when I'm the source of that smile, it's the most beautiful thing I've seen. "I'm going to be so good to you, Leila," he says, cupping my face with his hands. "You wait and see."

I lick my lips, staring up into his eyes. I know he's going to be the best boyfriend anyone could ever have. Too bad I'll likely never find out.

He pulls back, pulling out something out of his pocket. "I almost forgot," he says, placing the small rectangle box on the table. "Happy birthday, gorgeous."

He got me a gift too? I lift my brows at him. "What is it?"

He laughs, running a hand through his hair. "Well, I didn't have much time to get you something because I only found out it was your birthday this morning." He slides the box over to me. "But I couldn't come empty-handed."

"This is too much." First the restaurant, now this. I know he doesn't want me to worry, but I can't help it. Aiden needs the money. He works hard and gets almost nothing from what he makes. My stomach churns, making me feel guilty that he's spending all of his hard-earned money on me when I know he needs it.

"Just open it, Leila. You might hate it."

Not possible. I don't even care what's in here. Just knowing that Aiden went out of his way to get me something— anything—makes me want to cry and kiss him until I can't remember why I can't be with him.

I grab the small box in my hand, opening it up. Looking back at me is a small gold necklace with a small paw pendant. I press my lips together, staring down at the necklace, running my fingers over it. "It's not much, but I thought you could look at it when you miss your dad. I know you got the tattoo for him, but you can't really see it so…" I look up at him and he blows out a breath, shrugging. "It might be dumb, I just thought—"

"I love it," I blurt out, my eyes brimming with tears. I didn't even think he remembered what I told him about the tattoo, but once again, Aiden has proved me wrong.

"You do?" he asks, his brows lifting. A small grin appears on his face which makes me laugh.

I nod, closing up the box and wrapping my arms around him. "It's the sweetest thing anyone's ever done for me."

I hear his sharp exhale and he tightens his hold around me, pressing a kiss to my cheek. My stomach is twisting and turning and I never want this night to end.

When we pull back, the server is standing above us, holding up two plates. "Here you go," she says, chuckling as she places the plates in front of us. "Enjoy." She spins around, leaving us alone.

229

"This actually looks good." Aiden grabs his fork, picks up the risotto, and shoves it in his mouth. He groans, looking at me with wide eyes.

I laugh. "Good?"

He nods, picking up another forkful. "You wanna try?"

I lean in, loving how he smiles when I accept the food from him. I close my lips around the fork, my eyes rolling back when I swallow the risotto. "Damn, I should have gone with that."

He laughs, shaking his head. "Do you want to swap?"

"Really?"

He switches the plates, placing his risotto in front of me. "You should already know I'll give you anything you want." My heart races when he glances at me, a rush of emotions and warmth coat me, from my head to my toes. And when his thumb rubs against my cheek, looking at me with an admiration I can feel in my stomach, I know without a doubt that I'm falling in love with Aiden Pierce.

How did this happen? I promised I would never let myself fall for someone else. I told myself that no guy is worth the trouble and pain that is being in love. I thought I was in love with Jake, but what I felt for him was nothing close to what I feel for Aiden. It's completely different with him. Being with Aiden fills a hole in my heart that feels like it was empty for so long, filling it with contentment and comfort. We could be sitting on my couch talking about absolutely nothing and I feel at peace with him.

He lifts my chin with his finger and brings his lips to mine. I get lost in him whenever we kiss. No one else exists, no one's opinion matters and I imagine a world where I could be with Aiden. This kiss is soft and slow, like we have all night, and we do. We have the whole night to just pretend. Pretend that being his girlfriend is a possibility because when tomorrow comes, we'll be in the real world, with other people and their opinions, and it won't matter how well we fit together or how he makes me feel, I'll know it was never a possibility.

He pulls back and when I look into his eyes, I have this overwhelming urge to just blurt it out and tell him I love him, but I know better. I press my lips together, giving him an inconspicuous smile and pick up my fork, eating some of the risotto.

His hand disappears under the table, his fingertips running over my thigh. My breathing stops and when his hand travels higher on my leg, I force myself to swallow the food in my mouth, and glance up at him. "What are you doing?" My eyes scan the room to see if anyone can tell his hand is dangerously close to my panties.

"What?" he asks innocently, smirking. "I'm not doing anything." But his hands say something else as he trails his fingers higher and higher on my thighs, the tip of his middle finger brushing against my panties. I let out a heavy breath as the lightest brush of his fingers against my panties bring me pleasure.

"Fuck," he groans. "You're so responsive." Another brush against my panties, harder this time, pressing against my clit. "And so wet already," he whispers, running his finger along the damp underwear.

My hands grip his arm, pleading with him with my eyes, but my hips involuntarily scoot closer to his hand. *My body is a traitor.* "You want me to stop?" he asks, moving his hand back to my leg.

Hell no. I want his hands on me no matter how risky it may be. I reach underneath the table, moving his hand back into

231

place, letting out a breathy moan, biting my lip to stifle any noise when his fingers press against my clit.

His grin only turns me on that much more. "You're a little daredevil," he whispers, tracing my pussy over my underwear. "What if we get caught?" he teases, raising his eyebrow.

"I don't care."

He hums, moving the cloth to the side and runs his middle finger along my slit, covering it with my arousal. I spread my legs for him, allowing him to do whatever he wants with me.

"Wider. Let me feel how much you want me."

God, he's going to kill me, right here in front of these people. I do what he says though, opening myself wider for him, my eyes rolling to the back of my head when his thumb comes into play, rubbing circles against my clit.

I bite down on my lip, hard. "Aiden," I whisper, gripping his arm. "I can't keep quiet."

"Who said I'm going to let you come?" My eyes widen as I look up at him. His laughter makes his hand move against me, and I groan when it rubs against my sensitive, swollen clit. "I just want to tease you," he says. "A little preview for what's in store tonight."

"Can we leave right now?" I gasp when his finger penetrates me, fitting inside my wet center.

He shakes his head, pulling his finger out halfway and thrusting in again. My legs clamp shut around his arm, silently begging myself to keep it together. "We still have a dinner to get through," he says, thrusting in again.

A small moan escapes me, and my eyes widen, looking around the room. We're sitting pretty far back, so someone catching us is unlikely, but just the thought has me contracting around his finger, which makes him groan.

"I think you like the idea of someone catching you with my fingers stuffed in your cunt," he says, thrusting another finger along with the first. "You want them to know how much you want my cock right now?" He leans down to kiss my jaw. "How wet your pussy is for me?"

"Yes," I whisper, feeling the arousal build inside my stomach. Fuck, it feels so good.

He hums, pulling all the way out of me. "Can't let that happen," he murmurs. "Only I can know what you sound like when you're about to come." He licks his fingers clean, his eyes rolling to the back of his head. "And what you taste like."

My clit throbs harder, wanting—needing—his hands back on me. "Aiden," I whisper breathlessly.

"Eat your food, Leila," he says, picking up his fork, a mischievous grin on his lips. "You'll need the energy later."

27

Happy birthday

Aiden

I can't keep my hands off her.

I won't lie and say I've tried. I haven't. I don't want to. I want to keep touching her until all my senses are consumed with her and only her. Until I can think of nothing else but this beautiful girl beside me.

That Uber ride was pure agony, not being able to touch her the whole time, having to keep my hands to myself knowing that if I didn't, I'd be giving our poor driver a show he didn't bargain for.

The elevator barely shuts when I grip her waist and pull her back into me, laying a kiss on the top of her head. She drops her head onto my chest and my hands hold on to her hips, when I brush her hair to one side, pressing my lips against the small black ink I love on her.

"You owe me an orgasm," she says, looking over her shoulder at me when we walk out of the elevator.

I chuckle, grabbing hold of her hand and head down the hallway. "Don't worry, gorgeous. I'll make you come so many times, you won't even remember your name when I'm done with you."

Her breath hitches, lips parting slightly. I can't wait to be inside of her, but I also don't want to ruin the surprise, which is exactly why, as soon as the door shuts behind us, I grip her ass in my hands and lift her off the ground, wrapping her legs around me.

She gasps, pushing at my chest. "Aiden. Put me down."

"No fucking way." I love having her in my arms.

"I'm heavy."

I let out a snort. She clearly hasn't seen what I can do at the gym. "Leila, give me some credit. It's not my fault you were with weak-ass boys before me." I push through her bedroom door and drop her to her feet, turning her to face me so she doesn't see what's behind her just yet. My hands immediately grab her face, staring down at her, my thumb caressing her cheek as I look into my favorite pair of eyes.

I love you.

I want to tell her so bad. But knowing how reluctant she is on giving us a chance, I don't know how that would go down. I lean in instead and kiss her. I just want one more day with her. If this is going to end with her rejecting me and breaking this off, then I want one more chance to kiss her, to make love to her, to just hold her in my arms.

"Happy birthday." I twist her around and she gasps the minute she looks at her room. I wrap my arms around her from behind, bringing her back flush with my chest and rest my chin on top of her head.

Rose petals are scattered all over her bed, candles lit on her dresser and balloons resting on the ceiling. Damn, Gabi did a great job.

"What is this?" she asks, scanning the room. "How did you do this?"

I kiss the top of her head. "It's your birthday present." When I told her I'd make this night special, I wasn't lying. "And Gabi helped."

She turns around, brows knitted together. "Gabi?"

I shrug. "She already knows about us, right?"

A soft sigh leaves her lips which has me rethinking this whole decision. Does she hate it? "Aiden. I already told you I don't need all this big stuff."

I don't need it either. All I could ever need is her, sitting around and doing face masks or teaching her how to play basketball. It's all I will ever want, but what if Leila wants more? What if one day she wakes up and realizes I'm not enough for her? I will stop at nothing to make every one of her dreams and fantasies come true. No matter what it costs me.

"You didn't have to do this," she says.

I did. If I can't tell her how much I love her, I can at least show her. I run my thumb over her soft cheek. "Do you like it?"

She grins, wrapping her arms around my neck and presses her lips to mine. "I love it."

"Good." My hands grip her ass, pulling her into me. "Because I'm about to fuck every other guy out of your system." Hearing about her first time almost killed me. I want her to have a re-do, to have a night where she's not hiding and worrying about what she looks like and what the guy will think because I'm in love with every part of her and I'm also so attracted to her.

My lips press against her neck, every breathy moan from her making me rock hard. "Take off my shirt, gorgeous."

Her hands drift from my neck, unbuttoning every button one by one, agonizingly slow while her eyes lock on mine. "Fuck it." I rip the rest of my shirt off, buttons flying everywhere. I can't control myself when it comes to her, that much is obvious.

I walk us to the edge of the bed and sit her down on the edge. My belt goes next, those soft green eyes hooding with lust as she looks up at me. She licks her lips sending a jolt of lust shooting down my spine. Fuck, I want her so bad.

My hand trails down her face, my thumb brushing against her lower lip. Those juicy, pink lips open, wrapping around my thumb. Her tongue swirls around the skin, sucking my finger like she would my dick. That mouth of hers. Pulling my thumb out of her mouth, I grip her chin. "Take me out, Leila."

Her eyes never leave mine as she pulls my jeans off until I'm standing in my underwear.

Now it's her turn.

I lay her flat on the bed and her breath starts to quicken when I play with the hem of her dress. This fucking dress. It looks so good on her, hugging every one of those curves I love so much. It's been such a tease, this dress. It's made an absolute mockery of my self-control the past hour.

"Do you trust me?" I look her in the eyes, wanting her trust, needing it more than anything. "I want to see every inch of your beautiful body. I want to see all of you, but I need to know if you trust me."

Her heart beats with every move I make. I know how nervous she is, how much she struggles with exposing herself to someone. But I'm not just someone anymore. I want her to know that. Her lips part, letting out a shaky exhale and then she nods. That one small movement makes my heart skyrocket.

I lift the dress, slowly bunching it up in my hands as more and more of her skin is exposed. I swallow a groan. This woman is so sexy. Those thighs. It's criminal that I haven't had

237

my head buried between them yet. But not tonight. Tonight, I'm going to taste her, and show her what I've been dying to do to her.

I run my hands over the soft skin of her stomach. Every dip, every curve of her skin making me eager to see her. I lift the fabric higher and higher, until I pull it off her, revealing her to me.

Fuck. Me.

The material falls onto the ground when I take it completely off, and a low groan rumbles at the back of my throat as I stare down at her on the bed, looking like a wet dream. Her soft, tanned stomach exposed, her breasts covered by a black lacy bra, and those lacy panties completely drenched from the earlier teasing at the restaurant. I wanted to tease her, play with her, make her lose control but holy hell, I was so close to coming in my pants like a teenager that it was embarrassing.

I lift myself onto my elbows, looking down at her. "You're perfect." I admire her body, her golden skin in nothing but a flimsy piece of fabric. "Fucking perfect." I move down leaving a soft kiss on her stomach. Over and over again, I kiss the insecurities away, the harsh words of her mother, of other guys who didn't deserve her. I kiss all the hatred away and fill it with love.

I kiss my way up to her covered breasts. I can't wait to see all of her. My hands drift behind her back, unclasping her bra and pulling down the straps until the material drops. I drop my head to her chest. "I'm going to die." She laughs under me and I lift my head to look at her. "I'm serious." I tilt my head. "You're killing me."

She palms my back, running her soft fingertips over my skin. When her smile drops and her eyes widen, I know she feels some of the scars, her fingers running over the same marred piece of skin, examining it.

I don't give her time to say anything, I drop my head to her perky brown nipples, licking them, teasing her, driving her crazy. She starts to breathe heavy, her hips moving of their own accord. I palm one of her breasts, sucking her nipple into my mouth, wrapping my tongue around the hard bud. "So pretty," I murmur against her skin. "How wet are you, gorgeous?" I ask her, my hands drifting down her belly, getting closer to the sweet paradise between her legs.

"Bone dry."

I lift my head, seeing her lips pressed together. She laughs when I narrow my eyes at her, but the sound dies in her throat when I graze my fingers along the drenched material covering her pussy. "God," I groan, pulling the fabric to the side and slide my fingers along her slit. "You're soaked. I can't wait to eat you."

Her breathing turns heavy, her head lifting to look at me. "Aiden," she starts to protest, but I push her back down, covering her body with mine.

"You made me rush out of the restaurant to take care of this needy pussy," I whisper, running my fingers along her slick folds. "Now let me have my dessert."

I slide down her body, my knees pressing into the mattress as I grip her hips, pulling the hem of her underwear down her legs and throw it on the floor.

I stare at the spot between her legs, so wet, so ready for me. Fuck, I've been waiting for this moment for so long. I wrap my hands around her legs, spreading them wider making her completely exposed to me. Fuck. Yes.

"Aiden." My head snaps up, looking at Leila who's sat up, propped up on her elbows, looking down at me. "No one's ever… I've never…"

"I know." No one's ever seen her like this, no one's ever tasted her. But that's all about to change.

"Lie back." I press my lips against her thighs. "Let me show you what I've been dying to do to you."

Her head hits the mattress on a shaky breath when I leave an open-mouthed kiss on her inner thighs, barely touching her. This is going to be fun.

I press my lips to her thighs, my mouth getting closer to the place begging for me. When she groans, I give her what we both want and trace her folds with the tip of my tongue, letting it get coated in her arousal, the taste of her making me heady. It's too fucking good. I can't hold back anymore. I grip her hips, keeping her in place when a quick, hard lash of my tongue flicks her clit. She's so responsive to everything I do, but down here, where no one's ever been, after I spent the last half an hour teasing her, it's out of this world.

The desperate, filthy noises she makes when I devour her has me eating her with fervor, licking and sucking her clit into my mouth. She throws her head back as she grinds against my mouth, getting lost in the pleasure.

Another sweet little whimper escapes her when I lick her all the way to her entrance, her pussy contracting around the tip of my tongue as I stuff it in there. "I know baby," I murmur, attempting to soothe her, knowing how much I'm teasing her, driving her crazy, building up that pleasure inside of her. "You're okay." Her fingers bury themselves in my hair, wrapping around the short strands when I circle my middle finger around her sopping wet entrance, slipping it inside.

"Fuck," I groan when she starts grinding against my face again, trying to increase the friction. "That's it." I twirl my tongue around her clit. "Come on my tongue, Leila. Right now."

I wonder if she was holding back because as soon as the words come out of my mouth, she moans, loud enough to wake the dead, moving her hips against my face as I suck her into my mouth, the hot gush of liquid covering my finger and my face as she comes.

My dick scrapes against the mattress, letting her ride it out, ride my face until she's satisfied. I promised her I'd make her come until she couldn't remember her name, and that's what I plan on doing.

28

Mark me

Leila

"I'm not done with you yet," Aiden says, lifting off the bed. He brings his fingers that were just inside of me to his mouth, wrapping his lips around them and licking them clean. He lets out a low groan. "You tasted so good, gorgeous. Now my cock wants a taste."

His hands tug at his boxers, pulling them down until his huge erection bobs free, already so hard and leaking. "Lie back for me," he says, while stroking his dick, swiping a thumb over the tip.

I scoot back, lying flat and completely exposed to him. No one but Aiden has seen me this way, and even though I should be feeling self-conscious and trying to cover up, the way his eyes trace my body makes my core flutter with lust.

I watch as he walks over to my nightstand and grabs a condom, rips it open, and rolls it onto his cock. The candles glow behind him, making every move even hotter.

He approaches the edge of the bed again, and wraps his hand around my ankle, lifting my leg. "Hold your legs up," he instructs, lust coating his voice.

I do as he says, lifting my legs and holding them up in the air. I should feel so embarrassed being spread open like this, but the way Aiden's eyes darken, burning as he stares at all of me has me dissipating that embarrassment.

"Fuck," he groans, fisting his cock again. "Hold it right there and let me get to work." His knees hit the mattress, and he positions my legs onto his shoulders. I can't see much with him covering me and my legs up in the air, but I feel his dick nudge my entrance. He curses under his breath when he starts to push in.

I don't think I've ever been this wet in my life which makes it a ton easier for him to slide inside of me. He stops halfway, allowing me to stretch around him, He gruffs out a breath once he knows I've adjusted, and pushes all the way in. The moan I let out is anything but attractive, it's rough and dirty, desperate for him. His dick is so long and thick, fills me up so good.

"Shh," he soothes, not moving inside of me. I shake my head, attempting to move my hips so I feel some sort of friction. "Stay still," he warns, his hands firm on my hips. "Fuck, just let me feel you for a bit."

I squeeze my eyes shut, the feel of him inside me building a need so strong I can't take it anymore. "Aiden," I whimper. "I need you to move."

His hands grip my hips as he slides out and slams back inside of me with force. Yes. Fuck yes. "So fucking tight," he grits out. His hands roam all over my body, feeling every ridge of my rolls, touching all over my stomach, making his way to my tits. He grunts, speeding up his movements. "You squeeze me so good."

My hands run all over his shoulders and his back. Scars. I felt them. I've never seen them though. He's always behind me when we have sex, I've never been able to touch him, but today I am and I felt scars on his skin.

I shake the thought away and move my hips, wanting him deeper. It's not physically possible, he'll rip me in half. Somehow, he understands what I need and leans forward, my legs painfully straight on his shoulders as he thrusts all the way to the hilt forcing a moan out of me.

The feeling is so intense, so consuming that I squeeze my eyes shut, my nails clawing at his back until he groans. "Oh, fuck yes. Mark me so everyone knows I'm yours."

I let out a whimper at his words. We didn't really talk about what would happen once tonight was over. He wants something I don't know I can give him, no matter how much I want to.

I open my eyes, lifting my head. "You're so deep." My eyes drop to where we're connected.

"You want to see, baby?" he asks, pulling back and lowering my legs, wrapping them around his waist. He stares down at where his dick is thrusting in and out of me. "You want to see how good we look together?" He pulls out all the way, slowly pushing back in. "You feel so good," he groans. "So fucking good."

I shake my head, the pleasure building in my core with every thrust. "I don't remember it ever being this good," I cry out.

"That's because it's me," he says, grunting when he thrusts in again. "Because it's us."

Yes. I throw my head back and let myself get lost in him as the orgasm bursts through me.

"Oh shit, that's going to make me come, Leila." He speeds up, pounding into me, ripping away the last shred of control I had. He lets out a grunt when he comes, thrusting fast and deep until he's completely drained.

He doesn't pull out of me; he just leans in and presses his lips against mine, soft and slow while his hips thrust lazily, matching his kisses.

We didn't just fuck. Whatever just happened... we just made love.

29

There is no competition

Leila

"You want one?" Rosie asks, pulling out a croissant from a brown paper bag.

My stomach churns when I turn my head away. I *can't* eat. Just knowing that the issue where I'm standing in a swimsuit is out makes me lose my appetite.

It wasn't supposed to come out yet. I had another two weeks to prepare. I need those two weeks. I'm not ready.

"Are you ok?" she asks, furrowing her brows.

I haven't told her. I haven't told anyone. I didn't even know it was out until I saw a text from Amina this morning congratulating me, telling me we look amazing. I need some of what she has, some of that takes no bullshit from anyone attitude. It doesn't matter how many times I try to act like that on the exterior, trying to keep everyone at a distance, it changes nothing about how I feel on the inside.

"I'm good," I tell her, chewing on the inside of my cheek. "Just tired."

"We could hang out at Grayson's tonight if you want?" she offers. "Face masks, some snacks, and just talk."

"That's okay. I'm busy tonight." *Throwing up from stress. Big plans.*

"Are you sure?" She glances at me. "Aiden will probably be there."

My eyes snap towards hers. She munches on the croissant, but I can see a hint of a smirk on her lips. "What do you mean?"

"I saw you coming out of his room." She smiles at me sheepishly. "I went to get a glass of water around three in the morning after we… I woke up." I can't help but laugh when her cheeks tint with red. "And I saw you open the front door." She takes another bite of her croissant. "I was waiting for you to tell me yourself… but you never did."

That was months ago. "I'm sorry." My steps slow when I let out a sigh. "I wanted to keep it a secret," I tell her, lifting my shoulders in a shrug. "I didn't tell anyone."

"So no one knows?"

"Gabi knows."

Her brows knit together. "Gabi?"

I nod, scoffing at the reminder of how she found out. "She kind of walked in on us leaving the bathroom together."

She places half of her eaten croissant back into the bag. "So what does this mean? Are you guys dating?"

I shake my head before I even consider it. It's been three days since Aiden told me he wanted more and took me on a date. Three days since I realized I'm in love with him. And I haven't seen him.

I can't tell him what he wants to hear. I don't think I ever will. "That's not going to happen."

"Why not?" I glance at her, not daring to say anything else. She knows why. She was there. "Oh. Right." She swallows. "Jake."

Yeah, him. I let out a sigh. "I told myself I wouldn't let it happen again, but it's gotten a little… complicated."

"What do you mean?" The smile on my face is more than enough of an answer, which Rosie catches on to, stopping in her tracks, and grinning at me. A smile so wide I'm scared for her jaw. "You love him," she announces, everyone within a mile radius hearing her.

"Shhh." I glance around. "God, can't you keep a secret?"

She chuckles. "This is big news. You love him," she says again, unable to stop smiling. "So why aren't you guys dating?"

"It's not that simple, Rosie. I didn't want this to happen." I let out a groan. It's the last thing I could want and the best thing that has ever happened to me.

She smirks, glancing at me. "So are the rumors true?"

"What?"

She grins, holding out her hands about nine inches apart. My eyes widen when I catch on, bending over in laughter. "Oh my god." I shake my head. "Grayson has ruined you."

She drops her hands, laughing along with me. "That's a yes."

My eyebrow lifts. "That's a hell yes."

She gulps, eyes widening, which makes me laugh even more. She shakes her head. "I've got to go to class." She stuffs the croissants in her bag, waving goodbye.

The door of the café slides open when someone walks out and I head inside, approaching the counter to order my daily green smoothie when I hear laughter. Not just any laughter. I've heard it before. The cocky, bitchy laugh that girls do when they're making fun of you. Just the sound makes my skin prick with goosebumps when I look around, the noise haunting me from the years of modeling with other thin girls who acted like my body was a joke to them.

"I'm not lying. I saw them together at Vio last week." I stare at the counter in front of me, my ears perking and my heart racing when the name of the restaurant Aiden took me to comes up in conversation.

"Aiden Pierce doesn't go out with girls like her," another girl says. "There's no way they're sleeping together. They're just friends."

"I'm surprised she even fit on the page." My stomach drops when they laugh and I turn around, spotting three girls huddled together, the one in the middle holding a magazine. The magazine I'm on. Their eyes land on mine and the laughing stops, their faces visibly blanching. It doesn't matter how many times I've been through this, how many times I've heard comments just like it, it hurts every time.

"Hello, what can I get you?" I turn around, staring at the barista who's smiling at me. I don't even respond, I turn around and push through the door, walking out of the café trying not to fall and break down in front of a bunch of strangers.

I don't even know where I'm going. I just walk, my vision blurring as the tears threaten to drop. Why is it so much easier to focus on the negative over the positive? I've spent the whole morning on the post looking at comments and saw so many nice ones, so many supporting girls loving the diversity in the different body types. So why is it that one comment from a few girls has me rethinking everything?

"Hey." When I look up, Aiden's walking towards me with a grin on his face. I forgot how good his presence is. I almost forgot how he makes me feel when we're together. The settling feeling washes over me the closer he approaches, until he's right in front of me, reaching to cup my face.

249

My eyes widen when I realize he's about to kiss me and I take a step back, scanning the surrounding area. There are too many people here, people who know Aiden. This is not a good idea. His frown makes my stomach drop and I force myself to say, "We're in public."

I twist around and walk over behind one of the buildings. "Where the hell are you going?" he asks. I don't answer, I just keep walking until I'm certain no one can see us. His hand wraps around my wrist, halting me. "Talk to me, Leila. Stop running away and tell me why you're so hellbent on keeping this a secret." His frown deepens when I pull away from his touch and cross my arms, my heart pounding against my chest. "I thought we talked about this," he says, looking down at me, disappointed.

The problem was, we didn't talk about anything. We had one special night where I let myself pretend this could happen, but then I remembered it couldn't. "You talked," I tell him. "I said I couldn't do this."

He shakes his head, perplexed by how cold I'm being. I have to be. I can't give him false expectations, letting him wait around until I'm ready because I never will be. "What are you talking about?" he asks. "What the hell changed since a few days ago? On your birthday you said—"

"I lied." His mouth closes when I interrupt before he can give me a rundown of what I said that night. I know what I said, and I meant every word, but that was before I remembered how different Aiden and I are. "I didn't mean it," I lie, my heart breaking with every word. "I don't think this is a good idea, Aiden. We're not fit for each other."

"What the hell does that mean?" He stalks over to me, but when I take a step back, he freezes, letting out a harsh sigh. "Is this about my family?"

My eyes squeeze shut. Please, don't make this any harder than it has to be. "No," I tell him honestly. "I told you I don't care about that." His family have nothing to do with why I can't be with Aiden. This is all on me.

"Then what?" he asks, desperately. "What are you saying right now because you're breaking my fucking heart here, Leila?"

God. My heart aches when his voice cracks saying my name. I love him. I wish everything was different. "You don't like me like that, Aiden, you're just deluded. You like the sex or maybe it's just out of pity." I shrug. "I don't know. I just think we need to cool it." My throat burns when I spit out the next words. "I think we should—"

"Do not say see other people," he warns. "I thought I made it perfectly clear no one fucking touches you but me."

I don't want anyone else to touch me. I don't want anyone else to kiss me. I just want him. "I don't want to do this anymore," I tell him, dropping my eyes to the ground beneath us. I hate that I have to do this.

His thumb lifts my chin, the small amount of contact making my stomach flutter. When I lift my head and look into those blue eyes of his, my heart stops. I love him so much. "What happened?" he asks. "Just tell me."

I let out a bitter laugh. "What happened?" I repeat. "Look around, Aiden. I'm a joke. You're the king of Redfield. Did you honestly think it was going to go any other way than this? No one will get it. I barely do."

"You don't get what?"

"Why you want me," I yell back at him, wanting him to get it, to get what everyone else will think if they see us together. "Why you even looked at me when you can have any girl you want."

"I don't want any other girl," he yells, taking a step closer to me. "I want…" he closes his eyes, running a hand down his face. "Fuck, I just want you, Leila."

My lips press together as I shake my head. "Every girl in this school wants you," I tell him. "I can't compete with that."

"There is no competition," he says, taking a step closer. "You win every time."

His words make me press my lips together, my heart beating right out of my chest, so fast, so hard. "What we have works in private, Aiden. It doesn't work in public."

"Don't give me that bullshit. This has nothing to do with other people. This is between you and me. No one else," he says, stepping closer to me. "Just us."

"It's not just us," I say, gulping when I look at him. "Everyone will talk. You'll be ruined if people find out we're together." I let out a sigh, wanting him to understand. "They'll joke and give you shit for it. There's a reason they all want to keep it a secret." I throw my hands up. "God, even your teamma—" My lips press together when I realize I've said too much.

His eyes widen. "Repeat that for me," he says. "My teammate?" I let out a sigh, and when I don't answer, he asks, "Who, Leila?"

"You told me you didn't need names."

His brows rise even more. "If they said something to make you believe being with you should be kept secret, then hell yes I want their names."

"It doesn't matter, Aiden."

He doesn't buy it though. "Just tell me what happened," he says. "No names. Just tell me what they said."

My stomach drops. "I don't want to talk about this."

I try to push past him but he stops me, looking down at me. "Tell me."

I swallow, licking my dry lips knowing I'm about to break both of our hearts for repeating this but he needs to understand why I can't be with him. "Freshman year of college I was at a party and I saw him in the corner, alone and I approached him. I flirted, he kissed me and took me back to his place." I'm zooming past the information not wanting to dwell on it too much.

"He kept his hand on my mouth the whole time so I wouldn't make noise." I still remember how he kept telling me to 'shut the fuck up,' pressing his hand to my mouth so hard it was painful. "He told me to leave through the back exit and to never look at him in public."

Aiden's eyes darken and I can feel the anger brewing inside of him. "I'm going to kill him. Who the fuck said that?"

"You said no names."

"I take it back."

"Well, you can't. He wasn't the only one. Why you don't understand? This is what they do."

"I'm not them," he says. "I am not some silly little boy who needs validation from other guys about who I'm dating." He shakes his head. "I told you I don't give a shit what they think of me. I might have done once upon a time, but now…" His eyes bore into me. It feels like he's staring into my soul, seeing all of my bad parts and still wanting them. "I only care what

253

you think of me," he whispers, his throat bobbing. "So tell me, Leila. What do you think of me? Are you embarrassed of me?"

I sigh, closing my eyes. "No."

"Are you not attracted to me anymore, is that it?"

"No."

"Then what is it?" he asks again. I drop my head, feeling a tear roll down my cheek. His hands are on me again, pulling my chin up and before I know it, his lips are on mine, pressing a soft kiss to them, once, twice. "Nothing they say matters to me."

It might not right now, but how long will he last when all he hears are jokes and realizes he wants someone else? "I want some space," I mutter so quietly I don't think he heard me.

"Space," he repeats. "From me?" When I nod, his face shatters. "Right," he says, taking a step back from me.

"You have too much going for you to mess it up on a silly mistake."

He glances at me, shaking his head. "I would give it all up if it meant I could have you." My god, this man is breaking my heart. "You could never be a mistake."

30

Leila

"You could never be a mistake." Those words haven't left my head since I walked away and left Aiden standing there behind an old building, all alone. It destroyed me leaving him there, telling him I couldn't be with him when it's all I want.

He's been calling me nonstop, texting me that he wants to talk. But there's nothing else to talk about. What Aiden and I had was great when there were no feelings and no one else knew. But now that I'm in love with him and he wants more… it changes everything.

I let out a breath of relief when the door knocks, knowing Rosie is here. I told the girls about Aiden. Since two out of three already knew, one more wouldn't matter. Not when nothing would come of it anyway, but I needed my girls. I needed to talk and vent and just have someone that would help me forget about Aiden.

But when I open the door, Rosalie is not standing on the other side of it. Aiden is.

He steps back from the door and smiles when he sees me. The sight alone makes me want to ball up and cry, because it's not his usual smile. He's not grinning like he did when we first met. This smile is calculated, small and unsure, and his usually sparkling blue eyes seem dull… sad. I hate that I've done that.

He's so handsome. His hands are tucked in his pockets, and he's not wearing a cap this time. I love his hair, love when it's long, love when it's short. I just love him.

He visibly swallows, his Adam's apple bobbing when he gestures to my apartment. "Can I come in?" he asks when I don't say anything.

"Yeah." I open the door wider, stepping out of the way so he can walk inside. I close the door, pressing myself against it. I don't know what to do with my hands. I'm so nervous. I don't want to have this conversation again. I don't even know why he's here after last time.

I lift myself off the door, head towards the couch, sit down and stare at my hands—I still don't know what to do with them—fidgeting with the hem of my sweater. When I feel the couch dip beside me, my heart starts to race and the next thing I know, his hand covers mine, settling me.

"Will you look at me?"

I turn my head, staring at his beautiful blue eyes. He lets out a breath, and that's when I notice what's in his other hand.

He looks down, grabs the folded jersey and places it on the coffee table. The 23 on the back of it making me realize what's happening. He reaches into his jean pocket and pulls out a ticket, placing it next to the folded jersey. "I've been thinking a lot about what you said. About us." I pull my gaze to him, his frown creating a line in his forehead that I want to smooth out. "I can't make you change your mind if you don't want to be with me."

He twists on the couch, grabbing hold of both my hands. "But I want to be with you," he says, my heart racing with every word. "I want you to be my girlfriend. The hiding and sneaking around... it was enough for me before. I didn't want a relationship. Basketball was always too important to mess it up with a distraction. But you're not a distraction. You're my calm through the storm. You're the one person I want to be with when I feel my worst."

His eyes scan my face. "I've been on my own for most of my life," he continues. "I've never had a home or a family... but you're starting to feel like the closest thing to it."

I don't say anything, even though my heart is racing in my chest, no words seem to come out as I stare at the man in front of me, saying everything I've ever wanted to hear. "I thought the idea of us being friends was laughable when we started this. But you've somehow become my best friend." My god, this man is going to destroy me. "And I want to be with you." He sighs, shaking his head. "I want everything with you."

I swallow, licking my lips unable to take my eyes off him. his thumb sweeps over my hand. "I have a game tomorrow," he says. "I know you come to most of them, but this one's different." He lets go of my hands and grabs the jersey, holding it in front of me. "I want you to wear this," he says, placing the jersey in my hands. "I want you to come tomorrow and wear this jersey with my name on it for everyone to see." My heart's racing so fast I'm sure he can hear it. "If I see you there, and you wear this, then I'll know you want to be mine. But if you don't..." he blows out a breath. "If you don't, then I won't ever bother you again. I promise."

No.

"I can't do the casual thing with you anymore, Leila." He stands up from the couch and my eyes follow watching his large figure walk towards the door. He turns right before he reaches the door and the look in his eyes is so painful it buries itself in

257

my chest. "Congrats on the magazine issue by the way. You look beautiful." He smiles at me. "You always look beautiful."

I want to run to him, I want to stop him and wrap my arms around him. I want to tell him I change my mind. I want to be with him. I need to be with him, but I don't. I let him walk out the door.

31

Game time

Aiden

She's not here.

I really thought she'd be here. I gave her the ticket. I gave her the jersey. I gave her my fucking heart. What more could I give her?

I slow down my steps, blowing out a breath when I glance to the bleachers again where her seat is empty.

"Pierce." I snap my head to the right where Coach is angry as hell, throwing his arms up. "What the hell are you doing?" *Having a breakdown, that's what.*

"C'mon, Pierce. Move your ass," Carter calls out.

This is one of the most important games and I'm blowing it. I lift my head and see a guy from the opposing team racing towards me. My eyes drop to the ball in his hands and when he tries to move, I steal, grabbing the ball when it bounces behind him. I run towards the net, a nudge hits my shoulder and I twist, making sure he doesn't catch it.

"What the hell are you waiting for?" Jordan calls out from the side. "Shoot."

I spin on my heels, and shoot watching the ball fly through the air until it hits the backboard, bouncing down to the ground. Shit.

My ears grow heavy with the groans and booing in the place, weighing me down like a ton of bricks. What is wrong with me? That was an easy shot. I should have made it. I drop my head down, wiping the sweat off my forehead.

"What's going on with you, man?" Jordan asks.

"Nothing." I instinctively glance over at the seat which is still empty. She's really not coming, is she? I really thought she'd change her mind about us, that she'd see how good we are together and want to be with me as much as I want to be with her.

But that's not happening.

"Who are you looking for?" Jordan asks.

I narrow my eyes at him. "None of your business." Is it him? Is Jordan the guy Leila hooked up with on my team? It could be any one of them. And I have no clue. One of these guys kissed my girl, touched her and told her to be quiet, treating her like a dirty little secret.

"Jeez, Cap." Jordan's face contorts. "Calm down."

I blow out a breath and when the whistle blows my shoulders relax, heading towards the bench. Coach holds out a bottle of water to me, and I take it from him, downing half of it. I look up at the bleachers once again. I really need to stop doing that. She's not coming. I need to accept that.

"Are you out of your mind?" Ethan yells, throwing his arms up in the air. "You're costing us the game because of some pussy."

My ears burn when I turn around and narrow my eyes at him, stalking towards of him. "Don't fucking talk about her." Did this asshole touch my girl?

He scoffs. "I knew it was because of a girl." I grunt, grabbing his jersey.

260

"Pierce!" Coach's voice runs through me. "Back off. Do I need to bench you?"

I drop his jersey, Ethan scowling at me. "No, Coach." I blow out a breath. "It won't happen again."

"No girl is worth losing the game," Jordan says, nudging me on the arm.

"Jordan's right," Carter says. "You need to focus."

I know. I run a hand down my face. "I'm trying. Just lay off."

When the whistle blows again, letting us know time out is over I shake my head, jogging in place. Leila isn't coming. I need to focus on the game.

That's all I have left.

32

Let's go home, baby

Leila

I'm late.

I spent so long debating on whether I should go that I'm late. I have never missed one of Aiden's games. Not one. And now this one is the most important one; this one means everything and I'm not there.

When I push open the doors and the noises of the crowd fills my senses I start to panic, my heart racing as I stare at all these people who are going to know I'm dating Aiden. I glance down at the jersey on my body, the one with his name on it, the one that tells him I want to be his.

I lick my lips, swallowing down every emotion brewing inside of me and turn around. "What if he breaks my heart?"

Madeline's eyebrows lift. "You haven't even given the guy a chance to date you yet and you're already thinking of how it's going to end?"

"He's going to get drafted, Madi. We both know it. And he's not going to want me around when he can have his pick of every girl he could ever want."

Madi's eyebrows soften, grabbing onto my hand. "I love you, Leila. You are beautiful. You are perfect and Aiden knows it."

"For now."

"Look around," Gabi says. "He can have his pick of any girl right here, Leila, but he wants you. No one else. You."

Why? The question remains itself in my mind. "But what if…"

"Jake did a lot of things to you," Rosie interrupts. "But the worst thing he's done is make you believe you don't deserve love." My throat constricts at her words. Her eyes soften, holding onto my hand. "Jake was an asshole, Leila, but Aiden is nothing like him."

"If you want to be with him, then stop thinking of all the bad things that could happen and be happy for once," Madi says. "Make both of you happy and get in that seat."

I turn to look at her and laugh. She's got a point. I've been so focused on everything that could go wrong, I didn't even stop to think of how happy he's made me already.

I lean in, kissing her cheek. "I love you."

"Love you too." She smiles, pushing at my shoulder. "Now go get your man."

Yes, ma'am.

I make my way through the crowd to the seat he saved for me, right in the middle where I can see him on the court. I sit down, my hands sweating as I clutch at the material of the jersey with his name on the back. I try to watch the game, I love basketball, but right now I don't care about anything other than Aiden. He's still not looking up and I just want so desperately for him to lift his head and look at me.

Don't give up on me. I'm here. I'm right here.

I've always admired the way he moves on the court, handling every other guy there in a way I've never seen before. His shoulders slump when he loses the ball and my eyes scan the shape of his lips as he mumbles a curse. He runs his hand through his hair and glances up at the seat.

When his eyes lock with mine, my heart starts to race. His hand stops halfway in his hair, gripping it as his eyes widen. *God, I love him.* Why did I ever think about this? The choice was so obvious.

"Hi," I mouth smiling at him.

He shakes his head, blinks twice. My lips tip up, smirking as he tries to see if I'm really here. His eyes drop to the jersey on my body, the one he gave me. The minute he sees what I'm wearing he drops his hands, a massive grin exploding on his face. My poor heart is not going to survive this. I don't think I've ever seen this man as happy as he is right now. A laugh bubbles out of me when he throws me a wink, running towards the ball. The girls smile at me when I turn to look at them, Gabi though, is in her own little world, munching away on some popcorn as she shouts at the ref.

When I turn, my eyes stay locked on my soon to be boyfriend. Those words. Boyfriend. I haven't had a boyfriend since Jake and the thought of announcing to everyone that Aiden is mine makes my palms sweat. But as soon as I lock eyes with Aiden again, his smile makes all worries go away.

He grins at me, and then turns, stealing the ball and shooting. My eyes stay trained on the ball flying through the air, rimming the hoop once, twice before it sinks.

"Hell yes," I yell. The crowd goes wild, everyone around me standing up and cheering. Redfield's team crowds Aiden, hugging him but Aiden's eyes are on me as he taps his teammates shoulders, trying to get out of there.

My feet are stuck. I don't know whether to move and go to him or stay here. He rushes out of the court, heading up the bleachers. My heart races as I watch him come to me, moving past the mass amount of people trying to hug him or talk to him. He doesn't see anyone but me.

When he finally approaches me, his eyes locked on mine, he lets out a breath and smiles. "Hi."

"Hi," I whisper back. I don't know why I'm so nervous. No, scratch that, I know exactly why. Because this, this right here is going to change everything. No more hiding and sneaking around. It's going to be official.

He smiles. "You came."

"I did."

His smile drops a little. "I thought you bailed. I didn't see you earlier."

"I was late, I'm sorry." My stomach churns knowing I hurt him by making him think I wasn't coming when I know with everything inside of me that I want to be with him.

He shakes his head. "Don't you dare apologize." His hand grips my waist, his eyes dropping to the jersey on my body. "You're here. And you're wearing my jersey."

"I am."

He grins, laughs a little. "Remember when I said I'd love to see you cheering me on with pom-poms?" he asks, lifting his brows.

I narrow my eyes at him. "Do you want me to take this off?"

He drops his smile. "No. Fuck no." He lets out a content sigh and brings his forehead to mine. "Does this mean you're my girlfriend?" he asks, desperately.

I nod, pulling back and looking into his eyes. "Yes."

His gaze drops to my lips and I think he's going to kiss me but he swallows instead. "Everyone's going to know we're together," he whispers. Those big hands of his cup my face, running a thumb over my bottom lip. "Are you ready for that?"

More than anything. "You're going to ruin me," I say instead.

"You already have." He pulls me into him and crashes his lips to mine. A rush of gasps and murmur break out around us but I don't focus on them. I focus on my boyfriend, the way his lips feel against mine, how he lets out a groan when I brush my tongue against his. How his other hand grips my ass as he kisses me in front of everyone.

He pulls back and smiles. "Does this mean I get to call you baby now?" he asks with a grin on his lips.

I roll my eyes. "So cocky."

"I can't help it," he says shaking his head. "I just won the fucking lottery."

I lift on my tiptoes, leaning into him and leaving a soft kiss against his lips. "Take me home, boyfriend."

He shivers, his eyes darkening as he tightens his hold on me. "Holy fuck, say that again." I smile, laughing against his chest. He kisses the top of my head and grabs my hand in his. "Let's go home, *baby*."

I shake my head. What an asshole. How unfortunate that I still love him.

All the way

Aiden

This poisonous candy that tastes like crap should be illegal, but if it makes my girlfriend happy then so be it.

When I push open the door to her apartment, she's on the couch, snuggled up with a blanket up to her neck. She looks so adorable. It takes her a minute to realize I'm here and when she does, she smiles at me.

Jesus. Fuck. Prettiest sight I've ever been lucky enough to see. I remember when she wouldn't even smile at me, I remember when just the roll of her eyes would have me grinning—it still does—but now that beautiful smile is my favorite thing ever.

"Hey, gorgeous." I shut the door behind me, letting out an oomph when she attacks me, wrapping her arms around me. "Jesus," I wheeze. "I've been gone two days."

She shakes her head. "Way too long."

I agree. Going to Boston for a game was fun, even better when we won, but knowing Leila wouldn't be there, when she's usually at all my games put a downer on the whole experience. I couldn't wait to go back to my hotel room and call her, which ended in us having amazing phone sex as my congratulations. It made winning all that much sweeter.

I pull back, cupping her face in my hand and staring into those lime green eyes that I fell in love with. "Hi."

"Hi," she whispers back, leaning in for a kiss. Her lips brush against mine and I squeeze her waist, pulling her into me. Missed her. She flinches when a crinkling noise startles her and I laugh, pulling back and holding out her favorite—albeit disgusting—candy.

"Got you something." She narrows her eyes at me but I ignore it, holding it out to her. She gives up, letting out a sigh and takes it from me. I don't know how many times I'll have to prove to her that I can take care of her. I hate that she worries about my financial situation. I don't want it to be a burden on us. I'll gladly go completely broke and take whatever bullshit my brothers give me, if it means she'll be happy and taken care of. I'll do anything for this girl.

She flips the package, scanning along the back. My brows furrow, letting out a laugh. "What are you doing?" It doesn't take me long to figure it out which makes my smile fall. "Fuck no." I grab the package from her, watching as her eyes widen at me. "None of that."

I'll be damned if I let her look at calories or care about any of that shit. I rip open the package, walking over to the kitchen and drop it in a bowl, throwing the package away in the trash. "There," I tell her, pushing the bowl towards her. "Now you can eat whatever you want without worrying about how many calories is in it."

Her cheeks blush, a tint of red coating them when she realizes I noticed what she was doing. I'll spend the rest of my life telling her and showing her that she's the most beautiful woman to me. She takes a couple out of the bowl, dropping it in her mouth and I smile, rubbing my jaw, my eyes dropping to her figure, curvy and soft just how I fucking like her. "Have you eaten today?"

She rolls her eyes. It still manages to make me hard. "Yes," she replies.

"What did you have?" I ask her.

She laughs. "Really?" I cross my arms, raising an eyebrow, waiting for her answer. She finally gives in, letting out a sigh. "I had a baked potato with cheese and broccoli." She presses her lips together giving me an annoyed smile. Don't care. It's still a smile.

I grin, walking over to her and lean in, pressing my lips to hers. "Good girl. Glad to see you're taking care of yourself." My eyes drop to the shirt she's wearing... my shirt. "Is that mine?" I ask her, lifting the hem of my dark red t-shirt.

She eyes me. "I missed you."

I let out a laugh, my stomach fluttering. "Feel free to wear all my clothes," I tell her, burying my face in her neck, pressing my lips against her skin. "Every last one of them." I love seeing her wear my shirt.

"You smell good," she murmurs against me. My body breaks out into goosebumps when I feel her hands on my chest over my t-shirt. Love her. "Did you just come from the gym?"

"Yeah," I reply, wrapping my arms around her waist. "Coach has been busting my ass." After the game I threw at the start of the season, he's been watching me, making sure I don't make any more mistakes like that.

"It's okay," she coos. "You just need more practice. Not all of us can be as good as me," she teases.

I grin, looking down at her gorgeous face. I'm so gone for this girl. So fucking gone. Can't believe it's already been over two weeks since she agreed to be mine. "Really? Want a rematch?" I ask her, lifting a brow. "Last time I remembered, you flinched when I threw the ball at you."

She scrunches her nose, shaking her head. "I've changed."

I laugh. "You have?"

She nods. "Yeah. I have a boyfriend now."

I'll never get sick of hearing her say that. From the commitment-phobe herself, it's the best feeling in the world knowing she wants me.

"You do?" I tighten my hold on her waist, running my hands over her hips. She nods, her lips tipping up in a smile. "And what would he say if he caught you with me?"

She grins, mischievously. "He wouldn't like that."

"No?"

She shakes her head, standing up on her tiptoes until she's right in front of me. "He said no one touches me but him."

I let out a groan. "That's fucking right." I bring my lips to hers, kissing my girlfriend. "Missed you," I murmur between kisses.

"Missed you." She pulls back to take a breath, her hands gripping my hair. "You look so handsome."

My god I love her. I want to say it all the fucking time. Is it too early? It's probably too early. Definitely. I kiss her again instead, the words stuffed in the back of my throat threatening to come out.

"I wish I knew you were coming," she mumbles into the kiss. "I would have put on some makeup or something."

I frown, pulling back. "Don't do that."

"Do what?"

"Act like you don't know you're the most beautiful girl I have ever seen." Her eyes soften and she shakes her head but before she can try to deny it, I interrupt her. "I've seen you with your face painted green, Leila. I've seen you in pajamas, in little shorts, in underwear, in nothing. And every version is just as fucking gorgeous as the next."

Her lips part and I really wish I knew what she was thinking. I brush her chocolate brown hair behind her ear, running my thumb over her face. "You want me to compliment you?" I lean in, pressing my lips to her cheek. "You're sexy."

She groans. "Ugh, I hate that word."

I chuckle, leaning down to leave a kiss on her other cheek. "You're hot."

"Nope."

I pull back, my lips twitching. "You're picky."

Her eyebrow raises. "Is that supposed to be a compliment?"

I shake my head, laughing. "How about this? You." I kiss her cheek. "Are." I kiss her jaw. "So." I leave a hot kiss on her lips. "Fucking beautiful."

Her breathing picks up, her chest rising. "Better," she grits out.

"You're a hard woman to please." I kiss her one more time. "Luckily I love pleasing you."

"Yeah?" she says lust coating her eyes. "How much?"

"So much, baby." Being a boyfriend is so cool. There are so many boyfriend privileges. Like calling her sappy nicknames she claims to hate but secretly loves, like being able to kiss her whenever I want, and being able to tell everyone I have a girlfriend. It's the best and I'm glad I didn't have it with anyone before her.

I grab her hand and rush us to the bedroom. The minute the door shuts, I peel my shirt over my head, dropping it to the floor. Her eyes eat me up and I love it every time. "I want it

271

off," I grit out, grabbing the hem of my shirt that looks better on her than it ever did on me. "All of it."

She rips the shirt off and I groan when I see she isn't wearing a bra. Her pants go next, leaving her standing in her room in nothing but a pair of gray, cotton panties. I let out a groan when I see her gray panties with a dark, wet patch. And then they go next.

I grab her waist and pull her into me, laughing when she yelps. She might have an attitude when we're in public, but she loves letting me control her in the bedroom. I slam my mouth against hers, her tongue sliding against mine, tasting me, a moan rumbling out of her. Feels so good.

"Get on the bed, Leila." I don't even recognize my voice, it's thick and gravelly, consumed with lust. She sits on the edge and I part her legs, teasing her entrance with my middle finger. "So wet."

I lay her back, spreading her legs even wider and lean in, my tongue finds her swollen clit and I flick it until she moans, dropping her head back. I lap her up like she's my favorite meal, my tongue teasing her. She's so sensitive, it doesn't take me long until she's shaking and grinding against my face, coming all over my tongue.

I pull back when she's spent and wipe my chin, grinning at the sight of her spread open and wet for me. My boxers find themselves on the floor, and when she looks at my dick, licking her lips, I groan. I want her mouth on me, but there's something I want more.

There's one thing we haven't done yet that I'm dying to, so when she starts to scoot back, I shake my head and pull her off the bed, taking her place instead. Her lips part when I wrap my fingers around my cock and give it a slow, hard stroke, the pleasure curling up my spine. "Get up here."

"Aiden." Her eyes widen when she realizes what I want her to do. "I'll crush you."

I snort. "Not even close."

"Aiden," she says again, shaking her head.

I know her insecurities must be rambling away in that pretty head of hers, but nothing is sexier than the image of Leila impaled on my cock. "I want you to ride me." A hot breath leaves me when I watch her tongue run over her bottom lip, staring at my hand over my cock. So hot.

Uncertainty floods her eyes but when she sees how bad I want her, how much I need her, she walks over, climbing on the bed.

Yes.

She lifts her leg, straddling me on the bed, wrapping her arms around my neck and kisses me. The tip of my cock nudges her pussy, and she moans into my mouth, lowering herself and grinding her clit against my dick. Oh fuck. I pull back, both of us looking down at where she's coating my dick with her wetness. Jesus. "Sit on my cock, Leila."

She stares at me, pulling her bottom lip between her teeth and then lifts onto her knees, settling above me, positioning us so we align just perfectly. And then she starts to lower down. I let out a harsh breath, clutching her hips and helping her move. Holy fuck, she feels so good. So tight. So hot. So fucking wet. Her arousal coats the tip of my cock, gripping it inside of her. Why does she feel this good? How does she—

"Oh fuck." I grip her hips in place so she doesn't move. "Condom," I grit out.

She gasps, looking down at where she's impaled on my cock. She glances up at me and shakes her head. "I've never…"

"I know." She's never had sex without a condom. "Me either," I assure her. "My last test was negative."

Her eyes drop again. "Me too." She grinds her hips forward, providing glorious friction. I let out a moan, gripping her hips in place but it's impossible when she whimpers, doing it again. "You feel so good inside of me."

Oh Jesus, that's not helping. "Fuck, Leila." She feels amazing, so fucking good. Pleasure I've never felt before. Holy shit, how am I supposed to pull out? "We need a condom."

She bumps her hips again, white blinds my eyes. "Please," she moans, sinking down half an inch. "I don't want to stop."

Fuck. Fuck. Fuck. I let go of her hips, relaxing against the headboard while she sinks down onto me inch by glorious inch. Her tight heat coats me with her wetness. So. Fucking. Good. She stops halfway, her eyes squeezed shut. I smooth my hands over her hips. "All the way," I tell her. "I know you can take it."

She shakes her head, trying to sink down but bites her lips in a wince. "It's too much."

I position my thumb over her clit, letting her fall in pleasure. "You took me so well last time," I croon, hearing her sweet little whimpers. "You can do it again. I know you can. Just relax for me, baby, I'll make you feel so good."

She shifts on her knees, lowering her ass all the way so I'm buried deep inside her wet pussy. "Oh shit." I let out a guttural moan, dropping my head to her chest.

"I feel so full," she moans, grinding her hips forward. "You're so big."

Fuck. She needs to stop talking. The more she moans and talks, the closer I am to blowing my load inside of her. "I need you to move, gorgeous." I grip her soft hips in my hands, lifting her up. She slams back down creating the most perfect friction. We both moan. She's right. It's never felt this good before, with anyone.

"Like this?" she asks, lifting and dropping back down.

"Fuck yes, baby, just like that." I thrust my hips up, fucking her from below, going as deep as I possibly can. She groans, tipping her head back and lifts off my cock, burying me inside of her every time she drops her ass to my thighs. Our skin slaps against each other with every hard thrust we make.

I bring her lips to mine, and she moans into my mouth. I eat it up, swallowing down every desperate noise she makes. My lips leave her mouth, trailing kisses down her cheek, her jaw and suck the delicate skin of her neck, leaving my mark. I want everyone to know she's taken. She's with me. She's mine.

I wrap an arm around her waist and flip us over so her back hits the bed and I'm crowding her. I waste no time thrusting back into her, laying my elbows beside her head, leaning down to kiss her.

I love you.

Please love me back.

When another moan leaves her lips, I squeeze my eyes shut. I'm so close. Too close. But I don't want this to end just yet. I never want this to end. "Fuck, I don't want to pull out."

She wraps her legs around my waist, digging her feet into my ass to push me deeper. Her eyes roll to the back of her head, a filthy moan for my ears only coming out of her. "Then don't," she says on a gasp. "Stay inside of me."

I groan. "I don't think I want to be a dad just yet." She lets out a laugh which turns into a moan when I hit a spot deep inside of her. "I'm serious, Leila." I lift off my elbows, grabbing her hips and thrust into her. "We're too young, we're still in college. Do you even know how to take care of a baby?" 'Cause I sure as fuck don't.

"No, you idiot." She laughs. "I'm on the shot. Come inside of me."

I stop, gripping her hips in place when she tries to wriggle on my dick. "You're serious?"

She nods, licking her lips. "I want to feel you come inside of me."

I groan, bringing her hips to match my thrusts. She moans, throws her head back and her pussy squeezes around me, my cock flooding with a gush of hot liquid erupting out of her.

"Fuuuck." That's it for me. I thrust once, two more times and feel my balls tighten. I let out a low, agonized moan when her pussy contracts, squeezing every last drop out of me.

When I pull out and watch my cum drip out of her, an urge comes over me and I grab my dick, cleaning up the spilled cum with the tip and thrust it back inside of her, letting out a groan. "So good," I moan, pulling out an inch and push back in. "So fucking good." My head starts to feel dizzy the longer I go, the pleasure suddenly too much. "Shit." I flinch, pulling out of her, my dick spent from the overstimulation.

I drop beside her, burying my head in her chest. She wraps her arms around me and whispers, "I think you killed me." I laugh, leaving a kiss on her lips. "I'm serious. My legs won't stop shaking."

I look down where her legs are trembling, stretched out on the bed and I laugh, grinning as I look up at her. "Remember who fucked you so good your legs stopped working."

She laughs. "So cocky."

She starts to sit up and I stop her. "Wait," I tell her, looking down at her. "I want to take care of you."

Her brows furrow. "What do you mean?"

My heart aches for all the shitty sexual experiences she's had. The quickies here and there with useless, meaningless boys who didn't deserve her. After care is important, and I wish I could have done it before but Leila would always kick me out and tell me my job was done.

But now... now I'm not just her fuck buddy, I'm her boyfriend, and this is my job. I lean down and brush my lips against hers. "Stay here."

I get off the bed and walk into the bathroom, grabbing a towel and run it under warm water. When I walk back into the room, she's still laying there, right where I left her, tapping her fingers on her belly. I chuckle, leaning over her. "Open your legs, baby."

She glances at me, unsure and then spreads her legs open and I clean her up, swiping the towel gently over her, cleaning up all the mess we made and taking care of my girlfriend, just like I wanted to.

When I'm done, I turn around, dropping the towel into the sink and head back into the room, climbing into bed with my girlfriend and pull her into me. It's still weird, knowing she's my girlfriend. I love it. I love her.

She snuggles up to me, running her hand over my back. I know she feels the scars and when she sighs, I know it's coming. "I can't believe your brothers did that to you," she murmurs, pressing her lips against my chest.

I swallow the gravel stuck in my throat and blow out a breath. "My brothers didn't do that."

She pulls back, frowning at me. "Your mom?"

I shake my head. "My mom's ex," I explain. When her frown deepens and her tears start to well up, my hand reaches up, wiping the tears streaming down her face. "Don't cry for me, gorgeous. I'm okay. I promise."

She shakes her head, more tears falling down her face. "Why did he do that?"

I snuggle her closer, placing my chin on top of her head. "I walked in on him over my mom's unconscious body." I hear the sharp inhale from Leila and I decide to just push through. If I'm ever going to let anyone in, then it's her. "When I yelled at him, he picked up his belt and taught me a lesson." I run my fingers through Leila's hair, blinking when the image of Jerry reappears itself in my mind.

"Told me if I opened my mouth, I would hear from him again. I don't remember how old I was, probably about eight or nine." Most of my childhood was one messed up blur, all wrapped up in shit days after shit days. "But then he came back." I continue. "And when I heard my mom crying out again in the middle of the night, I grabbed the first thing I saw which was a frying pan and hit him over the head with it."

I shake my head, remembering the events of that night. "My mother yelled at me. Told me not to get involved," I tell her. "I still remember how my body froze when the first lash of his belt hit me again, but then my brothers woke up and took care of him. I don't know what they did, but we never heard from him again."

"Your brothers helped?"

I nod, pulling back and looking into her eyes. "They might have hurt me growing up, but they were there when I needed them."

She frowns. "That doesn't make it okay," she says, placing her hand on my face. "One good thing doesn't erase the years of abuse they put you through."

"You're right." I blow out a breath, wanting to say fuck it and just tell her how in love with her I am. "It doesn't."

She shakes her head. "I'll never let anyone hurt you ever again." She runs her hand up, playing with my hair. I used to hate people touching my hair, the thought of my mother pulling it as punishment a reminder every time I touched it, but when Leila does it, there's nothing but love there.

34

Bets and blackmail

Aiden

It's a great feeling being able to touch Leila without her flinching every two seconds and looking around for people.

I can't keep my hands off her. She's probably annoyed by how much I'm touching her, but she hasn't said anything so I'm not stopping anytime soon. Not when I've been deprived of this exact thing for months now.

When I lean in to brush my lips against hers, Rosie chuckles. "So cute." I grin when I pull back, looking down at Leila. She glances at me, rolling her eyes but her lips say another story when she smirks. "You guys are adorable."

"Just make sure you don't hog her like Grayson does," Gabi says.

I shake my head, smiling down at Leila. "I can't promise that." Now that I have her, it'll be impossible letting her go. I want to be with her all the time, it doesn't feel enough having her right next to me. Safe to say I'm obsessed with this girl and so fucking in love it blinds me.

The server comes out with our food, placing it in front of us. I feel my phone vibrate in my pocket and I take it out.

I pull my arm from around Leila, turning the phone away from her. What the fuck?

Unknown:

> You broke the rules.

Now? I hear from him now? I haven't heard a peep since I threw the game and did what he asked and sent... fuck. I haven't heard from him since I sent Leila's number. Why the hell is he texting me again?

"Are you okay?" I jump at the sound of my girlfriend's voice. My girlfriend who I betrayed.

I scratch my jaw, turning my phone off and stuff it in my pocket. My attempt at a normal smile falls flat when I remember everything that asshole told me to do. "Yeah, gorgeous."

"I'm going to throw up." Gabi fake gags and I snicker, watching Madi roll her eyes at her.

"Don't be jealous."

She sighs, shaking her head. "I'm going to be the last single girl here," she says. "I just know it. I'm going to be all alone."

"That's not true," Madi says. "I'm not dating anyone."

Gabi glances at her. "Yet."

"Ever."

Gabi shakes her head, letting out a scoff. "Right."

Madeline narrows her eyes at her. "I'm serious. The day you bear witness to me falling in love is the day I dye my hair red." She lifts her eyebrows.

"You're lying," Gabi replies skeptically.

"I'm not."

"You? The control freak? You would never."

"You're right." Madi nods. "I won't because I won't lose."

Grayson grins. "You sound confident," he says, his arm wrapped around Rosalie. My palms itch to do the same to Leila but after that text reminded me of how we started, I feel like a traitor.

"I am."

Gabi grins, turning her body to face Madeline. "You want to bet?"

"And what would your forfeit be when you lose?"

Gabriella shrugs. "Nothing."

"Come on," Madi says, rolling her eyes. "We have to make it fair."

"Fine," Gabi concedes. "If I date first, I'll dye my hair pink."

Madi scoffs. "That's not a bet. You've been wanting to do that for ages."

"Alright bossy, then what do you suggest?"

Madi stares into space, narrowing her eyes, thinking of a forfeit for Gabi. "You have to get a tattoo," I reply instead.

Madi seems to like that idea, and so does Gabi who shrugs and says, "That's not a big deal, I want to get a tattoo anyway."

I shake my head, leaning forward. "Madi chooses the tattoo," I say, gesturing to Madeline whose smile is getting bigger by the second. "And she chooses where you get it."

Gabi's eyes widen. "She's going to choose like… her name on my back or something."

I laugh. "Exactly."

Gabi narrows her eyes at Leila. "Your boyfriend is evil." Those words that made me so happy just ten minutes ago now feel like a heavy weight on my chest. How am I supposed to tell her everything without her thinking I was lying?

"Yeah," Leila replies, running her hands down my back. I let my eyes fall closed at the feel of her. Fuck, I love her. What am I going to do? "I'm fond of him though."

"Deal," Gabi says, turning back around to face Madi. "If I date first, then I'll get a tattoo of your choice."

"And if I date first, then I'll dye my hair red."

They shake on it, Madi shooting Gabi a grin. I chuckle watching them, this is going to be interesting. But when my phone buzzes in my pocket again, my body stiffens and I reluctantly take it out of my pocket, reading the message.

Pictures.

Not of my family this time, though. Of me and Leila, just now sitting in this café.

I lift off my seat, very aware of everyone staring at me as the chair stumbles onto the ground and look around. This person was here? Right in front of me, taking pictures and I didn't see them?

When my phone buzzes again, I glance down, my jaw clenching when I read the two words that make my stomach drop.

Unknown:

End it.

The feel of Leila's hands on me once brought me so much joy and peace, but now it's just a reminder of everything I did, and what they want me to do. I turn around, stuffing my phone in my pocket and my heart breaks when I see her frowning, placing her hand on my arm.

"What's wrong?" she asks, glancing down at my pocket. "Is it your brother?"

I shake my head, running a hand through my hair. Fuck. Fuck. Fuck. "No, gorgeous, I thought I saw someone." Before she can say anything, I lean down, pressing a kiss against her cheek and move past her. "I need to use the bathroom."

I don't even look back, knowing if I see her face I'm going to break down. When I shut the bathroom door, I pull my phone out and start texting.

Aiden:

Who the fuck is this?

Unknown:

Not important.

End it.

I don't understand. My fingers tremble with rage as I type away.

Aiden:

Why?

Unknown:

Do as I say or the pictures leak.

My teeth grind so hard it fucking hurts.

Aiden:

I thought you deleted them.

Unknown:

I lied.

"Motherfucker." The phone in my hand is seconds away from getting crushed like a bug. I should have known whoever got the pictures of my family would have kept them. I still don't know what they wanted from me. I gave them what they asked for and I hadn't heard from them. Until now.

Telling me to do the one thing that will break both my heart and the girl out there who owns it.

Fucked up family tree

Aiden

"I nearly had him."

Jordan swats him on the back of his head with a towel, laughing. "You had nothing. You nearly tripped over your own feet."

Ethan scoffs, shaking his head. "If he hadn't swerved, I would have had him."

I nudge Carter on the arm. "Who are they talking about?"

He pulls his shirt on, snickering. "Some kid who made a move on a girl Ethan is seeing. He found him outside of her dorm." He shrugs. "She swears nothing happened, but you know how girls are."

I lift my brow at him. Mostly because the only girls I spend time with these days is Leila and her friends, but also because… what the hell does this kid know about women?

He snorts when he sees my face. "Right. You're in love now and shit."

I laugh, lacing up my shoes. "You say that like it's a bad thing."

"It is for me," he says, sitting on the bench and lets out a sigh. "I'm allergic to relationships."

Funny. I used to be like that until I met Leila. I thought relationships were too much work, not worth the trouble. I was so wrong. It's been less than a month and it's been the best month of my life.

I nudge him, scooting closer so no one hears. "What happened with that guy you were seeing?" He glances around, but no one's listening. It's an honor knowing Carter trusts me with his biggest secret.

He shrugs. "We were just hooking up. We weren't seeing each other."

I shake my head, putting my cap on my head, letting out a scoff. "I don't miss the hook ups I've got to say." I'd been out of the game for a while before Leila came along. It just got... boring, repetitive, meaningless and I couldn't do it anymore.

When I first came to Redfield, I knew nothing about girls. Absolutely nothing. I hadn't even kissed one. And then I became captain and started winning games, and I earned respect around here, and a lot of attention from girls.

But I've never been as grateful to leave all of that behind in exchange for what I have with Leila. This sounds sappy as shit even thinking it, but I kind of wish I met her earlier. I wish I had held off on all the intimate stuff until I met her.

Because until her it was just a release, a quick escape that made me feel good. But with Leila? It was everything.

Carter laughs. "Of course you don't," he replies. "You can get laid whenever you want."

"Are we talking about Pierce's girl?" Ethan closes his locker, grinning when he turns around. "Not really my type, but she's got huge tits."

Jordan hits the back of his head again, making Ethan narrow his eyes at him. "What? It's true."

"Don't talk about his girl like that," Jordan replies.

I lift off the bench. "Do you have a problem with Leila?" I ask him.

Ethan laughs. "Who me? I don't even know the girl."

One of these guys does. One of them kissed her and slept with her and treated her like shit. I still don't know who it could be.

"Then why do you keep bringing her up?"

He runs his tongue over his teeth. "Sorry, *your highness*, won't happen again."

The door opens when Coach peers his head through, curling his finger at me. "Pierce," he says with a stern edge to his voice. His tone is cold, angry even. "Come with me." Coach turns around without any further explanation, the door closing behind him.

"Going to suck him off, are you?" Ethan calls out. I narrow my eyes at him wondering what his deal is before I walk out of the locker room.

When I push through Coach's office, he's sat in his chair, hands intertwined in front of him, his face reserved of any emotion. What the hell is going on? "You wanted to see me?" I ask, closing the door behind me.

He blows out a breath, staring down at some piece of paper in front of him. "I don't even know how to say this." My brows knit together when I try to look down at the paper. I can't read it from here, I have no idea what has him acting like this. When he lifts his head, the words that come out his mouth slice through me like a sharp blade. "You failed your drug test, son."

My spine grows cold, goosebumps rising all over my skin. "What? That's impossible."

He presses two fingers against the piece of paper on the desk. "The tests don't lie. You tested positive for

Amphetamines." My mind is running. How is this possible? "You know how bad using any drug, let alone a stimulant is, Aiden."

"Sir." My voice croaks and I shake my head, clearing my throat. "Coach, there has to be a mistake. I have never touched drugs." I scratch the back of my neck. "My family... they don't come from a good place." *Understatement of the year.* "I knew to stay away from them. I don't even drink," I throw the last one in there hoping he believes me.

The shake in his head gives me some hope, maybe he'll see it was a mistake. "I've got to say, it sounds a little unbelievable, but I can't take your word for it when the tests came back positive."

I don't understand. "Is it possible anyone messed with the results?"

He seems to mull it over, running a hand over his overgrown beard. "I don't think so." Fuck. "The samples are sent to the lab to get tested."

My palms itch. My head itches. Everything in my body screams at me. How the fuck did this happen? "What does this mean?" I force myself to ask.

"It means you're suspended for the time being."

"So, no game?"

He shakes his head. "You're not even on the team as of right now."

This is my worst nightmare. Basketball means everything to me. It was the only thing I had for so long, it's my way out of a life like my family have. It's the way that I make sure Leila is taken care of. It's all I have. "What else am I supposed to do?"

He lifts off his chair, rounding the table. "Focus on your studies," he says, grabbing a bottle of whiskey and pouring it into his mug. "Keep up with your school work."

"But if I'm not playing, then what happens to my scholarship?"

He takes a sip of the rank drink I can smell a mile away. "I'm not going to make any drastic changes at the moment." My shoulders drop. Thank God. "But we'll test you again, and if the test comes back positive a second time," he shakes his head, "I'm sorry, son, but you won't be on the team."

"Which means no scholarship." No future. No life. No Leila.

"I believed in you, Aiden." He places his mug behind him. "I still do. I know it's a lot of pressure to be under but this is not the answer."

"I didn't take stimulants," I assure him. "I would never touch them."

He crosses his arms, assessing me. "But you can't prove it?"

I throw my hands up, gesturing to the piece of paper that holds my future. "If my piss says the opposite, then no."

He nods, grabbing his mug again. "Come back in three weeks and we'll test you again." He takes a sip, shaking his head. "That's the best I can do."

I nod. Three weeks. "Thank you." I swallow. "For not taking the scholarship away."

He raises his brows. "This is the last time it will happen."

"I understand, Coach."

He gestures behind me, sitting back down at his desk. "Close the door on your way out."

I leave his office, walking into the locker room to find it empty. I pick up my gym bag from the floor, stuffing it in the locker and walk out. No more practice, no more game, no more team for at least two weeks.

When my phone buzzes I relax, thinking it's Leila. I'd love a text from her, a picture, even one letter. Doesn't matter.

But it's not Leila.

Unknown:

> Don't be so surprised. The apple doesn't fall far from the fucked-up family tree.

My heart races, threatening to beat right out of my chest. This guy did this?

Unknown:

> I warned you.

> End it or I end you.

36

You are worth
everything

Leila

Knocking on the door is a thing of the past for Aiden.

He doesn't even hesitate before his arms wrap around my waist from behind, placing his chin on my shoulder. I jump, looking behind my shoulder at him. "You scared me," I breathe, my heart racing.

His eyes widen when he looks down at the pot in my hand. "You're cooking?"

I turn back around, letting out a laugh. "I already told you I can cook."

His hands span the width of my belly, running his hands all over me. I used to hate touching my own stomach, every time my hands touched my skin it would find another thing to hate, to psychoanalyze over, but when Aiden does it, he isn't examining every roll and curve, he just can't stop touching me.

His lips press against my shoulder. "What are you making?"

I tilt my head at the watery rice in the pot. "I'm trying to recreate that risotto we had at the restaurant."

He chuckles against my skin, kissing my neck. "That was so good. We should go back there sometime."

I shake my head, turning back to face him. "No way, it's too expensive." I still remember nearly choking on my water when the bill came. I'm not letting him spend that kind of money on me again.

He lifts his head, gripping my chin. "I already told you to quit worrying about money. I will stop at nothing for you to have everything you could want."

Every day I fall more and more in love with this man. "But what about your brothers?"

He sighs, unwrapping his arms from around me. "They haven't called in ages, Leila. I sent them all I had and I'm not sending them anymore any time soon." He runs his hand down his face. "You have nothing to worry about."

I can't help it. Aiden takes care of everyone, works his ass off to then not get anything in return. No one's looking out for him. I have to.

His gaze drops to my legs, a cocky grin on his lips. "I never thought pajamas could be so sexy." When he looks back at me, there's hunger in his eyes. "You're way too pretty for my head not to be between your legs."

I let out a laugh, turning back around to mix the rice. I grab a spoon, picking some up. Damn, that's good. I pick up some more, holding out the spoon to him. "You want some?"

He smiles, stepping closer. "Yeah baby." He approaches me, trapping me with both of his arms against the counter. "I'll have anything you give me."

I raise my brow. "What if it's poison?"

He sighs, rubbing his thumb over my cheek. "It'll be the best way to die."

My cheeks heat. Who knew Aiden Pierce was such a romantic? His lips close around the spoon, swallowing down the risotto, and when his eyes widen, I know he liked it and that he finally believes I know how to cook.

"Good?" I ask him, my lips tipped in amusement.

He leans in, pressing a kiss to my lips. "So good," he murmurs. "I was wrong."

"As usual."

He shakes his head, laughing. "Not about everything. I was right about this."

"About what?"

"That we're good together."

Yeah. He's right about that. I was so guarded, not wanting him to break my heart that I nearly shut him out and turned away from all of this. I'm so glad I went to that game.

In a matter of seconds, something washes over Aiden and he steps back from me, his smile wiped clean off his face and turns around, burying his head in his hands.

I frown, watching as he groans. He's been acting weird all week. Especially at the café when he stood up abruptly and walked off without talking to me.

My hands run over his arms, his muscles hard beneath my palms. "Are you okay?" I ask. He almost breaks out of whatever he was thinking, turning around and letting out a breath.

"Yeah," he says, giving me a smile. "I'm good." It's not the usual, easy smile he has though. Something's wrong. I don't know what, but I know something is.

When the timer goes off, I turn around, turning off the pot and plating up the risotto. Aiden's right behind me, grabbing the plates before I can and places them on the table. We both sit down, digging into the food and when I look up, he's staring at me, intensely, scanning my features.

"Why are you looking at me like that?" I ask him, my face heating under his gaze.

The corner of his lips lifts a little, dropping back down a second later. "I'm ingraining this in my memory."

I look down at my plate, my smile growing by the second. But when my phone buzzes and I see the name on the screen I freeze, turning it over before Aiden can see and pick up another bite of risotto.

"Who was that?"

Shit. "Just Rosie." I shove a fork full of food in my mouth, not daring to glance up at him.

"Are you lying to me right now?"

There's no way out of this. I drop my fork, swallowing harshly when I look up at him and see him frowning at me. "Don't be mad."

He scoffs. "Great way to start," he says, his eyes narrowing. "Who was that?"

I have to tell him. It's been going on for way too long. "Remember when I said I had slept with one of your teammates freshman year?"

His jaw clenches and my heart starts to race. I hate that I'm doing this right now. "How could I forget?"

"He's been texting me for a while."

His jaw tightens even more, his fists curling up by his side. Before he can say anything, I hold my hands up. "I haven't been answering, I didn't even give him my number. I don't know how he got it." I shrug, hoping he believes me.

He takes a minute to breathe, his muscles tense as he leans forward. "You're telling me one of my teammates who I've had practice with every day has been texting you while we're together?"

Crap. I wince, fiddling with my hands. "Longer than that."

His eyebrows lift. "How long, Leila?"

I lift my shoulders. "A few months?" His face turns to stone, I can see the new information running around his head.

"Who?"

That one word makes my stomach drop. I can't possibly tell Aiden who has betrayed him, who has been texting me knowing we're together. I open my mouth, shaking my head.

"Who, Leila?"

I press my lips together. I've kept this from him for way too long. I let out a breath, knowing this is going to destroy him. "Jordan."

The silence cuts through me, settling over us as Aiden processes what I've just told him. "Jordan?" he repeats after a few minutes. "Jordan Wright?" He shakes his head. "No. No fucking way. Him?"

I don't know if he doesn't believe me or if he's just in shock so I push my phone across the table. "You can check if you want."

He rolls his eyes, letting out a sigh. "I'm not going to check your phone, Leila."

"I don't want you to doubt your trust in me."

His eyes soften, staring into my eyes. "I trust you. You're the only person I trust."

My heart flutters at his words, knowing I'm the only person who truly knows him. But I won't be able to relax until he knows the whole story. "Just check it, Aiden." I flip over my phone, inputting the code and open the text chain—the one-sided text chain—from Jordan.

He lets out a sigh and picks up the phone, scanning the screen. I know what he's going to find there. Endless texts from his best friend and teammate. Some of them talking about

296

repeating the night we had, and others calling me every name under the sun.

"Motherfucker." He drops my phone back onto the table, standing up and heading towards the door.

Panic washes over me when I realize he's leaving. "Wait, please." He halts at the door, turning around to face me. "Don't leave. I'm sorry. I should have told you."

He closes his eyes, his shoulder slumping as he grabs onto my face, running his thumb over my cheek. "Baby," he croons. "You have nothing to apologize for. But I'm not letting him get away with this."

"No. Don't." My tongue darts out to lick my lips. "It'll just make it worse. It's not worth it."

When he looks at me, I see so many emotions running through his head. "You are worth everything." He presses his lips against mine and in a matter of seconds, he turns around and leaves, closing the door behind him.

Aiden

Jordan.

It was Jordan this whole time.

I can't explain the anger that brewed inside of me when I read the texts he sent my girlfriend.

How did I not notice? I spent months, years with the guy and I didn't notice he was blackmailing me? It has to be him. Leila doesn't give her number out to just anyone and the texts started right after I sent the blackmailer her number.

I can't believe I did that. I should have tried to figure out who it was, to shut him down, but instead of I betrayed the trust and privacy of the only girl I loved and now this asshole is holding my past against me once again.

But this time, something else is on the line. Leila. One look at her and my heart hurts with the knowledge of what Jordan wants me to do. I can't end it with her. I can't. I let him blackmail me once, I'm not doing it again.

I don't even bother knocking when I burst into the frat house, the memories as a freshman needing a cheap place to stay coming back to me, the one guy who I hate more than Jordan right now in front of me.

Ben Reed. The asshole that shoved a line of coke in front of me calling me a pussy when I turned around and left. I hate this guy.

I remember lunging at him last year when he came after Rosie to get to Grayson. The things he was saying made me see red. No one speaks about a woman like that and gets away with it.

"What the fuck are you doing here, Pierce," he says, slurring his words. I should be shocked he's drunk before noon, but it's right on brand for him. "Did you come begging to join?" He grins, taking a sip of his beer. "You're out of luck, we don't accept pussies."

His dark chuckle does nothing but irritate me as I ignore him, taking the stairs twice at a time, looking around for the bastard that stabbed me in the back.

Grayson was there last year, holding me back from punching that asshole downstairs, saving me from getting suspended or even expelled, but right now? Not even Grayson could stop me. I have nothing to lose. Leila is on the line, my scholarship is on the line, and it's all because of Jordan.

I find his room in a matter of seconds, and fling open his door, stalking over to him, grabbing his collar in my fist and throw a punch to his face. Fucking asshole threatened me. Threatened the woman I love. He deserves this. He deserves worse.

"What the fuck," he sputters, trying to push me off. "Pierce, what the fuck are you doing?"

"I know it's you. I fucking know it's you that's been blackmailing me." I push off him, staring down at him. This guy was one of my best friends.

He laughs, wiping some of the blood sputtering from his mouth. "How did you find out?"

Hearing him admit it builds an anger inside of me I didn't know existed. I grip his jaw in my hand, tightening my hold on him. "You've been texting my girl," I grit out. "What the fuck do you want from her? From me?"

He pushes at my chest. "Get the fuck off me."

"I should kill you."

He narrows his eyes. "Go ahead. You'll fit right in with your family."

I let him go, my eyes widen when I remember he knows everything. The pictures of my mother passed out on the couch with a needle in her arm, the security footage of my brother stealing.

He laughs, bitterly. "You're such a pussy, this is why you don't deserve captain."

I blink at him, watching as he adjusts his jaw, spitting out blood to the floor. "This is what it's about?" I ask him.

He shakes his head, glaring at me. "You don't deserve it. I do. I worked hard for that spot and you swooped in and took it."

"That was on Coach." I didn't ask for this position.

He laughs. "Coach pities you, nothing more to it."

I can't believe just a few days ago, I used to think of this guy as a friend. "Coach doesn't even know. No one does."

"Of course he does," he says. "Do you think he doesn't do his research?" His brow lifts. "Did you think I wouldn't do my research?"

My jaw ticks. "How did you find out?"

He cracks his neck, and I can hear the pain he must be feeling. I wish I had punched him some more. "I needed something on you. It wasn't hard. You might walk around campus thinking you're a god, but you're a loser, Aiden. Always have been. Always will be."

"And Leila?" I ask the question that's running through my mind. "What does she have to do with this?"

He laughs again, my stomach churning. "That was interesting. She wasn't part of my plan but it was too fucking perfect."

I glare at him. "What are you talking about?"

"You might not remember, but I do." He crosses his arms. "She was all over me, flirting, smiling, licking those lips." The way he talks about my girlfriend makes me want to forget all about rational and punch him into the ground. "So of course I fucked her." He shrugs. "Never fucked a fat chick, first time for everything, right?"

I want to kill him. I want to kill him so bad.

"Then the next morning, she ghosted. Didn't like that."

I shake my head, remembering what Leila said about him threatening her not to tell anyone and now he's pissed she did exactly what he wanted? "Why do you care?" It's been over a year, why the hell is he still holding onto that?

He growls at me. "Because it was humiliating. I shouldn't have to chase her. She'd be lucky for me to stick my dick in her."

I stalk over to him. "Watch your fucking mouth," I grit out, gripping his jaw in my hand again. He winces when I squeeze it. "Or I will kill you. And I won't stop this time."

"Fuck you." He pushes at my chest. "You and that bitch are nothing but a means to an end. It was never supposed to be more than that."

301

"Then why tell me to get her number? Why do any of it?" My stomach cramps with the admission that the first few interactions we had were because of this asshole, wanting something from her.

"I was killing two birds with one stone." He sniffs, wiping the blood from his lip. "I wanted you to step down as captain and I wanted to humiliate her like she did to me."

"How were you planning on doing that?"

"Simple." His lips twitch. "I was going to make her fall in love with me."

I snort. "Leila wants nothing to do with you."

"Yeah." He narrows his eyes at me. "I figured. Which is where you come in. That day in class, you were all over her already, and she might have hated you but she talked to you." He was manipulating me the whole time. "I wanted to get her number, make her fall for me, but when that didn't work, I let you do the work for me." He laughs. "She fell right into your lap. It was too fucking easy."

"You're an asshole," I spit out. "You can't use people like that."

He shrugs. "I already did. And now you're going to finish what you started. You're going to end it. You're going to break up with her." His grin makes me violent. "Make it hurt, and make it public. It will be way more fun."

I lunge at him again, grabbing his collar in my fist. "You're not in charge anymore. I'm not breaking up with her and you're not going to make me."

"Careful." He pushes me off him. "I didn't delete those pictures, Aiden. If you don't want your basketball career down the drain, then you'll do as I say."

"You're bluffing."

He shrugs. "Maybe. Maybe not. Do you really want to risk being wrong?" When I don't reply, he grins like he's already won. "She's going to get what's coming to her, and you're going to do it."

"No."

He narrows his eyes at me, letting out a scoff. "Don't tell me you actually love her." My jaw is so tight it hurts. "Holy shit," he laughs. "I guess you should thank me."

I shake his words out of my head. Of course, I fucking love her, but he had nothing to do with it. He wanted her number. That's it. I wanted *her*. All of her. Her eye rolls and jokes, the way she could see through me and put me in my place. Her scowls and laughs, her smiles, her lips. She had my heart between those fingers of hers and this bastard had nothing to do with it.

"Well, that's too fucking bad. You have one week," he says. "End it or the pictures go out."

His words ring in my mind. I can't let her go. How am I going to let the best thing that has ever happened to me out of my grasp? "Why not just post it? If you wanted me off the team so bad just post the pictures and stop wasting my goddamn time."

He nods, licking the blood off his lips. "The thing is, Aiden. You're good. I don't want you off the team. I just want the captain position. I thought for sure making you throw the game would work," he says, his jaw ticking. "But if you don't give me what I want, I will expose you. And then," he whistles, "You're done. No one is going to want a loser like you on their team."

He's right. I know he is. My life as Captain of Redfield's basketball team would be over. No one would look up to me or respect me. It would be like high school all over again, joking and laughing, treating me like I'm a nobody. And there's no way in hell I would get drafted, no fucking chance they'd want someone with my background representing them.

I loosen my fists. I fucking lose. Either way, I lose.

"One week," he reminds me as I walk out of the door. "End it or I will."

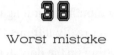

Worst mistake

Aiden

I'm a coward.

It's been almost a week and I still haven't seen Leila.

Any time she texts, my chest hurts. I want to race to her apartment and wrap my arms around her. I don't want this to end. I don't want to give up on her, I just don't know how to get out of this situation.

The pictures of my brother and mom constantly replay in my mind. There's none of Brendan because he's good at not getting caught. He's also good at beating my ass until I'm black and blue. I remember the first and last time I tried to tell a teacher about what was happening at home when I walked in with a split lip. It resulted in the police getting involved and me ending up in a foster home. I stayed there for a few weeks before my mom appealed to get us back.

I never knew why she bothered. She didn't care about me and my brothers. But that day when she showed up, she looked like a new person. She had to get clean before she could have us back and when I saw her standing at the door smiling at me my heart hurt.

She had never smiled at me before. *This time,* I thought to myself, *this time will be different.* She looked good. Healthy. I was so excited to go home and live my new life, but as soon as we got in the car, I realized that it was a ruse. She wasn't happy to see me, she backhanded me and called me a snitch.

I never opened my mouth about it again. I was so scared of getting hit again, it never really left me.

But seeing Leila sitting on the doorstep outside of my house makes this fear take precedence. The fear of losing her. Of hurting her.

I can't do it. I can't. All I want to do is pick her up in my arms and kiss the fuck out of her. If I have to give up my future to do so, then so be it.

"Leila." I take a step closer to my girl.

When she looks up, my heart breaks.

She knows.

Her eyes are rimmed with tears, and her lips are red and blotchy, and every part of me knows without a doubt that Jordan told her.

I stop in my tracks, looking down at her, my chest caves in. This is it. It's fucking over.

She stands up, anger in her eyes. "I can't believe I let myself fall for your lies."

"Leila—"

"I don't want to hear it," she bellows. "I just had to see if it was true."

"Leila." I take two steps forward, grabbing her arm but she flinches.

"Don't touch me," she growls, looking at me with such disgust I feel it all over my skin. "You don't get to touch me ever again."

"Let me explain, please, gorgeous."

"Don't!" she yells, closing her eyes as tears fall down her face. Fuck, I can't lose her. Please. Please. "Don't call me that."

"How did you find out?" I drop my hands, tears fighting to rise. I can feel my heart breaking. It hurts so bad.

She shakes her head, a bitter laugh coming out of her. "Not from you." She glances over at me, hatred in her eyes. "Jordan told me everything. How he told you to get my number, how he told you to kiss me. All of it."

The fact that she thinks I did all of this for fun breaks me in half. "I didn't kiss you because he told me to do it. I kissed you because I wanted to." Jordan might have told me to get her number but that first kiss was because she turned me the fuck on, because she liked teasing me and I liked teasing her right back. It had nothing to do with him and everything to do with us.

"Stop lying to me." She sounds like she's given up. On me. On us. She looks so tired, so exhausted over this. "I know everything, Aiden. I know it all."

"No, you don't." If she thinks I'm with her because Jordan told me to, she's fucking wrong. She has to know how much she means to me. I see the pain in her eyes, and I shake my head, trying to get her to believe me. "I am not him." I know exactly what she's thinking. I know she's comparing me to her shit of an ex, but that is not what happened. Not even close.

Her eyes cut through my chest. "You're worse. At least with him it was quick, he didn't drag it out like you," she cries out, tears falling down her face. "I told you what he did to me, and little did I know, you were doing the same thing. Playing me just like he did."

"No." Fuck no. That is not what happened. "Leila, Jordan blackmailed me. He had pictures of my mom, my brothers. He threatened to expose them, expose me. You know what that would do to my career."

"So, you played me."

I shake my head. "He just wanted your number. That was it. In the beginning, I knew nothing about you, I didn't know, Leila." She shakes her head, not looking at me. "When I first met you, I didn't know you were going to be this important to me." I stare into those lime green eyes that I love so much filled with tears. I did that. I hurt her. "You've got to know I would never hurt you."

"You hurt me more than anyone else," she says, slicing through my heart. "I trusted you with every part of me. God, I'm such an idiot." She closes her eyes, placing her fingers to her forehead. "I can't believe it happened again."

"No." I grab her hand in mine. "I didn't play you, Leila. It was real. All of it was real to me. How do you not see that? I told you about my family. I told you about everything. You are the only person I trust in this whole damn world. How would you ever think I would do something like that?"

"Because you did!" she yells, ripping her hand from mine and taking a step back. "You went along with it. You pursued me, chased me. I blatantly asked you what you got out of it and you said nothing." She laughs, more tears spilling out. "And I believed you. I genuinely believed you liked me."

"I do!" I yell throwing up my arms. "Jordan told me to get your number. That's it. That's all I was supposed to do. He didn't tell me to kiss you, or to sleep with you, or to fucking fall in love with you!"

"Don't," she warns, her voice cracking. "Don't you dare say that to me. You have no right to say those words."

"I love you, Leila. I am so in love with you. How do you not see that?"

"I don't believe you." She glares at me. "I don't trust you anymore, Aiden. Why would I ever believe you?"

"Because I'm telling the truth. You're the only person I have ever loved, the only one who has made me feel safe." I watch as her breathing quickens. "I love you."

She shakes her head. "No, you don't. You're just trying to save your ass." She walks past me, and I try to reach for her, but she moves out of the way, not bothering to look at me as she walks off.

She stops and looks back over her shoulder. "You are the worst mistake I have ever made."

Those words hit me like a knife as I watch her walk out of my life. But not out of my heart.

39

Never again

Leila

The smell of alcohol and sweat overwhelm my senses as I make my way to the makeshift bar, pouring myself another drink. The burn of the alcohol burns my throat and I let out a deep breath, closing my eyes and trying to shake off the memories that have been haunting every part of me for days.

Why is it so hard to forget? I don't want to sit here and think about everything that went wrong, I don't want to remember the sweet words he said, his hands on my body, his lips on my skin when it was all a lie.

My eyes catch on a couple dancing together, her arms wrapped around his neck as she smiles sweetly up at him. I swallow down my own jealousy and stupidity for thinking I could ever have that.

I turn back around, downing the rest of the drink, wanting, craving the burn, hoping the numbness will make the pain fade, make me forget even if it's just for a little while. I haven't had a drink in so long, since quitting for Aiden, and even though my stomach cramps, feeling guilty for breaking that promise to him, he broke an even bigger one.

My body tenses when a hand lands on my shoulder, jolting me out of my thoughts. I look behind my shoulder at Gabi standing behind me. My stomach drops when her eyes look at me with the one thing I hate the most. Pity. It's etched on her face as she shoots me a sad smile. "Are you okay?"

I close my eyes, letting out a hard sigh. "I'm fine." I can hear the lie in my own voice; I can hear how rough the words are coming out of my mouth. Her hand tightens on my shoulder and I look back at her. She doesn't look convinced, glancing at Madi who's frowning at me.

"I thought you quit drinking," she says.

I shrug, throwing the empty cup in the trash. "Guess not."

"Are you sure you don't want to just go home and talk?"

I hate talking. What is there to talk about? How I was stupid and let myself fall for another guy who was just using me for his personal gain, for fun, for… whatever he was using me for? "There's nothing to talk about."

"It's been four days, Leila," Madi says. "You need to wallow."

My heart beats even faster at her words. "Four days since what?"

"Leila."

"I need another drink." I grab another drink and tip the cup back. I walk away from them, hoping they just let me go and don't hound me about whatever it is I'm doing. I don't even know the answer to that myself. I don't want to think. I don't want to feel.

I push past the crowd, the music getting louder the closer I get. But when I look up, I don't hear anything. I don't see anything but the person in front of me. My heart starts to race when I look at the black cap on his head, the white t-shirt clung to his tall and hard body. I know how it feels under my fingers, I know how it presses against my skin when he's inside me.

311

I don't even notice the girl next to him at first, but when I do, I shatter, dropping the drink onto the floor, everyone around me jumping out of the way, the murmurs and conversation coming to a halt as they turn around and look at me, including Aiden. But when he turns around... it isn't Aiden. It's just a random guy.

My eyes squeeze shut, turning back around. Fuck, I need some air.

I head outside, push the back door open, sit down on the steps. What is happening to me? When Jake dumped me, I didn't feel this way. I cried for a few days but I didn't grieve what I thought I lost with Jake, I was just pissed about what he had done and how he exposed my texts.

This is completely different. It hurts. I can feel my heart shattering thinking about what I lost.

I miss him.

I hate him and I love him. And I miss him.

"Leila." My head snaps behind me, seeing Rosie standing at the door, looking down at me. She frowns, her brows tugged together as she shakes her head. "Let's go home, we can talk about this."

"I don't want to talk, Rosie."

She closes the door, sitting beside me. "You're allowed to be sad, you know?" She pulls her dress down over her bare legs. "I was a mess last year, and you helped me."

I scoff. "I dragged you out of bed." I would hardly say I helped her. I just needed my best friend back. Her smiles and bubbly personality were gone when she was heartbroken over Grayson and I couldn't let her rot away in that bed.

"And it helped." She leans in, resting her head against my shoulder. "We work differently. I wanted to cry, and you want

312

to move on and forget." My throat constricts. "But you still need to grieve the relationship you lost," she tells me, wrapping her arm around mine. "You can talk to me and I'll listen." When she lifts her head and looks at me, her eyes swimming with guilt and a little sadness. "Talk to me," she pleads.

I can't. I can't even think about it without wanting to break down, and I'm not going to let that happen. The sigh that leaves Rosie when I stand up riddles my stomach with guilt, but I don't give her any time to say anything before walking back into the party and grabbing another drink out of the ice bucket lying around.

One way or another, I'm going to forget.

"Fuck." My head pounds when my eyes open, squinting against the bright light that spills into the room. Damn those giant windows. My head feels like it's being hammered from the inside, a wave of nausea washing over me when I try to sit up.

I groan again, clutching my head, hoping it eases the throbbing pain. What was I thinking? How did I let myself get so drunk?

I turn my head, the pounding in my head a constant reminder of my mistakes, of the pain that I was so desperately trying to erase last night. I hear a soft groan from beside me and look down at Rosie lying haphazardly over the edge of the bed, her head buried into the pillow.

My heart squeezes when I turn, seeing Madi lying on the sofa, her dress from last night wrinkled around her body as she sleeps. Gabi's laying on the floor, using a cushion as a pillow.

Tears threaten to spill as I look around at my friends here with me. I haven't slept alone in so long. It was the best feeling, waking up beside him, our bodies together as we slept. He would kiss my forehead, pull me closer to him, and I would wrap my arms around his waist and bury my head in his chest.

But now all I get when I wake up is a reminder that none of it was real. That it was all a farce.

I swing my legs over the edge of the bed, careful not to startle any of them as I head to the kitchen. Grabbing a glass from the cabinet, I fill it up with water. I barely finish drinking before my bedroom door swings open and out comes the girls. Gabi groans holding onto the wall as she stumbles out. "Shit," she curses when she nearly trips over her feet. "I don't think I can stand."

Madi grabs onto her hands, catching her from falling over. "I thought you could handle your alcohol. How much did you drink?" She groans when Gabi nearly topples both of them over.

Gabi falls to the floor with an oomph, dropping her head back against the wall. "I lost count after the tenth shot."

Madi shakes her head. "Come on. You need to shower."

She groans. "Just let me die right here."

"So dramatic," Madi mutters, leaning down to wrap her arm around Gabriella, lifting her off the floor. She glances back at me. "I should get her in bed before she throws up on me. Are you going to be okay?"

No. Instead, I press my lips together, attempting a smile, my hands clutching the glass so hard I'm afraid it will crack. "Yes."

I can see the disbelief in her eyes when she shakes her head, walking over to the door, Gabi holding onto her like a lifeline. She reaches the door, holds onto the handle and turns back to me. She swallows. "If you need anything. Anything at all. Call me."

I nod.

"And me," Gabriella buts in.

Madi snickers when Gabi nearly trips again. "You can barely take care of yourself right now. Come on." They both leave, closing the door behind them.

Rosie comes out of the room, phone in her hand. When she looks up at me, her brows are knitted together, her lips pursed as if she wants to say something but she's holding back.

I sigh. "Go, Rosie."

"It's just Grayson. He was worried because I didn't tell him I'd be staying over."

I look up at her, smiling at her, trying to make her see that I'm okay. Even if it's not true, I will be, eventually. "Rosie, I'm okay, you can go."

She smiles, walks over to me, and presses her lips to my cheek. "I'll be right back, I promise."

She heads out, closing the door and the silence takes over. My eyes land on the camera on the table, my Polaroids next to it. I know I shouldn't do it, but it doesn't stop me from grabbing them and finding the exact one I look at every day. When I find it, I debate ripping it up and forgetting all about him, but that won't work.

Ripping a picture won't rip him out of my heart. He'll always be there, lingering, a heavy weight on my chest from all the memories I had with him that I thought were genuine. My finger traces his smile in the picture and I stiffen, wondering if this too was a lie. Was every smile and laugh and kiss just a means to an end to him?

My phone buzzes on my lap and I stiffen, afraid that Aiden is texting me again.

He hasn't stopped. Ever since I told him it was over, he's been calling, texting. But I can't find the strength to block him. No matter how much he hurt me, his texts are a little reminder of how it used to be, of everything we went through and every word that left his lips.

Sometimes, I scroll, reading the good morning texts he would send me, the goodnight texts and late-night calls we used to have.

I clutch my phone, forcing myself to look at it. The hope I was holding onto disappears when I realize it's not Aiden. It's my dad.

I take a deep breath, trying to settle my nerves before I pick up the phone. "Hey, Papi."

"Leila." His voice settles me a little, making me miss him. "You sound different."

I squeeze my eyes shut, keeping the tears back. "No, Dad," I attempt to keep my voice normal. "I'm fine."

He laughs quietly. "You're always so strong," he says. "Eres una tigresa."

I clutch the necklace with the paw print that Aiden got me hanging around my neck, my fingers running over the indents of the paws. My lip wobbles as his words roll through me. I'm a fake. I'm not strong at all. "Yep." My voice breaks and it's too late. Tears spill over as a sob catches in my throat.

"Mija." I shake my head, his gentle tone making me cry even harder. "What happened?" I can't find the words, the line fills with my quiet sobs as I try to restrain them.

"Dad, please. Can we not talk about it?"

He grunts, I can almost picture him shaking his head in disapproval. "What happened?" he asks again.

I shrug even though he can't see me, holding onto the necklace as if it's life support. "There was... this guy." I close my eyes at the use of past tense. "We broke up."

"Broke up?" My mother's voice makes me stiffen, my tears freezing as anger rolls through my body. "You told me you didn't have a boyfriend."

"You were listening?"

She scoffs. "You talk to your father but not me? Pass me the phone," she says to my dad. I press my fingers against my temples. God, I don't want to talk to her.

I hear shuffling and then my mother's voice. "No puedo creer que me hayas mentido," she chastises. *I can't believe you lied to me.*

"I didn't lie," I tell her. "He wasn't my boyfriend at the time, ma. Just a friend."

"And now?" she asks. "He broke up with you?"

"Yes."

She hums. "I can't say I'm surprised. Te dije." *I told you.* "Guys these days don't care about personality, mija." My spine stiffens at her cruel words. "If you had just listened to me, this wouldn't have happened."

I let out a bitter laugh, more tears spilling out. I can't believe this. Actually, that's a lie. Of course, she is saying this. Of course, she's telling me the reason I got my heart broken is that my body isn't good enough.

I wipe my tears with my hand, tasting the saltiness coating my lip. "I've got to go."

"Leila, escúchame."

317

Listen to her? If she thinks I'm going to sit here and listen to her insult me, she's dead wrong. I hang up the phone and throw it on the couch.

I don't even realize what I'm doing until the cabinet is wide open, and I have every single snack Aiden bought for me in my hands. I rip open one packet, drop some of the multi-colored candy into my hand, and shove it into my mouth. The sweet taste covers my tongue, invading my senses until I can focus on nothing but this.

Alarms ring in my head. I know I'm eating too much. I know what I'm doing. I can't even taste the food anymore, my stomach cramping as I keep eating. But I can't stop, this food is my only comfort, my only solace.

My stomach cramps when I swallow the first bite, the memory of doing this so long ago coming back to me. The urge has the best of me as I turn the package in my hands, scanning the back, but when I see what's on the back, my heart stops.

I can't see how many calories I've just stuffed in my mouth because in place of the nutritional value is a white piece of paper stuck to it.

Food is energy. Eat what you want.

The plastic shakes in my hands as I stare at his messy handwriting. When did he do this? Why? If it was all a lie, why would he do something like this?

I grab another snack, turn it over, and see another white piece of paper covering the back.

You're so beautiful. My heart skips a beat every time I see you.

I let my eyes drift closed, another tear falling down my cheek. I flip over another one.

These should be illegal. But if you enjoy them, eat away.

318

I almost laugh, almost smile at the thought, but then I remember everything that happened between us, and I push the packet away from me, staring at the words that mean so much but are all lies.

Keys jingle in the door and I freeze, my mouth drops open at the sight of Rosie walking in.

Shit.

"Hey," she says, walking through the door. "I went home and told Grayson I was coming bac—" She turns around, her words getting stuck in her throat and her eyes widen when she spots me.

I collapse onto the floor, the empty wrappers trailing down, littering everywhere around me. I bury my face in my hands, feeling my heart race at the realization of what I've done.

Fuck. What did I do?

A sob explodes out of me, tears falling onto my hands as I press my head into them.

"Leila." Rosie's voice breaks and she falls to her knees beside me, wrapping her arms around me.

I shake my head, pulling back and looking at her. "It happened again," I cry out. "I got played again. How did I let it happen again?"

"I'm so sorry." Her eyes fill with tears, my own watching her blurry face frown, crying along with me. "I'm so sorry, Leila."

I bury my head back in my hands, wishing I could go back and do everything again. I wouldn't give in this time. I would never have known what it was like to have his hands all over me, whispering words of affection. I wouldn't have been heartbroken.

"I loved him," I admit.

Her hand freezes on my shoulder and she sniffs. "I know."

I pull back, wiping the tears. "I thought it was real. I thought I meant something to him." She sighs, pressing her lips together, wiping her eyes, and looking away from me. "What is it?"

She glances back at me, biting her lip. "I talked to him."

A frown fills my face. "You did?"

She shrugs. "I don't think he meant to hurt you."

I glance at her, feeling betrayed. "You're joking."

"Don't get mad," she pleads, placing her hands on mine. "I live with him, Leila. I had to talk to him about what he did and… I don't think he did it on purpose."

I sigh, wanting to bite the bullet and ask her how he's doing, but I shake my head instead. "I heard what Jordan said, Rosie. The asshole waited until I left class and pulled me aside and told me everything. How he told Aiden to kiss me at that party, he told him to get my number, to sleep with me, all to get back at me for rejecting Jordan. How could that be an accident?"

She lays her head on my shoulder. "Why would Jordan be honest? Didn't he lie to Aiden about texting you?"

I pull my bottom lip between my teeth, shrugging. "That could have been another lie." But as I say the words, I don't know if they're true. "Aiden could have been in on it."

"I don't think so," Rosie says. "The guy is miserable." She lifts her head off my shoulder, glancing at me. "He hasn't left his room. He hasn't worked out, hasn't eaten, hasn't talked to Grayson." A frown paints her lips. "He's just as heartbroken as you."

I shake my head, squeezing my eyes shut. "None of it was real."

Rosie sighs, laying her head back on my shoulder, not saying another word. She looks around the floor at the empty packets laying by our feet. "You did it again," she whispers, quietly. "You promised me you wouldn't do it again."

I shut my eyes, tears filling my eyes. The reminder of Rosie catching me binging in high school a painful image. I spent so long trying to fix my issues and in a couple of weeks, I've ruined all progress. "I'm sorry."

She snaps her head up, her lip quivering. "*I'm* sorry." She shakes her head. "I should have been there for you more."

"You haven't left my side, Rosie. There's nothing more you could have done."

She lifts her pinky at me and I let out a breath, knowing what she's going to say. "Never again."

I nod, wrapping our pinkies together. "Never again."

"You come and talk to me, or Gabi or Madi." She frowns. "We love you, Leila. We'll do anything for you."

I nod, attempting a smile at my best friend. I know she's there for me, and I know what I did was a mistake, but I didn't even think about it. It was almost instinct. My stomach screams at me, pain racking through my body. I look around at all the wrappers on the floor. I didn't even realize I ate this much.

When I wince, she looks down at my hand pressing against my stomach and lifts off the floor holding her hand out, beckoning me to take it. "Let's go," she says. "We're going for a walk. Get your shoes."

I groan. "I don't want to leave."

She shrugs. "Remember when you ripped my curtains open and forced me to get out of bed?" she says, eyes glimmering as she smirks. "This is revenge, baby."

I roll my eyes, picking myself off the floor. "Grayson's a bad influence."

"Yeah," she says, smiling. "But I like it."

40
Too late

Aiden

I don't know what I'm doing here.

I'm not even sure if I'm still part of the team or if I'm going to lose my place here, so the gym is the last place I should be.

I should be getting my spot back on the team, I should be finding a way to get Jordan to drop this whole thing, but instead, I've spent the last week buried in bed with nothing but my thoughts to keep me company. Just the reminder that I royally fucked up. I was winning. I had the best thing in my life right there in my arms, and I fucked it all up.

I've always liked working out, exerting all my energy into what I'm doing, and if it means I'll focus on something else for a while, it's worth a try. When I get on the treadmill and the speed picks up, my legs feel the pain of laying in bed all week and I let out a curse, blowing out a breath. Fucking hate running.

It's not working.

I can't think of anything but her.

I miss her so much. I took the time we had for granted. I thought this was just the beginning, that I'd have forever to be with her, and hold her and kiss her, but I was so wrong. And now I've lost her.

I lift my head, shaking all thoughts out of my head. Fuck, heartbreaks suck. When I look up my heart stops and I tear my headphones off when I see a familiar brown ponytail swinging in front of me.

Fuck.

Leila.

I turn down the speed as I look at her. I haven't seen her since she was outside my doorstep, crying over how I broke her heart.

My eyes trace down her body. A body I once had my hands all over, kissing her, telling her how beautiful she was to me. I hate that she thinks everything between us was a lie. It was nothing but the truth. Being with her was the easiest thing in the world.

She looks so good. Her long brown hair is tied up, allowing me to see every inch of her face. A face I once held onto and kissed with so much love. My eyes trace her lips, remembering how sweet she tastes, how good her kisses felt. And when she turns her head and those beautiful green eyes lock on mine, my heart races out of my chest.

Fuck, I miss her.

And I love her.

But I've lost her.

I see it in the way her lips part and her eyes widen with shock, only for a second before her features contort with hurt. I know at that moment that she's done with me. And when she stops the machine, twisting her head and grabs her bags off the floor like she can't run away any faster, I step off the treadmill, heading towards her before she can leave.

Just one touch. Just my hands grabbing onto her elbow and my heart soars. My body breaks out into goosebumps from one touch. I am so fucking in love with this girl. She sucks in a breath when she feels me and steps back, staring at me with wide eyes. All I want to do is touch her and pull her into me. I just want to look into her eyes and tell her how much I love her.

I should have said it before. I should have told her the minute I fell in love with her because shouting it across the street when she was bawling her eyes out was the hardest thing I've had to do.

I didn't want to tell her I loved her to keep her. I wanted to tell her I loved her when I knew she was mine and when I was certain she'd feel the same for me.

"Don't leave," I tell her, my throat constricting with the words. "I'll go, Leila."

It's the first time I've spoken to her since that day. I just wish it wasn't this that I had to say. There's so much I want to say to her.

She doesn't say anything to me, her face stricken with anger, lips pursed as she stares back at me. I wish I could pause this moment, just to have her eyes on me for a second longer before I have to leave and never look at her again.

"I'm sorry." I take a step closer to her and she takes a step back, away from me, sucking in a breath. I let my head drop. "I'm so fucking sorry." I turn around and turn off the treadmill, walking out of the gym, with my heart back there clutched in her hands.

I've barely opened my front door when my phone buzzes in my pocket and when I see the name on the screen… I'm done. I'm fucking done.

Putting up with some guy blackmailing me, living in constant fear someone is going to find out my secret, giving up the woman I love, and all for what? To protect my family who never gave a shit about me?

There is no other reason he's calling. He doesn't care about me, he wants nothing but money.

When I answer the call, my stomach is riddled with guilt, knowing what I'm about to do, but I've lived in constant debt and I'm sick of it. I know if I don't put an end to it, it will never end.

"Listen, I need—"

"It's over."

A silence ticks and then he laughs. "What?"

My hands clutch my phone tighter. "This little arrangement we had? It's over. I'm not sending you any more money."

"What about Mom?" he asks, a bite to his tone. "Jerry's back. I can't leave her."

This excuse has gone on for way too long. Jerry hasn't been back in years, why would he be back now? "I thought you two handled him?" I ask my brother once again. "You told me you handled it. What exactly did you mean?" Silence. My brother is never silent. "What did you do, Brandon?"

"You wanted him gone, didn't you?" he yells, my bones chilling at the sound. "You wanted him out of our lives, out of Mom's life, and now he is."

My spine chills, a shiver running up it when I catch onto what he's telling me. "Tell me you didn't."

"We got it handled."

My body relaxes at the thought of Jerry not being alive, like knowing he can't hurt anyone ever again brings me peace, but it also makes my brain race a million miles per second. "So you've been lying to me?" My throat clams up. "You've been telling me he's back to get money out of me?" Another stab to the back. One after another, after another. "You used Jerry against me, knowing it's a sore subject." There are times that I can't get the image out of my head, and my brother knows this. He knows how much it fucked me up.

"You wouldn't give us our money."

"I've given you everything!" I shout into the phone. "I've given you everything I had. I have nothing else to give. Nothing." I run a hand down my face. "I should have done this a long time ago. I should have cut you off the minute I got away from you."

"Who the fuck do you think you're talking to?" My brother replies, venom coating his tone. "You'll do as I say or—"

"Or what?" I ask him, gritting out the words. "You have nothing on me. You and Mom have been punishing me for doing what none of you had the courage to do. I left, I fucking escaped that hell hole and now I have a good life, without any of you."

The more I speak, the lighter my body feels. I've been holding onto their dead weight for so long, wanting to make it right between us, wanting us to reconnect and be a real family even if I lost everything but what is the point? None of them would do the same for me. They spent my whole life beating me down—literally and figuratively—and I am fucking sick of it.

"Tell Mom I love her." I swallow down the emotions clogged in my throat. "I know she hates me but I will always love her. Tell her if she wants to get sober—really sober—then I will help her. Take her to a facility, find a professional, whatever she needs but I will never give any of you money again."

327

My brother scoffs on the other end. "The offer stands for you too," I tell him. "And for Cam when he gets out of jail." My voice softens when I hear silence on the other end. He isn't yelling… that's a start. "I will always help you, but I won't let you guys use and abuse me anymore."

When he doesn't answer, I let out a breath and hang up the phone. I've said what I needed to say, and if he's not happy with it, there's nothing I can do about it. When I stuff my phone in my pocket, my hand grazes against cold plastic. My eyes close, knowing exactly what's in my pocket and I take it out, looking over the picture of us both with green faces, my lips against hers in a kiss I can still feel.

She hasn't answered any of my texts, she's probably blocked me, removed me from her life, but I can't do the same. She's so wrong about it all. She doesn't know how much she means to me, how I can't think of a world where I'm not with her. She's ruined me for everyone else.

My thumb runs over her face in the picture. So goddamn beautiful. I had everything right here, and I lost it.

I sigh, stuffing my phone back into my pocket and head towards the kitchen, opening the fridge.

"You're out of your room." I turn around and see Grayson leaning against the door, arms crossed over his chest. His brows sit so high on his forehead, his shock almost makes me laugh.

I face away from him, grabbing the cheese and lettuce, out of the fridge. "I went to the gym." I grab the bread from the counter, placing the cheese on it. "Left early."

"Why?"

Annoyance nips at me, my jaw clenching as I take a bite of the sandwich. "She was there."

He nods, pressing his lips together. "Did you talk to her?"

I don't bother replying, turning my back and opening the fridge again. I reach for the Diet Coke, my eyes flashing back and forth to the six-pack of beer sat in there. My fingers itch, the urge to grab it and see what it tastes like so strong it's almost hard for me to stop myself. My hand twitches, getting closer to the cans.

"Don't do it."

Grayson's voice snaps me out of the quick fascination with wanting to know what it would be like. Just once. Would I feel better? I grab the Diet Coke, close the door behind me, and turn back around. I crack the can open and stare down at it to avoid looking at Grayson. "What do you mean?" I feign ignorance, taking a sip.

"Aiden," he says again in a tone that makes me feel guilty as fuck. "It's not worth it."

I place the can down on the counter, my eyes squeezing shut. Fuck, what did I just almost do? "I just don't want to hurt anymore." My voice cracks when I bury my head in my hands. "I want it to stop." I press the palm of my hands to my eyes. "It hurts all the time."

"Drinking is not going to solve it."

I lift my head, peering at my best friend. It wasn't that long ago that he was in the same position I was in. Heartbroken and wanting the pain to go away. "Remind me how you reacted," I tell him, nudging my head to the beer on the counter. "Last year with Rosie."

He sighs, shaking his head. "I get it, man, I do. I turned to alcohol because I couldn't control my feelings. I didn't understand what was going on, but you're not me. You're better than this."

"No, I'm not." Every bitter word and thought burning my body with the admission. "It's ingrained in my fucking DNA, Grayson." I press a hand to my chest, pressing it hard against the muscle that won't stop beating, hurting. "I'm destined to be a fuck up. She just realized that sooner." My eyes drop at the mention of Leila.

She looked so good today, but her smile was missing. That smile that she spent so long before allowing me to see. I did that. I took that happiness away trying to protect my family, my reputation. So stupid, so futile.

"That's not what happened," he says, narrowing his eyes at me. "And you know it."

I don't know anything. "Then what happened?" I ask him, shaking my head. "Fucking tell me because I'm at a loss here." I press my fingertips to my chest. "I love her and I fucking lost her."

"You hurt her," he says. "You did the one thing I told you not to do. I warned you to make sure you knew what you were doing."

The weight of his words hit me like a semi-truck. How many times did he tell me not to hurt her, to step away and leave her alone? I should have listened. I shouldn't have gotten involved with her and let Jordan release those pictures.

But I couldn't. I couldn't stay away. The more time I spent with her, the more intrigued I was. And the short moment I had her was the happiest I have ever been. It was worth it. It was worth all of this heartbreak for one second of her time, her affection.

"I didn't mean to hurt her." My eyes drop, the excuse too weak to hold up. I didn't mean to. But I did. "I was trying to protect my future." I close my eyes, tipping my head back. "I just didn't realize what I was giving up at the time."

"You didn't know?" Grayson asks, making my eyes snap open. "Because I've got to say, I'm having a hard time believing you would use her like this just for your own personal gain."

"Fuck no." My head shakes. "The bastard only asked for her number at the start and I thought... what's the harm?" I shrug. "She didn't even like me back then. It was an easy thing to do in exchange for not risking my future here." I blow out a breath. "But now, if I knew..." I let my words trail off knowing they mean nothing.

It's too late to change what happened. The only thing I can do is either hope she forgives me and realizes I wasn't lying about us... Or let her move on without me, even if it kills me.

"I don't know what to do," I admit, my shoulders slumping. "She won't talk to me." I shake my head, remembering how she barely looked at me in the gym. "She can't even look at me."

He blows out a breath. "You fucked up. I'm not going to lie." His lips twitch when I glare at him. "But there must be something we can do."

I peer at him. "We? I thought you were pissed at me," I say.

He huffs out a laugh. "I was. But Rosie doesn't seem to think you hurt her best friend on purpose."

"I wouldn't." My hands drop. "I would give everything else up for another second with her." Nothing is worth losing her. Nothing. Not even basketball. "Fuck." My head snaps up. "That's it."

"What is?"

"That's fucking it." I grab the can from the counter, drinking the rest of it. I throw it in the trash, heading out of the kitchen.

"What are you doing?" he asks.

"I have to go."

"Aiden. Don't do something stupid." His voice rattles on as I head for the door.

Too late.

41

Nothing else to lose

Aiden

My phone rings in my hand, Grayson's name flashing on the screen. I tuck it into my pocket as I push the door open. I find him right away sitting on the couch, lip locked with some girl. I whistle, getting his attention, and he rips his mouth away from her, eyebrows furrowing when he sees me.

"The fuck do you want?" Jordan asks.

"Release it."

His brows deepen. "What?"

"The pictures," I clarify. "Release them."

His eyes widen when he catches on to what I'm saying and whispers something to the girl, setting her aside and gesturing to the stairs with his head.

I follow him upstairs, the urge to pull him down and beat his ass so fucking strong.

"Are you out of your mind?" he yells when we reach his room.

"You want the captain position, right?" His eyes look at me uneasily. "Then release them."

"Why now?" he asks skeptically. "You were so hellbent on doing whatever I said to keep it hidden."

I glare at him. "Because it doesn't matter anymore."

He shakes his head, looking at me with confusion. "All for some pussy?" He scoffs.

My jaw tightens, my fists curling up by my side, knowing I can't hit him. "Release the fucking pictures," I grit out.

He blows out a breath. "Can't do that," he says on a shrug.

"What?" The longer I spend around him, the more I want to punch him. "Don't you want the captain position? Isn't that why you blackmailed me?"

"I do," he says, narrowing his eyes at me. "But like I said, Aiden, I don't want you off the team." He shrugs. "Besides, with your little drug problem, I've stepped in as Captain." His grin is so smug and I almost smile, knowing I have him right where I want him.

"How did you do it?" I ask him. "How did you mess with the drug tests?"

"I didn't." My brows furrow in annoyance. I know it was him. I need him to admit it. "That was all you."

"What are you talking about? I haven't taken any drugs."

He laughs, shaking his head. "You did. You just didn't know you did."

"What?"

"You're so careless with your drinks," he says, crossing his arms. "It was almost too easy dropping it in there."

My heart races at the realization of what he did. "You drugged me?" I grit out.

He rolls his eyes. "Relax. It's not like you're not used to it." Motherfucker. I want to hit him so bad. "It was half a pill. Not enough to affect you, but enough to show up on the test."

I wipe a hand down my face. The more he talks, the less control I have, and I need control right now. "All of this because of jealousy?" I ask him, shaking my head. "Just release the pictures, Jordan. You'll get what you want."

"And you?" he asks. "What will you get?"

"Maybe nothing. Hopefully everything," I admit, clenching my jaw. "Either way I have nothing to lose."

He laughs, shaking his head. "Is she really worth all of this?"

Without a fucking doubt. "Yes."

"Well, that's too bad." He shrugs. "I don't have them."

"What do you mean you don't have them?"

"I deleted them," he says. "You did what I wanted you to do." He runs his tongue over his teeth. "You hurt that bitch, just like she hurt me."

"She didn't hurt you. She rejected you, and you were too much of a man-child to accept she wanted nothing to do with you."

He glares. "Doesn't change anything. You still dumped her like I wanted you to." My fists curl. "I have no reason to release the pictures."

Fuck.

I played right into his hand.

I shake my head, racing out of that place before I put him in the ground. My hands reach for my phone, scrolling through the messages he sent on his burner phone. The pictures are all still there.

I've got nothing else to lose.

42

Secret's out

Leila

The girls are all crowded together, looking down at their phones when I walk into the café.

"Hey," I say, approaching them. They all look at me and then look back at each other. My brows knit together. "What's wrong?"

"Have you checked your phone?" Madi asks.

I drop my bag to the ground, sitting at the table. "No, why?"

They all share a look again. What the hell is going on? I pull my phone out of my pocket and unlock it. I'm not even sure what I'm looking for but I find it immediately. Right there, when I open my phone are pictures.

My heart races, knowing these pictures are of Aiden's family. His brother has a darker shade of brown hair, but that face… there's no doubt this is Aiden's brother. I scroll down, another image pops up. The name on the mug shot reading Cameron Pierce.

I swallow the gravel in my throat, scrolling through, seeing more pictures. There's a short, blonde woman in one of them and my heart aches when I realize this is Aiden's mother. Wrinkles coat her skin, her eyes sunken into her skull. She looks so small, but I know the kind of pain she inflicted on

Aiden. The kind of pain he still carries with him, on his body and in his mind.

Jordan did it. He posted the pictures.

I glance around, seeing everyone murmuring and looking at their phones. They've all seen these pictures. Everyone has seen who Aiden's family really are.

All of his efforts were for nothing. All the time and the lies and making me fall for him… it was all for nothing.

"Have you guys ordered?" I ask, tucking my phone into my pocket. They don't answer me. I look down at the napkins on the table but I can feel their eyes on me, assessing me, questioning me.

"Are you okay?"

My eyes snap open, glancing up at Gabi, who glances down at her phone screen that's turned off now. I tilt my head at her. "Why wouldn't I be?"

Rosie presses her lips together. "You knew, didn't you? He told you about his family."

I shrug, wishing I had a drink to wet my dry lips. "He said a lot of things. Who knows what was true?"

"Leila," Madi says, placing a hand on my arm. "You're not concerned? I know he hurt you," she says frowning. "But just imagine what he's going through. Have you talked to him?"

"We're broken up. Why would I talk to him?" Thoughts of seeing him in the gym yesterday run through my mind, ripping my heart to shreds. I can't stop thinking about it. Can't stop seeing the look of desperation and guilt on his face. Of how he grabbed onto me desperately, almost as if he didn't want to let go.

"I'm going to order." I get up from the table, avoiding their pitied looks. I don't even make it to the front desk without hearing murmurs and Aiden's name. I should hate him. I should be thankful that it all blew up in his face and he got what he deserved... but I hate it.

I don't bother ordering, leaving the café and going to see the one person who I wish I could avoid forever.

I knock on the big blue door to the frat house. Some other guy opens the door, furrows his brows at the sight of me, glancing behind him. Oh, for fucks sake, I don't have time for this.

I push past him, hearing him curse an insult at me as I do. It's impossible not to notice Jordan instantly, legs spread open as he sits on the couch, a controller in his hands. He spots me and groans. "Jesus," he spits out, throwing the controller to the side. "Not you too."

I lift an eyebrow. "I don't want to see you any more than you want to see me."

He laughs, rubs his mouth. "Are you here for your boyfriend?" he asks. "You're late."

My palms itch. "I don't have a boyfriend."

He snorts. "Right. Hurts, doesn't it?"

I don't want to stay here any longer than I have to, but I've been racking my brain for answers. "Why did you do it?" I ask.

"Do what?"

I glare at him. "Don't play coy with me." After all, he was the one who told me all about his plan, his texts with Aiden, how he manipulated everything. "Why did you tell him to kiss me?"

He shrugs. "I didn't."

"What?"

"I didn't tell him to kiss you," he says, staring at me. "I just told him to get your number."

"But you said—"

"I lied," he says with a shrug, grabbing the controller in his hand, and staring back at the screen. "Wanted you two to be over."

"Why?"

He laughs, shakes his head, but doesn't reply. I stalk over to him, ripping the controller out of his hands. "Bitch," he scolds. I almost laugh. How original. "I needed to get back at you," he admits, flaring his nostrils.

I flinch, taking a step back. "Back at me? For what? What did I ever do to you?"

"You don't remember?" He tilts his head.

"Remember what?"

"The party, Leila," he growls. "Freshman year, two weeks after we hooked up." He sniffs, turning to the side. "I came onto you and you pushed me away."

My mind starts spinning, remembering back to when Jordan was getting too touchy, grabbing me when I didn't want him to, whispering in my ear about how he was going to fuck me so good.

"You threw your fucking drink on me, in front of everyone." He turns back to face me, his face hard. "Made me seem like a loser after some fat chick."

I've got to say, even after everything, that word still manages to hit like a punch to my stomach. And knowing I was intimate with this guy, even after thinking I was in control of the situation, thinking I had him right where I wanted him, it hurts knowing I was right. I was nothing but a challenge.

"You wouldn't let me go," I tell him.

"I just wanted to talk to you," he says, taking a step closer to me.

339

I take a step back, creating space between us. "I didn't want to talk to you. I still don't. I just needed to know why you would do all of this."

"You humiliated me. Pierce was my main goal," he says, dragging his eyes down my body. "Getting my revenge on you was just the cherry on top."

"That was over a year ago." I narrow my eyes at him. "I didn't even remember it."

He sniffs. "You act like such a stuck-up bitch, but you came onto me first," he says, pointing at me. "You approached me. You kissed me. You wanted it."

I tilt my head at him. "Must have been the alcohol." My eyes snake over his body. "Because nothing's appealing about you right now."

He snarls. "You ghosted me right after. Didn't even look at me."

"You told me to act like you didn't exist. Besides." I lift my shoulders in a shrug. "The first time was bad enough. Didn't want a repeat."

He laughs, bitterly. "You should consider yourself lucky I threw you a pity fuck."

"And yet, you did all of this because I rejected you." He blows out a breath through his nose, agitated. "Why Aiden?" I ask. "Why bring him into it?"

His lips twitch, smirking and I hate it. "That's a different issue," he says. "But who better to do a job I couldn't do?" he says. "He would do anything to save his reputation."

"Aiden's not like that," but the words die on my tongue right after I say them.

He smirks. "Got him to do it, didn't I?"

My heart breaks all over again. No matter how much I think I know Aiden and what his true intentions were, I don't. I don't know anything about him, or if everything he said was just to keep up his end of the deal.

"I just didn't expect him to fall for you," he says, running his tongue over his teeth. "Thought he'd do his job, lead you on and leave."

"What do you mean?"

He tilts his head, looks me up and down. "He sent your number a long time ago. I had what I needed."

"Then why did he keep pursuing me?" I gave him my number before anything even happened between us. Why didn't he just quit as soon as he got what he needed?

He laughs. "Because he lost his mind."

I love you, Leila.

Everything was real.

Aiden's words race through my mind, making me think of how he looked at me, begged me, desperately to hear him out. Could he... Was it real?

"I've got to go."

A hand on my arm stops me and I look up at Jordan who's got a grin on his face. "You know," he says, looking me up and down. "This can all be fixed." His eyes meet mine, filled with heat. "I could learn to forgive you."

I nudge his hand off my shoulder and glare at him. "I'd rather fuck a hundred guys over you."

He laughs and tilts his head. "Haven't you done that already?"

I spin on my heels, push his front door open, and walk out of that house. My head spins, thinking back to the one guy I let go that meant everything to me.

Was he being real? Did he mean what he said to me? Does he… love me?

I pull my phone out, scrolling through the pictures that Jordan posted on social media. The comments are brutal, endless, and soul-crushing.

I can't imagine what Aiden's going through right now. I don't even know If he would want to talk to me after everything. I was the one who made these pictures leak. His life is ruined because of me.

Aiden

The first thing I hear when I walk into the living room is a little kid cursing at Grayson.

"Dude, you're like ten."

"Eleven actually, grandpa."

Grayson snickers, turning his head when he spots me. "Hey, how are you?"

"Who are you talking to? Your mom?" The kid's voice booms through the headset Grayson has around his neck. His eyebrows shoot up, a smirk on his lips.

"My friend," Grayson replies.

"Oooh. A girlfriend?"

Grayson laughs, shaking his head. "Nope, a guy friend."

"BOO." Grayson winces when the kid's voice bellows through the headset. "I'm off, you're boring."

The kid disconnects, leaving the game.

"I swear I'm never playing multiplayer again," Grayson says, looking at me. "I'm terrified of kids."

A scoff escapes me as I sit beside him. "I'm sure you were worse than him at his age."

He laughs, running a hand down his face. When he turns to look at me, he squints, assessing me. "You did it, didn't you?" he asks. "You uploaded the pictures."

"Yeah."

He nods. "You really think it's going to help?"

I blow out a breath, fixing the cap on my head. "I don't know." It was the only thing I thought to do. "I'm sorry," I tell him. "You took the fall for me freshman year and I just blew it."

He shakes his head. "I don't care about that shit. The only people I care about know who I am." He lifts his chin at me. "What about you?" he asks. "What if everything else turns to shit?"

There's a high possibility of that happening. But at this point, I don't care about anything else. There's one person in my head at all times of the day, it's the only thing I care about. "I don't have basketball anymore." I lift my shoulders in a shrug. "I don't have Leila. What else do I have to lose?"

His eyes narrow, shaking his head. "You still have school."

"Without a scholarship I'm out of here, and then what? Where do I go? I can't go back home." I shake my head, the mere thought of it sending shivers down my body. "I *won't*." I have what I need. If everything goes well, I'll have my scholarship back, but if not... I lose everything.

"I would never let that happen," he says. "The scholarship won't be a problem."

"No." I shake my head. "I'm not taking handouts from you." It's bad enough he doesn't let me pay rent here, I'm not letting him pay for school too.

"It's not a handout. I just want to help you."

I rub my hand down my face. "I promised Leila I would be good for her. That I would be someone worth her time." My heart starts beating at the sound of her name. "I told her she'd

344

never have to worry about my shitty past. If I accept handouts, I'm proving her wrong."

"You told her?" he asks. "About your family?"

"Every fucking bit," I admit, pressing my fingers to my temples.

"Damn. That's more than you've told me." It's more than I've told anybody. She knows everything. Every part of me. "You really love her, don't you?" he asks.

What a stupid question. "More than I ever thought possible."

"You could have come to me." He throws the controller to the side, turning to face me. "I would have helped you with Jordan."

My jaw tightens. "I thought I had it handled." Truth is, I didn't want anyone to know. Grayson knew some of what I went through back home, but not enough, not to the point where I'd be willing to show him those pictures and put all of my vulnerability on the table.

"And it all blew up instead."

I glare at him. "Yeah, I got that. Thanks."

When my phone rings, I pull it out of my pocket, my heart thrashing against my chest when I see the name on the screen. "It's Leila." I swallow down the lump in my throat. She's calling me?

He taps me on the back. "Good luck, man." He stands up and walks out of the living room.

I don't know what to do. I just stare at the screen like a jackass, looking over the five letters over and over again. Is this really happening? I press the green answer button and bring the phone to my ear.

There's silence on the other end, just the soft tone of her breathing. I clutch the phone in my hands, letting my eyes fall closed. "Am I dreaming?" She doesn't answer though, her breathing getting a little faster, a little harder. "Leila." My voice is thick, desperate. "Please, talk to me."

"How are you?" I tip my head back at her beautiful voice. I've missed it so much. I've missed her. My heart beats so fast it's almost still. Is this what dying feels like?

"Right now," I say with a low chuckle. "Fucking amazing."

"Why's that?" I can almost picture her cute little smile, or maybe that's what I want her to be doing. Maybe she's not smiling at all. Hope she is, though.

"Because you're talking to me." I don't even know what this means, I don't really care at the moment. She's talking to me.

The sigh that comes out of her destroys me. "Aiden."

"Fuck. Not yet," I interrupt before she can hang up or say this was a mistake or anything else. "Please, just a little bit longer." She might not forgive me, or believe me, but I just want to hear her voice a little longer. "Don't hang up yet."

Each second of silence breaking me apart, until her soft voice says, "Okay."

I smile, stretching out my legs over the coffee table. "So, how was class? Is Professor Wilson still giving the same boring lectures?" I don't want to talk about us right now. There might not even be an us, I just want to talk to her. "I don't miss his classes, that's for sure." I've always been interested in business. Basketball was my main goal, but having a business degree would be a good fallback if my dream didn't happen. But Professor Wilson manages to turn a simple subject into a drag. I should be attending classes, but knowing my scholarship is on the line and everyone sees me differently... I couldn't go. I barely had the energy to get out of bed.

"Yeah," she says, I can hear the ruffling of her favorite blanket that she always has around her shoulders. "He's moved onto accounting." The little laugh that comes from her sounding like a symphony from the angels themselves. "I swear I nearly fell asleep last week."

I can't hold it in any longer. I blow out a breath. "I've missed you." When she doesn't reply, I worry I've fucked it already, I went too fast. But it's hard thinking about anything else when I have her on the phone with me.

"How are you?" she asks. "About everything."

My gorgeous girl, always worried even after I hurt her. "I've been better," I tell her.

After a few minutes, she sighs. "I'm sorry Jordan did that to you."

Well, now's as good a time as ever. "He didn't."

A few seconds tick by. "What do you mean?"

"I uploaded them, Leila," I say, blowing out a breath.

"What?" she says breathily. "Why?"

I barely know the answer myself, just that I needed to do it. "I had nothing else to lose," I tell her. "Basketball was the one thing I thought meant everything to me, but it felt dull and pointless. It wasn't worth losing you."

"Aiden."

"Nothing was a lie, Leila," I blurt out, squeezing my eyes shut. "Nothing. Jordan manipulated me. I played right into his hands and did exactly what he wanted. I should have done this from the start, I should have let him release the pictures and say fuck it."

347

I hear the sharp intake of a breath from the other end and continue, throwing my heart on the line. "Basketball was my priority and I would have done anything to protect that. I wanted people to respect me here, and that wouldn't have happened if everyone found out the truth. But I didn't know what his intentions were."

I shake my head, hoping she believes me. "He wanted your number. I didn't even know you back then, I just thought this loser—whoever he was—just wants a shot with a girl he can't have. It was easy to do in exchange for keeping my reputation intact. But the more time I spent with you…" I trail off, letting out a harsh breath. "Everything that happened between us had nothing to do with him. It was us. All fucking us. Nothing was a lie."

She's quiet for so long, I pull back to check she hasn't hung up. "How do I know I can trust you?" she asks.

I run my hand down my face. "I've given up everything just for the possibility that you would know I wasn't lying to you. I can't tell you to trust me, that's your decision to make, all I'm asking is to believe that I would never hurt you on purpose. I didn't sleep with you or kiss you to save my ass, I did it because I liked you. I did it because I love you."

She sucks in a breath, and I force myself to continue. "I don't even know where to go from here or what's going to happen. People aren't going to look up to me anymore, that's for sure." I let out a sigh. "They know I'm a nobody now."

"You're not a nobody," she says, my chest aching for her.

"I don't even care about that," I admit. "I don't care what they think of me." I press my lips together, my hand squeezing the phone. "I only care what you think of me." I open my eyes, wishing she was in front of me, wishing I could look into her

348

beautiful eyes and say this. "You're the only one who really knows me."

"You know me too," she says with a harsh breath. "Better than I know myself."

I smile, picturing her. "I know," I tell her. "I know how much you love cats and wish you had one of your own. I know how much you love those disgusting candies but never let yourself have them." I pause, gulping. "I know how much I hurt you. And how you think I did exactly what your prick of an ex-boyfriend did."

"Aiden."

"I know how much you love your dad," I continue. "He's right, you know. Eres una tigresa." She lets out a laugh at my bad Spanish pronunciation. "So confident," I say, remembering how scared she was to do that photoshoot and did it anyway. I've always admired how she seemed to do whatever she wanted, even if it scared her to sometimes. "So fearless, and so strong." I swallow. "But tigers are also warm-hearted, soft. They're sensitive and emotional and capable of great love."

I let my eyes drift closed. "You deserve that great, huge, earth-shattering love, Leila," I say. "And I'm willing—dying—to give that to you. If you let me." My heart beats so fast for this woman. "I love you, Leila."

This is it. I've said everything I needed to say. My whole heart is out there for her. If she tells me she doesn't want to be with me, that she doesn't trust me, or doesn't believe me, there's nothing I can do. I want to fight for us, but I don't want to keep hurting her.

"Where are you?"

I lift myself off the couch, opening the door. "Anywhere you want me to be."

She laughs. Fuck, I love that sound. "Can you be here in ten?"

I'm already out of the door when I say, "Make it five."

44

He loves me,
he loves me not

Leila

I never thought my heart could race so fast from just a knock at the door, but when I open the door and those bright blue eyes are looking down at me, it manages to beat even faster.

Aiden licks his lips, staring down at me. "Leila." I smile at my name coming from his lips. He doesn't say anything else, his head shaking slightly as he looks at every inch of my face, from my lips, to my eyes, to my cheeks; there isn't a part of me that doesn't feel the burn of his gaze.

The door opens wider when I take a step back, allowing him to come in. The moment he enters my apartment and I close the door behind us, it feels like he was never supposed to leave. "It's weird," I breathe out. "This place has felt so empty without you, and as soon as you come in, it feels like home again."

He turns around to face me, his brows shooting up, the meaning of my words lingering between us. I pull my bottom lip between my teeth, trying to avoid him. When I look up, his eyes aren't on mine, they're on my chest, or more specifically, on the gold necklace dangling around my neck. I watch as his Adam's apple bobs with a gulp. "You're still wearing the necklace."

I haven't been able to take it off. It's the only thing I had of him, the one thing that meant the most to me. My head drops, a tear falling down my face. His hands are on me in a second, cupping my cheeks and lifting my head until I can see him. "Please don't cry," he pleads, running his thumb over my cheek. "It breaks my heart all over again."

"I'm just so lost." I drop my eyes again, the feel of his hands on me too much to think straight. "I don't know what to think, Aiden." I blow out a breath, and when I look back at him, the look in his eyes almost makes me break down again. "I have so many thoughts running around in my head," I admit. "I feel like I'm five again, picking flower petals. He's lying, he's telling the truth. He loves me, he loves me not."

"Loves you," he says, staring into my eyes. "He loves you so fucking much." He drops his eyes, grabbing my hand and brings it to his lips, pressing them softly against my skin. "I am so in love with you it hurts."

I squeeze my eyes closed, stopping the tears pooling in my eyes. "I loved you too."

I can *feel* his heart breaking as he drops my hand and takes a step back from me. "Loved?" he asks. "Past tense?"

I look to the side, avoiding eye contact. "I believe you," I admit. "I believe you didn't sleep with me for your benefit. But that doesn't change the fact that you still played me. You flirted, asked for my number constantly until I gave in."

"I gave him your number before we even slept together, Leila. It was before everything. Before you entered my life and twisted it upside down." I force myself to look at him, my heart aching when I do. "Nothing has been the same since. And I don't want it to be. My life had no meaning before you. Basketball, graduate, get drafted. That's all I ever wanted."

When I take a step closer, he shakes his head. "But now all I want is you," he continues. "It's you that makes me want to get up in the mornings, it's you that makes me smile. It's you that makes me happy." He takes one step towards me, closing the distance between us and leans in, brushing my hair behind my ear. "It's you I'm so desperately in love with."

I let my eyes flutter closed, pressing my hands against his chest. He stiffens between me, not knowing whether I'm going to push him away, or tell him to leave, but I do something else. I raise my hands, feeling every ridge of his torso until I wrap my arms around his neck, finding my place at the crook of his neck. "Aiden," I whisper, looking into his eyes.

He shivers under my touch. "Yeah, gorgeous?"

"Kiss me."

He breathes hard, his lips parting as he looks at me. "Are you serious?"

I nod, the corner of my lips tilting in a smile as I lift myself onto my toes until our lips are stacked, less than an inch between us.

His hands drift down to hold on to my waist. "You need to be one hundred percent sure about this, Leila. I'm not letting you leave me ever again. Not a fucking chance."

"I'm sure."

"Thank fuck," he murmurs before crashing his lips to mine. I let out a yelp when his hands grab onto my ass, tightening his hold on me. His touch lights me up inside, feeling him everywhere, on my body, on my lips, in my heart. When he pulls back, he grins. "This means what I think it means, right?" he asks.

I nod, smiling up at him. "It means you're all mine."

He laughs, shaking his head. "I've always been yours," he says, brushing his lips against mine. "From that very first kiss, you marked yourself into my heart. It will always be you. Always, Leila."

My heart races, my brain screaming three little words at me until I let them out. "I love you, Aiden."

"You do?" His hands freeze on me, squeezing my hips.

"So much," I admit. "I tried to hate you, I tried to push everything I felt for you deep down, but I couldn't." And I wouldn't want to. "You're the only person I have ever loved this much." I let out a laugh, loving how he smiles at the sound. "It's killing me. You've ruined me."

He presses his lips to my forehead, chuckling. "You ruined me a long time ago, baby. Time you caught up."

I roll my eyes, nudging him and he lets out a laugh. "I love you," he says, whispering the words over and over again over my skin, kissing my cheek, my eyebrows, my lips.

When he pulls back though, his expression sombers. "Things are going to change, Leila," he says with a sigh. "People might say some nasty shit to you for being with me. Are you sure you're okay with that?"

My stomach drops at the thought of Aiden thinking I don't want to be with him because of what other people think of him. I didn't fall for his reputation. I fell for him. I shrug, cupping the back of his neck. "I've heard every nasty thing I could have. It won't bother me."

He frowns, lifting my chin with his thumb. "You're lying," he says. "I know how much it bothers you." He shakes his head, letting out a sigh. "I hate that people have hurt you." His frown deepens, a line forming between his brows. "I hate that I was one of them."

I let out a breath. "It's inevitable, Aiden." There are always going to be people who have hate inside of them, and there's nothing I can do to stop them. I glance up at him, uncertainty building in my chest. "Are you sure you're okay with being seen with me?"

His shoulders drop, cradling my face in his hands. "It breaks my fucking heart when you say that," he admits. "I don't want to keep you hidden; you're not a dirty secret, Leila. You're my girlfriend." He leans in, pressing his lips against mine. "It would be my fucking privilege."

45

Whatever it takes

Leila

I'm so comfortable right now, I don't want to move.

Aiden's breath hits my skin, and I know he's awake. I wonder how long he's been watching me sleep, how many times he's pressed his lips against my forehead and whispered 'I love you' against my skin. I've caught him doing that a few times.

It's the best way to wake up. My leg flung around his waist, my arms wrapped around him, not wanting to let go. It's crazy that mere months ago, he wasn't in my life. I couldn't ever imagine getting this close to another person like I have with Aiden.

When my eyes flutter open and I look up at his face, he's smiling down at me. God, I really like his smile. "What time is it?" I slur, still half asleep. We may have stayed up all night kissing and talking and making love… and more kissing. It was so much fun.

"A little after two," he says, brushing the strands of my hair out of my face and leaning in to kiss my forehead. I let out a sigh, melting at his touch. He hasn't stopped kissing me since, and I revel in it, loving every one of his touches.

"We should get out of bed soon," I murmur, pulling the covers down.

He stops me, pulls me into him, and buries his head in my neck, pressing his lips all over my skin. "A little longer," he mumbles. "Don't want to let you go yet."

I let out a laugh, turning to look at him. "You've had me all weekend."

"Not long enough."

I have to agree. I don't think I'll ever get enough of him. But I have a feeling that It's not the only reason he doesn't want to leave this room. "Are you nervous?" I ask him, running my hands along his abs, smiling when I feel him flexing under my touch. I love his body, love the hard ridges of his torso, how he's so hard against my soft. "About the drug testing?"

He lets out a sigh. "Unless someone snuck drugs in my drink again, then I'm clean."

I still can't believe Jordan did that, knowing how Aiden feels about drugs it must have scared him out of his mind that someone he considered a friend would ever do that to him. "Then why are you so tense?"

He turns, wrapping his arms around me and places his chin on my head. "Everything is going to be different," he says. "None of the guys are going to respect me anymore. I probably won't be captain." I know how hard Aiden has worked to make the team look up to him, and the thought of him being made a fool of brings an ache to my chest. "I don't really want to think of anything else right now," he whispers. "I just want to be in bed with you a little longer."

A flutter of guilt flashes through me, knowing he's only in this mess because he wanted me to forgive him. "I didn't tell you to do that, you know?" I peer up at him. "I would never have let you release the pictures if I knew."

He shakes his head, pressing a kiss against my cheek. "I know Leila. It was all on me, I needed to do it."

My hand freezes on his stomach. "Are you worried about seeing Jordan?"

He glares, his hand squeezing my bare hip. "Please. Don't say his name when you're naked in bed with me."

I laugh, pressing my lips together. "Sorry."

"I hate the thought of that asshole ever seeing you like this," he says running his hand over my skin. "I wish I would have met you sooner. Seen you right when you came to Redfield." He stares into my eyes. "You wouldn't have ever had to meet guys like him."

I love him for saying that. The smile on my face tries to convey that, but it falls weak. "You probably wouldn't have even given me a second look."

His smile is wiped clean, his face shattering. "You're kidding, right?"

"Aiden," I sigh. "You didn't even notice me until you needed to get my number. I don't hold that against you, but it's the truth."

He shakes my head, breathing out a laugh. "I remember a very different first impression of you."

I narrow my eyes. "You do?"

He nods, shuffling closer to me. "At the bar, about a year ago," he murmurs, running his hands over my body like he physically can't stop touching me. "When I was working, Rosie came over and ordered a beer for you. I told her it was on me."

I still, flashes of the night Aiden bought me a drink flooding my mind. "I didn't think you'd remember that." When I looked at him, he was talking to another girl and I thought nothing of it. I didn't know it would eventually bring me here, with him.

"You were talking to someone else," he says, smiling down at me. "Laughing, smiling, all for some other guy. I didn't think you even noticed me."

I did. I noticed him even though I desperately didn't want to. "If I knew…"

He shakes his head. "Don't worry about that, gorgeous. I have you now."

I smile, my heart thumping against my chest. "I wouldn't want to go back."

"No?"

I shake my head. "I like our story."

He smiles. "I *love* our story." He rubs his thumb over my cheeks. "Who knew a game of spin the bottle would bring me to you," he jokes, shooting me a smirk.

I let out a laugh. "You'll have to thank Gabi for that."

"Thank you, Gabi," he mutters, pressing his lips against mine.

I reluctantly pull away from him, and turn toward the phone ringing on my nightstand. I reach over to grab it, smiling when I see my sister's name on the screen. I accept the FaceTime call, Laura's face filling the screen.

"You're still in bed?

I let out a laugh. "Hi to you too."

She squints. "Who does that shoulder belong to?"

I turn to Aiden, who's grinning when he pops his face into the screen. "Hi."

My sister's eyes widen when she sees Aiden sitting next to me in bed, shirtless. "Well, it's nice to meet you…"

"Aiden," he finishes for her.

She turns to face me, and I shrug. "It's new?" I offer.

She laughs, letting out a sigh. "I can see that you're happy." I can't help but look at Aiden when she says that.

"Yeah," I say, looking into his eyes. "I am."

"¿Laura, con quién estás hablando?" *Who are you talking to?*

My sister's eyes widen at my mom's voice. "Oh shit."

"Leila?" Her face pops up on the screen, my sister mouthing 'I'm sorry' at me. I haven't spoken to my mom since I hung up on her, and seeing her again makes my stomach cramp. "Leila, mija, quería hablar de—" The words die on her tongue when her eyes dart to Aiden who smiles at her. "Leila," she says in a serious voice. "¿Por qué hay un chico en tu cama?" *Why is there a boy in your bed?*

My sister laughs, pressing her hand to her mouth, and I let out a breath. "Because he's my boyfriend, Ma," I tell her, hating how her eyes squint, questioning me. "This is Aiden. We're dating."

"Hi, Mrs. Pérez," Aiden says, squeezing my hand under the covers. "It's nice to meet you."

She presses her lips together, eyeing me. "Leila, mi amor," she starts, my heart beating with the anticipation of whatever words are going to come out of her mouth and make me question everything about myself. "¿Estás feliz?" *Are you happy?*

I freeze, wondering if I heard that right. My sister glances at my mother, also in shock and Aiden squeezes harder. I clear my throat. "Yes, Mom," I reply in English, so Aiden knows exactly what she asked me. "I'm very happy."

My mother nods, her lips lifting in a smile. "Then It's wonderful to meet you too, Aiden," she says to my boyfriend. When she turns to me, her expression sobers. "I wanted to talk to you. I'd like to apologize," she tells me. "I should have never said any of those things to you, Leila. You are my daughter, you are beautiful, and smart and talented. I just wanted you to have the best life you could have."

Hearing her apologize is all I've ever wanted. I've dreamed of hearing these words from her, that she loves me, that she still sees me as beautiful even if I'm bigger than her, that she wants me to be happy. But actually hearing her say it, makes my heart ache for what I went through as a little girl, all the pain she caused me. "I can still have that, Mom," I tell her. "My weight has nothing to do with my happiness. I am happy, and I want to love myself, but it's hard to do that when you don't love me."

Her mouth drops as she shakes her head. "Of course, I love you, Leila. I just—"

"You just told me I wasn't pretty enough." Aiden's hand tightens around mine. "You just said I would have a better life if I was thin. Well, I'm not. I'm not thin, and I probably never will be, but I'm okay with that. I just need you to let me live my life without the comments about my body. That's all I need you to do. Can you do that, Mom?"

She's quiet for a while, and my eyes dart to the corner of the screen where my dad is standing by the door, arms crossed over his chest. The smile on his face says everything without him ever uttering a word. *I'm proud of you.* And I'm proud of myself too, for finally telling my mom how I feel, and putting myself first.

"I can do that," she finally says.

All the tension in my shoulders lifts when I let out a breath. "Thank you."

She nods, smiling at me before she turns to Aiden. "You better take care of my daughter," she tells him.

"I will," he tells my mom, smiling at her. "I'll do whatever it takes to make sure she's happy."

46

Payback

Aiden

When I push the door open and I see all of my teammates on the court, it brings me a kind of hurt I can't explain. Basketball has been all I've had for so long that knowing it could all be taken away from me today makes me nervous.

Coach turns his head when the door closes, spotting me approaching him. "Pierce," he says. "The test is scheduled for tomorrow. You're still under suspension."

"I know, Coach, I was wondering if I could talk to you."

He lifts his chin. "Can it wait?"

"Not really." The longer I hold on to this information, the longer Jordan thinks he won, but he hasn't, not even close.

I spot him on the court, narrowing his eyes at me, his cheeks blazing with anger. How did I not see it before? These guys have been like my family since freshman year, knowing that one of them stabbed me in the back hurts like hell.

Coach's whistle goes off, and everyone comes to a halt. "Practice is over," he shouts.

"Hell yes," Carter mutters, running to the locker rooms.

"Nice to see you, Cap," Andre says, patting me on the shoulder.

When everyone leaves, the asshole approaches me. "What do you think you're doing?" Jordan asks, narrowing his eyes at me.

I shake my head, almost laughing at how much of a piece of shit he is. "You want to ruin my future? I can do the same." His nostrils flare, but I don't elaborate. Jordan scatters when Coach approaches me.

"What did you want to talk about?" he asks, walking ahead of me to his office.

The minute the door shuts, I let out a breath. "I have proof."

"Of?" Coach asks, sitting at his desk.

"That the drug testing was tampered with."

His brows shoot up. "What proof?"

I pull out my phone from my pocket and open up the recording I have of Jordan admitting everything. Admitting to blackmailing me, admitting that he messed with the drug testing. All of it.

When the recording ends, Coach looks up at me. "This is Jordan?"

I made sure to say his name so that there would be no confusion. That asshole might have controlled me for the past few months, but I'm not letting him get away with it. "Yes, Coach," I say. "He wanted the captain position and was willing to blackmail and drug me to make it happen."

Coach lets out a sigh, shaking his head. "He's been coming to me for a while asking to reconsider him being captain." My eyes widen at the admission. All this time? "I didn't think he would be a threat, but this is serious," he says, shaking his head. "This is damning evidence."

My heart starts to race. "So what does this mean?"

"It means I was right all along in believing in you," he says, nodding. I'll always be grateful for Coach seeing something in me and giving me an opportunity. "And it means you're back on the team."

"And the scholarship?"

"Still very much intact."

My shoulders drop, all the weight lifting off them. "Thanks, Coach."

"I didn't want to have to do this," he says, lifting off his chair. "But Jordan is out, and my guess is he'll no longer attend Redfield University."

"Really?"

Coach nods. "This is very serious. Not only is blackmail a criminal offense, but tampering with one of his teammates' drug testing is not the kind of guy I want for this team." He glances at me. "I'm sorry you had to go through that, Aiden. I know how hard it must be, with your family."

"You knew?" I didn't really know whether to believe Jordan when he said Coach knew about my past. He never made any comments on it, never treated me any differently.

"Of course I did," he says. "As soon as I saw you in that janky high school gym, I knew you'd be one of the greats. And I still believe that. You're one of the best damn players on this team." He presses his lips together. "And I'm proud to have been your coach. You've become like a son to me," he says, making my throat clam up. "I can't wait to watch you play in the NBA."

Fuck. I've never had someone be proud of me, or want me to succeed. "What about the pictures?" I ask him. "If I get drafted, they won't want someone from a background like mine."

He shakes his head, offering me a smile. "That doesn't matter to me, and it won't matter to them," he says. "Nothing is going to stop you from achieving your goals unless you stop working for it. Coming from a background like yours doesn't mean anything. It doesn't impact how you play," he says, pressing his finger to my chest. "If anything, it makes it more impressive that you managed to work as hard as you have knowing you didn't have the best environment."

His mouth tips up. "I've already had teams interested in you." He has? "Just keep working hard and show up. You play like you always do? There's not going to be a damn team that doesn't want you."

Well shit. "You're serious?"

"I sure am, son."

I nod. "Thanks, Coach."

He gestures behind me. "I was going to wait until everyone left, but... do you want to do the honors?"

I grin. "Hell yes." He tried to ruin my life, it's just as fair I get to do the same.

"Glad to have you back, Pierce." Coach says before I walk out of his office and head to the locker rooms.

"Holy shit," Ethan says when I walk in. "Look who it is."

"Where have you been, Cap?" Andre asks.

I turn to Jordan who's avoiding me, stuffing his clothes in his locker.

"You ok?" Carter asks.

What the hell is going on? I fully expected to come in here and see the guys laughing at me, talking shit and looking at me like I'm a pile of trash. It's what I'm used to back home. Pushes from my own teammates, pranks in the locker rooms. It was brutal, but I kept at it because basketball was my only escape from home.

But these guys are still talking to me, calling me cap? I don't know what I expected, but this wasn't it.

"I'm good," I tell him. "Finally back on the team."

Jordan twists around, his eyes in slits. "Aren't you suspended?"

I grin, shaking my head. "No, but you're off the team."

"What?" Jordan asks.

The anger on his face makes me laugh, knowing that after everything, he lost it all. Jealousy got the better of him and he lost. "You should have checked my pockets, asshole." I shake my head at the guy who I thought was a friend here. "I recorded every goddamn word you said. Coach knows I haven't used. You, on the other hand, have been caught tampering with drug tests and blackmail."

The guys murmur, their faces contorting with what I felt when I found out Jordan was the blackmailer… betrayal. Hurt. The team is supposed to be a family, not turn on each other.

"You can't kick me out," he says.

My shoulders lift. "Coach thought I should do the honors." His gaze darkens, finally realizing he has nothing. "You're off the fucking team. None of us want to work with someone like you."

Jordan laughs, looking around the room at the other guys who've iced him out. "Please," he says, turning his eyes to me, shooting me a glare. "He's a fucking loser." The words still manage to hit deep even after all this time. "He shouldn't be captain. The pictures are proof enough. He's a nobody."

Everyone is silent. I wonder if they're thinking over what Jordan said, maybe warming up to the idea of agreeing with him. I'm not a nobody. I know that now. My past or my family don't make up who I am. I'm my own person, I have my own morals and beliefs and goals, and guys like Jordan aren't going to make me feel like that anymore.

When Carter stands up, everyone's eyes turn to him. "I had next to nothing growing up," he says, swallowing hard. I flinch at his confession. "Tell me I'm not supposed to be here." He glares at Jordan. "Fucking say it."

He lets out a scoff, ignoring Carter. "You're all just fine with having him as captain?" When no one agrees with him, he laughs. "You're all losers," Jordan says, shaking his head.

I don't even acknowledge the irony in his statement. "And you're not supposed to be here. Leave."

"Fuck you," he says, picking up his shit and shoving it in his gym bag. "Fuck this school." He turns around, but before he can leave, Ethan grabs him by his collar and swings, landing a punch to his face.

Jordan jumps back, his eyes wide and the room settles in silence. He shakes his head, his jaw clenching, and then walks out of the door.

Ethan turns back around, eyes blazing as he runs a hand through his hair. "He played me," he admits, shaking his head. "He fucking told me you had rich parents who paid off Coach to make you captain."

My eyes widen at his admission. Jordan really wanted that position, and he was willing to turn everyone against me to do it. "That's not true." Furthest thing from it.

Ethan nods. "I know that now." His eyes dip, running his tongue over his bottom lip. "Fuck, I'm sorry, Cap. I really thought…"

I nod. He was misled, nothing we can change about that. "Thanks for that," I gesture towards the door.

He shakes his head, letting out a scoff. "He had it coming."

Yeah, he did.

I blow out a breath knowing he's no longer a threat. But if Jordan could do that to me, then any one of these guys could turn around and do the same. "He isn't a problem anymore," I tell him. "He's off the team and out of this school. We need to have each other's backs, not stab them." I turn to the rest of the team. "Anyone else have a problem with me being captain or where I come from, then say it now. Because these petty little arguments are exhausting."

"I'm good," Carter says, raising his hands.

"I have nothing against you," Andre replies.

"Me neither," Brent says.

My shoulders drop. "Glad to have that sorted."

"We all saw the pictures," Andre says, making my face drop. "I know how hard it must be to have your personal business out there."

"Yeah," I breathe out.

"We're here for you, Cap," Carter says, lifting his chin. "Whatever you need, you can count on us."

I'm glad to have a team that has my back, even if no one else does after this. I give him a nod. "You too," I tell him, admiring him for standing up for me today, even if it meant exposing his business. When I turn to leave the locker room, his voice stops me.

"Where are you going?" Carter asks.

"Home to my girl."

EPILOGUE

Kittens and birthdays

Aiden

"They're plants, Leila. They all look the same."

"Shhh." Her eyes widen, tucking the plant to her side. "They can hear you."

She's adorable. I want to kiss her. I always want to kiss her. Every moment of the day, every second. "But you already have so many." Understatement. Her apartment is covered in green. I've got to say, I kind of love it. It reminds me of her.

She shakes her head, examining the leaves. "They bring me comfort and oxygen. Do you not want me to breathe?" The way her eyes narrow at me, makes me want to laugh, but I know better so I press my lips together.

"Of course I do, gorgeous."

"Do you have anything else to say about my plants?"

I snicker, pressing my lips to hers. "No, baby. Where do you want them?"

She points to the ground, outside of the small flower boutique, at the basket filled with ten other smaller plants. "In there."

Whatever my girl wants, she gets. I take the plant from her, placing it in the basket with the others. "You're lucky I love you," I say, brushing strands of that chocolate brown hair out of her face. I'm lying though, I'm the lucky one. So fucking lucky to have found her. I lean in to kiss her forehead. I can't seem to stop kissing her, looking at her, thanking every God there is that she forgave me and loves me.

"Yeah?" She smiles, her eyes shining at me. "Say it again."

I'll say it a million times if necessary. "I love you," I whisper against her lips.

"Hmm," she hums. "That sounds so good coming from your mouth."

"It would sound even better coming from yours." I love hearing her say those three little words that make my heart skip every time.

She lifts her eyes, looking at me through her eyelashes. "I love you, Aiden Pierce. All of you. Every part, even the annoying ones."

"Annoying?" I ask her, amused.

She nods. "Like when you snore."

I scoff. "I do not snore."

"You do," she says, scrunching her nose. "It's so unattractive, I should have known that before I slept with you."

I shake my head, leaning into her. "Too fucking late. I'm never letting you go." The second our lips meet she melts into me, wrapping her arms around me, her fingers tangling in my hair. I love her so much my heart feels like it's about to burst.

"Leila?"

We pull back, Leila's head snapping up, staring behind me. Her eyes widen, a smile sprouting on her face which makes me frown as I turn around, seeing who belongs to the deep voice that seems to make my girlfriend smile.

My eyes trail down his clothes that look like they were tailor made, his curly brown hair complimenting his tan skin. He rubs a hand over his trimmed beard, making him look manly as fuck. Holy shit. This man is handsome. I hate him.

"Lucas?" Leila says, walking right past me and pulling him in for a hug. Who the hell is this guy and why is he touching my girl? "What are you doing here?" Leila asks him, pulling back from their embrace that lasted way too fucking long.

He smiles down at her. "I was just buying some flowers for my mom's birthday. I didn't want to tell you until it happened, but I moved back home," he says. "I changed agents." Fuck, he's a model. Of course he is.

"No way," my girlfriend says, sounding way too excited. "So I'll get to see you more often?"

The fuck she will. I take a step closer to her, wrapping my hand around her waist and pull her into me, staring down at this asshole, showing him that she's mine. All fucking mine. "Who's this?" I ask, lifting my chin at him.

"This is Lucas," she says. "He's a model, we work for the same agency." She laughs. My eyes widen. He's making her laugh now? Absolutely not. "Well, not anymore, I guess."

"And this is?" Lucas asks Leila.

"Aiden." I tighten my hold on Leila's waist. "Her boyfriend."

His eyebrows shoot up. "Boyfriend?" He shakes his head. "Well, congrats to you both." When he notices my frown, or glare, maybe both, he holds his hands up. "Listen man, you have nothing to worry about. We're just friends, we have been since she was modeling in Barbie pajamas." He grins at Leila, and even though he just gave me a whole spiel about being friends, I can't help it... I'm jealous.

She laughs. "I was like ten, give me a break."

He smiles at her. "It was so nice seeing you, Leila, hopefully we can catch up soon. I've got to go." He leans in, presses a kiss to her cheeks and heads off.

"So, that's your friend?" I ask her, unable to hide the bite in my tone.

She glances at me, narrowing her eyes. "Don't be jealous. I'm yours. You have me."

I blow out a breath at her words, turning to face her and grab onto her face. "I do," I say, staring down at her green eyes. I grab her hand in mine. "And you have me. My heart is clutched between these fingers right here. You own me."

She smiles at me, and I'm about to lean in to show my girlfriend how much I love her when I hear a noise.

"What was that?" Leila asks, pulling back, a frown on those pretty lips.

When we hear it again, it's faint but sounds close. We turn around, looking around until we hear it again. A cat. The soft meow comes again and when I hear Leila gasp, I turn to look at the basket filled with plants where she's staring at.

"Oh my god," Leila whispers, staring at the black and white kitten laying in the middle of our plants. "He's so tiny."

He really is. The poor thing looks like it's months old. He brings his paw to his face and licks it with his tongue. "He doesn't have a collar," I tell her, watching as the kitten stretches out.

"Can we keep him?" she asks me, eyes widening.

We. It's her place, her decision, but I love that she's including me in this. Like he's ours. Like a little family. I press my lips to her forehead to hide my grin. "Of course we can." I know how much she loves cats, and this little kitten coming to us almost feels like… "It could be fate, you know."

STEPHANIE ALVES

She rolls her eyes. "I don't believe in fate."

My brows lift, staring down at her. "Fate brought me to you."

She scoffs, laughing. "More like a game of spin the bottle." Whatever it was, I'm thankful I found her. I gave up on love a long time ago, I just never thought I would have it. I'm so glad I was wrong.

I approach the little guy, letting him take my hand until I can pick it up. Leila fawns over the kitten instantly, petting his head, his purrs making her melt. "What should we call him?" she asks.

I glance at my girlfriend, looking at the gold paw necklace I gave her for her birthday hanging around her neck. "How about Tiger?" I ask her.

Her eyes widen, a smile pulling at her lips. "I love it."

"Okay," Leila says before she opens the front door to my house. "Before we go in, let me just remind you that I looove you," she drags out the word, giving me the sweetest smile.

I narrow my eyes at her, holding onto Tiger. "What have you done?"

I get the answer to that when she opens the door, and I get blasted with a bunch of people yelling, "Surprise."

The basketball team, my best friend, my girlfriends' friends, they're all here, surrounded by multi-colored balloons and holding up party horns. Grayson even has a party hat on that I have no doubt Rosie made him wear.

374

I look down at Leila, who's got the biggest smile on her face. "You did this?" I ask her.

"Is that a cat?"

"Yeah," Leila replies, wrapping her arms around my waist.

My whole heart is inside this woman. "How did you know?" I ask her. I've never told anyone when my birthday is. I didn't see a point to it when I had already missed out on so many growing up.

"I'm your girlfriend," she replies. "It's my job to know these things."

I shake my head, grinning down at the love of my life. "Have I told you I love you yet?"

She mulls it over, shaking her head. "Not yet," she teases, knowing damn well I've said it about a hundred times today.

I press my lips to her forehead. "I love you, gorgeous," I tell her, holding Tiger with one hand and holding her face with another. "I am so in love with you," I murmur before bringing our lips together.

"All right," Carter says, making us pull back. "We get it, Cap. You're in love. But we have a cake to cut."

I've never had a birthday cake and Leila knows this, which is why she's smiling when I look at her. "I couldn't help but think of everything you missed out on. I wanted you to have a normal birthday." She squints at me. "Do you like it?"

Every day I fall even more in love with her. "You know I would have been more than happy spending the day in bed with you watching movies, right?"

"Seriously," Gabi says. "Why is no one talking about the cat?"

Leila shakes her head. "You deserve the best. You deserve everything."

I look down at my girlfriend when I say, "I already have it."

THE END

Acknowledgements

Thank you for purchasing this book and reading it.

I hope you enjoyed Leila and Aiden's book as much as I loved writing it. This book was honestly so fun to write and I had the best time with these two characters.

I relate a lot to Leila's character and it was so important for me to write her story to help heal a little piece of me. I'm not quite as confident as Leila is, and even though she's a bad ass, she still has those moments of doubt that I never quite see represented, and wanted to include in my book.

Aiden was the MMC of my dreams. He's completely obsessed with Leila and I had the best time writing his story so much.

I would like to thank all of you who read this book and loved it. I would like to thank my beta readers, my street team and my arc readers and anyone who supported me on social media.

I never thought life would bring me here a few years ago, and the comments and likes and shares leave me astounded every day. I can't believe how many of you actually enjoy the stories I put out there and for that I am so grateful.

As always, thank you to my best friend who kept me sane when I was losing my mind while drafting this book, and thank you to Tatiana for helping me turn the early drafts into something readable.

If you enjoyed Spin The Bottle then please consider leaving a review as reviews help out indie authors a lot.

About the Author

Stephanie Alves is an avid reader and writer of smutty, contemporary romance books. She is English / Portuguese and she loves happy endings, whether it's in a book or a romantic comedy. All of her books are available to read on Kindle Unlimited.

You can find her here:
Instagram.com/Stephanie.alves_author
Stephaniealvesauthor.com

Made in United States
Troutdale, OR
10/04/2024

23380293R00235